Rush

Part One & Two

Bridget L. Rose

Editor: Selina Ruf
Proofreading: Selina Ruf & Bridget L. Rose
Cover Designer: Selina Ruf
Formatter: Bridget L. Rose

This book is dedicated to
all the girls and women out there with a dream. Never give up on your dream,
even if it feels like your dream is giving up on you. And if you have already, start dreaming again. The world needs you to be the change.

Rush: Part One

Chapter 1

After an exhausting fourteen-hour flight from LA to Monaco, my legs ache, and my feet are throbbing. The latter is not because I spent most of that time sitting, but my brother's elephant feet stepped on mine as we got off the plane. I scowled at him as soon as it happened, but my childish brother was too busy laughing at a guy whose butt crack was on display. I shoved him off my foot, causing him to lose balance and almost fall. With his eyes wide and in complete shock, he glared at me and cursed. I pointed at the sore area and then flipped him off before walking away.

Now, he's walking at a noticeable distance behind me, asking why I'm limping. He's obviously still trying to figure out what happened, but I don't dignify his questions with a response. I'm too annoyed, and my foot is hurting too badly. After a couple of minutes of me silently walking ahead, I take a deep breath and turn around only to realize he's disappeared. I frantically search for my phone to call him but quickly give up since it doesn't have any data yet.

"Adrian!" I hiss, hoping he will hear me. He appears in front of me with a smug smile on his face moments after I first called out his name.

"You look like a child, who lost their parent in a crowd," my brother says, laughing at his joke.

"Where the hell have you been?" I ask angrily, and he cocks an eyebrow.

"I told you I had to go pee, but you were too busy pouting to notice. I'm pretty sure the whole airport knew where I was, except for you, Ms. I'm-limping-for-no-apparent-reason."

"Ten, nine, eight, seven..." I count down out loud, enunciating each number and probably spitting in his face. When I finally reach 'one', I take a deep breath. "So, taxi?" I ask with the fakest smile and chippiest tone in my voice. Adrian wipes my saliva from his face and follows me toward the taxi line outside the airport.

"Grandpa's house is ten minutes from here," he informs me nervously for the third time today after telling the driver where to go. I only nod absent-mindedly.

A couple of minutes into the drive, we pass the Zoological Garden of Monaco. I vaguely remember my grandfather taking us there once when Adrian and I were still very young. Afterward, we never went again. Adrian detested that the animals were forced into such small cages with nowhere to run. I soon adapted the same mindset.

The Mediterranean Sea captivates my attention next. The landscape is just as breathtaking as I remember it, making me feel guilty for not coming back sooner. I tear my eyes from the water and close them to keep my emotions at bay. The nostalgia is overwhelming.

When I open them again, we are pulling into my grandfather's driveway, and I suck in a sharp breath. This house represents family. Adrian and I spent most of our childhood here, learning about manners, how to write and read, and who we are.

"Valentina." Adrian's voice brings me back to reality, but his hand waving in front of my face doesn't. I slap it away and glare at him, but he reaches it out again and, suddenly, there is a compassionate expression on his face. My brother wipes away my involuntary tears and forces a smile. "I know. I miss him too," he admits, leaning toward me and placing a swift kiss against my temple.

Grandfather's house seems bigger than I remember it. The white columns on the front of the house, including the stone facade, are still the same ones my grandparents had used to build the house. I can feel my heart drop. He left us his home five years ago when he died of lung cancer. Until now, Adrian and I haven't been able to come back, but half a year ago, we decided to renovate it and move in.

The familiar smell of roses and freshly watered plants hits my nose. The sun burns my skin. I take off my flip-flops before I step onto the lawn and let the feeling of the slightly wet and cold grass envelop my feet. They carry me toward the large front door, which Adrian and the taxi driver patiently wait for me to unlock. We bring the luggage inside and put it in the foyer. Our antique chandelier catches my attention, reminding me of the day my grandfather explained what a 'chandelier' is.

"Val, are you okay?" Adrian asks when I don't move or talk. I nod and feel his hand on my shoulder before he squeezes it comfortingly. My eyes move to the glass doors leading to the kitchen, the living room, and the dining room.

"Are *you* okay?" I ask him when he studies our house in the same way I am.

"Yes, I'm just feeling a little nostalgic, I guess," he admits and runs his hand through his dirty-blonde, curly hair.

Adrian and I look a lot alike, too much alike for siblings with a four-year age gap. Our hair is the same color; our eyes are the same combination of green, blue, and a little bit of brown. However, I am pretty short, have a rather large bust and butt, whereas Adrian is pretty much a straight line on feet. Many people think he is too tall to drive in a Formula One car, but he proves them wrong with every race he wins. He and I have the same set of straight teeth, round lips, and small ears. Adrian is a young championship contestant with merely twenty-three years of age. He is a fantastic driver, just like our father and grandfather were.

Formula One is a fast-paced racing sport with twenty drivers competing in the championship. The open-wheeled cars race around unique tracks at a speed of over two hundred kilometers per hour. A specific number of laps have to be completed within a two-hour window for each track, and whoever crosses the finish line first wins. The race weekends are held from Friday to Sunday, with press events and fan meet and greets on Thursdays. The main event is the race, the Grand Prix, on Sunday.

The sport was founded in the United Kingdom, and more than half of the races take place in Europe, making it very Eurocentric. This is why it made sense for Adrian and me to move back to Monaco.

"Want to go out with me tonight? I'm meeting up with some of the other drivers," he offers, and I smile. As serious as they take their competition, all of the drivers make up a tight-knit community.

"Who is coming?" I inquire with a curious expression on my face.

"James, Leonard Tick, Cameron, and Gabriel." Gabriel Biancheri... My heart beats faster against my ribcage, but I hide my excitement. Gabriel Biancheri is the goofiest, most compassionate, and most gorgeous guy I've ever seen. For three years, I've had the biggest crush on the Monegasque. He is kind, intelligent, and an incredible racing driver. "Oh, and Gabriel's girlfriend is also coming," he adds, and I am no longer excited. I don't want to see him with that annoyingly beautiful actress girlfriend of his, Kira Delgado. They have been dating for three years, about as long as I have known Gabriel.

"Okay, what time?" Adrian cocks an eyebrow at the change in my mood, but I simply ignore his inquiring look and focus on opening the glass doors to the living room.

"Seven o'clock," he replies and follows me into the kitchen. The tiles feel cold under my feet.

The kitchen has a modern electric stove in the middle connected to an island, which has three brown leather chairs standing against it. There are brown, wooden cabinets all over the walls, and an oven and a microwave are on the left. My eyes drift to the clock by the oven, and I see it's only two in the afternoon.

"What do you think we should do?" I look up at my brother and think about his question.

My stomach growls uncontrollably at the thought of food. "It may be better to go grocery shopping," I tell Adrian, and he winks knowingly at me. A grin spreads over his face, and I furrow my brows.

"Excited to see the cars?" Realization washes over me, and I jump up and down in excitement. We walk to the garage, and my heart explodes into a million pieces. A black 1955 Chevrolet Bel Air stands at the front of the garage, followed by a blue 1973 Ford Mustang. However, Grandfather possessed more than just classic cars. He also bought a white 2014 Audi Q7 and a grey 2014 BMW X6 before he died. I love those cars, both classic and new, although nothing will ever come close to the adrenalin rush I feel when I see an F1 car. "Which one?" Adrian asks, and I point at the Mustang.

With a simple smile, he gets the key and throws it to me. Thanks to years of reflex training to prepare for racing in Formula One, I catch them with ease. Without wasting any time, I get into the baby blue car. My fingers run over the black leather steering wheel, and I sigh when my eyes drift to the air refresher hanging from the inside mirror. It's the first one my grandfather had ever gotten. He always kept it there as a good luck charm, even after the scent faded. My heart is pounding, and my knees are weak when I turn on the engine of the first automobile I ever drove.

After our trip to the grocery store, I head upstairs and unpack my things. The walls in my old bedroom are a soothing, light blue. My curtains are thick and dark, and my golden-brown wooden bed stands in the middle of the left wall.

I finish unpacking within an hour, making sure to put all my pictures on my nightstand, and sit down at the foot of my bed, staring at the art Grandfather chose not too long ago. The painting of the last Formula One car Dad drove, a much smaller version of Adrian's Ferrari, stares at me, and my mind drifts to him. A memory I have been suppressing since the day he died appears in my head, and I let it consume my thoughts.

"Daddy, how fast can you go?" I look up at my father, and a bright smile appears on his face. We are walking past tall people, who wear all different kinds of colors. I see blue, yellow, and green. My dad says all teams have a different color, but my favorite is the one he is wearing: red.

"Very fast. At our fastest, almost 300 kilometers per hour," Daddy explains, and I stare at him, completely mesmerized. My six-year-old brain has no grasp of how fast that is. My daddy stops walking, and someone starts talking to him.

I wait impatiently for the woman to leave him alone so I can ask my next question. "Can I drive one?" He only shakes his head. His blonde hair hides underneath a hat, which has a picture of a black horse on it. Dad calls it the Ferrari symbol, but I call it 'Champion', like my daddy.

"It's too dangerous for children. When you're older and become the strong woman I know you will be, you can drive one," he assures me, but I pout anyway. I want to drive one at this moment.

My dad leads me to the bright-red-colored car, and he allows me to touch it. My tiny fingers run over the smooth metal, and I jump when I feel how cold it is. I lift my eyes to look at Dad again, but he is talking to another man. Even though it is very cold, I leave my hand on the car and tilt my head to the side. It is much bigger than the one I sit in when Grandpa takes me karting. It has a long, pointy nose with a mustache at the front, reminding me a bit of my grandpa. It gets bigger where the cockpit is. Adrian calls it the belly, but I like the word 'cockpit' better because my daddy and all his friends at work use it. Another word I like is 'wing', and it is behind the cockpit. It is the tallest part of the car, a lot taller than me.

I pull on my daddy's arm. "Not now, Valentina," he scolds, and I frown. He does this to me a lot. My eyes go back to the car, and I smile. It's very loud here. I barely heard my dad yell at me before. People run from one side to the other, screaming at each other. Almost everyone has a serious expression on their face. They look like Adrian when he concentrates really hard on coloring inside the lines. I always tell him he can't do it, and I'm always right. I don't think he likes my coloring books very much.

I bring my eyes back to the car. It must be a lot of fun to sit in it, but I'm never allowed. Dad doesn't want me to break anything, which is why I'm only allowed to touch the nose and mustache. I'm not sure what it's actually called. My dad's best friend stands next to me, and I poke his leg to get his attention.

"What is that thing?" I point at the mustache. At first, he seems confused, but then he gives me that same weird smile many adults give me.

"That is called a front wing. It makes sure the airflow is redirected so the car can go faster. With the shape of the car and its lightweight, it needs a–" He stops, and I blink cluelessly at him. "Uhm, how can I explain it to you? The air goes... swoosh." I nod, although I still don't get it. My eyes stay on the car.

"I'm going to drive you one day," I whisper right before my dad pulls me away.

Chapter 2

"Valentina Romana," Adalene Beaumont pulls me from my memory. She never fails to make me grin from ear to ear, even now.

"Madame Beaumont," I say and hug her tightly. I contacted Mrs. Beaumont a couple of months ago, hoping she would take her old job back, but my efforts were unsuccessful. "How are you?" I ask in my mother tongue because I remember she only speaks French and Spanish. Even though I'm fluent in both, I prefer French.

We fall into a casual conversation, which makes me realize how much I've missed her. The delicate woman in front of me was Grandfather's housekeeper until the day he died, but she was always a part of the family. She taught me about fashion, making my bed, laundry, and just in general how to take care of myself.

"I heard you're going to dinner tonight," she states, and I smile shyly.

"Yes, but I'm not too excited," I admit, and she frowns.

"Why not? Monsieur Biancheri will be there. He is a very polite man. I've known him since he was this big." She holds her hand three feet above the ground, and I half-smile.

"I know, but he will be busy," I mumble in response. I know Mrs. Beaumont sees right through me, but, luckily, she doesn't push.

"Shall we do your hair and makeup?" Mrs. Beaumont asks sweetly. I stand up and follow her to my closet.

"Thank you, madame." Before I can get emotional, she *shoos* me to the bathroom, so I take a shower.

The warm water relieves all the tension in my body. I don't remember a day I've not been sore from training. When I walk into my room again, she has laid out a stunning outfit for me to wear. The top half of the dress is decorated with lace, and the bottom is a simple cream color. There are white wedge heels next to it and some silver jewelry. I put the dress, heels, and accessories on before sitting down in the chair in front of the vanity. Mrs. Beaumont curls my hair, so it falls down my shoulders in waves and draws a simple line of white eyeliner on my lid. She then adds mascara and puts a pink, matte lipstick on my lips. Usually, I would do all of this myself, but she's told me how much it pleases her to help me. Mrs. Beaumont doesn't have any children, and this is the only time she gets to dress up her 'daughter'. It's a win-win because she likes doing it, and I end up looking incredibly gorgeous, just like today.

"You've grown to be a stunning woman, Valentina, inside and out," she tells me when I admire myself in the mirror. Speaking French with her makes me feel truly at home. I shift my eyes to her face and see a single tear falling down her cheek. "Oh, look at me, getting all emotional." Mrs. Beaumont laughs slightly. "I should go back home. Early day on Monday, lots to take care of here," she says with a wink and disappears from my room.

"You are not wearing that," Adrian snaps when he walks through my door. He put on some white shorts and a cream dress shirt. He looks handsome, but it does bother me that we are matching. How does this always happen? "Three out of the four guys that are coming tonight are single and young, and you are not wearing that." He shakes his head and, even though I know he is serious, I don't care what he says. I know those guys too well. Cameron is my friend and not interested in women, Leonard doesn't like me, and the feeling is mutual; James and I have been friends for years, and Gabriel has a girlfriend.

"Thanks, I agree with you. I do look gorgeous," I tell Adrian and grab my purse from the dresser. "Plus, you can't hide my irresistible charm and humor anyway." He simply shakes his head at my innocent facial expression. "Ready?"

Chapter 3

The drive is silent, and I enjoy being behind the wheel of the Mustang. My heart beats rapidly when I think about seeing Gabriel for the first time in weeks. I make a plan in my head: who I'm going to talk to, James and Cameron, and who I'm going to avoid, Kira. Although she is kind and polite to everyone else, she doesn't seem to like me.

We arrive at *Les Perles de Monte-Carlo*, and I park my car at the valet booth. Adrian gets out, and I adjust my hair while waiting to give my keys to the valet. To my surprise, Adrian opens my door and holds his hand out. A smile takes over my entire face.

"When did you become so chivalrous?" I ask him, and he rolls his eyes but doesn't hide his amused smile. His attention drops to my feet, and a wicked grin appears on his lips. "What's with the face?" I ask.

"Well, I'm just surprised to see you are wearing heels, you know, considering you were limping this morning," he replies before imitating what he perceives I looked like after he hurt me. I attempt to kick him in the ass, but he dodges the attack of my vengeful foot. "I knew you were being dramatic." I glare at him and cross my arms in front of my chest.

"How about I get an elephant to step on your foot, and then we'll talk," I retort, and his mouth falls open.

"With an ass like yours, you're the closest thing to one. Bring it on." He presents his foot to me, inviting me to step on it. Naturally, as soon as I try to, he moves it away and lets me stumble forward.

"That's it," I yell and manage to jump on his back. "Go, donkey, go," I tell him, pointing toward the restaurant.

"So, what am I? A donkey or an elephant?" I can't help but laugh.

"You're a donkey with elephant feet. Now, go!" I slam my knees into his sides to get him to move already. I should be embarrassed this is happening in front of such an expensive restaurant, but I'm too busy laughing to care.

Adrian gently drops me back onto the ground, and we walk inside to where Leonard, James, Cameron, and Gabriel are already sitting at a table. When my eyes focus on Gabriel, I giggle a little. He's playing thumb wars with Cameron and making grimaces to distract his friend. As Cameron presses his thumb on Gabriel's, the Monegasque makes a farting noise so loud, it throws his opponent completely off-guard, earning him the win. People at the surrounding tables frown at his child-like behavior, but I burst into laughter. *If they only knew who he was.*

"Adrian," Leonard says and gets up to hug him. He gives me a slight nod, and I give him half a smile.

James Landon walks over to me, and I smile at the tall, twenty-two-year-old. He looks handsome in his blue jeans and green polo shirt. His blonde hair complements his blue eyes.

"Hey, gorgeous," he greets me before his arms wrap around my upper body. "You look lovely," the English man tells me, and I blush. I have known him for most of my life, and I know his compliments are entirely platonic. Even the kiss on the cheek is. He turns to Adrian and sighs. "I see you're embracing the Californian culture of casual wear for any occasion," he jokes, and everyone laughs.

"VAL!" Cameron Kion picks me up from the ground, and I giggle. He is slim and relatively short, but he is still strong enough to lift me. Cameron is the nicest guy. He was Adrian's first teammate in Formula One.

Finally, I allow my eyes to shift to Gabriel again. His brown, curly hair is slightly tousled but still looks perfectly in place. Gabriel's green eyes have shimmers of brown in them, which I know even from far away. His lean, trained body is covered by black pants and a white dress shirt, and his dimples are breathtaking as he smiles at the makeshift trophy he made for his thumb war victory. When he catches me staring, a blush settles on his cheek, but he winks anyway, probably to look more relaxed. I walk over to greet him. *Where is Kira?*

"Hey, Gabriel," I say before he pulls me close and wraps his arms around me. He smells of mahogany, and my senses are heightened as I feel his lips brush my cheek. Feeling his body so close to mine is heavenly.

"You look unbelievable," he tells me and takes one of my curls between his fingers. His behavior is so odd, I'm not even surprised when he sits down and pretends nothing happened. James takes the spot next to me across from where Gabriel is.

"How have you been?" he asks but also hands me a menu. His English accent is insanely thick.

"Good now that I've finally graduated," I laugh, and he joins in. James knows I had to repeat a grade because I moved to Los Angeles to live with my aunt, and the school system was different from the one in Monaco. "How about you? How do you feel about your new contract with Red Bull?" I ask, and he sucks in a sharp breath. Every driver signs a contract with a team, depending on salary, duration, and additional benefits. They then race for that team for however long their contracts last. James recently switched from McLaren to Red Bull.

"Great, I'm really excited." A nervous laugh escapes him, and he runs his big hand through his heavy hair. He has gained a lot of muscle, which I already felt when he hugged me, but I can also see by looking at him. James is still lean but also very trained. Formula One drivers need to be slim to fit in the car, and they cannot be too heavy either as it slows them down; every gram matters in racing. However, they still have to be strong because their bodies have to withstand the heavy forces of steering the car around the track. "Any plans for this year since we last spoke?"

"Not really. I'm going to keep training for now and see what opportunities present themselves," I reply, and James nods. His eyes focus on mine, and his hand inches closer to where my arm lies on the table. I cock an eyebrow, and he retracts his hand, an embarrassed blush settling on his cheek. What is going on? My eyes drift back to Gabriel, who is watching James closely.

"Val?" Adrian asks, and I turn my head to look at him. The waiter stands next to him now, and I order before he moves on to James.

The ambiance of the restaurant is pleasant. It's not too loud, and the instrumental music is slow and soothing. I listen to Leonard, Cameron, and Adrian talk about the brutal workout regimes they have to endure every day in preparation for the start of the season. I do the same routine and don't find it as painful, but I won't point it out. Then, James and I fall back into a conversation about his work. He tells me how ready he is to travel and see all the places he likes. It seems like forever since we last spoke, even though we texted yesterday.

Cameron grabs my attention when he asks how the flight home was. I tell him the whole story of Adrian's assault on my foot. Everyone at the table laughs, except for Adrian. He nudges me in the ribs and glares at me. It doesn't hurt, but I nudge him back anyway. Of course, I do it a lot harder, and he almost falls off the chair. Gabriel snickers in response.

"Anyhow," James starts, and I shift my attention back to him. "Have you thought any more about coming with us when the season starts?" I'm not surprised by his question, but I still don't have a clear answer for him. "As I've said before," he continues, "you could focus a little on yourself, keep training, and you'll have a better chance to find opportunities," he adds with an excited smile.

The first time he asked me was a little over a month ago, but I haven't made up my mind yet. It's not something that's easily decided, but I do get excited when I imagine what it would be like. Watching Formula One is my favorite thing to do, besides actually racing. The atmosphere on track is an entirely different world. The thrill is overwhelming, with the fans in the stands cheering throughout the weekend and the drivers' passion for the sport. Additionally, I would get to spend more time with Adrian and James... and Gabriel.

"It's a great idea, and if you want to, you know I'll make it happen," my brother chimes in. I know Adrian can. He is driving for Ferrari this season, so rather, I know they can make it happen.

"I still need to think about it," I state, and Adrian nods, taking my hand in his and squeezing it.

Gabriel gets up from the table and disappears. After a moment of hesitation, I decide to follow him. I'm worried and want to make sure he's okay. The cool summer air sends shivers down my spine when I find him outside. At least I'm telling myself it's the air. Gabriel runs his hand through his hair and bites his bottom lip. A frustrated expression plays on his face.

"Gabriel," I say, my voice almost a whisper. He hears me anyway and turns to me. His expression doesn't change.

"Please, go back inside, Valentina," he begs, and I cock an eyebrow. When I don't move, he takes three steps toward me. "Just leave me alone, please. I don't want to talk right now." I wish he would share what's on his mind, but I don't push. Instead, I head back inside to our table. This behavior is very unlike Gabriel. We usually have no trouble communicating.

"Is he okay?" Adrian asks me, and I bend down to his ear.

"No, but he doesn't want to talk about it," I reply, and he shrugs.

"Maybe he's having an off night," he suggests, and I sit back down in my chair. *He didn't seem to have an off night before we arrived...* Eventually, Gabriel comes back inside, but I leave him alone.

"What happened to Kira?" I finally ask Adrian once my curiosity gets the better of me.

"They got into a fight before coming here." I nod and focus on my dessert. *It must be why he is acting so strangely.*

We all finish our food, and Cameron tells everyone how thrilled he is to start the new season in three weeks. Leonard chimes in and agrees while Adrian sits back in his chair, watching everyone closely. Gabriel's eyes are on me when I glance at him, and I wish I knew what he's thinking. He looks guilty, the way his eyes are pleading with me, and his lips are slightly parted as if he wants to say something.

Adrian and I leave the restaurant around midnight, without Gabriel showing any sign of his usual playfulness. I let my brother drive since I'm too tired and want to give my mind a break, to let it roam free.

"About you coming with me–" Adrian starts, and my head flips in his direction. "I'll be flying back and forth a lot, and sometimes I will be staying in one place longer than in another." He pauses and frowns. "I would love for you to travel the world with me. The past four years, every time I left, I wanted to take you with me." I understand what he means. Adrian and I have been through a lot, and we are each other's most important people. Yet, there is a war going on inside my head. One side tells me I have a better chance of realizing my dream if I travel with him. The other thinks I should stay in one place and keep training here while also finding a job to make some money. It's challenging to make a decision when I don't know what the right choice is. However, I know that my chances are pretty low either way, and I want to spend as much time with my brother as possible.

"Get ready for months of greatness then because I'm going with you," I tell him excitedly, and the biggest smile appears on his face.

"Alright," he replies just as giddily. Adrian taps his fingers on the steering wheel as I get back to my thoughts. Back to Gabriel, my subconscious reminds me, and I roll my eyes involuntarily. I don't understand what is wrong with me, why I've spent years crushing on a guy who is not interested. He is dating someone else. So why is it so damn hard for me to get over him?

I lie in bed and stare at the ceiling, feeling beyond weird sleeping in Grandfather's house without him here. After half an hour of struggling, I get out of bed and walk down the hall to Adrian's room. I knock twice before he tells me to come in. He sits up in the bed that is way too big for him, and I stand awkwardly in the door.

"What's wrong, Val?" he asks with a frown on his face.

"I can't sleep. I feel... odd," I mumble, and he pats the side of the bed next to his. I walk over, and he holds the blanket up for me.

"I get it. It feels like he's here, but he's not," Adrian admits, and I nod. "Well, you can sleep here until that feeling goes away." Again, I nod and close my eyes, relieved my brother is there for me when I need him most. "Just remember, we are going to have months filled with excitement, traveling, and, most importantly, winning ahead of us. I'm so happy you're coming with me." He squeezes my shoulder before falling backward onto his pillow, making me laugh.

"Goodnight. Love you," I say as my eyelids get heavy.

"I love you too," he replies and turns the other way.

It gets quiet when suddenly, Adrian's silent but violent fart fills the room, and a soft chuckle escapes him. *What an idiot...* I kick him in the shin. *It's good to be home*, is the last thing on my mind before the smell knocks me out.

Chapter 4

"You know, Valentina, if you want to achieve your dream, you have to stay in the best physical shape you can be," Grandfather informs me as I watch him closely. His grey hair stands up at the sides. "When you sit in that fast car, the limits of your body are tested. You have to be mentally, emotionally, and physically ready. The first step in succeeding is understanding they are all interconnected." Grandpa stops to pull out a piece of paper while I shift impatiently in my seat. Adrian is absentmindedly listening as he plays with his Nintendo, but my full attention is on Grandpa. I want to hear everything he has to teach me. Grandpa writes the three criteria on the paper, and I watch him draw arrows to connect them. "If you are out of balance in one, you will have an imbalance in all. Do you understand?" I nod, but Grandfather's thin lips form a frown. "Do you understand me?"

"Yes," I reply. "But why do I have to be in control of all three?" A smile replaces his frown. Grandpa likes it when I ask questions.

"If you're not in control of your emotions, they will lead to mistakes. You can't be too aggressive. You have to be mentally strong to focus entirely on the track ahead of you. You need to be aware of the other drivers, identify

the track conditions, adapt, and monitor your vehicle. Lastly, you have to be physically strong to drive for a very long time. Your body will be exhausted after each race." I stare at him in awe. I want to be that strong. He pauses for a brief moment, clearly contemplating his following words. Grandpa seems unsure about something. "I don't want to scare you, but there is a lot at stake. When you sit in the cockpit and compete for the win, there are risks involved. Your body has to be prepared for any case, even if it is a crash into the barriers or one with another driver. Your muscles can help you take the force of the hit." His words are a lot to process and not something I can take lightheartedly. Racing is risky, but I love it more than anything. It will be different when I train and learn how to do it properly. As long as I'm careful and prepared, I will be on top. It's my dream.

"Can we start today?" I ask, and Grandfather nods.

"Yes. We will start by going for a slow, short run," he tells me, and I get up from my seat.

"Adrian, are you coming?" My brother looks at me and then at our grandfather before bringing his attention back to his toy.

"No, not today," he simply responds.

"Ready?" I nod. I'm ready to be just like him.

It is only six in the morning, and Adrian is sound asleep, just like I should be after the dinner we had. My body probably won't run well on four hours of sleep, but I can do nothing about it now. A small groan leaves my throat as I aggressively remove the blanket to get out of bed. A hot bath will help my muscles catch up with my mind.

When I walk down the stairs to meet Adrian in the kitchen, I almost choke on my breath. Gabriel is sitting at the island, drinking coffee with my brother.

"Morning, Adrian," I say, giving him a brief hug. "Morning, Gabriel," I go on but move over to the fridge without giving him more of a greeting.

"Val," I hear Gabriel call out in the softest tone behind me. I take a sip of my orange juice before turning to him with a curious expression.

As always, his hair is tousled, a green shirt sits on his muscular body, and simple blue jeans hang from his hips. Gabriel's sunglasses dangle from his neckline, and the single necklace he always wears is under his shirt. His eyes scan my body in a way they never have before, and he stops at my breasts three seconds too long. I look down and remember that I didn't put on a bra, and my nipples are hard against the thin fabric. I cross my arms but can't stop the smile from spreading across my face. What is wrong with me? I should be embarrassed. Instead, I feel good about catching his attention. I look around the kitchen to realize Adrian has left the room.

"I'm so sorry about yesterday," Gabriel starts. "I was upset because I got into a fight with Kira, and then I saw..." he breaks off, and I cock an eyebrow. "All that matters is I am truly sorry. I hate pushing you away." The way he pouts and pokes my cheek with his index finger makes a grin spread over my lips. I was never upset with him for not wanting to speak to me.

"You didn't have to apologize," I inform him, but he nods.

"Yes, I did." His proximity is confusing my senses, and I move away from him, toward the cupboard with the glasses.

"You want some orange juice?" I ask to change the subject.

"I actually have to go. Kira has an entire day planned for us." The moment is over, and the smile disappears from my face. "Again, I'm really sorry," he says before wrapping his arms around me. My heart races, my skin catches on fire, and his mahogany scent makes my head spin. "Bye," he mumbles and smiles, flashing me his handsome dimples before disappearing.

After minutes of mindlessly sipping on my juice, I cook breakfast for Adrian and me. I make some eggs, bacon, pancakes and cut up some more fruits before calling my lazy brother into the kitchen.

"How did you sleep?" I ask as I turn to Adrian, who just put the biggest chunk of pineapple into his mouth. With a full mouth, he smiles and shrugs before he attempts to answer. All I hear is gibberish as juice starts dripping from his mouth. "Never mind," I laugh and shake my head. "Also, next time we have a visitor, please let me know so I can put on a bra," I beg, and he chokes on his coffee. His laughter fills the kitchen. I nudge him in the ribs, and he catches himself.

"That's why he was walking so weirdly," Adrian points out, and my mouth drops. "Yeah, wide legs and all." I swat his arm, but he seems to enjoy his joke too much.

"Did I miss something?" Gabriel asks from behind us, and I shoot up in my seat.

"NO," I quickly reply and glare at my insensitive brother. If Gabriel knew, he would be incredibly uncomfortable.

"I forgot my phone," Gabriel explains as he walks over to it. An annoyed expression appears on his face, and I wonder what he is reading. My curiosity vanishes when my eyes focus on his three-day stubble, and I get lost in his handsome features. "Well, apparently, I'm free today after all. Kira just canceled on me. Mind if I join you?" he asks me specifically.

"Sure, but Adrian and I are going for a run soon," I tell both men, and Adrian's eyes go wide right before they plead with me. I've always been more serious about the workout routine. When his trainer isn't around, I make sure to push him, as I do myself.

"Great, I'll join." Gabriel sits down, and I get up to bring him a plate. "I'm not hungry, chérie." My heart skips a beat, and I feel the need to turn around and stare at him. He has never called me 'chérie' before.

"You need to eat a good breakfast," I state, and he smiles. "We have a lot of training to do." Again, Adrian's eyes plead with me, but I ignore him and put my plate in the dishwasher. I am rushing to go upstairs and put on some workout attire.

"You guys are having a party without me? That's not cool," a voice with a heavy English accent calls out, and I shake my head. *I am starting to regret moving back to Monaco. And how do they keep getting into my house?* James appears in the kitchen seconds later with a single sunflower in his right hand.

His eyes focus on mine before they drop to my body, and he swiftly looks away. *It is a bad day to decide to go braless*, I tell myself. "Good morning, beautiful," he says and hugs me tightly. "This is for you." He hands me the lovely flower, but I don't know how to deal with this level of affection.

"Thank you for the sunflower," I reply, and James winks at me. He is probably the only man other than Grandpa and Adrian, who knows that sunflowers are my favorite. My eyes shift to Gabriel, but his expression is unreadable.

"What are you doing here?" Gabriel asks James frustratedly, and I give him a confused look. His gaze momentarily meets mine but shifts it back to James almost instantly. The testosterone stinks up the whole room, and I think about opening a window. Instead, I simply go upstairs, change into some sportswear, and pack a bikini for later.

Once I'm dressed, I sit down on the edge of my bed and take three deep breaths to calm myself. It would be better if Adrian and I were alone, but I also know it's good for Gabriel and him to spend time together. After all, they are teammates this season. Ferrari acquired two strong drivers for their team this year, but I can already predict the chaos that is to come. While the drivers compete for the same team, they also individually fight for the championship. Adrian and Gabriel are both very competitive and eager to be first-time champions.

Twenty minutes later, it is time for me to face the trio again. To my surprise, they are all ready to go for a run, both guests clad in my brother's clothes. I smile when I see Gabriel doesn't fit in them since he is much shorter. He catches me grin strangely at his outfit and tugs the shirt into the pants before tightening the waistband to make himself look even more ridiculous. I shake my head as I laugh.

We start running soon after. The guys are trying to keep up with me as I lead them down the path Grandfather started taking me to when I was eight years old. That's why running is second nature to me. My whole life, I trained harder than everyone else because I had a dream. A dream, which was crushed, when they decided I wasn't good enough.

Gabriel runs past me in a sprint, and I try to keep up but have to slow down earlier than him. He sticks out his tongue at me, and I run into him on purpose. Sadly, he catches me and spins me around before wrapping his arms around me. Laughter escapes his throat. I join in because I love how playful we are. Gabriel has been through a lot in his life, about as much as I have in mine. It is why he and I usually get along well.

"You still have more practice to do if you want to beat me, chérie." I push away and scowl at him. His dimples are deep as he smiles brightly.

"Yes, either I get better or grow taller. Your legs are double as long as mine," I complain, and the smile on his face starts to annoy me.

"Stop making excuses," he says teasingly, his accent thicker than I have ever heard it. Gabriel has the typical Monegasque accent. He chooses to speak in English with me because it's good practice for him. The Formula One press conferences and interviews are primarily in English, which is why it's so crucial for him to learn.

A warm breeze runs down my spine, and I lean my head back to let the sun shine onto my face. When I look at Gabriel again, he's staring into the distance. His forehead creases, and he bites his bottom lip absentmindedly. It's not the most flattering facial expression, but it does show how upset he is.

"How come you *really* had time today?" I ask him, the curiosity threatening to eat me alive. Gabriel's expression changes to an uncomfortable one.

"How come you are as red as a tomato right now?" he asks in return, and I laugh at his joke.

"Okay, no need to attack," I reply and place my hands on my stomach to imitate being stabbed. Gabriel laughs at my dramatic reaction before we grin at each other. My eyes shift to James and Adrian, who have *finally* caught up to us. They are both out of breath and seem entirely exhausted. *Slackers.*

I convince them to work out for half an hour longer. When we finish, we are all beyond exhausted. Our tired expressions remind me of something my grandfather used to say to me every time I wanted to quit.

"You can give up if you want, you can throw it all away and pretend your dream never existed, but if you clench your teeth, scream at the top of your lungs, and go through with it, you will end up more than happy with yourself." There were many times in my life when I wanted to give up on my dream, but I didn't. *I haven't.*

"What do you want to do now?" Adrian asks the group, and the other two shrug.

"Well, I'm going to the beach," I inform them and grab my backpack before changing into my flip-flops. "I'll see you at home." I look at my brother, and he swiftly nods before he gets up as well. I turn around and start walking toward the beach.

"Do you mind if I come with you, luv?" James yells after me, and I stop dead in my tracks. I don't know what to tell him. On one hand, all the time we've spent alone together has always been platonic and comfortable, but he has been acting strangely toward me these past twenty-four hours. Then again, he's my friend, and I love hanging out with him.

"Sure," I assure him. I never want to hurt James by pushing him away. He is my oldest friend. We have many embarrassing memories together, but we also have unforgettable ones.

"So, how are you feeling?" James asks me after I've changed into my bikini. I give him a confused expression, and he elaborates. "About the move? About being back in Monaco? About living in your grandpa's house? It can't be easy, darling," he states, hitting the nail on the head.

"I'm managing," I reply, and he frowns at me. We sit down close to the ocean. "After everything, I'm just glad to be home." My eyes drift to the trees near the beach and then to the nearby restaurants. I'm trying to avoid eye contact with James because I know I will break down if he looks at me. I will cry because I don't want to be in the house without my grandpa and being back in Monaco reminds me of everything I've lost. "Tell me how *you're* feeling," I say after moments of absolute silence. "You're taking a big step driving for Red Bull." Although we've already talked about this, I need to change the topic.

James looks down and picks a single, small rock out of the sand before twisting it around in his fingers. "Well, today is my last day of somewhat relaxation before I have to take everything more seriously again," he admits, and a nervous laugh escapes him. "But it's fine. I'm fine," he mumbles, a childhood habit of his. When he says 'fine' twice in under ten seconds, it means he is freaking out. I smile.

"All right. Well, since it is your last day, let's forget all about work and have a great time." He nods eagerly, and I know it's exactly what he needs. It will be good for me too.

"Bring it on, gorgeous," he yells as he sprints toward the water, and I run after him.

Chapter 5

After spending three hours at the beach, I've soaked up enough sun and saltwater, my stomach growls, and James and I are ready to go home. It takes us a while to walk back to my house but seeing all the different cafés and restaurants I used to go to as a child makes me feel better. We make small talk, yet I am not paying much attention. My mind is preoccupied with our surroundings. Eventually, I link my arm through his, like I've done countless times in my life, and laugh at something he tells me.

James moved to Monaco when he was only eight years old. His dad was convinced James had a great future ahead of him if they moved from London to Monte Carlo. His family still lives here, and they are not planning on moving any time soon.

For a little while, our conversation focuses on his sister and how worried he is. Mia is making questionable choices with questionable people, and James has no idea how to help her. She is careless because she's convinced her parents' money makes her invincible.

My mind drifts to Gabriel and his younger brother, Jean, who also had a terrible phase a couple of years ago. He lashed out because he couldn't deal with his grief and with all of the pain he was feeling. I couldn't blame him then, nor can I now, because I have felt hopeless, devastated, and broken more than once. Jean is the only one who had the courage to say, 'I'm not okay, please help me.' And we did. Adrian took him to therapy, Gabriel took him to the most beautiful places around the world, and I simply spent a lot of time talking to him on the phone, helping him work through his feelings. After a couple of months, he seemed much better, and now he's happier. If Jean could fight through the grief that made him lash out, I'm sure Mia's spoiled phase will pass too.

We arrive at home, and my heart rate speeds up to an unhealthy level when I see Gabriel sitting on the veranda with Adrian. Gabriel has a serious expression on his face as he studies James and me: arms linked and smiling brightly.

"How was the beach?" Adrian asks when I put my backpack on the table and pull out my towel to hang it over the chair.

"It was great. The water was cold, but it was worth it." I smile at him, but he only nods absentmindedly. He is probably reading an email from his team, which is why he's behaving rudely.

"I have to go home, Val, but thank you for the lovely day," James tells me, and I grin at him.

"Thank you. I had a great time." His face lights up, and he gives my cheek a quick peck before he leaves. I put on my shirt from earlier when a phone rings. My head snaps up, and I see Gabriel stand up and walk toward our pool area.

"No, Kira!" is the first thing I hear Gabriel say into the phone. "You always do this! You always put yourself first, and that would be okay if, once in a while, you would put me first. But you don't. All you do is yell at me, tell me I should prioritize you, but you know what? My career matters, too!" I try not to listen, but Gabriel is screaming. Adrian and I exchange worried expressions. A growl roars from where he is standing, but I refrain from looking at him. "Valentina?" he says in a soft voice. My eyes move in his direction, and I see his face is red, his eyes are half-closed, and his hand is in his hair. I wait for him to say more. "May I have some water, please, chérie?" I simply nod before going inside to get what he asked for.

"Here you go," I tell the upset man, who is sitting in the chair I previously occupied. "Excuse me, you're in my seat," I tease, but he's too caught up in his thoughts to sense it's a joke.

"Oh, shit, sorry," he mumbles and attempts to get up, but I only laugh as I push him back down.

"Stay, I'm just kidding," I add, and finally, he chuckles.

"Thank you." His words are soft as they leave his mouth, and it makes my knees weak.

"Of course, you're a guest in my house," I tell him, and he shows me his brilliant, white-teethed smile with dimples. His adorable personality, combined with his sexy smirk, is why he's so dangerous. My eyes shift away from his face to make my head stop spinning and heart stop racing.

I decide to go upstairs and take a shower. It has been a long day, and I am ready to sit down with my favorite book until it's time for dinner.

I try to focus on the words on the page with all of my strength, but nothing works. My thoughts only want to concentrate on LA, Aunt Carolina, Luke, Grandfather, my parents, and other fun things that still haunt me. Groaning and moaning, I put the book aside and fall back onto my bed.

"What's wrong, chérie?" I look up and see him standing in my doorway. His trained arms are crossed in front of his chest in a sexy, brooding way. One of his eyebrows is higher than the other, and all I want to do is smooth out the creases in his forehead, bring a genuine smile to his face, and make him happy. He deserves to feel joy instead of negligence.

"Nothing," I lie and cross my legs on the bed before I pat the space in front of me. "Do you want to talk about what's bothering you?" I ask, hoping he'll finally open up to me. He nods slightly and places his hands on the bed, followed by his round butt.

"I don't know what to do anymore, Val. Kira and I want such different things, and everything between us hasn't been right. We haven't been right, and all I keep thinking is that I have known this girl for three years. Kira is talented, kind, and funny. She has watched me grow into the man I am today, kind of like you have..." He pauses with a thoughtful look on his face. It's brief, and he shakes his head to focus on the conversation again. "...and I don't know how to let her go," he admits in a rant, and his honesty takes me aback. He's never opened up to me about Kira. Usually, he keeps his business just that, his. However, hearing him talk about his relationship shows me he needs my help and advice.

"Instead of screaming at each other, why don't you sit down with her and talk about everything? She needs to know what is going on in your head in a calm manner. Don't let your emotions get the better of you. I think you guys can work it out. All you have to do is explain and listen." Gabriel's eyes are on mine, his lips are slightly parted, and his breathing is steady. For a minute, no words fall from his full lips, but when they do, I wish I wasn't such a good friend.

"You're right. We're going to make it work. We always do." Gabriel gets up from my bed and walks closer to me, his lips brushing over the top of my head. "Thank you, Val." He leaves my room seconds later, and I am alone again.

"Good job, Valentina," I whisper to myself.

Chapter 6

Approximately Three Years Ago...

“Come on, Val, we have to get going,” Adrian yells, and I put on the finishing touches of my makeup. I walk out of the bathroom of our hotel room, and Adrian smiles at me. “You look beautiful,” he says, and I tug at my plain, blue dress before smiling shyly.

“You don’t think I look stupid?” Usually, I don’t dress up unless I have Mrs. Beaumont’s help. However, the dress is so simple, I know I can’t go wrong with it.

“Not at all.” For a brief second, I see tears glistening in his eyes, and a confused expression settles on my face. “Sorry,” he quickly mutters and sits down on the bed. I walk over to him. “You’re growing up, and I’m not quite ready to see that happening, as absurd as it may sound,” he tells me, and I wrap my arms around him.

“I understand. You grew up faster than I did, and all I wanted was for you and me to stay the same age we were five years ago.” I feel Adrian’s arm wrap around my shoulder and swallow down the tears. Five years seems like a lifetime ago. Grandfather was still teaching me, training me; he was still alive. Now, it is only Adrian and me. Well, Adrian, me, and that witch Carolina.

"I'm sorry I always leave. I wish I could take you with me, but you need to finish high school. You need a good education, but I am sorry. You're my everything, Val, my whole life. I need you to remember that," he says in a strong voice, and tears drop from my eyes.

"And you're mine." I wipe them away with my index finger and smile. Adrian and I are unlucky in many ways, but we are also fortunate to have each other.

He pats me on the shoulder and says, "Okay, let's go." I nod and get my purse before following him.

It takes us about half an hour to get to the room Peter Weizer, former Formula One driver and current head of McLaren, rented for the party. It is dark outside, and I put on my jacket when I see it is only ten degrees Celsius. Adrian and I flew out to England for this party, and I've been enjoying my time away from our aunt. However, I would like it even more if the weather wasn't so disappointing.

We get out of the car, Adrian holds out his arm for me, and I hook mine through his. I'm thrilled to meet all the other drivers, but I'm also nervous because, after all, they are celebrities. At least my oldest friend James is going to be there to keep me entertained.

The room is packed with people, and I feel intimidated. Luckily, James walks toward us and opens his arms for me. I hug him, and he picks me up, just like he always does. "I've missed you, darling," he says and puts me back down on my feet. He kisses the top of my head before turning to greet Adrian.

"Hey," Adrian greets him, and they do the typical handshake-hug-pat-on-the-back, which a lot of guys do. They fall into a conversation, and my eyes drift around the room.

There are a lot of middle-aged white men and their wives at the party. Then my eyes wander to the group of drivers standing near an enormous table in the middle of the room. I recognize Killian Grand, Leonard Tick, Cameron

Kion, Ian McCaugh, and a few more faces that seem familiar. My eyes stop, and my heart drops when I spot the most handsome man I have ever seen. His brown hair looks messy yet somehow is still in place. He is slim and of average height. The dimples that appear when he smiles make my heart stop.

"What's caught your attention, lovely?" James asks me, and I look away from the gorgeous stranger.

"Who is he?" I've known James long enough to feel comfortable asking him almost any question. He takes a sip of his beer and turns his head in the direction of my not-very-subtle finger.

"*That* is Gabriel Biancheri. He is a new driver, starting in a Williams." I nod and look at James again.

"You're driving for McLaren this season, right?" I ask, making sure I remember correctly.

"Yes, ma'am," he says, his English accent thicker than honey. I look at Gabriel and feel James' eyes on me. "He's nineteen, luv." I roll my eyes and focus on my friend. I already figured he would be older.

"How is it going between you and Katie?" James starts swooning over his girlfriend, and I try my best to only pay attention to him. But every now and then, I look past him and toward Gabriel. He is in a conversation with Peter and his wife, Brigitte Weizer. For the first time, Gabriel's eyes find mine, and a confused yet curious smile spreads over his face, making my heart tingle. Again, I shift my attention to James, who, luckily, hasn't noticed.

"Ah, James, it is very gut to see you," Peter Weizer interrupts us with his almost incomprehensible German accent. His wife is smiling and nodding next to him. "And who are you?" He holds out his relatively small hand, and I shake it politely.

"My name is Valentina. I'm Adrian Romana's sister. He brought me tonight. It's nice to meet you. I'm a huge fan of what you do," I ramble nervously and have to catch my breath. The man's tired blue eyes widen, and an amused expression spreads over his face.

"Ohh, slo down, yung laidy. You are tu fast. My English is not zat gut," he responds and squeezes my hand. "Adrian, ja ja, I know him. Gut Mann. Very gut! Ah und zis is my waife Brigitte." He motions to the woman standing next to him. "Brigitte das ist Valentina. Sie ist Adrians Schwester." I have a tough time understanding him as is, but I'm convinced the last sentence was not English. I smile at the wife, and she returns it. The blouse she's wearing is a blue color, which complements her brown-colored hair. The neckline is higher than I would usually wear my own, but it fits her perfectly.

"I like your blouse," I tell her, and she looks away from me and toward her husband.

"Was hat sie gesagt?" Again, I'm unable to understand anything, and I look at James for help. I'm worried I said something to offend her, but he smiles at me and squeezes my hand to assure me everything is fine. Peter says something back, and the woman turns to face me. "Ah danke, I mean, zhank you, zhank you." A blush settles on the older woman's cheeks, and I manage to bring the smile back to my face.

James introduces me to the owner of Formula One, Claudio de Michael. We talk a little about the new regulations before I build up the courage to share what happened to me personally last year. I was racing in Formula Three after dominating the karting circuit when, after a year, my team dropped me. No one else wants to sponsor me, despite my success. F3 is similar to Formula One, except the cars are smaller, and there are a few format differences for the race weekend. It is a steppingstone to come closer to racing in F1, but all of a sudden, the ground was pulled from under my feet.

"Well, Ms. Romana, I'm sure they had good reason," Mr. de Michael replies, and I shake my head. I've been given the same ridiculous excuse from more people than I can count.

"I'm sorry to interrupt. Val, this is Cameron Kion, a good friend of mine," Adrian introduces us, and I smile at the man with the kindest face. He has smooth features, blue eyes, and just, in general, a face that makes you want to trust him. Cameron makes small talk about my school, my favorite music, and I ask him about racing and his favorite movies. The Australian seems genuinely interested, and I'm fascinated with his accent. James and Adrian disappear to talk to some of the other drivers.

"Cameron, you forgot to show me a picture of your helmet design." His voice is just as attractive as the rest of him. He has the Monegasque accent I love. It is beautiful and smooth in my ears, and at the same time, it reminds me of home. "I really hope it's a kangaroo, and you're in its pouch," he jokes, and I chuckle. Gabriel's eyes focus on mine, but I look away, embarrassed.

"Oh, Valentina, have you met Gabriel?" Cameron asks, and I shake my head.

"Hi," Gabriel says and holds out his hand for me. Instead of shaking it, I simply hold his awkwardly. He cocks an eyebrow and lifts our hands to his mouth before placing an unsure kiss on the back of mine. He seems amused then. "It is lovely to make your acquaintance, Lady Valentina," he teases, and heat rushes into my cheeks. I let out a nervous laugh, which sounds more like a hyena when it sees food. I retract my hand before mentally slapping myself. Cameron excuses himself after almost bursting from holding back the laughter and leaves Gabriel and me alone. "So, who did you come with?" he asks me, obviously trying to fill the awkward silence with casual conversation.

"Um, my brother brought me along. Adrian," I quickly add and point at the tall guy with curly, blonde hair. I feel weird talking to him, but I also don't want to stop.

"Ah, yes, the resemblance is uncanny," he says, a small laugh escaping him. His accent does something to me I don't understand, but it feels incredible. My whole body almost vibrates with each word he speaks. "Where are you from?" he asks, and it tells me he hasn't met Adrian yet. He also wouldn't be asking me if I had the same accent.

"Monaco, just like you, I'm guessing," I respond, smiling sweetly at him. I am terrible at flirting.

"Oh, no way! Yes, I am," he says in French, and it takes me a second to process his words. I hardly ever speak French. Adrian and I grew up bilingual since our dad only spoke to us in English, but our grandparents only in French. In school, we also learned both, but when I moved to LA, I had a strong accent, similar to Gabriel's. Aunt Carolina shamed it out of me by only speaking English at home until there was no hint of it left. "I can't believe how good your English is."

"I grew up bilingual," I explain in the best French I can muster, and he continues to smile. If a smile could make someone fall in love, his would. "I hear you're driving for Williams." I don't know what else to say and hope he will lead the conversation and tell me more about himself.

"Yeah, it's my first season in F1, and I'm excited. I have worked incredibly hard most of my life to get here, and I honestly can't believe it's happening." As he grins, I finally notice his eyes are a unique combination of green and brown. I smile back at him, and a slight blush settles on his cheek. "Sorry," he mumbles and looks at his feet. *He is shy?*

"What for?" I ask, perplexed by his apology.

"I don't know." He shrugs. *Why is he nervous? I'm the one who is supposed to be nervous! I'm talking to this handsome man, who is older than I am and not only hot but also charming. So, why would he be nervous?* "Would you like to sit next to me during dinner?" I can't hide my shocked expression. *Why does he want me to sit with him?* I turn around to see who he was addressing. "I would love to hear more about life in LA, *Valentina.*"

"Yes." The words leave my mouth before he even finishes his sentence. For the second time, he holds out his hand for me, and I take it. This time, I get to enjoy the touch instead of feeling embarrassed for holding his hand. My entire body is covered with goosebumps, and I shiver.

"You're cold," he states, a frown on his face. *He could not be more wrong.* My body is on fire from his touch, and the only reason I shivered is because, for a brief second, I let my mind drift. "Do you want my blazer?" I shake my head to let him know I do not need his jacket. The last thing I want is to make his blazer wet from my sweat. He smiles at me, and we sit down at the table. We fall into a passionate conversation about Formula One, led mainly by my opinions, and he watches me with a smile the entire time.

“I’m sorry,” I eventually blurt out, but he shakes his head.

“Don’t be. I’m very intrigued by you. I’ve never met anyone as interesting and strong-minded as you. You fascinate me,” he admits. “And on top of that, you’re gorgeous.” I’m sure I misheard him, but when James chimes in, I know I didn’t.

“And very young. She’s sixteen, mate,” James says so blatantly I want to punch him in the face. All my hopes Gabriel could like me are blown away.

“Oh, okay, so I can’t tell her she’s one of a kind?” My head turns in Gabriel’s direction, and he is glaring at James, who is sitting down on the other side of me.

“You can, but you need to keep your hands off her. Understood?” James tells him more than he asks. His voice is deep, and his accent is fading as he growls at Gabriel.

“If I were uncomfortable, I would have said something, *James*,” I point out while glaring at my oldest friend. Without listening to another word of their ‘conversation’, I get up and walk over to Adrian. He smiles brightly at me, and I try to return it genuinely. “I’m going to get some air. I’ll be back.” I squeeze his arm, and he winks at me.

As soon as I’m outside, the cool air freezes my body, and I stand completely still. I am not necessarily mad at James for telling Gabriel how old I am, I would have done that sooner or later, but I do not like how it happened. *And what does he care anyway?* I catch myself. To him, I’m like a little sister he has to protect. I’m this fragile thing who cannot defend herself, but that’s why I don’t think of him as a brother. My actual brother knows I can protect myself. He knows he doesn’t have to interfere unless I ask him for help. It’s why James is my oldest friend, not my best friend, and not my brother. Those two titles belong to one single person: Adrian.

After minutes of freezing, someone wraps their jacket around my body. I know it’s James. A moment of hesitation later, I turn around to look at him. He rubs the back of his neck with his hand, and I wait for him to talk.

“I’m sorry. I shouldn’t have said that. Please forgive me,” he says. The defeat is evident on his face. "Come on, Val," he pleads when I don't respond to his apology. I can tell he is freezing.

"Okay, but I am keeping your jacket," I let him know, and he smiles.

"It looks better on you anyway," he replies.

Adrian sits at the table, far away from where I sat before, and I see an empty seat next to him. Without hesitation, I take it. He grins at me with a full mouth, and I shake my head, smiling.

James' jacket keeps me warm for most of the night, and I'm sad when I have to say goodbye to Cameron and Gabriel. I know I will see James soon, but I don't know when I will see Gabriel again.

I stand in front of him, a sad smile on my face. "It was nice to meet you, and I'm sorry about earlier. James is overprotective when it comes to me," I inform him, and he simply nods.

"I understand. I'm sorry, too, if I made you feel uncomfortable in any way. I didn't mean to, and to be honest, you were the one making me a little nervous." He grins, and I don't know what to say.

"You didn't make me uncomfortable." *You make me feel incredible, you make my body react to your touch within seconds, you take my breath away, and I have no doubt you will be on my mind for a while.* But I don't say any of this. All I say is, "I guess I will see you around." I hold out my fist without thinking.

"I'll see you soon, *Lady Valentina.*" He fist-bumps me with an amused grin. Embarrassment washes over me, and I leave before I do anything awkward again. *Fuck me, I'm an idiot.*

Chapter 7

Present...

It's been two days since I've seen anyone but my brother, and I enjoy the peace and quiet. Adrian asked me if we could host a dinner tomorrow night, inviting Jean, Gabriel, and, *ugh*, Kira. After giving it a lot of thought, I agreed to co-host. There is no point in avoiding them when Adrian needs to have a good relationship with his teammate. However, I'm dreading to see Gabriel and Kira cozied up the entire evening. There are better ways to spend my time.

Since I got back, I have been trying to find somewhere to buy clothes, but I've been unsuccessful. For the third day in a row, I am strolling past cafés and restaurants when I spot a single boutique in-between two coffee shops named *Rush*. The place has an antique style, and my interest is piqued. It is charming, and the light-red-colored bricks which build up the tiny clothing store are captivating.

There are three mannequins in the window display. The first one is wearing a simple blue skirt with a white tank top and a matching blazer. The second mannequin is wearing black jeans, a green blouse, and black high heels. The last outfit, however, is the one that catches my attention the most. It is a long red dress covered in white flowers. *I want to have it.* My feet move before my mind catches up.

The inside of the store is just as elegant as the outside. The same bricks decorate the walls, and the racks of clothing are neatly placed around the room.

"Bonjour," a petite woman says behind me, and I turn to her. She must be at least seventy with long, gray hair and crystal blue eyes. The woman is breathtaking, and the smile on her lips is inviting. "Can I help you?" she asks, continuing to speak to me in French. It is good to be back because it allows me to practice my mother tongue.

"Yes, please," I reply with the same level of warmth in my smile, I hope. "How much is the red dress from the mannequin in the window?" A knowing smile appears on her face, and I cannot explain the comfort I feel around her.

"Fifty euros," she informs me, and I almost take out my wallet to buy it. "There are more sizes on the far left." I find a medium and go into the small changing room to try it on. The silky fabric feels smooth against my skin, and the dress highlights my curvy body in a sexy yet classy way. "How was it?" she asks when I come back out, and I beam at her.

"I love it. I'm going to buy it," I inform her, and she nods, the same kind smile as earlier spreading over her face. "Do you mind if I keep looking?"

"Not at all. Take your time, mademoiselle." Her French is flawless, and so are her clothes. I go through the racks and find seven more items. "Are you from here?" the sweet lady asks me.

"Oui, madame," I reply.

"I thought so. I can hear it in your French." I am glad I don't sound like a foreigner, which is why my smile brightens.

"How long have you had this store for?" I inquire, wanting to make conversation.

"My husband bought it for me after he won his first Formula One championship." I almost drop the clothes I'm holding and turn my full attention toward her.

"My brother is an F1 driver!" Her eyes go wide as well.

From there on, we talk for hours about her husband, whom I then find out is Carlos Klein, the youngest driver to win a race and a championship thus far. She tells me about his first race and his last one. However, I refrain from sharing my racing story because it's too embarrassing. After all, she is married to a Formula One legend.

"How did the two of you meet? If I may ask," I say, hoping I don't offend her in any way. She and I have more in common than I would have ever expected at first glance.

"In school. I was a junior when he was a senior, and we were paired together for a project. I was in his math class since I was very good at it, and that is where we met. However, it took months for us to become more than friends." She lets out a small laugh, and I love the way her cheeks flush and eyes sparkle as she talks about her husband. "I thought his career would take him far away from me, and I didn't want to fall for him, but I had no choice. Luckily, he didn't have one either and fell at my feet. It's something for the books, I tell you." Her index finger waves around in front of me, and the smile on my face becomes permanent. "But enough about me. Is there anyone special in your life?"

"I used to have a boyfriend, his name was Luke, but he was not good for me. I broke up with him and never looked back. There's been someone else on my mind for a very long time." I don't know why I am opening up to this woman, but I enjoy talking to someone about how I feel.

"Does the other boy know about your feelings?" I blow raspberries but recover quickly when she cocks an eyebrow.

"No, madame. He has a girlfriend he seems very serious about, and I am not ready to embarrass myself. We're good friends, and I wouldn't want to ruin that either. Not to mention, he is friends and teammates with my brother, which complicates the situation even further." Her eyes narrow slightly, and I'm afraid of what she will say next.

"You never know. Maybe he isn't happy; maybe he has feelings for you too. Some relationships take too much work, and both people end up being unhappy. Or he could be doing the same thing you did when you were dating Luke. He could be distracting himself." Boy, she is good. I didn't even have to tell her about my motivation behind being with Luke.

"Maybe, but I can't take the risk. He means too much to me." She nods, and we move to the small, wooden table at the front, where the cash register is. "It was really nice talking to you. I hope I can see you again," I tell her, and she nods in agreement.

"That would be lovely. My store is always open, dear. I'm here Monday to Saturday, ten to eight." I hand her my card, and she swipes it on the machine. "Whenever you need someone to talk to."

"I will take you up on that offer," I reply, and she hands me my card back. "I never got your name," I say, realizing I haven't.

"My name is Evangelin." She holds out her hand for me, and I shake it cautiously.

"Valentina. It is a pleasure to have met you." Evangelin hands me the bag with clothes and grins.

"Likewise. And here, take this, dear." She hands me a black leather jacket, and I gasp. "Please, don't tell me you cannot accept it. You bought so much, and I know you will look stunning in this," she adds, and I have no idea what to say to her. I simply take it and put it in the bag.

"Merci." Evangelin walks around the table and squeezes my arm ever so gently.

"Good luck, Valentina." My cheeks flush, and I nod, hiding the embarrassed expression on my face with a polite smile. We exchange goodbyes, and I make my way home.

Adrian, James, and Gabriel are at work, which means I have the whole house to myself without possible interruptions. Whenever I do, I go upstairs to the training room. There is a racing simulator, weights, a treadmill, and bands for neck exercises... Those are the worst yet most important ones. I start by doing some cardio before moving to the weights and then going through the pain of strengthening my neck. The last part is the simulator. Adrian used to call it a fancy video game, but for me, it has always been a way to stay connected to the sport.

I put on the helmet I bought when I first started training with the simulator in L.A. and sit down in the seat, which looks exactly like those in a Formula One car. It's a bit uncomfortable because it's fitted for Adrian's body, but he lets me use it whenever I want. The screens in front of me are bright, and as always, excitement courses through me. I choose the Singapore track since part of it drives through the city and part on the permanent racetrack. In real life, it's one of my favorites because of how beautiful Singapore is.

Once I've selected the track, I close my eyes and take a deep breath. All of my senses heighten while I feel the adrenalin rush through my veins. This is as close as I can get to racing in a Formula One car, and it's always a thrill, even if it's only a simulation. When I open my eyes again, I wait for the lights to go out and push down on the gas pedal, pressing the right buttons simultaneously.

I could stay in the simulator for hours, but unfortunately, it's exhausting, and my body gets tired quickly. By the time I get out of the seat again, I smile like a happy child, satisfied with my performance. Adrian arrives at home minutes after I finish showering and getting dressed. He comes to my room to let me know he will wash and be right down to have dinner with me.

As I place the lasagna between our plates, Adrian reappears with a big grin on his face and a towel in his hand. He rubs it over his wet hair, and within seconds, it is dry. *How unfair...*

"How was your day?" I ask, and he shrugs as he places some food on my plate.

"It was good. Daniel and I got a lot of work done." Daniel is Adrian's performance coach, supporting him in his mental and physical training daily.

It's almost as if they shadow the drivers, and, during the race weekend, I often compare them to moms, carrying everything the driver might need in their bags. The performance coaches are in charge of warm-up exercises, muscle regeneration after the races, and countless other things. Daniel and Adrian are very close like many drivers are with their coaches. "I'm getting ready to get back in the car. I'm also getting more nervous every day, Val. So fucking nervous," he says and slightly laughs. "How was your day?" He takes a bite of the lasagna, and a happy moan escapes him. "This is so good." He talks fast and hurriedly as if he is running out of time, but instead of pointing it out to him, I go along with it. I don't want to make him feel worse by telling him how on edge he seems.

"I had a good day. I met a very kind woman. Her name is Evangelin, and she is so sweet. And you won't believe who her husband is!" Adrian waits patiently, and I smile brightly. "Carlos Klein!" He drops his fork, and it makes a loud *clink* with the porcelain plate. Carlos Klein has been Adrian's hero ever since he was five years old.

"You have to introduce me to him. Valentina Esmèe Cèlia Romana, you *have to* introduce me to him. *Please*, please, please," he begs, and I let out a small laugh.

"Okay, relax. I haven't even met Carlos, and I have only met her today. Please, don't make this uncomfortable for me. *If* I ever meet him, I will let him know how big of a fan you are, and he may do what he wants with that information. Maybe, and only if you're nice, I'll ask him if you could meet him." Even though I'm giving him a lot of hypotheticals, he smiles childishly. "Anyway," I go on, and he focuses on my face once again. I notice how much curlier his hair is when it is roaming free after a shower. "I bought a really nice dress for tomorrow, and Evangelin gifted me a leather jacket." Adrian hearkens politely to the events of my day.

I take a bite of my food and listen to all of the changes Adrian has to figure out this season. Driving for a new team is very challenging, especially when the cars are ever developing. It is impressive to hear about the technological advances the team has engineered, and something inside of me gets incredibly jealous. There is little I want more than to sit in a Formula One car and feel the adrenalin course through me as I race down the track. I push the thought aside because this is not about me.

After Adrian is finished talking about his work, we eat in silence for a while until he starts a conversation about Gabriel. I only listen to half of it because my mind battles with whether it's time to share how I feel. My mouth is quicker than my restraints can hold me back. "I have feelings for Gabriel." Adrian doesn't seem surprised by this new information, and I don't know whether he is mad at me or just speechless. *Why isn't he reacting? This is huge!* I expect some kind of response. It doesn't matter if it's good or bad, *just something!*

"I know, Val," he says, and my mouth slightly drops. "I've known for a long time."

"Oh," is all I can say, and when he finally smiles at me, I feel relieved. "I know it's stupid, and he is with Kira, but I don't know what to do." He puts his fork down again and takes a deep breath. His face is serious, but he also seems pleased in a way.

"I don't know either," he admits and crosses his arms as he leans back. His eyes never leave mine, but he runs his tongue over his teeth. It makes his face look weird, and I wait impatiently for him to continue. "What I do know is that he doesn't deserve you in the slightest. Yes, I'm biased because I think you are my favorite person on the planet, but I also know who he is." *What the hell does that mean?* He takes another brief break, and I don't think I'm going to get an explanation. "However, I'm here for you whenever you want to talk about your feelings." I get up and walk over to him before wrapping my arms around his shoulders and pressing a kiss to the top of his head. "*Thank God*, you finally admitted it. I was making secret bets with myself."

"I'm very worried about you," I say and laugh a little.

A weight has been lifted off my shoulders because I finally know how Adrian feels about this.

Chapter 8

Approximately Three Years Ago...

Gabriel has been on my mind constantly for the past two weeks. I've never had a crush on anyone before and don't mind it at all. Every time I think about Gabriel, a smile spreads over my face, and my heart thumps against my ribcage.

I sit in my bedroom when Adrian comes in and lets me know he invited Gabriel over for dinner. I didn't even know Gabriel was in LA, but I'm excited. James is already staying at our house, visiting from Monaco. Hopefully, James and Gabriel behave this time.

Without putting too much effort into how I look, I stroll out of my room and find James and Adrian sitting on the couch. They're watching a show and laughing at whatever is being said. When James notices me, he winks before turning his attention back to the TV. I sit down on the arm of the couch and wait for the doorbell to ring.

My mind makes up all the different scenarios of what might happen tonight. At one point, I even jerk my head toward the direction of the door because I'm convinced the bell just rang. My heart goes wild when I think about seeing him so soon. *I hope he will be happy to see me. I hope we'll have some time to talk. I really hope James and Gabriel will get along this time.* I almost sigh when I imagine them getting into an argument. For some reason, I also start doubting whether Gabriel is the guy I remember from the party. *What if he isn't the great person I've imagined him to be? What if I was completely wrong about him and just wasted two weeks obsessing over an asshole?*

I force myself to think about something else when the doorbell finally rings. I jump up from the couch. Both heads turn in my direction, and my eyes go wide when I realize my behavior isn't normal.

"I'll just, uh, open the door," I mumble, and they both give me a slight nod.

Before I open it, I take three deep breaths to calm myself, but Gabriel quickly knocks it out of me. His beautiful eyes seem greener today, and his curly brown hair complements them perfectly. The blue shorts and white t-shirt highlight his tanned skin, and I forget how to talk.

"Hello, Lady Valentina," he says and chuckles. His damn dimples make my cheeks flush and heart pound rapidly.

"Please tell me this isn't going to become a thing," I beg, and he chuckles again. My lips betray me when they reveal a smile.

"Not if you do not like it, Your Majesty," he jokes, and I shake my head, still grinning like a child.

Politely, he presses a kiss on my cheek to greet me and then walks past me to say 'hello' to his friends. My skin tingles from his touch long after he is gone. I roll my eyes and slightly groan. He makes me shy, nervous, and I hate the control he has over my usual confidence. *Then again, isn't a crush supposed to make you feel like this?*

Everyone shares stories for most of the dinner, and I laugh harder than I have in a long time. It is so different with them than it is with my peers. I have much more fun with those three guys than I have with twenty classmates. Maybe it's because I have more in common with the men sitting around my dining table. After dinner, I sit on the couch while the guys stay at the kitchen table. I have homework to do and, as much as I would love to continue talking to them, I have to stop procrastinating.

"Mind if I sit down?" Gabriel asks while taking a seat, and I grin. For a split second, I look at him. "What are you doing?" he asks, and I frown while looking at my paper.

"Biology homework," I reply and look up at him once again. His eyes are focused on my face, and his dimples deeply bury themselves into his cheeks. I love this. I love how my mind, heart, and body respond to him. It is new to me but also fascinating and wonderful. My skin is tingling, shivers are running down my spine, and there is throbbing in places I haven't experienced like this before. *I enjoy feeling this way.*

"May I steal your attention, or is the homework important?" he says, and I smirk.

"It is, but you're more interesting," I reply smoothly and mentally pat myself on the back for being cool about this. Gabriel takes my papers in his hands and places them neatly in my folder before putting them on the table. "Okay, what would you like to talk about?" I tug my feet under my butt and intertwine my fingers. I'm so nervous, mainly because his cologne is strong and delightful. *Mahogany.*

"You," he simply states, and I roll my eyes before I touch my tongue to the roof of my mouth. He is smooth and incredibly cheesy at the same time.

"Well, as you know, I'm a huge Formula One fan," I start, and he laughs a little. "I also love books, and I spend a great deal of time at school, studying things I couldn't care less about."

"I felt the same way when I was still in high school. I was always bored because I wanted to spend all of my time racing." He runs his hand through his hair nervously, and I reflexively cock an eyebrow. *I make him nervous?* "I came across an article about you recently," he starts, and I hold my breath. "You were in Formula Three and a fantastic driver. If you don't mind me asking, what happened?" he goes on, making me look down at the couch.

"I don't mind that you ask, but I also don't have an answer for you. Your guess is as good as mine," I admit. The only explanation I have for being kicked from the team is because I'm a girl. I followed all the rules, showed nothing but respect, and was rewarded with the opposite. Gabriel's eyes reveal compassion.

"From what I've seen and what you've shared with me, you deserve a seat in Formula One more so than I do. I'm very sorry, Val." His fingers slide on top of my hand, and I suck in a sharp breath. This is a very emotional subject and combining his touch with it overwhelms my head.

"Well, I'm not giving up yet. I'm still training, and an opportunity will come, I'm sure of it." He nods in agreement. "Okay, so you know a lot about me now, and I barely know anything about you. What do you like to do in your free time?" A grin tugs at the corners of his mouth.

Gabriel is an artist. He has been drawing since he was seven years old. I ask to see some of his works, but he only shows me one of his drawings. It is enough for me to realize how talented he is. The girl in the sketch is gorgeous and, to my surprise, fully clothed. I would have expected Gabriel to have muses who strip for him. *I would strip for him...*

"You look shocked," he points out, making me shift my gaze from the woman to him. "Should I be offended that I don't look like an artist?" he says, but his smile reveals he's merely teasing.

"Not at all. I just wasn't expecting someone who puts as much time into his career to be this good at such a difficult hobby," I state, and Gabriel winks playfully at me.

"My mom bought me my first art supplies," he explains after a brief moment of silence. His smile has faded, and a serious look replaced it. "She had a brain aneurysm and dropped dead in the grocery store. My dad followed her and died a year after," he admits, and I almost choke on my breath. I reach out to take his hand in mine and run my thumb over his smooth skin. Gabriel and I have more in common than I could have ever imagined. "It's just my brother Jean and me now. Although we do have my aunt and her wife, who look after

Jean, but that's it, they are all that I have left," he says, and a single tear escapes his eye. He's witty, kind, has a great sense of humor, and doesn't mind being vulnerable. This is a very dangerous combination.

"I understand," I tell him, and he looks up at me. I lean forward and wipe the tear away. It's instinctual, and I fear I may have overstepped my boundaries, but he closes his eyes in response to my touch. "My father died in a car accident, and my mother ran away before I could walk." I shrug, and he is watching me closely. "The pain never stops. As hard as we try, as much as we want it to end, it never does. But I wish I could make you feel better," I say, and he leans closer toward me. I don't move; I simply can't. His breath is hot on my lips, and I can taste his gum on my tongue before he even touches me. Gabriel's lips are a centimeter away from mine, and I wish he would kiss me. But I soon snap out of it and remind myself that what we are about to do is wrong. I push him back gently. "We can't. I think it's best if you go back to the others," I remind him, and his face falls. I stand up but lean down to press a kiss on his cheek. "Good night."

I go upstairs, my homework in my left hand, regret in my right. With a groan, I drop onto my small bed, slightly hitting my head on the headboard and making another one leave my lips.

The following morning, I feel as horrible about what happened as I did yesterday. Without even trying to make myself look better, I walk downstairs in my pajamas and tousled hair. I stop and almost turn back around when I notice Gabriel is sitting on the couch, where he clearly slept. I should have known Adrian would insist he stay here. Instead of running the other way, I am too mesmerized by the way his hair is still in place, his lips somehow fuller, and his upper body without a shirt. His lean body looks delicious on the sofa, and it drives me crazy to see his muscles on display like this. When he sees me, I can tell he regrets yesterday.

"Morning," I mumble and continue to make my way down the stairs in my Hello Kitty pajamas, which I am just now becoming aware of. I attempt to control my hair at least, but I'm convinced it is without success.

"Hey," he replies simply. "I'm so sorry about yesterday," he starts, and I stop halfway to the kitchen. "I don't know what came over me. You and I have a lot in common. For a minute, I forgot..." I wish I could turn around and look at his face, but something tells me not to.

"Don't worry, I'm not upset," I assure him.

"Okay, I just wanted to say I would have never attempted to kiss you if–" he starts, but I cut him off because his words are hurting my feelings.

"You're not my type either, so don't worry about it," I inform him, and he flinches.

"Oh," he replies, and I go into the kitchen. *Well, this is it, this is why I never liked anyone, to avoid this awful feeling spreading from my chest into my stomach.* "Val," I hear him say right before he comes into the kitchen. Luckily but disappointingly, he has put a shirt on. "I hope we can still be friends. I really like you. You're smart, funny, and wonderfully passionate. Plus, you understand me in a way no one ever has, and I don't want to lose you over a small moment of weakness." I nod, and he holds out his phone for me. I put my number in, making him smile. "I'll talk to you soon," he states, and I go about my day without speaking to him again. I don't even notice when he leaves my house because I'm too busy finding distractions.

Chapter 9

Present...

Jean, Gabriel, and Kira are on their way. I've been dreading this dinner for more than a day, but at least I get to cook. I made all kinds of dishes: salad and fish for Kira since she's a pescatarian, and I made some steaks for Jean, Gabriel, Adrian, and myself. I also made some potato wedges and a broccoli salad for Jean; he loves those. Mrs. Beaumont finishes her work, and I hand her a bag with some of the food and a piece of the marble cake I made for dessert.

Adrian comes downstairs in a dress shirt and jeans, and I look at myself in the reflection of the coffee machine. I flinch at the horrendous state of my appearance: hair messy and flour over my cleavage and face from the explosion I created earlier. My brother hides his laughter when he sees me. I squirm upstairs and quickly take a shower before putting on the dress I bought yesterday, some makeup, and even some eyeliner.

The doorbell rings, and I rush downstairs. Jean is the first to walk through the door. My arms wrap around his neck, and I realize how much I missed this boy. He looks a lot like Gabriel, except his hair is black instead of brown, Jean is much taller, and he doesn't have the stubble Gabriel always has.

"How are you? How have you been? What has been going on?" I know most of the answers to those questions, but I ask them nonetheless.

"Can I come in first?" he asks, and I smile. His voice is higher than Gabriel's but still very similar.

"Of course. I'm sorry," I laugh, but my happy expression soon fades when I see Kira and Gabriel walk through the door, holding hands. *Bleh.* The smiles on their faces are genuine. *Double bleh.*

"Hello, handsome," Kira sweetly greets Adrian and ignores me completely. She does this a lot. I'm annoyed at how breathtaking she looks. Her brown hair falls straight down her back, her blue eyes are highlighted by the smoky eye she put on, and a skin-tight pink dress covers her slim body.

"Hi, chérie," Gabriel says, pulling me out of my thought-trance and pressing a swift kiss to my cheek. His eyes scan my body, and his mouth falls open ever so slightly. "You look gorgeous." Panic flashes over his face, and he moves back to his girlfriend. Kira presses a kiss to Gabriel's lips, and I turn away before feeling Adrian's hands on my shoulders. He leads me toward the living room and bends down to whisper something into my ear.

"If it gets too much for you, let me know." I nod and smile at him, thanking him with my eyes. Jean follows closely and starts talking to me about his grades. He recently finished high school and is applying to the *International University of Monaco* to get his business degree. Kira and Gabriel converse with Adrian, and I'm glad I don't have to talk to them. She is so genuine and friendly to Adrian...

"You're so lucky you get to travel with them this season," he says with a jealous expression on his face. "You're going to leave for Australia soon, aren't you?"

"Yes, on Monday." Excitement washes through me at the thought. The qualifyings, races, free practices; I love watching them more than anything else. My mind drifts to Grandpa, and I think about how happy he would be to see Adrian and I travel the world together.

"Val, Valentina." Jean pulls me out of my thoughts, and I glance at him. We are sitting at the table, eating the food I made. When I look at him, he smiles brightly. "I just wanted to say thank you for making this dinner. Everything tastes incredible."

"Yes, it really does. Thank you," Gabriel chimes in, and I grin at him. Kira notices our exchange and places her hand over his possessively. Adrian thanks me for dinner, too, and the only person who doesn't comment is the one for whom I made a completely different meal. I ignore it until she does comment.

"The fish is a little dry, I have to say." She pushes her plate away, ninety percent of the food still on it. My eyes go wide, and anger settles in my stomach. In the corner of my eyes, I notice Adrian tense as his eyes go wide as well.

"Excuse me?" My voice is calmer than I expected it to be, but everyone's eyes follow mine and widen. I don't know if it is my reaction or her words.

"The fish is dry. It does not taste good." She emphasizes every word like I'm an idiot who didn't hear her the first time. My blood is boiling in my veins, and I try to control myself, but I can't. I ball my hands into fists and watch as Gabriel takes a bite from the fish.

"Kira, it tastes amazing. What are you talking about?" That is when she gets angry, too, but I don't care. They can fight later. Right now, I'm not having her insult a dish I spent hours making for her. It is petty, but I really can't help myself.

"I spent hours making this for you, *specially* for you because you're a pescatarian. Most of us don't like fish, but I made it for you anyway. I tasted it seven times, ensuring it is neither dry nor salty and has just the proper amount of spices. Just. For. *You.*" Again, my voice is calmer than I intend it to be.

"Well, clearly, you don't know how to cook then." I jump up from my seat and am about to lunge forward and rip out her hair extensions, but Adrian holds me back. I calm down quickly and take a deep breath while Adrian's arms still detain me.

Turning to Jean, I say, "I'm sorry, I think I've lost my appetite." Then, I turn to my brother, who is worried and also angry. I know he isn't mad at me; he is mad at Kira for insulting me in my home. "Excuse me." He nods, and I walk upstairs into my room.

My feet bring me toward my bed, and as soon as I sit down, I start to cry tears of anger. It takes me a couple of minutes to settle, and when I do, I go to the bathroom and wipe my face. I pull off the dress and am about to put on shorts but groan loudly instead. *Great, now I'm on my period too!* I realize why I snapped.

Sometime after I have gone upstairs, a knock on my door startles me. I sit down on the bed, but the person doesn't bother waiting for me to say 'come in'. When I see it's Gabriel, my heart skips a beat, and I want to start crying again. *Fucking hormones...*

"Can we talk?" he asks, and I nod. He walks over and sits down in front of me.

"Why aren't you with Kira?" I ask, pulling on a loose thread hanging from my shorts and avoiding his gaze. His hand covers mine, and his other lifts my chin, forcing my eyes to meet his.

"Because you are more important." I swallow hard, and my stomach twists. The tingles and sparks leave my skin when he removes his hands. "I'm sorry about Kira. I don't know what came over her. It is not okay for her to treat you this way. I'm so sorry," he tells me, and I nod before sucking in a sharp breath when I feel a cramp in my lower abdomen. I try to hide the pain with a neutral expression, but he notices anyway. "What? What's wrong?" His hand covers mine again, and I am incredibly irritated by his actions. I take my hand back and wince when I get a worse cramp. "Val."

"Nothing. Please, just leave me alone." The pain gets worse and worse by the minute, and I have to get up and move around, which is precisely what I do. Every month, the pain is overwhelming, and I don't know how to handle it.

"Let me help you," he says and follows me around the room. His arms reach toward my body, and tears leave my eyes.

"No, just go away. You and your girlfriend have done enough! You've ruined my evening, and you–you–" I stop talking before I let my words get the better of me; before I say something I will regret, like admitting my feelings or even the fact that I was jealous of Kira.

"What did I do? I even defended your fucking fish," he replies, his voice firm.

"Stop talking to me like that!" The tears stream down my cheeks, and I am hopeless and defeated.

"Like what, chérie?" He is gentle then. I have to sit down on my bed when the cramps become too much. "Okay, tell me what to do! Please, chérie, please tell me what to do." His entire attitude changes, showing how worried and confused he is. I lean back on my bed and crumble into a fetal position. Everything is amplified, mainly because we are fighting, and I can't take the pain. "I'm sorry, I didn't mean to fight with you. Just tell me how I can help." His hand rests on my thigh, and everything inside of me lights on fire.

"It hurts," I whine, and he nods.

"Okay, okay. Wait here, don't go anywhere." I frown at him, and he gives me an apologetic smile. "You know what I mean."

When he returns minutes later, he pulls me into an upright position and wipes the sweat off my forehead with a small towel. He hands me a glass of water and two painkillers. I take them gladly, and he removes the glass from my hand once again. Gabriel holds out a hot water bottle he has made for me, and, for the first time in half an hour, I smile. It soon fades when another cramp shoots pain through my whole body. I lie on my side.

"I'm sorry I yelled at you," I mumble, and his hand lifts to touch my cheek.

"It's okay. I'm sorry, too. I'm so sorry, chérie." Gabriel lies down next to me until we are facing each other. My eyes close, and crinkles appear on my forehead as I furrow my brows and breathe loudly. Gabriel's hand lifts to smooth them out before dropping to my arm, where he starts running his fingers up and down.

"It hurts," I complain again, and his thumb wipes away the tears which continue to stream from the corners of my eyes. The way his skin feels on mine is heavenly. His hand moves to my arm again, and he rubs along there. "Make it stop." Pain flashes in his eyes, and I know it hurts him to see me like this.

"I would give anything to make it stop, chérie, *anything*." His voice is so soft as he talks to me. "You're the only girl who has ever been this vulnerable with me. I can't begin to describe how much it pains me to see you like this. Maybe it's because you mean so much to me, or maybe it's because there is nothing I can do to help you. Either way– I guess what I'm trying to say is–" He cuts off before he finishes his sentence, but I sense he is not done speaking. "You're so very strong," he informs me, and my head spins. The mahogany scent coming off him, his smooth accent, his handsome face, all of it clouds my senses, and if I gave in, I would ask him to kiss me. "Stronger and more beautiful than anyone I have ever met." I must be imagining his words because they don't make any sense to me. *He is drunk*, I tell myself. He must be intoxicated somehow because Gabriel wouldn't say this to me, not while he is still dating Kira. *Would he?*

"I don't understand." He smiles at me, and his dimples are deep and sexy, making my head spin even more.

"Neither do I. You've turned everything upside down for me." *Okay, now I know* he's making all of this up to distract me. It is working too. After all, it's been minutes since I've last felt a cramp. "How are you feeling?" he asks when I don't respond.

"Better. Your distraction helped." Gabriel's eyes go wide momentarily before he plays it off and smiles.

"Yeah, there you go. I knew it would." He sits up, and I follow him, still clinging to the hot water bottle.

"I'm sorry you had to see me like this, and I'm sorry about our fight and just, in general, the way I behaved," I apologize, and he puts his hand on my cheek, his thumb caressing the soft skin slightly. *Kiss me. Just kiss me.* He doesn't.

"Don't apologize. None of this was your fault. I'm sorry for it all." He shakes his head. I don't know what to think anymore, but my eyelids get heavy, and my eyes close. "I have to go," he whispers, and I nod. I thank him for bringing all the things I needed. He leaves my room with a swift kiss on the cheek, and I fall asleep shortly after.

Chapter 10

The following day, I wake up early and decide to go for a run. I leave a note for Adrian on the fridge to let him know where I am, grab some water, and start running the same track the guys and I followed almost a week ago. The events of last night come crashing back when I sprint down the same path where Gabriel and I raced last time. The way he talked to me and called me 'strong' more than once replays in my head. I'm out of breath, my mind is running wild, and the cramps come back to my lower abdomen. The sound of the steady waves as they crash onto the shore relaxes me. The smell of saltwater fills my nose, as well as the sweet scent of chocolate from a crêpe stand not far from where I'm sitting.

For years, I wanted to hear Gabriel talking to me the way he did yesterday. Although, I would never have expected that he would only do it to distract me from the pain when he finally did. I get up and start running again out of frustration. I don't know where I'm going, but I gasp when I arrive at Evangelin's store. It is crowded, and she looks overwhelmed, which is why I quickly move toward her.

"Bonjour," I say, and her face lights up when she sees me. Evangelin is holding thirty different articles of clothing, and the look of panic is even more evident on her face up close. "Can I help you?" She nods, and I glance at the lineup at the cash register. I readjust my ponytail to try and make myself look more presentable. Evangelin follows me and gives me a brief introduction to her system. Once I understand, I start cashing people out. After another hour of absolute stress, the store clears up, and only a handful of people are left.

"Thank you so much," is the first thing she says to me when we finally have a second to breathe. "Danielle quit this morning, and my other employee has the flu. They left me to take care of the store all by myself on a Saturday!" The petite woman throws her hands into the air and shakes her head.

"Don't worry, I don't mind helping you at all. Here is my phone number. Whenever you need me, and I'm in Monaco, I'll come in and help out." Her small eyes study me, and a warm smile appears on her face.

"Thank you. I will, of course, pay you," she assures me, but I shake my head.

"No, please don't pay me." I don't want her to waste money on me.

"Okay, at least let me repay the favor someday." I smile at her.

Evangelin shows me everything I need to know about the clothes, prices, sales, and so on. I pay close attention, hoping I will remember everything when more people come into the store again. I also notify Adrian where I am so he doesn't worry about me.

At lunchtime, she disappears for a little while but holds up takeout in her right hand and coffee in her left when she returns. We eat and talk a little more about the store. Evangelin even offers me some clothes to change into, and I gladly accept. I don't want to scare off any customers because of my sweaty workout attire.

"So, how are things going with the guy you like?" Her question is so simple, and I wish I had an answer like 'good' or 'not so great', but I have no idea what is happening between us. I tell her about yesterday and watch as an amused grin spreads over her lips. "It sounds like he didn't say those things to you because he wanted to distract you," she comments with a melodic tone in her voice before biting off a piece of her sandwich.

"Of course it was! Gabriel has no interest in me other than being friends. There was one time when we almost kissed, but it wasn't the right time." I play with the bread from my sandwich and tear off a small piece.

"It sounds like he did like you, but you rejected him, and he got into a relationship with someone, and so did you. The only difference is that you broke up with Luke when you realized there was someone else for you. He is still dragging the other girl along. Then, yesterday, he made another advance, and you shot him down again. It makes me think he truly does like you." I want to shake my head, but it feels impolite. "Nowadays, love is something rare, as if it is something which only happens to people who understand what it takes. You can't give up on someone you love after one fight, and you can't give up when you drift apart in the slightest bit. If you truly love someone, you have to fight to make it work because these days, it is so rare to find a person who makes you want to breathe forever." The wisdom flowing from her makes me speechless. I never looked at the world from her perspective, but I'm glad she gave me something to think about. Love is a lot more complicated than I could have ever imagined it.

"I want to say you're right, but it is undeniable how I feel about him." I let out a small sigh before I focus on the uneaten piece of bread in my hand.

"Oh, child," she says and puts her food down. "Some people can be so blind when it comes to figuring out how the other person feels." She cocks an eyebrow, obviously meaning me. "Communication is crucial. People tend to forget this. So, I am reminding you, tell him how you feel. It's better done sooner than later." If it were that simple, I would have admitted my feelings to Gabriel a long time ago, but it's not. I only nod and force a smile onto my lips.

A couple of hours later, I walk home. It is still light outside, and the wind is pleasantly warm. I see a message from Jean asking if I want to hang out with him. We agree to meet at my house in half an hour. Jean arrives as I'm done putting on fresh clothes, and I run downstairs to open the door for him. Adrian is still with his performance coach, so we are all alone.

"Hello," he says as soon as I open the door.

"Hi," I reply, and he gives me a quick hug. "How are you?" I ask and lead him outside onto the veranda. I like to spend most of my days out here.

"Good, I wanted to check on you, though. Yesterday was a disaster," he simply states, and I chuckle.

"Yes, it wasn't the best." We both laugh, and I enjoy the calm after the long day. Jean is smiling at me, and I can tell there is something on his mind.

"Can I ask you for a favor?" he eventually says, and I nod. "I haven't seen my brother since everything happened last night, and I'm getting worried. Will you speak to him? I think he's unhappy, but Gabriel doesn't share his feelings with me, not like he does with you." His eyes are pleading with me, and his hand is on the table, reaching out.

"If he comes to me, I will talk to him. Otherwise, it is his life, and I have nothing to do with it," I inform Jean in a firm tone. He nods and leans back in the chair.

We play some card games before he has to head home. As much as I like spending time with him, I am also glad to be by myself. My cramps have worsened again since the painkillers are wearing off, and I sit down on the couch in the living room with a hot water bottle, some water, and a few crackers. I put on a movie and curl up into a ball on the couch. I wince when the pain gets worse and close my eyes to try and let it go.

It feels as if a hand appears on my forehead and gently runs over my face. The softness of the touch reminds me of Gabriel's. I must be imagining the way his index finger runs over my cheek, the way it drops to my neck and makes goosebumps spread over my entire body. His name leaves my lips uncontrollably, and I feel his thumb as it caresses my cheek. I want this to be real. His name leaves me for the second time, and I still don't know if I'm dreaming.

"Chérie," Gabriel's voice says, and I shoot up on the couch. He is really here. "I'm sorry, I didn't mean to scare you," he states, and I wipe my eyes, hoping I'm not hallucinating.

"What are you doing here?" I ask him when I finally find my voice. My eyes focus on his handsome face, and I notice he's wearing a black long-sleeved shirt and jeans. His hair is messily neat, as always, and his lips seem fuller and pinker than ever before.

"I wanted to check on you. Adrian let me inside, and I found you sleeping on the couch." I nod, but it doesn't explain why he touched me and ran his fingers over my face. "You were saying my name in your sleep," he whispers, and I blush instantly. Embarrassment washes over me, and I want to pull the blanket over my face. I don't know if I should be honest with him like Evangelin told me to be.

"Why were you touching me?" I counter, putting him on the spot instead. He leans back and looks directly into my eyes.

"I'm sorry, I tried to wake you gently," he explains, confusing me more. "How are you feeling?" he asks, completely changing the subject. Worry is evident on his face.

"I'm fine," I lie. "Where have you been? Jean was concerned about you." He looks away from my face as he answers.

"I needed some time to think," he replies, and I frown. He's acting so weirdly. "Okay, well, I've got to go. I just wanted to make sure you're feeling better." He gets up from the ground, and when he leans down to press a kiss to my cheek, I twist my head so his lips are only a centimeter away from mine. If he feels anything, he will kiss me. My eyes are on his, and it feels like time is standing still. I need him to do something, anything.

"Kiss me," I beg without even thinking about it. For a second, I'm convinced he will.

"We can't," he whispers and rushes out of my home. I am left with my thoughts, and I let anger wash over me. *This is getting ridiculous.*

Chapter 11

Approximately Three Years Ago...

I'm out of breath, and my heart is beating rapidly in my chest. It has been a week since I've last worked out, and it is already affecting me. School is piling on the stress, making it impossible for me to do anything I genuinely enjoy. After finishing my run, I walk back to Aunt Carolina's house, briefly stopping by my favorite smoothie shop.

When I get back to the house, Aunt Carolina is luckily out with her friends. Adrian is racing in Spain this week, which means I'm all by myself. Before I can feel lonely, my phone vibrates. Gabriel's name flashes on my screen, and I get excited while my stomach turns upside down. It's been a month since I've last seen him, but we speak on the phone almost three times a week. We also text a lot or send each other content over social media, which we know the other person will enjoy.

Quickly, I take a shower and make myself somewhat presentable. Gabriel and I usually video call, so I must look as attractive as possible. My phone vibrates on the bed, and I throw myself on it, briefly fixing my appearance.

Gabriel is lying on his hotel bed, a beautiful smile on his tired face. He's slowly been growing a beard, but it is still patchy. I don't mind it because he looks sweet and sexy with a bit of stubble. The yellow shirt he's wearing complements his green-brown eyes. We make conversation about how our week has been so far, and when he flashes me his breathtaking smile, which is decorated with charming dimples, *I melt.*

"How is your brother doing? Jean, right?" Gabriel's face lights up, and he smiles brightly.

"Yes, Jean. He's doing okay. He's got a lot of schoolwork he likes to complain about," Gabriel informs me as he rolls his eyes. "Jean is a bit dramatic when it comes to school." I chuckle, but I can't help but feel bad for his brother. I understand how challenging school can be. After all, I'm still going through it myself.

"So, what else is going on?" I ask him after we make awkward faces at each other and laugh. His smile slowly fades, and he bites the inside of his cheek before he speaks.

"I met someone. Her name is Kira Delgado, and she is an actress. She is brilliant and funny, and I am going to see her again when I get back to Monaco." I am close to hanging up.

"Gabriel, I gotta go do homework," I excuse myself after listening to him gush about Kira for almost five minutes, *even though it feels like he's been talking for an eternity.*

The initial excitement of talking to him over the phone has faded and left nothing but hurt and disappointment in its place. I text my brother and see if he has time to talk to me. Adrian responds instantly and tells me he is 'preoccupied'. I shake my head and smile at my phone. He seems to be 'preoccupied' a lot recently, which is good. Adrian is usually too responsible, which is precisely why I am happy he is enjoying life. However, I am sad I can't talk to him right now. I need someone to take my mind off Gabriel, and the only other person I can think of is James. I text him to see if he has some time, and within minutes, my phone rings, and James' name flashes on my screen.

"Helloooo," I say, relief washing over me. I need James to tell me about his life and make me forget about my own.

"Hi, gorgeous," he chimes into the phone. "You miss me?" I let out a short laugh before I assure him I do. "I miss you, too, luv." I hold back the tears that threaten to leave my eyes and scold myself for wanting to cry. "Katie and I broke up," he informs me, and my mouth falls open.

"How come?" I ask, still shocked by this new development. James and Katie have been dating for two years, and the last thing I knew was they were happy together. This is as much of a surprise to me as Gabriel having a girlfriend.

"I don't love her; I don't know if I ever did," he plainly admits, and my mouth opens wider. I am glad we are not on a video call because my facial expression would only make him feel worse.

"I thought you did."

"So did I, but I don't think it was love I felt," he whispers in the softest voice.

"Have you ever been in love?" He stays quiet for a very long time. It isn't a bad question, and most of the time, James opens up to me about everything, but the silence on the other side of the line drives me crazy.

"Your brother is outside of my hotel room. I have to go. Bye, darling," he lies and hangs up. I know Adrian is busy and wonder why James would lie to me.

For the rest of the day, I stay in bed and do my homework. Aunt Carolina comes home eventually but doesn't bother to let me know. She simply goes to bed, and I figure she has already eaten. Everything is routine in Los Angeles. I go to school, get home, work out, train in the simulator, do my homework, prepare some food, take a shower, and go to bed before waking up and repeating the *same shit.*

Chapter 12

Present...

I feel foolish, *so incredibly foolish.* My legs refuse to help me walk, the embarrassment has taken over my whole body, and my mind is allowing every question and feeling about Gabriel to enter. I shake my head repeatedly to let go of the thoughts and emotions. *Why did I have to say something? Why couldn't I leave it alone? He has a girlfriend! But he was so affectionate...* Anger settles in my chest, and it is directed at Gabriel. I am so mad at him for being a caring person.

Adrian walks into the living room, and the tears start streaming down my cheeks. "What the fuck did he do?" he asks and sits down on the couch next to me, wrapping his arms around me. I tell him what happened, and Adrian holds me close to him, comforting me. "Dickhead," he whispers, and I laugh. "Say the word, and I'll give him a black eye." I sit up and look at my brother.

"No, I don't want you to do that. I'm sorry for crying. I just had to let it out." Adrian wipes away my tears and nods. The last thing either of us needs is for him and Gabriel not to get along. After all, they are going to have to work together for at least a year.

"Don't apologize for sharing your emotions with me. I love you, and I would do anything for you," he reminds me and presses a kiss to the top of my head. "I have to go to sleep, lots of packing to do tomorrow." Adrian gets up but stops halfway to the stairs. "By the way, Gabriel is taking the same flight as us on Monday. So..." he trails off, and I roll my eyes. *Fuck!*

"Does that mean we have to go to the airport with him?" I ask, and Adrian chuckles.

"Yes, he lives a couple of houses over. It wouldn't make sense to take two cars." I groan and lean back on the couch. "Don't worry, it will be okay. At least Kira is not coming," he assures me, and I cock an eyebrow.

"How come she's not coming? It's the first race of the season!" I almost feel bad for Gabriel but dating her is his choice. Adrian shrugs before he leaves me to my thoughts.

My phone vibrates, and I decide to see who is texting me. James is asking me if I want to meet him tomorrow after I finish packing, and I let him know when to come over.

Something inside me doesn't want to get out of bed when I wake up the next morning. My body is tired from only getting five hours of sleep and from the events of last night. Instead of dwelling on them, I pull the blanket off my body and saunter into my bathroom. I get ready, pack, and let James know when I'm done so he can come over.

He stands at my front door with yet another sunflower in his hand. I laugh, but he simply smiles brightly at me. "Hey, luv," he greets and holds the flower out for me. I take it from him with a genuine grin on my face.

"Thank you." He winks at me and leans down to press a kiss against my cheek. James always smells amazing: minty and woody, a combination I never thought would smell good. For as long as I can remember, I associate this smell with security.

"What do you want to do today?" he asks after I put the flower in the same glass as the first one that he brought me a week ago. To my surprise, it is still alive and blossoming. I shrug and look at James again. "Feel like boxing?" A smile spreads over my face, and I go upstairs to get the gloves and focus pads.

James puts on the focus pads first, and we move to the garden. The sun is hot, yet the grass is still wet. We are both barefoot. I'm hitting hard against the pads, and James is clearly having difficulty not asking what is bothering me. Eventually, he does open his mouth but just makes casual conversation. He asks me how I'm feeling about flying out tomorrow and how I am doing in general. We switch, and James starts to hit the pads.

"Gabriel called me yesterday. He was upset with me," he says out of nowhere.

"What?" I ask and lower my hands, not realizing James would keep hitting. His hand reaches forward, and he punches the left side of my throat. I gasp for air immediately before ripping off the pads so I can wrap my hand around the ache.

"Oh my God, Val. I'm so sorry." He gets closer to me, but I hold up one of my hands, still gasping for air. The area is burning with pain, and it starts throbbing almost immediately. It takes me a while to breathe evenly again, and James wraps a bag of ice around my throat. "I'm so sorry, darling, I'm so fucking sorry." There is pain in his eyes, and it shows that hurting me brings him more agony than the physical one I am feeling.

"Don't worry, I'm going to be fine." My voice cracks, and he flinches. "You were telling me something," I say to distract him. James shakes his head, his expression still filled with worry.

"Never mind, luv. Can I bring you anything else?" He reaches his hand out and runs the back of his fingers over my cheek. My heart skips a beat, and I am surprised by it.

"No, I'm fine, really," I assure him, and he takes his hand back. "Please, tell me what Gabriel did," I beg, and his expression becomes unreadable.

"He was upset about something, but I couldn't understand him. It had something to do with work, but I'm not sure that's why he was furious." I wonder what possibly came over Gabriel, but my neck is distracting me. After a little while of complete silence, James' phone lights up on the table, and I see his manager is calling him. He completely ignores it, still studying my injury.

"Go answer your phone," I croak and press the device in his hand. He hesitates, and I glare at him. James lifts his hands and excuses himself to take the call. When he returns, an upset expression lingers on his face. "What's wrong?"

"Nothing," he lies and sits down next to me again.

"If you have to leave, go. I will be fine, I promise," I assure him, but he frowns.

"I'm not leaving you, especially not after I hurt you," he says with a frustrated tone in his voice.

"We both know when your manager calls, you drop everything and go. So, I'm kicking you out of my house, and you better see what she wants," I command, yet he hesitates again. "I'm alright. Go," I tell him, and James nods. He gives me a swift kiss on the cheek, gathers his stuff, and leaves, but not before looking over his shoulder one more time.

My throat is burning. The ice eventually numbs my entire neck, and I have to put it down. Luckily, the pain and throbbing stop, but I wince when I look in the mirror. The mark is significant and a flaming red color. It runs from the middle of the left side of my throat to my collarbone. I shake my head, regretting it immediately.

"Val?" Adrian screams through the house. He sounds concerned, which makes me worry.

"In my room," I inform him. Within seconds, he is in my door frame and running toward my bed.

"James told me what happened. Are you okay? Let me see," he says and almost rips the ice pack from my throat. When I cry out, he mumbles, "Sorry," and gently removes it. "Fuck, that's bad," he states, and I frown at him.

"Oh, is it? I hadn't noticed."

"I'm sorry," he mumbles once again. "Is there anything I can do?" Adrian is still examining my throat, but I shake my head. All I want to do is get dinner ready and then go to bed.

Chapter 13

"Passport? Plane tickets? Backpack?" Adrian sounds nervous, which brings a smile to my face.

"Got it. Got it. Got it," I promise, but he still doesn't calm down. He's running around the house, searching for who-knows-what, and never even stops to think about what he's doing. "Adrian, we've got everything. Relax," I say with a firm tone, and he stops to look at me. He nods and picks up his backpack before squeezing my arm. His hand reaches out to my throat, and he gently tilts my head to the side.

"It looks awful, Val," he tells me, and I roll my eyes right before I zip up my jacket and put my hood over my head.

"There, nothing to see anymore." Adrian frowns but doesn't argue with me. He calls for a taxi. Today, we're flying out to Melbourne for the first race of the season. The circuit is located around Albert Park. Our trip to Australia will take a day, and I don't look forward to sitting for that long.

The taxi arrives at the same time as Gabriel. He is wearing black sweatpants, sneakers, and a simple, white shirt. Gabriel stops walking as soon as he sees me, and I have to grab Adrian's arm. *I can't talk to him. I can't have the same conversation again.*

"Valentina," Gabriel says, and I squeeze Adrian's arm.

"Back off, mate. If she wants to talk to you, she will." Gabriel's eyes narrow, but when he sees my pain-filled expression, he drops it. Usually, I wouldn't hide behind Adrian, but I don't have the energy to deal with Gabriel.

When we get into the taxi, Gabriel sits in the front, and I sit behind him. The drive is primarily silent, except for a few things Adrian and Gabriel discuss. Involuntarily, my eyes shift to the outside mirror of the car, and I find Gabriel's reflection staring at me. I look away and pretend I never saw him. My phone vibrates, and I look down to see a text from Evangelin, wishing me a safe trip.

For so long, I've had bad luck meeting people I could connect with as I have with Evangelin. She listens to me, understands me, lets me vent, and I love hearing about Carlos and their relationship. Evangelin is much like the grandma I never had. My real grandma never understood my dream. She didn't understand why I wanted to become something so 'unfeminine', in her words, something mostly men are.

Grandma died when I was very young, and Grandpa was devastated. He hid it well from us, but Adrian and I knew he was heartbroken. It took him years to be able to smile when Grandma's name was mentioned. Now, he is with her again, probably talking about who ate the last barbajuan. Every Sunday, they would have the same conversation, arguing over who was the culprit. To this day, neither of them knew it was either Adrian or me who ate it.

The three of us walk through the airport, check in our luggage, and find the security check. I make sure no one notices the bruise, and as soon as I'm through security, I pull my hood over my head again. We sit down on the seats near our gate, and Adrian excuses himself to go to the bathroom. Like an immature teenager, I put on my headphones and turn up the volume. I'm afraid Gabriel wants to talk to me.

A couple of minutes pass when all of a sudden, Gabriel holds up a piece of paper. Can we talk? I shake my head and pull my feet onto the chair. There is a sad expression on his face, but he looks down at the paper again and starts writing. Please, Val. I'm so sorry. Once again, I shake my head. It's not that he rejected me, but this whole chaos threatens our friendship. Valentina Esmèe Cèlia Romana, you know we have to talk. He is right; we do need to speak, but not now. As soon as we start talking, I'm going to start feeling things.

Adrian comes back, looks at Gabriel and me, and frowns. I focus on myself and close my eyes when my favorite song starts playing through my headphones. My fingers fumble with the string from my hood absentmindedly, and I think about what to do. Naturally, I come to no conclusion.

They call our flight for boarding, and we make our way onto the plane. I sit down in my seat, and Adrian attempts to take the one next to me, but Gabriel appears behind him and whispers something into his ear. I don't know what it is, but it makes my brother move away and sit down in a different one.

"I broke up with Kira," he states as soon as he sits down, and my mouth drops.

"What?" is the only thing I'm able to croak out.

"Yeah, it was time. We were both miserable. She wants to pursue her acting career, and I need to focus on mine. Kira is nice, but she'll be better off with someone else. I don't want to be with someone who disrespects you," he adds in the last sentence, and I look at him with shock. He flashes me a wonderful smile with his dimples.

"Well, I'm sorry then," I blurt out, but he can tell I don't mean it. The selfish person inside of me is thrilled to hear he broke up with her.

"No, you're not." I look away from his smug smile and shake my head while one dances onto my lips as well. "I care a lot about you, chérie, and I hope what happened yesterday won't stand in the way of our friendship." *There it is, the reason I didn't want to have this conversation.*

"We both know the uncomfortable situation from yesterday will always be embarrassing for me. I put myself out there, waited for you to kiss me, no, I asked you to kiss me, and you let me think you were going for it..." I pause and take a deep breath before I can continue. "How do you expect us to go back to just being friends? We're screwed, Gabriel, because I can't go back." I've been waiting years to tell him this. Gabriel leans back and pulls his bottom lip between his teeth. He's thinking about what to say.

"Val, I'm terrified of my feelings for you. I won't deny them, but I also can't address them without risking everything between us. You're one of my best friends, compassionate, open, and I know I can always count on you. If things go wrong between us, I will lose you forever, and I can't," he rants so quickly, I have trouble keeping up with him. Once his words have registered in my brain, and I understand his fear, I can finally speak.

"I get it, Gabriel, but how do you expect me to keep on suppressing how I feel?" I ask, turning him speechless.

When he doesn't say anything for a few moments, I get nervous, but I don't push him. It wouldn't be fair of me to expect him to have an answer ready for something like this. I simply put my headphones back on and play some random songs. My eyes drift to the window, and I feel his hand reach for my hood to force me to look at him, but I resist. My hood falls completely, and I glare at him.

"What is this?" he asks, concern laced in his voice. I have no idea what he's talking about for a moment, but when I realize, I panic.

"It's nothing," I snap. The last thing I want is for him to get mad at James. They seem to have enough problems with one another as is.

"Valentina, please tell me who did this to you." I choose to ignore him, and he groans beside me. "Why are you so stubborn?" My blood boils, although I know the only reason why he called me that is because he's worried about me.

"Why am I stubborn? Why are you so confusing? Why do you act like you have feelings for me and then decide that 'we can't'? Why do you have to be the only guy I've ever-?" I stop myself and flinch. *Great job, Valentina, really fucking smart.*

"What?" His lips move away from each other, and the shock is evident on his face.

"Never mind," I tell him and attempt to pull my hood back up, but he takes my hand and stops me from doing so.

"Does it hurt?" he asks me, the concern stronger than the shock.

"Yes, but you hurt me more." Gabriel lets go of my hand, and I'm finally able to put my hood back on. I look out of the window again.

Ten hours go by without Gabriel speaking to me; ten hours of listening to music and trying to sleep. Eventually, I give up and pull out my favorite book. I get lost in Vincent and Kate's love story. *They don't have it easy either*, I tell myself, *but they also have the supernatural to deal with.* Gabriel and I don't. We only have to deal with the fact that Gabriel can't decide what he wants. When I get to my favorite part of the book, I swallow the lump in my throat. I look over at Gabriel, but he's asleep. W*hy can't I like someone who's available, I've known for years, who cares about me, and I know will treat me well? Someone like James... wait? James?* Yet, here I am, stuck on a man who keeps finding ways to hurt me without even realizing it. My mind lingers on James a little while longer.

Then my focus shifts back to Gabriel. He told me he couldn't lose me, but I am prioritizing my crush over our friendship. People have been dying, leaving, and disappearing out of our lives, and I don't have the heart to break both of ours.

I poke his arm, and his eyes shoot open. Ten hours gave me enough time to think and make a decision I am probably going to regret. Gabriel removes his headphones and looks at me, confusion on his face.

"What's wrong, chérie?" His hand reaches out, and I take his in mine.

"I'm sorry about earlier. If you give me a little time, I can go back to being friends. I promise, I just need time." Gabriel studies my features. There is a short pause. No one says anything, neither of us moves, but I can see the conflict in Gabriel's eyes.

"I don't want this to be painful for you like it is for me," he says firmly, and I suck in a sharp breath.

"The alternative is not speaking at all. Would you prefer that?" His eyes reveal his indecisiveness.

“Of course not, but you’ll suffer with me constantly being around you. Trust me, *I know*,” he points out, making me realize he’s right.

“Don’t flatter yourself,” I try to tease, but this whole conversation is dreadful. I’m embarrassed, whether or not he admitted he has feelings for me too. I should be excited knowing he does and that he’s finally single again, but instead, we’re having one of the most confusing and draining conversations I’ve ever had.

“I can’t be the only guy you ever dot dot dot, or wherever that sentence finishes. You need to be with someone who isn’t as broken as me, chérie. I can’t do that to you,” he admits with shame, and instead of trying to understand him, I get angry.

“Okay, then leave, Gabriel. Please switch seats with my brother and don’t speak to me again.” I place my headphones on my ears and turn away from him. This was, by far, the worst way I could have reacted, but it’s what I do. As soon as I realize ultimately where this would end up, I push him away to avoid humiliation. It’s wrong, and it hurts him, but it protects me.

Adrian is next to me then, and his hand wraps around mine. I tell him nothing but that I am tired and probably going to sleep for the next two hours until we have to catch our second flight. He nods, and I rest my head against his shoulder. My heart hurts in my chest, and I remind myself to breathe every once in a while.

Chapter 14

Approximately Two Years Ago...

My cheek burns, and the tears are hot on my face. *I should have never lied to her in the first place*, I remind myself. The ice feels soothing on my sore skin, and I wish Adrian were home. Not that I would have told him Aunt Carolina slapped me, but he would cheer me up and comfort me after I made up a story. However, Adrian is out with James, who has been visiting us since Monday. James and I have hardly spent time together since he came to Los Angeles, but I'm still glad he is here. It's been a while since I've seen him, and I have missed him.

To keep my mind from focusing on the pain, I start doing my homework. The distraction mostly works. Then, I think about the evil woman, who is casually sitting in her living room right now, with no regrets about slapping me across the face. *What possible reason could she have to hurt me? What justification?* I stop myself before I fall into that hole. *There is no justification; there is no reason.* People like her never have a good reason to do what they do. They think they have the right to hurt their dependents, to discipline them.

"'Ellooooo," James says as he walks through the door. "Adrian didn't want to leave his date yet, but I got bored of watching him attempt to flirt. It's only amusing for so long," he goes on, and I panic, but he notices the mark before I can hide it. "Good God, Val, who did that?" I scramble for words, not finding the right ones. "Did Carolina do that to you?"

"No," I squeak, mentally slapping myself. *Like he's going to believe that.* Anger flashes over his face, and he starts walking toward the stairs with his hands balled into fists. "James!" I pull on his arm, and he spins around. "In my room, now," I demand, and he obeys.

"What the hell, Valentina? How long has she been abusing you?" James drops onto my bed and runs his hand through his thick hair. I sit down on the ground in front of him and look up to meet his gaze. "Why haven't you told me?" Pain flashes in his eyes, and I am not prepared to tell him what Aunt Carolina has been doing for the past three years. His hand touches the cheek without a mark and caresses it gently with his thumb.

"You can't tell Adrian. No matter what you do, you cannot tell Adrian." I beg, but James only nods. "No, no nodding. Swear on our friendship that you will not tell him." The sad expression lingers on his face.

"You want me to sit back, knowing you're getting abused, and not do anything about it? Who do you think I am?" He storms out of my room and downstairs, but I cannot catch up with him this time. "You think you can lay a finger on her without facing any consequences? You're very wrong!" he screams at my aunt, and I flinch.

"Excuse me?" the short, curvy woman asks, and I pull on James' arm. Her face is red, and her breathing is uneven, as is mine. "How dare you speak to me like that?"

"How dare *you* lay a single finger on her?" James points at me, but I hide behind him like the coward I am. James, however, moves closer to Aunt Carolina and leans down just enough for her to hear the following threatening words that fall from his lips. "If you ever hurt her again, if I ever find out that you hit her again, I will call the police, and I will have them arrest you. Then,

I'm going to make sure you lose your house, all of your money, and any good reputation you might have. If I ever hear anything about you abusing Valentina again, I will ruin your life." James moves away from the horrible woman, gently takes my hand, and pulls me upstairs. When we get to my room, he slams the door and holds me against it. His arms are on each side of my face, and his hands press against the door. James' breathing is heavy, and I can tell he is frustrated. "You let me know if she ever harms you again. Do you hear me? Nothing can happen to you, Val. Nothing." His face is inches away from mine. His emotions are all over the place, and so is he. I can't make out what he's going to do next. "Valentina, promise me on our friendship that you will tell me."

"I promise," I assure him, and he wraps his arms around me. I can hear his heart beating at an abnormal speed in his chest. Mine mimics the rhythm. "Thank you," I say, and he squeezes me harder.

"I wish you would have told me sooner," he whispers, and I shrug.

"Adrian would have to take care of me, or even worse, I would be put into the system." James steps out of the hug and puts both of his hands on my cheeks.

"You don't have to worry anymore. Carolina isn't going to ignore my threat. She knows better than to do that," he assures me, and I nod. "Now, is there any homework you need help with?" I laugh, and he wipes away the tears of relief that escaped my eyes seconds earlier.

James is brilliant. He graduated high school at seventeen but decided that instead of going to university, he much rather wanted to keep working toward his dream. He was nineteen when he first started racing in Formula One.

James has helped me with my homework for as long as I can remember, especially because Adrian never really liked school. It takes me an hour until James' explanation of how to calculate velocity finally makes sense. I hate physics, I am terrible at it, and I don't know what it is. With patience, James repeatedly explains how to do this simple problem, and I finally understand.

The whole time we're studying, my mind keeps drifting. *What if Aunt*

Carolina is going to hurt me worse next time? What if she doesn't care about James' warning? What if she will come for me tonight? Am I going to scream, knowing Adrian is in the next room? I have no control over any of these answers, and it scares me.

"What's on your mind, beautiful?" He pokes my arm, and I try to smile but fail.

"I'm scared," I admit. "I'm scared that once you're gone, she will hurt me again." I can do nothing to her, but there is a lot she can do to me. James wraps his hand around mine. He knows he can't convince me she won't touch me, which is why he doesn't even try to.

"What can I do to make you feel better?"

"Can you stay with me tonight?" His eyes slightly widen, and his hand briefly tightens around mine, but he soon disregards his surprise and smiles at me.

"Of course. Whatever you need." We get ready for bed, and James brings the pillow from the guest bedroom and his blanket. He attempts to lie on the floor, but I pick the pillow up again and move it onto my bed. "What are you doing?" he asks, confused by my actions.

"You're not sleeping on the floor. We're old enough to sleep in the same bed and not make a big deal about it, aren't we?" I cock an eyebrow and wait for his response.

"Yes, I guess we are." I lie down in bed, and he joins me but lies as far away from me as the bed possibly allows. I am facing him, and he is on his back, staring up at the ceiling.

"Can I ask you something?" James turns his head so he can look at me, and he smiles brightly. It is easy to understand why James has hundreds of fan accounts from people who admire him. He is gorgeous, cute, talented, and kind. His smile alone could make anyone fall in love with him within a second.

"Anything," he replies and puts his hands under his head.

"Why did you really break up with Katie? It's been four months, and I thought maybe you're ready to tell me the truth." His expression never changes, but his body language does. He goes from lying openly to closing it and turning toward me.

"I was in love with someone else; I am in love with someone else. There, is that honest enough for you?" A smile grows on my lips, and suddenly, I am so much more curious.

"Who is she?" I ask, scooting closer toward him.

"I will not tell you her name, but I can tell you this: She is beautiful, the most beautiful girl I've ever seen, and I've known her for a few years. I love her smile, her sense of humor, her eyes, and how they sparkle when the sun hits them, her determination and wit, her fascination with the tiniest things, and the way she always fights for what she wants." He pauses briefly. "Actually, I love everything about her. I have for a while, too. I never had any time to fall in love with someone else. I told Katie from the beginning about the girl, and she was very understanding until she started to want more, which I couldn't give her. Katie was good for me for a little, but this other girl, she has me all kinds of messed up," he tells me, and I grin. I love hearing him talk about her.

"Have you told her how you feel?" James' eyes drift from my face, and he sighs.

"She doesn't feel the same way, trust me. I wish she did, but she only has eyes for another guy," he explains and shrugs.

"Well, she is an idiot. You're an amazing guy. I'm already sure she doesn't deserve you. You're way too good for everyone, *trust me on this*, I know. I don't even deserve you as a friend." He shakes his head and puts his fingers on the back of my hand.

"What a silly thing to say," he replies. "I have to sleep. Good night, luv."

"Night," I say and turn the other way around, facing away from him. My screen lights up, and I read Adrian's text message, informing me he will be home tomorrow. I am confused, but if he's having fun, then good for him.

Chapter 15

Present...

It is Tuesday afternoon when we finally arrive at the hotel in Melbourne. James is already there and welcomes us at the entrance. A big smile spreads over my face, and I sprint over to him as soon as I get my luggage from the taxi. I wrap my arms around his neck and enjoy his comforting scent.

"Hi, darling," he says and takes my luggage. "Let me carry this."

"I'm more than capable of carrying my own suitcase, thank you very much," I respond, and he rolls his eyes.

When I get to my hotel room, I take a shower. Adrian does the same thing before meeting up with his team to go over the strategy for this weekend. He needs to familiarize himself with the track and weather conditions in preparation for any race weekend, attend press conferences, and fulfill other obligations like filming team challenge videos. Those are always my favorite, and with Adrian and Gabriel in one team now, I can't wait to see the finished product. They are both incredibly silly and awkward in front of the camera, which is why I know the videos will be pure comedy.

A few hours after the guys left, Adrian texts me, inviting me to dinner with James and James' teammate, Eduardo Marquez. I put on a plain, light orange skirt which fits me snugly, a white tank top, and a dark orange cardigan. I only put on mascara and lip balm before I finish off the look with some white sneakers. Adrian is waiting for me in the lobby, and a sweet smile appears on his face when he sees me. He holds out his hand and leads me outside.

"Val, this is Eduardo. Eduardo, this is my sister Valentina," Adrian introduces us, and I smile at the handsome man. He has full lips, a pinched nose, light brown eyes, a clean-cut beard, long lashes, and a lovely bronze skin tone. He is lean and muscular but not too bulky, and when he smiles, I see his slightly crooked set of white teeth. His brown hair fits his thick, well-shaped, dark brown eyebrows well. I've seen him on television before, but I've never met him in person. Until this year, Adrian and James didn't have much to do with him.

"It's a pleasure to meet you," he says and holds out his hand for me. I shake it politely and return his smile.

"The pleasure is all mine." Eduardo is relatively short, but he is still at least a few centimeters taller than me.

The dinner is lovely, and I find out a lot about Eduardo. He is twenty-six, from Spain, has three sisters, a completely functional family, and it is his sixth year in Formula One. Eduardo is kind and open, and he asks me lots of questions too. I tell him about my plans to travel along this season, and he gets excited when he hears I will be around a lot. Talking to him is easy, although we don't seem to have much in common. Luckily, my love and passion for the sport make having a conversation with any of the drivers very natural.

"Valentina is a stunning name," Eduardo compliments with his enchanting Spanish accent. I enjoy listening to him talk, hearing him pronounce words in such a unique way. "You and your brother look a lot alike," he states, and I nod. James and Adrian are deep in conversation, but I look at my brother anyway.

"Yes, I agree, and, sadly, so do a lot of people, apparently," I reply and let out a nervous laugh. Eduardo also laughs, a deep, sexy laugh, and to my surprise, my insides warm. Not in the same way they do when Gabriel smiles at me, but still. "So, did you bring any family members this weekend to support you?" He smirks at me and plays with the condensed water which runs down his glass.

"My sister Angelina," he replies, and I nod absentmindedly. When I look at him again, he smirks at me, half of his bottom lip between his teeth. My eyes linger on his mouth, which makes him lean forward over the table. "Has anyone ever told you how intriguing you are?" I roll my eyes at his cliché question, but my smile soon fades. Gabriel told me many times he thinks I am. "Can I take you out on Thursday? On a proper date, not a dinner with your brother." He chuckles, and my mouth drops open.

"Eduardo," James warns, but when he sees me flash him a glare, he holds up his hands and backs off. I turn to the handsome man in front of me and smile. I want to tell him 'No', decline politely, and move on, but I'm unsure why. Eduardo is very attractive, and he seems mature. There is no reason why I shouldn't go on a date with him. *Except for Gabriel*, my subconscious reminds me.

"What time?" I ask him, and the smile on his face grows.

"I'm working until seven. So, seven-thirty?" I nod, and his rough hand wraps around mine. Eduardo lifts them to his mouth and presses the tiniest kiss to the back of mine. "Good night, hermosa." I smile at him, and he releases my hand again.

"Buenas noches," I reply, earning me a smile from him. Eduardo leaves, and both of the other boys scoot closer to me.

"You're going out with Eduardo? How come?" Adrian asks, and I know what he means. A day ago, I was crying over Gabriel, and now, I'm agreeing to go on a date with a guy I only met a couple of hours ago. It's very unlike me, but that is precisely why I am doing it. "You know he's twenty-six, right? He's seven years older than you."

"So? He's a nice guy and incredibly easy on the eyes," I swoon, and both boys scrunch their noses.

"All right, Val, we don't need to know what gets you going," Adrian complains, and I laugh. "We should go too. Long day tomorrow." He yawns and stretches his arms into the air.

We get back to the hotel, and I drop onto my bed. Adrian is already passed out before I am even ready to go to sleep. I check my phone and, out of habit, my Instagram. I click on Cameron's story and choke when I see Gabriel. He is sitting at a table, surrounded by other drivers, but, of course, the main focus is Gabriel. There is no smile on his face, his eyes have dark circles underneath them, and he simply looks exhausted. I force myself to think about Eduardo, and it kind of works. *Eduardo's smile, Eduardo's laugh, Eduardo's beautiful eyes, Gabriel's dimples... NO! No, no, no, no, no!*

Everything feels upside down, and the only thing releasing me from the chaos is sleep.

Chapter 16

Adrian and Dad stand in front of me, the picture of a Formula One car in Dad's hands. They have been quizzing me on the names of the parts for the past week. It is surprisingly easy for me, even though I'm only nine years old and some of the words are difficult to pronounce. Dad starts to point at the different parts, and I name them with ease.

"Front wing, rear wing, engine intake," I say as he continues to move his finger over the page. "Suspension, disc brake, also engine intake, brake cooling intake," I go on, and a proud smile appears on his face.

"That's correct," Adrian tells me, but I need Dad to reassure me. He knows more than my brother.

"You're absolutely right. The mechanics who work on the car would be very pleased with you. Maybe if you can't become a driver, you can be a mechanic," he assures me, and I frown.

"Why wouldn't I be able to become a driver?" I ask, confused. Dad always tells me he believes in me.

"Because it is difficult to become a Formula One driver. If it were easy, everyone would do it, but they can't. There are many factors involved, and,

sadly, talent is not the main one. However, I strongly believe you have what it takes to live your dream. Just like I believe in your brother." He stops and puts his hand on my shoulder. "I'm so proud of you." This is one of the rare moments he ever shows affection. When he does, he makes sure I will never forget it. I hug him as fiercely as I can.

"I love you, Daddy," I say, and he hugs me back.

"I love you, too, little champion."

Adrian takes me with him to work this Thursday morning. Today is an autograph session and press conference. I haven't spoken to Gabriel or seen him in two days, but I'm sure I can no longer avoid him unless I don't want to see Adrian at all. I remind myself I might also see James and Eduardo and immediately feel better.

James briefly greets me before I get into the car with him, Adrian, and Daniel. We arrive at the track and walk toward the paddock. I smile brightly as I take in my surroundings. Here is where I'm meant to be, where I want to spend years of my life. Looking at the track and feeling it underneath my fingertips as I bend down has always been my highlight from the race weekend. This is all my grandfather and I have wanted, but only Adrian gets to live his dream.

"Valentina." My heart stops. *What in the hell could he possibly want from me?* "Can we talk?" he asks, and I look at him with an annoyed expression.

"I told you not to speak to me," I snap at him, and he flinches. "I'm busy forgetting about you."

"I think I can help with that." I spin around in surprise to see Eduardo standing behind me, wearing his Red Bull shirt and a pair of plain, black jeans. His bronze skin looks lovely in the blue color of his shirt. I smile at him, relieved he is interrupting. His sunglasses are on his face, and the smirk on his lips is inviting. Eduardo greets me with a kiss on the cheek, and the displeasure is evident on Gabriel's face. "I look forward to our date tonight," Eduardo informs me, and I bite my bottom lip before grinning victoriously.

"Me, too," I reply, and he squeezes my hand before walking away, turning around one more time to smile at me.

"You're going out with *him*? He's like ten years older than you." I can't tell if he's sad or angry.

"*Seven*, and why do you care? You've made it pretty clear you're not right for me." I try to walk away, but he wraps his hand around my elbow and pulls me back. "What? What do you want?" We're making a scene in front of everyone, which is probably why he leads me out of sight to a private room. "Stop it, just stop." He lets go of my hand immediately. "Three years of friendship, all ruined because you are not mature enough to deal with feelings. So, Gabriel Matteo Biancheri, go fuck yourself because I am done." I am out of breath, and it feels like a weight lifts off my chest. My bottled-up emotions are spilling everywhere, but I don't care anymore.

"I can't give you what you need, what you deserve. I need you to see that for yourself." He's way too calm about something so heavy.

"Oh my god, you are ridiculous. Telling someone who has feelings for you something like that doesn't make the feelings suddenly disappear." *It hurts them, breaks their heart, it can even destroy them. Lucky for me, I did not give him such power over me. I'm smarter than that.* I feel the need to tell him all this, but he doesn't deserve to hear it. Gabriel is studying my face closely, and his expression is soft.

"Please don't go out with Eduardo." I blink a couple of times because if I start counting down out loud, as I do with Adrian, he might think I'm crazy.

"What?" I bark, and he takes a step back when I move closer to him, my hands balled into fists. "You are out of your goddamn mind." I push him out of the way and open the door.

"I am out of my mind," he pleads, and I shut the door once more. "I want what's best for you," he explains.

"Okay, then why can't you be what's best for me?" I challenge, and his fingers appear on my arm before he slowly spins me around.

"All I do is upset you," he replies, shame laced in his words. His face falls, and I lift my hands to his cheeks to force his eyes to meet mine. Gabriel never shies from being vulnerable with me, which is one of the things I admire most about him.

"Because you push me away, and you don't need to," I whisper, and his hands wrap around my wrists. I lean forward, but he backs away, sending a brief and sharp pain through my chest.

"Val, I can't," he mutters, and I let out a sigh.

"That's fine, Gabriel. You tell me you want to be with me but can't, and it's fine. There are people who do want me, and even if there weren't, I don't have to stand here and fight with your indecisiveness," I snap and leave him before he can say anything in response.

I've wanted Gabriel to have feelings for me for three years, but I never thought they'd be so complicated. This whole situation is a mess, and he needs to figure out what he wants. I won't stand in the way of it, but I also won't wait. My feelings are strong, but they most certainly do not control me.

I go back outside and find Adrian standing with his strategists and engineers. He looks concerned, but he is busy and doesn't talk to me. I don't mind since I am just searching for a distraction. I talk to a few people on Adrian's team and make conversation about the new front wing of the car. The people I speak to are mechanics and listening to them explain its workings is fun. I've been studying Formula One cars since I can remember, and Grandpa always took me to work. He was a consultant for McLaren after he retired, and he used to explain everything to me. I was little and barely understood anything, but now, I am fluent in the language they speak. It's a beautiful connection I still have to him and my father. Even though Dad was barely ever home, we still had good moments. He worked in different areas for Formula One. First as a driver and then as a reporter, until the day he died. It's been seven years since his death, and I miss him every day, though not even close to how much I miss Grandpa.

The day is long and exhausting, and I am excited when I finally get back to the hotel room and start to get ready for my date. After the disaster with Gabriel, I'm looking forward to a carefree dinner.

Chapter 17

Approximately Two Years Ago...

Today is one of the most important days of my life, and my nerves prove it. Adrian used his connections to get me a special test drive for some of the driver academies. Usually, they recruit drivers based on their karting results and points they have collected, but since my case is quite different, they made an exception. I get to set a time to see if I can compete with the drivers who are already part of the academy. Adrian flew me out to Barcelona for this because a lot of testing for Formula One is done here. James and Gabriel decided to come with us and are impatiently waiting at the sidelines. My oldest friend being here isn't a surprise, but Gabriel coming to support me was a big shock. We're good friends, but I didn't think he would travel to Spain for me. I can't help but like him more for it.

My eyes scan all three men, and I can tell how nerve-wracking this is for them, especially Adrian and James. Since I was kicked out of Formula Three, all they've done is help me make it back into the racing world. It all seemed hopeless until today.

"Ready?" my brother asks me once I'm seated in the familiar F3 car. It's been a while since I've sat in one, but I've been training, studying every single track and footage I can to prepare myself for an opportunity like this.

"I'm ready," I assure him, but my heart is racing in my chest, and my palms are sweating under the gloves. The helmet is snug on my head, and the racing suit is tight, making it difficult to breathe properly.

"You've got this," Adrian assures me, and I nod. I can barely hear him, and my mind is preoccupied with calming my body. I love this sport more than anything, and this is important. My lap time has to be outstanding for me to get a spot in the driver academy. I've waited two years for another opportunity, and today is the day of my second chance.

I'm given the green light and make my way out of the pit box. After I familiarize myself with the track for a couple of laps, I'm ready to set a time and grab my opportunity by the horns. Once the start and finish line is in my sight, I speed up and race down the track as quickly as possible. The force of the turns is strong, but I lean into them as I have done countless times. Adrenalin runs through my veins, and suddenly, I feel completely calm. This is where I'm meant to be, and I will do anything to prove it to the people watching me. With every bumpy turn and curb I take, my smile gets bigger. I calculate the different angles I have to take to speed down the perfect racing line, something I could never do in my day-to-day life but is second nature to me in the race car.

By the time I reach the start and finish line, I feel sweat dripping down my back. That was exhilarating, and my time was better than any I've ever set before. I'm told to do a slow, cool-down lap and then return to the pit box. James, Gabriel, and Adrian each give me a thumbs up, and pride replaces anxiety inside of me. Once I'm out of the car, I remove my helmet and balaclava. My hair clings to my scalp, but I don't mind it one bit. It takes me back to the races, and so does the exhaustion my body experiences post-driving.

"That was bloody fantastic," James congratulates me before picking me up from the ground to spin me around. I feel like crying out of happiness.

"I'm sweaty," I remind him, but he hugs me tighter.

"Good, that's how you're supposed to be," he assures me, and I laugh.

"That was phenomenal," Adrian says next, but when I go to hug him, he holds me back. "Just because James is okay with your sweat doesn't mean I am," he states, and when my mouth falls open, he pulls me into a hug and chuckles. "Have you lost your sense of humor today?" he asks before I push him back and smack his stomach, making him lean forward and cough dramatically. "She has wounded me, mortally wounded me," Adrian almost screams, and I shush him. I'm smiling so brightly, my face hurts. Gabriel is the last one to come up to me.

"Did I make your trip worthwhile?" I ask to make him smile, which he does.

"Seeing you already made it worth it. Watching that lap was the cherry on top," he says so calmly, it knocks the breath out of me. Gabriel hugs me as well, and I grin against his shoulder.

Then comes a long wait. Adrian, James, Gabriel, and I are led to a room while the people from the driver academies decide my fate. Adrian hands me electrolytes and something to eat to keep my energy from dropping drastically. I thank him with a smile, and Gabriel and James sit down at a table with me. James repeatedly informs me how proud he is, but my leg bounces up and down anyway. This was all a test, and there are people now judging me. I feel nauseous.

"I compared your times to the other drivers in the academies, and you were second fastest. If they don't take you, then I don't know what their problem is," Adrian states, and I'm not sure who he's addressing. It could be me, but it could also very much be himself. Gabriel takes my hand in his, grabbing my full attention.

"There is no driver out there like you, Val. Your determination is priceless, and if they can't see it, they are fools," he says so sincerely, a warmth spreads through my chest.

The moment is soon over when the door opens, and the recruiters from the three different academies walk into the room. They all have serious expressions on their faces, and I know whatever they have to tell me will not be pretty.

"After analyzing every category, we've all concluded that Ms. Romana would not make a good fit in our academies." My heart sinks into my stomach as tears shoot into my eyes. I didn't need all of them to take me. One would have been more than enough. *I only needed one.*

"What, why?" Adrian blurts out, and as much as I'd love to talk, I'm devastated and speechless. "She's one of the fastest drivers you've ever had!" My brother is angry then, maybe too angry to have a rational conversation with the people who are denying me the opportunity to live my dream. I'm about to get up to hold Adrian back when Gabriel places his hand on my brother's shoulder to calm him.

"We have to consider more than her lap time," says a man with grey hair and blue eyes. Gabriel tenses visibly.

"Okay, then consider the other categories. Talent: she has more than just talent. Money: it is not an issue. Time: this is her dream; she'll do anything to make it happen. Fitness: Valentina works out every single day and is in the best shape she could possibly be. There are your categories, and she is perfect in every one of them. Tell us, how do you justify turning her away?" Gabriel's words surprise all of us, especially me. He came here to support me, but I would have never expected him to fight while I try to compose myself.

"We don't have to justify ourselves. We simply don't think she'd be a good fit for any of our academies." Those three men can really stand there and say those words without hearing the problem behind them. Well, not on my watch. I'm so sick and tired of getting turned down because of who I am.

"So, your justification for not giving me a chance is because I'm a girl, correct?" Everyone turns to me. Gabriel and Adrian move out of the way to let me speak to the three men whose eyes have widened.

"Now, young lady, how dare you accuse us of–" I have to interrupt the middle-aged *man* with a beard then.

"I'm not accusing you of anything. If you take offense from my question, it only proves me right. You have not given me a single reason why I don't belong in your academies, simply that I am not a 'good fit'. If you cannot come up with any other reason despite my gender, how can I see it differently?" For a moment, there is absolute silence. They look at each other, but none of them seem to have an answer that will make them look less sexist.

"You were already kicked from a team once. Doesn't that speak for itself?" The other man, who hasn't addressed me before, points out, and I nod in agreement.

"I was kicked out probably for the same reason you are refusing me now." My tears have long dried, and I'm starting to feel numb.

"We cannot take a risk on you. I'm sorry, Ms. Romana. We did this as a favor to Mr. Romana, but it didn't work out." They are about to leave when I stop them dead in their tracks.

"Then tell me what I can improve on!" I demand, and the man with blue eyes turns to me one last time.

"Improve your ability to let it go. You'll never reach Formula One." They all leave, and Adrian wraps his arms around me to hold me up.

I'll never score enough points in a junior league like Formula Three or Two. I'll never get the Super License every Formula One driver is required to have. I will never meet all of the criteria to fulfill my dream. Everything my grandfather and I have worked toward is moving further away with each step I take forward. 'You'll never reach Formula One'. Well, it sure is starting to feel that way...

Chapter 18

Present...

I scan all of the clothes I've brought, hoping something will stand out and make my choice easy. I'm nervous, *really nervous.* This is my first proper date since I've broken up with Luke. My fingers trail over the same three dresses, but I can't decide on any. Eventually, I give up and sit down on my bed, the towel from my shower still clinging to my chest.

Someone knocks on the door, and I look through the peephole. I open the door despite being barely dressed, but his eyes only focus on my face.

"Hi," he says with a sad smile, and I cock an eyebrow.

"What do you want, Gabriel?" I finally bring myself to ask, and he starts to shift uncomfortably from one foot to the other. His hands are behind his back, only confusing me more.

"Oh yeah, sorry," he replies nervously, his eyes drifting to the floor. "I got you something." He brings his hands to the front and gives me a small package. "It's for you to wear on your date," he states, and both of my eyebrows lift in surprise. "I know, it's very unlike me to do something like this."

Gabriel lets out a sad laugh, and I open the top to reveal a claw hair clip in the shape of a butterfly. I gasp loudly, catching his attention. "If you don't like it, I can return it," he promises, but I shake my head.

"It's stunning, but I don't understand why you bought me a gift," I reply. Gabriel only shrugs.

"I saw it and thought of you. Maybe it'll complete your outfit," he suggests, but I'm still confused.

"It might, once I figure out what I'm going to wear," I tell him with a small laugh, and his eyes focus on mine once more.

"If you want, I can help you choose something," he offers, and I can't hold back my following words.

"Okay, what is going on with you? Why do you want to help me choose an outfit for a date with another guy?" He looks uncomfortable now, and I almost regret asking. Yet, I also know I have every right to question his strange behavior.

"To be completely honest, chérie, I just miss you as my friend." I lean against the door for support and study the man in front of me. With all of my strength, I try to understand him. Gabriel asked me not to go out with Eduardo, said he has feelings for me, but at the same time, doesn't think he deserves me. As much as I try to convince him otherwise, he's not ready to listen.

"Well, I do have three options I can't choose amongst," I reply, and, finally, a sincere smile appears on his face.

Gabriel helps me pick out my green maxi dress combined with black heels and a matching purse. I add the hair clip, and he gives me an approving grin when I've finished my subtle makeup. His eyes then shift back to the floor, and I let out a long sigh.

"Now, what will I wear tomorrow?" I walk back over to my clothes while he watches my every move.

"I'm not sure what you mean, chérie," he answers sweetly, and I wish for the millionth time we weren't in this situation. Gabriel is a great guy, and I want to be with him. *Why does everything have to be so complicated?*

"For our 'friend date'. It's been a while since it was just the two of us," I explain, and Gabriel jumps up from the bed, excitement evident on his face.

"That would be great. I'll arrange it!" We both smile at each other, and he leaves my hotel room soon after. I can't tell if this is going to be good for us or a complete disaster. I guess I'll have to find out the hard way.

The date is lovely. Eduardo takes me to the track, where he set up a table. I smile brightly when I take in the rest of the scenery. The lighting is dim but still bright enough so we can have a clear view of everything. There are two plates filled with food, and candles stand between them. It's cheesy and very cliché, but also thoughtful and romantic. Eduardo pulls out a chair for me, making me roll my eyes while a grin plays on my lips.

The dinner goes by faster than I would like, but I'm enjoying myself a lot. Eduardo has a great sense of humor, is mature, likes to make me laugh, I can tell that much, and he is charming. He shares stories about his childhood, and I listen closely. Eventually, he offers me wine, but as soon as I tell him I don't drink, he puts the entire bottle on the ground, out of our way.

"You don't drink either?" I ask, and he leans back in his chair, running his hand through his wavy hair.

"I do, but I don't feel like it tonight. I'd much rather focus on you." *Smooth, really smooth, Marquez.*

We continue our conversation, and he tells me about his experiences in Formula One. I share stories about growing up with Adrian and about my life in Monaco. It's easy to share a connection with someone who has lived a similar lifestyle in another European country. We then talk about the most random things, and I laugh harder than I have in a while.

Eduardo and I drive back to my hotel four hours after he first picked me up. The drive is silent, but his hand feels comforting in both of mine. There might not be a tingle, an ache, or anything that Gabriel ignites inside of me, but it's pleasant. I enjoy holding Eduardo's hand and feeling the butterflies in my stomach.

"Are you ready for tomorrow?" His head moves to the side, and he looks at me.

"Yes, it's only free practice," he assures me and gently squeezes my hand as he repositions it. I nod, and his eyes drift back to the road. His thumb caresses the back of my left hand in a steady motion, and I smile.

Eduardo gets in the elevator with me and walks me back to my hotel room. The butterflies continue to fly around in my stomach, and I feel a sense of victory because of it. We stop in front of my door, and I face Eduardo with a big grin on my face.

"Do you think I can kiss you without getting a black eye from your brother?" I laugh at his question.

"Yes. My brother will only attack at my command." Eduardo nods and smiles at me. His lips melt onto mine a second later. This is, without a doubt, the best kiss I've ever had. It's not rushed or sloppy, just sweet. When he steps back, I leave my eyes closed for a moment to enjoy the effects of the kiss for a bit longer.

"I'll see you tomorrow," I eventually say, and we exchange one last smile before he leaves.

Chapter 19

Today were the first two free practice sessions of the season. During, the drivers can familiarize themselves with track and weather conditions while driving in their cars. They can also try different strategies and tires, and set lap times to compare with the other teams. Gabriel and James did well, but Adrian struggled visibly today. He'll have another chance to improve in the third practice tomorrow, and, hopefully, it will allow him to set a good time during Qualifying.

Thousands of fans were already in the stands today, supporting their favorite drivers by cheering, wearing their teams' colors, and holding up posters and flags. This is something that always warms my heart. The excitement of the fans every time the cars race by them is wonderful. I barely had fans when I was racing for Formula Three, but the few who supported me meant the world to me.

As much as I tried not to think about Gabriel and our 'friend date', my mind kept drifting to it the entire day, up until now, while I'm standing in the shower, letting the warmth of the water calm me down. There is no reason for me to be nervous, but here I am, water dripping down my back from my hair and looking through my suitcase once more. A knock on the door startles me, and I shake my head at Gabriel when I open it.

"Do you get an inner alarm every time I'm in a towel?" We both laugh, and he shrugs with a wicked smile.

"No, but I most certainly wouldn't mind having it," he jokes, and I step out of the way so he can come in. "I brought you something else," he informs me, but I frown at him.

"Stop bringing me things," I complain, but Gabriel only grins as he holds out a Ferrari team shirt.

"It's important for where I'm taking you," he simply replies, and I tilt my head to the side ever so slightly, hoping he'll elaborate. "Come on, Lady Valentina, we have somewhere to be," he teases me, and I smile involuntarily.

"You haven't called me that in years," I mumble, overwhelmed by the sudden wave of happiness. After all of the chaos between us, I'm glad to see our friendship isn't ruined. Gabriel tells me to get ready, probably to give us both a break from the emotional tension between us.

The shirt fits me snugly around the top, and when I inhale, I realize it's Gabriel's. The mahogany scent is impossible to miss. Wearing it gives me a strange feeling of belonging and comfort. I add a pair of shorts and the hair clip he gave me before putting on my sneakers and following Gabriel to his rental car. He stays quiet the whole drive to the track, and I wonder what we could be doing there at this hour. My mind even makes up a scenario where Gabriel organized a dinner like Eduardo, but he's more creative than that.

Not knowing what he has planned is slowly driving me crazy. "Can you give me a hint, at least?" I beg, but he only laughs at my impatience.

"We're almost there, chérie. You'll see soon enough," Gabriel promises, and for the first time tonight, I study his outfit. He's wearing a white dress shirt and simple blue jeans. I feel underdressed next to him, but my outfit was his choice. Once the car is parked, he turns to me with a sincere smile. "Now, the question is, do you trust me enough to let me blindfold you?" he asks, and I furrow both of my eyebrows in response.

"I think we had different ideas about what this was," I joke, but Gabriel's cheeks turn a bright red.

"Jesus, Valentina, get your head out of the gutter," he laughs, and I join him. A weight lifts off my shoulders. *We're okay.*

"Okay, then you may blindfold me," I permit him, and his fingers carefully tie the fabric of one of his bandanas around my head to take my vision away.

Gabriel does a pretty good job not bumping me into things, *for the most part*, but it takes a while to get to wherever we're going. Eventually, he stops me from going any further, and I hear him speak to someone else about whether or not everything is ready. This only makes me more impatient.

"Okay, finally. I had to pull a lot of strings for this, but it will be so worth it," he says before pulling the bandana from my face and revealing his Formula One car. "I know your dream is to race in one, but for now, you can sit in it." This wouldn't seem like much to anyone else, but to me, it means the world. I've only ever been allowed near the car, never in it. One of my biggest dreams has always been to know what it feels like to sit in one. I stare at Gabriel in disbelief, and he smiles brightly.

"You did this for me?" During a race weekend especially, this should be impossible. The car and driver are the most protected components because, without them, there is no race.

"Of course. It's long overdue." His green-brown eyes stare into mine, and I wonder how someone can remain so pure after losing so many people. "Go, sit," he pulls me from my moment of awe and helps me into his car.

The seat is tight at the sides and incredibly uncomfortable at the back, but that's because it is made to fit Gabriel perfectly, not me. It would be different if this were my seat... I look straight ahead at the halo, one of the most important additions they've recently made to the car. It's a safety measure in the shape of its name that sits over where the driver's head is. It has saved the drivers many times when they crashed. The thought almost makes me shiver. Formula One is not to be underestimated. My eyes focus on where the steering wheel usually is, and I stretch out my arms to imitate a driver's body position during a race.

"How do you feel?" Gabriel asks after a while of me admiring the car.

"Like one of my fantasies has just become a reality," I admit, and he cheers victoriously.

"So, you're happy?" he goes on, and I nod. Tears have been threatening to leave my eyes since I've sat down, and when he celebrates my joy, I let them fall. Gabriel allows me to stay in the car for a bit longer. He even takes a few pictures of me in it to capture this moment. "You know, the first time I sat in one, I was so nervous, I kept pressing the off switch instead of on. But, at first, I didn't realize that, so I started complaining. 'Why is this stupid car not turning on? Something's not working. It's fucking broken.' Eventually, someone came up to me and had to remind me what the right button is. Val, I almost died from shame," he tells me, and I burst into uncontrollable laughter.

"No, you didn't," I reply, still too amused by his story to keep from laughing at him.

"It was so embarrassing," he admits, and I finally catch myself. The smile on my lips remains, but at least I'm calm enough now to see his shy grin and red cheeks. It's not fair that his outside is just as beautiful as his inside.

"Will you share more stories?" I ask. Gabriel squats down next to the car to tug a loose strand of hair behind my ear. I stop breathing until he retracts his hand and runs it over his stubble with a thoughtful expression on his face.

"Would you like to hear about the time I almost soiled myself in the car or the time I was incapable of putting my balaclava on?"

"Both!"

We stay in the Ferrari garage for a bit longer, eating and talking, until he brings me back to my hotel. Like Eduardo did yesterday, Gabriel walks me all the way to my room, but instead of kissing me, he tightly wraps his arms around me.

"Thank you for tonight," he mumbles before kissing my cheek and leaving.

If only things were different, and he'd kiss my lips instead of my cheek for once...

Chapter 20

Adrian and I sit on Grandfather's couch as we stare at the television. Our dad didn't want to bring us to the race, which is a normal thing now. Grandfather has been making sure we aren't too excluded, and he's been training us for years, but it doesn't make it hurt any less. Our father has abandoned us for his career. This is a pain, which isn't easily overcome. However, Grandfather is doing his best to raise us. Adrian and my dreams are his priority, and my brother has been taking it more seriously the last couple of months. Not as serious as me, but still.

"Look, the safety car is out," Adrian informs me, and I bring my attention back to the television. There are many reasons why the safety car might be required. It could have been a crash between two drivers, a driver crashing into a barrier, engine failure leading to a car in the middle of the track, or many more reasons. The safety car is a sports car and usually comes when the conditions on the track are unsafe. The rest of the drivers are instructed to follow behind it at a much slower speed.

"What happened?" I ask because I didn't pay enough attention to the screen. Adrian turns to me and shrugs.

"Silver drove into the wall because they didn't properly screw on his tire. It fell off, and he spun off track. He's fine; he walked away without a scratch. They just need the safety car because his is in a dangerous position for the other drivers." My eyebrows lift, and I gasp. Patrick Silver is my father's biggest rival and the only one who was in his way of winning the championship. My daddy is going to win the championship! I jump up from my seat to run into the kitchen where my grandfather is. Excitement overwhelms me.

If I am this happy for my father, how happy will I be when I win? Well, I guess I will have to find out.

Saturday morning comes faster than I want it to. Today is the first Qualifying of the season, which determines the starting positions for the drivers on the grid for the race the following day. Adrian and James are beyond nervous. I can see it in the way they walk, the lack of communication, their body language, and especially how they keep checking the time. They're still operating, but inhumanly so. This is important for them. The first race is always the most nerve-wracking for Adrian. Today, everything is amplified because it's his first Qualifying with Ferrari. They are one of the top three teams in the sport, and in the last five years, they have been attempting to eliminate Mercedes AMG's dominance. Although Mercedes has won the Constructors Championship three years in a row, Ferrari has always been a close second. Winning the Constructors Championship means their team has collected the most points over the season. A driver can secure up to twenty-five points for their team with every race, depending on their position at the end of the race. The points from both drivers are totaled into one sum for the Constructors Championship. Those points also count to the Driver's Championship, where each individual driver competes for the title.

This year, Ferrari has younger, more motivated engineers, the drivers are eager to prove their worth, and the whole team has improved immensely. Something inside me wants to sit down with the strategist and listen to their

Qualifying plan, but I can't do that. All I'm allowed to do is stand at the sidelines and hope everything will run smoothly.

My eyes scan the Ferrari garages, but I can't find Gabriel anywhere. That means he probably already put his game face on and doesn't want to be distracted. It works this way for most of the drivers. Adrian is in his red suit; James is in his blue and so is Eduardo. When he sees me, a huge grin spreads over his face before he goes back to work.

When Qualifying starts, I'm tempted to bite my nails as I look at the small TVs inside the garage. Eduardo gets a good lap in Q1, which makes me happier than I would have expected. James has a good lap, too, and I'm waiting to see how Adrian and Gabriel fare. By the time Q1 is done, Gabriel completed the fastest lap, Adrian has the second best, and then the Mercedes AMG team occupies the third and fourth positions. Five drivers are out in Q1, and Q2 is set to start soon.

In Q1, the drivers who place anywhere between sixteenth and twentieth are eliminated from the next Qualifying round. That means their positions are set for the Grand Prix on Sunday. They have eighteen minutes to complete as many laps as the team deems necessary without using their regulated amount of tires. In Q2, the same principle applies, except the session is only fifteen minutes long, and any position after the tenth is eliminated. In Q3, the remaining ten drivers race twelve minutes for pole position, which is the primary position, and then are placed anywhere between one and ten, depending on their lap time.

James, Eduardo, Adrian, and Gabriel all make it to Q3, and my heart is racing in my chest. Cameron is positioned in eleventh place, Leonard occupies thirteenth, and the Mercedes AMG drivers, Jonathan Kent and Kyle Hugh, are also in Q3. I constantly switch between standing and sitting, depending on how nervous I am. The time starts counting down on the clock, and I jump out of my seat. All of the mechanics in the garage follow my lead and are probably as anxious to see the results as I am.

These twelve minutes feel like the longest of my life, but when the Qualifying finally ends, I can't believe my eyes. Adrian gained pole position, Jonathan is second place, Gabriel is third, while James and Kyle occupy the fourth and fifth positions. My eyes scan the leaderboard for Eduardo's name, and I notice that he came in seventh. I'm jumping up and down and clapping my hands together in joy. I feel overwhelming pride for Adrian as he snatches the first pole of the season. After what feels like forever, I finally get to hug my sweaty brother, who picks me up and squeezes me tightly.

"Congratulations! I'm so proud of you!" I tell him, and he puts me back on the ground. "I can't believe you did it!" Adrian has gotten poles before, he's also won races, but I'm still surprised he got the first pole of the year.

"You don't have to sound so shocked," he says and smiles at the same time. "I gotta go, but I'll see you back at the hotel tonight. Love you," he adds, kisses the top of my head, and jogs out of the room.

A couple of hours go by while I talk to Martin, Adrian's press officer, and we have a great time discussing the strategy for Adrian's Formula One future. Martin leaves me in the conference room, and I pull my phone out of my pocket to check my messages. I enjoy the brief moment of solitude because I know it probably won't last very long.

"Hola, hermosa," Eduardo says from behind me and lightly presses his fingers to my elbow. I turn around and almost immediately feel his lips on my cheek, making butterflies storm around in my stomach. A big smile spreads over my face because I'm unable to contain my happiness. I must be moving on; otherwise, I would not feel like this.

"You're not satisfied with seventh place, are you?" He shakes his head and puts one of my curls behind my ear. His hand cups my face, and his thumb caresses my cheek. My skin isn't on fire, but his touch feels pleasant.

"Although, I'm happy because I get to look at you now," he says with his Spanish accent, and I melt a little.

"Don't you have to go and let your performance coach massage your tired muscles? That sounds much better than spending time with me." I laugh, and he joins in.

"No, I like spending time with you," he tells me sweetly. "But yes, I do have to go. I'll text you later." He gives me another innocent peck on the cheek before he leaves, and I wonder why he's not kissing me. I don't have time to dwell on it when my heart rate picks up speed from another interruption.

"Is he treating you right?" Gabriel's familiar voice drowns into my ears, and I turn around to give him my full attention. He's casually leaning against the wall, but I can tell something's bothering him.

"So far, yes," I reply truthfully, and he gives me a small smile.

"That's good. I'm glad," he mutters absentmindedly before shifting his weight from one foot to the other.

"It bothers you to see me with him," I state because it's obvious. Gabriel's eyes lift to my face, and his lips part in an attempt to speak, but he closes his mouth without saying a single word. "Why does it bother you?" I challenge, and he looks away then.

"It bothers me that I can't be him." That wasn't the response I was expecting. "Eduardo has always had a picture-perfect fucking life. No one's ever left him; no one's ever truly hurt him. He can deal with emotions better than someone like me, but it still breaks me that I can't be good like him." He pushes off the wall and takes three steps closer, making my heart beat rapidly in my chest. His words give me hope. "Chérie, you are the most incredible woman anyone could ever ask for. You're so kind and, at the same time, a complete badass." I chuckle at his word choice. "You're not afraid to speak your mind, and I love how forward you are," he informs me, and I almost choke on my spit. I like Eduardo, but if there is any chance Gabriel will let down his walls, I have to try. I want him, even if I attempt to convince myself otherwise.

"Okay, if you love that about me, then here it is: stop fighting your feelings. I understand how terrifying they are, but we're both suffering from your fears when we don't have to be. You want me," I state, and he nods. "You make me happy, Gabriel, can't you see that?" He shakes his head, and I take a step toward him. "Think of yesterday, would you?" Gabriel puts his hands in his pockets, closing himself off from me. I reach out to touch him, and to my surprise, he lets me. My hand rests on his cheek, and I can see the hurting boy inside of him. Gabriel is only vulnerable with me, and I love how close it makes me feel to him. "Stop pushing me away," I almost whisper, and his eyes fixate on mine.

"I'm sorry, chérie," he replies. His apology is sincere, and I can genuinely see now how lost Gabriel is. Nothing makes sense to him, as it doesn't for me.

"Stop being sorry and do something about this," I say and point my index finger between us.

"Kiss me," he begs, relinquishing all control and giving it to me without a moment of hesitation.

My other hand lifts to touch his cheek, and I step on my tiptoes to press my lips to his. I've been waiting for this since I've met him, for this exact moment. Gabriel is surprised I'm giving him what he wants, but his lips melt onto mine soon enough. Shivers run down my spine as heat takes over my body. I'm aching, I'm exploding into a million pieces, but it feels incredible. It feels better than anything I have ever experienced. The mint I can taste from him is heavenly. Gabriel's hands drop to the small of my back then to my butt, and he squeezes gently. I part my lips slightly, and Gabriel's tongue enters my mouth with ease. A small moan escapes me, catching both of us off-guard. I've never moaned from a kiss, and he tightens his grip on my bottom in response. Our lips move in perfect harmony, which is why I whimper when he removes his from mine.

"Not here," he whispers, and panic settles in my stomach. I wasn't even thinking about anything past kissing him, but now, it is all I can think about. He tucks a strand of my hair behind my ear, and it surprises me how much better it feels when he does it instead of Eduardo.

"Then let's go to your hotel room," I suggest, and he tugs his bottom lip between his teeth.

"Okay, but I think we should talk some more before we go any further," he says, and I almost groan before we both let out a small laugh. His lips come to mine one more time, and he hands me a small envelope with his key card and his room number. Gabriel lets go of my hand and runs out of the room.

Chapter 21

The red dress I brought on the trip highlights my body, and I feel incredibly sexy. I put on mascara, lip balm, and some perfume, even though I doubt I need any of it to impress Gabriel. Luckily, Adrian is not back at the hotel yet, which makes 'sneaking out' a lot easier. I simply text him I'll be back late. My feet bring me to Gabriel's room, and I unlock the door with an excited smile. I call out his name once, but he isn't back yet. I sink down on the bed and let the butterflies storm around my stomach. My mind goes through many scenarios of what will happen, and they all excite me.

A knock on the door startles me, and I look through the peephole to check who it is. The breath is knocked out of me when I see Kira. For a moment, I debate leaving it closed and ignoring her, but it wouldn't do any good. Her eyes go wide in surprise as they fixate on me.

"Valentina? What are you doing here?" she asks so calmly, it surprises me. "Am I at the wrong room? I'm looking for Gabriel." Again, Kira is calm and polite toward me, something she never is.

"What are you doing in Australia?" I ask, completely disregarding her questions. I'm too shocked she's here to focus on anything else.

"I came here to win him back, but apparently, I'm too late," she replies, pointing at my outfit. "Oh my God, it's all so clear to me now. You're her. You are the reason why he broke up with me," she barks, and I flinch. Her words hurt me. I stay completely silent because I have no idea what to say. "He doesn't want to focus on his career. He wants you!" Kira is angry then. She steps into the room, pushing me out of the way. "Gabriel," she screams, and I stay by the door in case it's better to run. "Where is he?" she demands to know, but I still can't respond.

"Where is who?" Gabriel replies, and his eyes immediately go wide when they focus on his ex. "Kira? What are you doing here?" His hand reaches out to grab mine, but I move behind him and out of the way of confrontation.

"Really? You left me for her?" The familiar disgust Kira feels toward me returns, and I'm almost glad.

"I left you for myself, Kira. Leave Val out of this," he replies firmly, and I let out the breath I've been holding.

"Bullshit. Look at how she's dressed. She came here to have sex with you, and you obviously wanted her to," Kira yells at him, and I cover my chest reflexively. When Gabriel sees how uncomfortable I am, he turns around and hands me one of his jackets. I give him a small smile before covering up.

"Kira, I don't even know why you're here. We broke up. My life is no longer your business." I don't know how Gabriel can stay so calm.

"I came here to prove to you that your career matters to me too, but Valentina has ruined everything!" Gabriel's shoulders tense from her words, and I place my hand on his back.

"If you attack her one more time, I'm not going to be civil anymore," Gabriel warns, but Kira doesn't seem to care.

"I'll attack her as much as I want. She ruined everything!" Again, I feel sick from her words. Gabriel turns to me with a sad expression on his face.

"Val, I think it's best if I sort this out while you're not here," he says gently, but I feel anger settling in my stomach. *He's throwing me out of his room to stay with her?* I put on the fakest smile I can manage, smack the key card into his hand, and leave. As soon as the door closes behind me, I hear them arguing. Maybe he's right to do this without Kira constantly having to look at me, but he shouldn't have asked me to leave. He could have gone into the hall with her, but instead, he's decided I should leave, making me feel humiliated whether it was his intention or not.

I make my way down the hallway to James' room and knock. If Kira leaves, I feel Gabriel will come to my room, and I don't want to see him right now, not while I feel guilty and embarrassed. James opens the door seconds later, tousled hair and half-naked.

"Luv, what's wrong?" I wrap my arms around his naked torso and start crying against his chest. "Okay, babe, it's okay. Come on in," he tells me in a soft voice, and we sit down on his bed.

It's time I told him everything. I share my feelings for Gabriel and what is going on with Eduardo and me. Then I explain how it felt kissing Eduardo and how different it was with Gabriel. James is patient, listening to every word, but I also notice a wave of anger washing over his face. By the time I finish my story, James' hands are wrapped around mine entirely.

"I'm so sorry this is happening. If you want, I'll push him off the track during the race tomorrow." We both start laughing. "I'm truly sorry to say this, darling, but I have to go to sleep. If anyone finds out I didn't get my eight hours, I'm in big trouble." I look at the watch and see he's right. I nod and attempt to slide off the bed, but he holds me back and pulls me close. "There is nothing I wouldn't do for you, Val."

"I love you, James." I wrap my arms around him and don't linger on the fact I just admitted this out loud. I've never told anyone who isn't part of my family I love them, but it feels good to say it to James.

"I love you," he simply replies and presses a kiss to the top of my head. "You can sleep here if you want," he offers after a few moments, and I smile before curling up next to him on the bed.

"Good night," I say as we face each other.

"Night, gorgeous." James must have called me every sweet pet name that exists throughout my whole life, and I love it. It would be so much easier if he were the one I wanted, instead of Gabriel or even Eduardo. *Do I even really want Eduardo?* After the kiss I shared with Gabriel, I'm not sure anymore.

Chapter 22

Adrian is sitting in his Formula Three car right before his first-ever race in it. My heart beats quickly in my chest, and my breathing is uneven. I'm nervous for him. Grandpa stands next to me and waits for a chance to talk to Adrian.

"Breathe, race, and win, as long as it doesn't cost you a limb," Grandpa states slowly, and I look at him. These are the only English words he ever says to us because he likes how they rhyme. Grandfather gives me a brief smile, revealing how happy he is. There is nothing more important in this world to him than us. We are his life and his pride. He gives us the affection, respect, and attention which our father has long found unnecessary. Winning is important to Grandpa, but our health and happiness are even more so. Succeeding has nothing to do with winning for him.

"I will give it my all," Adrian assures both our grandfather and me, and I smile proudly at him. Adrian is one of the youngest drivers in Formula Three, but he is also one of the most talented. Grandfather takes my hand and leads me away from the car, which is much smaller than an F1 car.

"Don't worry, little champion, your day will come," he guarantees me,

and I chew on the inside of my cheek. He adopted my father's nickname for me a few years ago. In his words, it will help me reach my potential. It will give me confidence and faith. I never doubt myself because I know I want this more than anyone else. I want to be the first female championship contender in Formula One.

Staring at the small screens, I can't calm the anxious feeling which turns my stomach upside down. There are so many things that could go wrong, and I can't bring myself to look when the lights go out, and the cars start to race.

"Don't be scared. Adrian is doing well," Grandfather informs me, and I remove my hands from my eyes. Adrian is indeed doing well. He's in the sixth position, which is excellent considering he started tenth.

"Go, Adrian," I cheer and clap my hands together with excitement. I am filled with pride.

The loud noises around me have become familiar and pleasant. It would be odd not to hear them anymore. It would be strange if I didn't see people running around and having heated arguments. It would be unusual not to see the mechanics with helmets on, staring at the screens as I do too. I have grown used to all those things, giving me a sense of belonging. I understand more of the language spoken here now, and I can even ask Grandfather questions to expand my knowledge. He always has patience as he explains new aspects of the sport to me.

Today, I ask him about the different penalties drivers can receive. He tells me about time penalties, grid penalties, and drive-through penalties. For time penalties, additional seconds would be added to the gap between the different drivers, which might result in the loss of positions for the person who received the penalty. A grid penalty means the driver has to start certain places behind what he qualified for. The drive-through penalty requires the driver to go through the pit lane once. Since it is the only part of the track with a speed limit, they usually lose a lot of time and even a certain number of places, depending on how far ahead they are. This decision is made by the FIA, who is in charge of ensuring rule-abiding.

"Thank you for teaching me," I say to the person I look up to the most.

"I will do so until there is nothing left to teach you. I promise."

"Are you ready?" I ask Adrian, and he nods his head too quickly for me to believe him.

"Breathe, race, and win, as long as it doesn't cost you a limb," we say in perfect harmony. Grandpa used to say it to Dad before his races and then to Adrian and me before ours. It's a tradition to say because it brings good luck. Adrian gives me a quick hug and then joins everyone to listen to the Australian anthem.

All twenty drivers stand in a line as they respectfully listen to the anthem sung by a young woman. Fans are quiet in the stands but soon cheer when it is over. The drivers then move on to have a group picture taken. The nervous feeling in my chest is overwhelming as they move back to the cars that are already on the starting grid. The crew works hard to warm the tires with tire blankets and make any final adjustments to the car. All the fans get more impatient, including me, as the time runs down to the start of the race. I see Gabriel smiling at his performance coach on the monitors right before putting on his balaclava and helmet. My mind briefly drifts to last night and his attempts to speak to me today, but I push those thoughts aside to focus on my brother.

Once all the drivers are in their cars, they take one lap called the formation lap to heat their tires, allowing for better grip on the track. They do that by swerving from left to right. After they return to the start and finish line, I wait for the lights to go out. This is always the most nerve-wracking for me because the cars are so close together, and it is all about the drivers' reaction times. I'm at the edge of my seat, watching the screens, and when the lights go out, I have to bite down on my bottom lip. Adrian gets an incredible start and stays ahead; Gabriel overtakes Jonathan and moves to second place; Kyle overtakes James for a brief second, but then James moves back ahead. So much is going on, and I have no idea where to look. I bite on my fingernails as I watch the race.

After the first couple of laps, I start to worry less as Adrian creates a time gap between himself and Gabriel to ensure he stays in first place. But when it's time for the pitstop to change the tires, I hold my breath. Adrian's stop is incredibly slow, closing the gap he worked so hard to achieve. Gabriel is merely two seconds behind him since he already stopped to change his tires a lap earlier. I start to feel nervous for my brother then, and everyone in his garage is glued to the screens.

Toward the end, Adrian and Gabriel are still one and two, fighting for first place. Gabriel comes closer and closer until he overtakes my brother a lap before the end of the race. It's a head-to-head battle until the very last second, but Gabriel manages to snatch the win from Adrian. Kyle comes in third place, James is fourth, Jonathan is fifth, Eduardo comes in eighth, Cameron is tenth, and Leonard Tick's car never makes it over the finish line. The whole Ferrari paddock celebrates as the two drivers get first and second-place finishes, and I do so with them.

When the three guys stand on the podium, I am at the bottom, mouthing the words to the anthem of my home country. The trophies are distributed, and Adrian is forcing a happy expression. The smile on Gabriel's face makes me sick to my stomach. I'm delighted for him, but at the same time, I'm so angry about what happened yesterday.

The rest of the day goes by in a blur. There is a lot of cheering, many different interviews Adrian has to go to, and eventually, I go back to the hotel. I decide to call Evangelin and see how she's doing. She picks up after the third ring, and we fall into a casual conversation. She tells me about her store, and I fill her in about the weekend and the results, although I know she watched the race. We hang up minutes later, and I fall asleep as the events of today overwhelm my body.

Chapter 23

There is a loud banging on the door, and I jump up in bed. Adrian is sleeping in the one next to mine, and I pick up my phone while I wonder who could be bothering us at... three in the morning? I move toward the door and open it before almost slamming it shut again.

"Please, Val, I don't understand why you're avoiding me," he pleads, and by looking at his frustrated frown, I can tell he doesn't know why I'm upset.

"You kicked me out of your room while she stayed! I was humiliated, Gabriel. I went to your hotel room so we can have sex, yet I was the one asked to leave," I whisper, and his eyes go wide. Whether I planned on it, or it was only something that crossed my mind doesn't matter. The important thing is, I wanted to spend the night with him, not be thrown out while Kira stayed. "Can't you see the problem there?"

"My only intention was to protect you, chérie," he informs me, but I only roll my eyes. "Don't do that, Valentina. I'm telling the truth. She was attacking you, blaming you, and you didn't deserve to stand there and take it. Please, tell me, how is that wrong?" he asks, shutting me up for a moment.

"Chérie," he says softly and reaches out to me, but I step away from him. Pain flashes across his face, and he drops his hands in defeat.

"I understand how difficult the situation was, but you told me to leave while she stayed in your room. Don't you understand how embarrassing that was for me?" Mainly because it gave Kira the satisfaction.

"What did you want me to do? I didn't want to cause a scene outside of my hotel room, which she did. Kira was screaming at me, and I had to calm her before reminding her that we are broken up. It took an hour to get rid of her, and when I went to your room, you didn't open the door. You've been ignoring me the whole day when all I wanted was to celebrate with you!" he blurts out, and as logical as his words are, I'm still upset.

"I don't want to fight anymore, Gabriel. I want to go to sleep." I open the door, but his words stop me.

"Val, you told me not to push you away, but you're being a hypocrite." He's probably right, but I'm sick and tired of always being the fool with him. I disappear into my room without speaking again. Maybe I'm not ready to face my feelings either.

James sits next to me throughout the flight, for whatever reason, and I use most of it to sleep. Every now and then, he makes small talk with me about the race or the weekend, but then he concentrates on his book again. James loves to read, which is something I've always admired about him. When we were younger, he read all those great classic novels and then gave me the ones he enjoyed. James waited patiently for me to finish the books before we discussed them. It started when I was ten, and he was thirteen, and it hasn't stopped. This time, however, I gave him the book I'm reading. I gave him a copy of Die For Me, my favorite book of all time. He's reading it on the plane right now, and I love his facial expressions.

"This back and forth between them is killing me, Val," he complains, and I smile.

"But that's the best part. Their love story isn't easy. They don't just fall in love and live happily ever after. They fight to be together," I tell him, and he nods. "Also, when they finally do get together, it's beautiful." He puts on a dramatic shocked expression.

"They end up together? Jesus, Val, you just spoiled the ending," he jokes.

"I'm so sorry," I say and push my bottom lip forward teasingly. James glares at me but then smiles and shakes his head.

After a day of traveling and mainly sleeping, Adrian and I are back home. James left to go to his house, and I haven't seen or spoken to Gabriel since that night at the hotel. It's eight in the morning when we arrive at our house, and I am awake and ready to start the day. I take a quick shower, watch Adrian attempt to load the dirty laundry into the washing machine, load it myself to make sure our clothes won't be ruined, and go downstairs to bake. After five minutes of looking through Grandma's recipes, I decide on some easy blueberry muffins.

The doorbell rings the second I've placed the muffins in the oven. A small package addressed to me sits on my doorstep, and I carry it into the kitchen. My fingers reach for the beginning of the tape, and I rip it off the box right before opening it and pulling out a single envelope. Frustrated with the packaging of whatever this is, I tear open the envelope and take out the hand-drawn picture of... me. It's a drawing of me sitting on a chair in the waiting area of an airport. I'm reading a book, biting my lip, and my legs are crossed. It's breathtaking, and I know without looking at the back that it is one of Gabriel's. I turn it around and find a note attached to the back.

Chérie,

I'm so sorry for disappointing you. You've made me realize my mistake, and I can't stop thinking about how you felt when I told you to go. I promise I didn't mean to upset you, but that doesn't matter right now. What matters is that

I apologize for it. I'm sorry, chérie. No other woman will ever compare to your honesty, resilience, loyalty, kindness, and self-confidence. You captured my full attention from the day I met you, but we lived so far apart, and I was convinced you didn't like me as anything other than a friend. When you moved to Monaco, and I was around you, I couldn't help but constantly think of you. You are the only person I want to be with; I think you've always been. Please, I hope you know now that no one compares to you. You're Valentina Romana, future Formula One champion.

Only yours,
Gabriel

I drop to the floor and let my heart calm down by itself. It feels like it is being squeezed and shaken, but I can't make it stop. The drawing, the letter, and the feelings are all too much for me. This chaos between us is too much for me.

Chapter 24

My head is still spinning, but I push all the thoughts of Gabriel aside. I finish baking the muffins, pack some of them in a bag, and start walking. Evangelin is waiting for me to help out at the store. The walk to *Rush* helps me clear my mind of anything that pains it, and I focus entirely on seeing my new friend. When Evangelin spots me, a huge smile breaks out on her face. Her small, short arms wrap around me, and she places a kiss on each cheek.

"It's so good to see you," she says in French, and I smile.

"It's good to see you! I brought you something," I reply before handing her the muffins.

"Oh, you shouldn't have," she opens the bag and gasps. "Blueberry muffins are my favorite! Thank you." She squeezes my hand and puts the bag behind the counter.

There is hardly anyone in the store, allowing Evangelin and me to catch up. She tells me about the surprise trip that Carlos took her on over the weekend, and it sounds like the sweetest gesture. They went on a road trip and drove to Elba, an island in Italy. Our conversation drifts to the race and how disappointed Adrian was when Gabriel won.

"Do you maybe want to come over for dinner this week? I would love to meet your brother, and I'm sure he would enjoy meeting Carlos," she offers, and my mouth drops.

"That would be great, but I should warn you, my brother is a Carlos Klein superfan." We both laugh a little. Evangelin waves her hand in front of me as if to dismiss my worry.

"It will be fun." Her eyes study my face for a moment, and I can see the smile slowly fading from her lips. "Do you want to tell me what's going on?" Her question brings tears to my eyes. I swallow them back down and tell her about what happened this weekend. Something inside me is mad that I'm sharing this story with so many people, but Evangelin is my guiding compass. She usually has the right answers for me, and she's more of a mother than my actual one ever was. Considering I've only known her for a couple of weeks, it amazes me how comfortable I am around her. "That's a lot," she simply states, and I let out a small laugh.

"I know, I'm sorry." I fumble with my ring and bite down on my bottom lip.

"Have you decided what to do?" This back and forth between Gabriel and me isn't healthy. We go from friends to more to not speaking at all, and despite how we feel, I can't do this right now, not while I'm trying to focus on my career. He's messing with my emotions, and therefore with my mental and physical health too. Grandfather taught me about the connection amongst them, but he would be disappointed to see how imbalanced I am because of Gabriel.

"I think Eduardo is good for me. He's open and incredibly nice," I say more to myself than to Evangelin.

"You know, you can decide to date neither. You shouldn't commit to one right now, especially when you're so confused," she assures me, and I smile.

"I know, but it's not about needing a boyfriend or about getting into a serious relationship, commit, and then have lots of babies. I don't want that.

I'm young, and I'm free, but I just can't get Gabriel out of my head. There needs to be a different way." Evangelin studies me for a second, then says something I would have never expected her to say.

"Why don't you try being friends with benefits with that Eduardo guy. This way, you get to enjoy yourself without committing. If you ever do like him as more than just a friend, you can talk to him, or if you realize your feelings for Gabriel are too strong, you can talk to Eduardo about that, too." Maybe I'm going insane, but her plan sounds genius. Instead of going through the trouble of having an actual relationship with Eduardo, who lives in Spain anyway, I could just have fun with him. All I need for this plan to work is distance from Gabriel and Eduardo's corporation.

"You're quite brilliant," I tell Evangelin, and she smiles at me.

"Yes, so I've been told." She whips her hair back, and I laugh. My whole life, I've been missing a person like her: a female role model who helps me through difficult times and finds solutions with me. Mrs. Beaumont and I are close, but I can't imagine her talking to me about having friends with benefits with a guy I'm interested in.

After a couple more hours of working and laughing together, I decide to head home. I need to do laundry and make dinner unless Adrian made some, which in my experience, is highly unlikely. It's been a long day, and I am ready to fall into bed and sleep. When I get home, there is another package on the doorstep.

"Have you opened my first package?" His voice appears behind me, and I jump.

"God!" My hand lifts to my chest, and I try to calm my heart. Gabriel is wearing blue sweatpants, which hang perfectly from his hips, and his black t-shirt is loose. His hair is messy as usual, and my body is drawn toward him. Luckily, my mind is stronger.

"Did you read my letter?" he asks, his voice hopeful. His hand runs through his hair, and I melt.

"Yes, I read it. I read it a hundred times," I admit without shame. "But we don't work, Gabriel." There are so many emotions that flash over Gabriel's face, and I only notice a few: panic, anger, pain, and fear.

"You're throwing everything away because of one mistake?" he asks and stares at me in disbelief. "What can I do to make you forgive me? I'll do anything," he begs, but I've made up my mind.

"I'm not throwing everything away over one mistake. All you've done is push me away, and I have to protect myself instead of your feelings for once. We're too complicated, Gabriel, and I see no way that we can make this work," I lie because I've fantasized enough about us to see many ways. However, none of them are easy, and I need that right now, not chaos.

"Then why won't you let me show you? Val, I only need you, nothing else," he replies, his voice cracking and a tear falling down his cheek. I walk through the door and hear him follow me up the stairs. "At least take this and read the other letter." He's begging, and I take the box from him. I don't plan on reading the letter or even looking inside. I close the door because I can't listen to his words anymore. They'll only convince me to discard all of my plans.

Gabriel screams outside, a scream of frustration and pain, and I want to let one out myself, but I can't. No sound leaves my lips. I've never seen Gabriel shed a tear because of me, not until today. My heart aches, my stomach turns upside down, and I don't know how to make any of it stop.

Chapter 25

"This one, or that one?" Adrian is holding up a white dress shirt and a dark blue one. He's shifting his weight from one leg to the other, and his arms are shaking as he holds up the clothes.

"You'll look good in either," I assure him absentmindedly. I'm looking through my clothes to find an outfit to wear to dinner, but Adrian pulls me out of my closet and sits me down on the bed. He holds the two shirts up again, and I laugh. "The blue one," I say, and he frowns at the shirt.

"I'm not sure," he mumbles, and I throw my head back onto the bed.

"Good God, just wear something. As long as you don't show up naked, you will be fine." My hands are in the air as I wait for him to pull me back up. When he does, he does it way too aggressively, and I fall forward onto the floor.

"Oops, sorry," he teases and runs out of my room.

Laughing, I get up and walk back into my closet. I flinch when I see the dress I wore the night I went to Gabriel's hotel room but simply push past it and find something else. I decide on a yellow dress, which reaches just above my knee. It's tight around my breasts, just like every other dress, and falls loosely from thereon. My curly hair is tied into a ponytail, but a few strands hang around the sides of my face. After putting on some makeup, I go downstairs to pack the dessert. The tiramisu looks mouth-watering as I cover the top with some cling wrap.

"Hey, Val, are you expecting a package?" Adrian asks, and my heart drops into my stomach. "It says it's from Gabriel." Then it sinks into my shoes. I didn't even open the package he gave me last time, and it has been almost a week. Adrian walks into the kitchen, wearing a completely different shirt, and hands me the box.

"Thank you," I mumble and bring the box upstairs before standing in front of an impatient Adrian. "Are you sure you want to wear that?" His eyes go wide, and he starts to fumble with the hem of his black dress shirt. "I'm kidding. You look handsome," I inform him, and Adrian lets go of his shirt.

"Thank you, you look beautiful as always," he replies, and I smack his arm when he stares at me, tears flooding his eyes. "Sorry, sorry, it's just difficult for me to believe that you're all grown up sometimes. You don't need me as much anymore, and it scares me a little." Adrian is a very emotional person, and he's never been ashamed of showing his feelings. I admire that about him a lot.

"I'm always going to need you more than I need anyone else. You're my family, Adrian, and you will *always* be the most important person in my life. Now, stop crying because if you cry, you're only going to get your shirt wet, and then you'll have to change it for the thirtieth time," I scold teasingly, and he laughs.

We make our way to my favorite car, the baby blue Mustang, and Adrian holds onto the tiramisu while I drive to Evangelin and Carlos' house. When we arrive, my jaw drops, and I can't believe my eyes. Their house is much smaller than I would have ever expected. It's a two-story house, with a single garage door and a small yard. Adrian fixes his appearance three times, looking in the small mirror on his side of the car, and then gives me a small smile before opening the door. I shake my head and chuckle. I can't even begin to imagine how nervous Adrian must be.

We walk the small stone path toward the wooden door, and I ring the bell once. I can hear Adrian swear nervously next to me and squeeze his arm to comfort him. As soon as Evangelin opens the door, everyone starts to greet each other.

"I apologize, Carlos is preparing dinner, but he will join us shortly," she assures us and leads us inside the house, which is just as simple as the outside. There are no fancy furniture pieces, no chandeliers hanging from the ceilings, only simple white furniture, and a few paintings. "The tiramisu looks delicious, Valentina," Evangelin says.

"I hope it tastes as good as it looks. We better put it in the fridge." She nods. Evangelin hurries into the kitchen and returns a minute later with Carlos Klein. The famous man isn't much taller than his wife, very slim, has thin white hair, and an inviting smile, which he uses to greet us.

"Valentina," he says and reaches out his hand so he can shake mine. "My wife has told me many great things about you. It's a pleasure to meet you, dear," he informs me in the most perfect French I've ever heard anyone speak. It's hard for me to believe his mother tongue is Spanish. "And Adrian, yes? I've heard you are a fan of mine." He's not cocky or arrogant; he's merely stating a fact. He faces my brother with the sweetest smile. "It's very nice to meet you, too." They shake hands, and Adrian is speechless. He looks at Carlos with the utmost admiration, and if I didn't know better, I would think he is about to cry.

"I'm so sorry, sir, I've always wanted to meet you," Adrian stutters, but Carlos isn't freaked out or annoyed by him. He simply starts talking to Adrian about Formula One and that he has been watching him for years. The way my brother's eyes light up makes my heart ache. I have always wanted him to be this full of joy.

Evangelin and I fall into a conversation, and Carlos serves dinner. I notice my brother following his every step closely, like a lost puppy that just met its new pack leader. I have to suppress a chuckle.

"So, Valentina, what is your goal for the future?" Carlos asks while we eat the delicious gnocchi with seafood he cooked.

"Oh, I'm taking a gap year to try and figure that out," I lie because I don't want to make things uncomfortable.

"Actually, Valentina has been training her whole life to become a Formula One driver, but no one has given her a proper chance so far," Adrian chimes in, and I drop my spoon into my plate. Carlos and Evangelin both look at me, but I simply blush and look away. "She was the best in every race as a kid. When she turned fourteen, she got a chance to drive in Formula Three, but a year later, they dropped her. Nobody wanted to sponsor her anymore. Valentina fights harder than I ever did, but no one wants to help her reach her potential for some unknown reason." I don't know why my brother is sharing this sad, terrible story with them, but I also can't tell him to stop. His big mouth seems to have gotten the better of him in the presence of the great Carlos Klein.

"I'm sorry, Valentina," Evangelina replies, and I force a smile. "That must have been horrible. I'm so sorry, my dear." Her hand reaches forward on the table, and she squeezes mine tightly.

"That's terrible, Valentina," Carlos says with a frown. "There haven't been many women who were allowed or 'fast enough' to race in a Grand Prix, and sadly, it's not always because they weren't talented. I'm not surprised to hear you're a gifted driver. You seem like a remarkable young woman." The forced smile on my face turns into a real one.

The rest of the evening goes smoothly, and I realize Evangelin and Carlos are genuine and down to earth. They talk about their marriage and share stories from their life together, and Adrian and I listen attentively. We also share a little bit more about our past.

We leave their house around midnight, and I let him drive to give myself some time to think. I should be mad at Adrian for telling my personal story, but I know what he would say if I complained. *"In order to move on, you have to speak about certain things. The more you address them, the easier it will get every single time. Why do you think it's so much easier to talk about Mom?"* This is precisely what Adrian would say to me, and he would be right. That is why I'm not giving up yet. I'm still training, and as hopeless as it seems, I'll keep trying. This is my dream, and I'm not done fighting for it.

We arrive at home minutes later, and my feet bring me upstairs to my room. I pick up my phone from the nightstand and see two new messages from Eduardo. He's letting me know he is arriving at ten tomorrow. We've been talking on the phone almost every day since we left Australia, and a couple of days ago, we agreed on him coming here. This way, I'll be able to talk to him and clear some things up.

Chapter 26

Approximately One Year Ago...

"Happy birthday to you, happy birthday to you, happy birthday, dear Val, happy birthday to you." Cameron, James, Adrian, and Gabriel sing to wake me up. I pull the blanket over my head and groan but also smile. No one's ever stood in front of my bed with a cake and sang to wake me up.

"Come on, Val, it's your eighteenth birthday. You've got to get up and blow out your candles," Cameron tells me with his thick Australian accent and removes the blanket from my body. I wipe my face with my hands before I do as I'm told. Adrian and I flew to Palma de Mallorca to celebrate my birthday, and all of my friends decided to join us.

"Happy birthday, my love," James says and hugs me tightly. He presses a kiss to my cheek and lets go of me so Adrian can congratulate me too. Cameron hugs me as well, and when I get to Gabriel, I'm nervous.

"Happy birthday, Valentina," he simply states and wraps his arms around me. My heart does three jumps when he puts his hand on my cheek. The moment lasts about two seconds, and then he retracts his hand and moves on.

"Go and get ready because I have a full day planned," Adrian lets me know, and I smile. All the boys are already dressed, which is why I run into the bathroom and get ready in record time. I put on some long, loose pants and a simple white top, brush my teeth, and add light makeup.

When I leave the bathroom, the four boys sit on my bed, discussing something to do with work. My eyes drift to Gabriel, and I finally acknowledge how attractive he looks today. He put on some light blue denim shorts, which are slightly ripped on his thigh, and a white t-shirt, which allows me to admire his handsome muscles underneath. Gabriel loves wearing white shirts. He also put on a bandana, letting his sexy and messy curls fall over it effortlessly. When he sees me stare, he cocks an eyebrow, but then for a second, his eyes wander over my body, too.

James gets up from the bed and walks over to me before he picks me up and throws me over his shoulder. "Hey," I complain, but he simply chuckles.

"I got her, boys, let's go." James carries me to the elevator and finally puts me down when he sees people approach. I smack his chest playfully but can't keep the smile off my face. We all step into the elevator seconds later. "Sorry, luv, but as soon as they're gone, you're going back over my shoulder."

"Is that right? I guess you gotta catch me first," I say, press all the buttons, and run out of the elevator right before the doors close. If they want to play, I'm game for it. I run toward the staircase and make my way down to the lobby when I hear Gabriel walking up the stairs toward me. I get out on the second floor and close the door. There is a small slit of glass that allows me to look through it and into the staircase. Luckily, Gabriel runs past and further upstairs. I smile victoriously and get back to running.

"Valentina," he sings through the staircase, and my heart stops, and so do my feet. "Come on, Val, where are you?" On my tiptoes, I keep going and open the door to the lobby just to get caught by James and thrown back over his shoulder.

"Hey, there are people around," I complain, but James doesn't seem to care any longer.

"Too bad, we're kidnapping you for today, and you are going to have to deal with it." My hands are on James' muscular back. I finally look up to see Gabriel, Adrian, and Cameron all walking either next to or behind us. They're laughing at the picture in front of them, which makes me a little mad but also smile. "By the way, Valentina, your arse is blocking the road on my left side completely. Now, not that it's not a hot view, but my good God," he says, and my mouth drops.

"You're just jealous because yours isn't that nice and trained," I fire back, and he laughs.

"Maybe you're right," he agrees, and I look over at Gabriel, who is smiling at our conversation. *Gabriel has a nice ass...* I shake my head and push my subconscious back into her horny corner.

Eventually, James puts me back on the ground, and I start walking by myself. They bring me to a breakfast place near the hotel, and we order within minutes. All of us seem to be extremely hungry.

"Are you ready for your presents?" Adrian asks, and I frown.

"No, because I don't want anything. We've been over this, I"

"Yeah, yeah, shut up and open the presents," Cameron chimes in and hands me a box. I smile at him before opening it and pulling out a beautiful purple dress. I would have never expected to get a dress from Cameron, but it is breathtaking. The fabric is soft between my fingers, and I can tell it must have cost him more than I would like. They shouldn't spend any money on gifts for me. I made that clear more than once. Yet, I know if I complain, they will only be disappointed.

So, I simply get up and say, "Thank you so much," before I hug him and press a kiss on his cheek.

"Damn, is everyone going to get a thank you like that?" Gabriel asks, and I want to tell him 'No', but I'll use any excuse to feel his skin against mine.

"Mine next," James chimes in and hands me a smaller package than Cameron. Somehow, I know whatever's inside is going to be three times more valuable. The package is heavy. My fingers wrap around the ribbon, and I undo it in a swift movement. I open the box, and my mouth drops to the floor. Inside it sits a helmet, the size of maybe a small melon, in the helmet design I drew when I was twelve years old. The flowers run from left to right, and the blue and red colors harmonize perfectly. The number nine is written on the sides, and a yin and yang symbol is in the center of the back. Tears flood my eyes, and I stare at James in disbelief. "Do you like it?" All I can do is nod and look down at the small helmet again.

"I love it," I eventually say and get up from my chair. James gets up too and hugs me tightly. I've always wanted to get the full-sized one, but I didn't get to choose when I was racing in Formula Three. Gabriel, Adrian, and James know why this is so emotional, but I'm still a bit embarrassed about my reaction. I wrap my arms around James' torso.

"I'm so sorry you haven't yet gotten the chance to get your full-sized one. You more than deserve it," he says, and I almost let a sob escape me.

"Thank you," I whisper, and James pulls back to press a kiss to my forehead. We sit back down, and I take the helmet into my hands one last time before placing it back inside the box. My eyes drift to Cameron and Gabriel, who are looking at James with a confused expression. "Sorry, guys," I mumble when I pull myself together. They assure me it's not a problem and all smile at the same time.

"Here, although I don't think it's as good as James'. He should have gone last. Now the expectations are fucking high," Gabriel jokes, and I laugh a little. He hands me an envelope, and I take it from him with a grin. His stubble makes my heart stop for a second before I can focus on the present in my hand again. I open the envelope and take out two tickets to *Les Misérables.* They are for next year, August, which is more than a year away. I smile because I remember the first movie Gabriel and I watched together was *Les Misérables.*

"Does this mean I have to take you with me?" I ask, and he laughs.

"You can take whoever you want but remember who got you the tickets and who is a huge fan of the musical," he says with a wink, and I melt.

"Okay, fine, I guess I'll take you," I reply, and he chuckles.

"Does that mean I will also get a kiss?" I roll my eyes and watch Adrian's face change.

"Careful," he warns Gabriel, who simply lifts his hands in surrender. I get up for the third time and give Gabriel a hug, then a swift kiss on the cheek. I know Gabriel is just teasing since he is very happy with Kira. Adrian hands me an envelope, too, and I shake my head. "I know you didn't want a present but trust me on this." With a soft sigh, I open it and pull out the card. It reads: I gave James your drawing, so I kind of helped with his present. I laugh, and my brother smiles at me. I blow a kiss at him and put the card back into the envelope.

The food arrives, and we finish it much too quickly. Before anyone else can take out their credit card, I go to the front and pay for the meal. We get into a taxi and drive for a while until we arrive at *Catedral-Basílica de Santa María de Mallorca.* Excitement shoots through me, and I can't wait to get out of the car and go inside the beautiful cathedral. I love architecture, especially European architecture from hundreds of years ago.

"Isn't this a great way to spend your birthday?" Adrian asks, and I nod enthusiastically. We walk inside, and I gasp.

"It's breathtaking," I mutter, and I hear Gabriel mumble something which sounds like 'so are you', but I'm sure I misunderstood. Maybe it was wishful thinking.

The cathedral looks like many I've seen before, but it doesn't make it any less gorgeous. The ceilings are high, the columns are square cut, the choir stalls are close to the altar, and the way the light shines into the cathedral through the rose windows is beautiful. The benches, on which the people may sit, are normal wooden ones. The sculptures and paintings are unique and incredibly pretty, and it takes us an hour to walk around and look at the entire cathedral. The boys' stomachs start to growl, and I laugh.

"Lunch?" I ask the four guys, and they nod. Athletes, I think to myself and smile. "Okay." I hook my arm through James'.

"What are you doing?" My grandfather asks, and I look up from my paper to answer his question politely. He has taught me that when somebody speaks to you, you should give them the respect of making eye contact.

"I'm drawing my dream helmet," I inform him. He sits down next to me, his light eyes scanning the drawing. I asked Adrian to print out a plain helmet, and I've spent the past two hours drawing on it.

"Looks lovely." I am not terrible at art, especially not at drawing flowers, and since most of my design includes such, it looks stunning. At least to me. "How come you wrote the number nine on it?" I stare back at the helmet and shrug.

"I'm not sure. I think the number picked me," I say, embarrassed, and Grandfather puts his hand on my shoulder.

"Then it is your number." He walks away, leaving me to finish my design.

Chapter 27

For the second time today, I'm getting ready in the hotel bathroom. Adrian told me to put on something I can party in. Some tight jeans and a see-through glitter shirt will do the trick. I'm only wearing a black bralette underneath, and I feel incredibly sexy. The dark eyeshadow I applied fits my outfit very well, and so does the red lipstick. I walk out of the bathroom to face the men who are yet again sitting on my bed. Adrian is still in his room. James' mouth falls open when he looks at me, and I smirk at him. I move over to the chair on the other side of the room where my purse is and feel three pairs of eyes on me. When I look up, they all have the same expression of shock on their faces.

"What?" I ask them, and Cameron and James look away. Gabriel's eyes stay on me, and I get nervous.

"You look gorgeous," he compliments me, and I see James shoot him a glare. I thank him and go back to packing my small purse with everything I need.

"No, no, no, no, no. No," is all I hear when Adrian walks into the room. "No," he repeats, and I laugh. "Look at them. If they're already drooling, what do you think other men are going to do?" Gabriel and James start to blush and immediately get up. Cameron simply smiles. He would be more interested in Adrian, which is why I can't help but smile either. However, Adrian is very insensitive when it comes to pointing out things like that, and I don't appreciate how uncomfortable he's making our friends. "What do you think you're doing, wearing something like that?"

"I think for the first time in my life, I feel smoking hot," I simply reply and throw my purse across my chest. "So, I'm going to wear this and feel this way the whole night. And I'm not worried about other men. James is going to be with me the entire time anyway." James nods and runs his hand through his hair.

"That's true. I would never leave her alone," he says, and I hold out my hand as if to say 'see'. "Especially not when she looks like pure sex." My eyes go wide, and he shrugs.

"Fine, but I am not leaving your side either," Adrian tells me, and I roll my eyes.

"That's fine by me." I make my way over to Adrian and squeeze his arm. "Now, let's have an awesome evening." He nods, and I walk past him to my door.

All of them put on something casual yet still attractive. James is wearing jeans and a dress shirt, Cameron has a similar outfit on, Gabriel is dressed in black jeans and a green shirt, and Adrian is in shorts and a polo. I feel overdressed with them around me, but it's also my birthday, and I'm only going to turn eighteen once.

The bar is filled with people, it is loud, and I am excited. It's my first time at one, and it is not like I imagined it. It's much better and worse at the same time. The music is decent, and the people seem to be having a lot of fun, but it is also hot and loud. When we walk into a more crowded space of the bar, people push against me, and I struggle to move forward with the rest of my friends. I feel a hand in mine, and sparks ignite on my skin. I don't even have to check to know it's Gabriel's. We find a table close to the dance floor, and he drops my hand as soon as we reach it.

James suddenly appears with four shots and places them on the small, round table in front of me. I've never had alcohol before, but I'm curious about it. Adrian sips on the water James brought him, and I reach for the shot glass.

"Ready?" James asks me, and I nod. He hands me a lemon and some salt. I put a little bit of salt on the back of my hand like James is showing me and lick it off before I pour the burning liquid down my throat. I quickly put the slice of lemon into my mouth and suck on it. It's such a weird feeling. The drink is warm as it burns like fire in my throat, and the sour of the lemon contrasts the bitter tequila. It's worse than I thought it would be, but I also really enjoy it.

"How was that?" Cameron asks me, and I smile.

"Incredible," I admit, and he grins at me. Adrian rolls his eyes, but I ignore him. "Come on, James, let's dance." The English man stares at me for a few seconds without moving. I know he doesn't care for dancing. "You said you wouldn't leave me alone," I remind him and hear him sigh. I hold out my hand, and he takes it. He spins me around once, making me laugh softly. I run my hands through my hair, and my hips move to the music. James is standing awkwardly next to me, so I take his hips in my hands and move them for him. "It's not that hard. Come on," I complain, and he sighs for the second time.

"Fine, but remember you asked for this," he says and grabs my hand before pulling me close to him. He spins me around, so my butt faces his front, and he starts moving my hips for me in rhythm with the music. His lips move to my ear. "I've been with girls who dance in all kinds of ways. I picked up a few things," he admits and spins me around again. His feet move with the beat of the song, and I can't believe how good he is at this. After a few more minutes, I feel the alcohol settling and a little lightheaded. It's not bad at all. I still have control over everything but also seem to enjoy things the slightest bit more. James and I go back to the group, and Cameron comes with another round of shots. I repeat the process from earlier, and so do James, Gabriel, and Cameron.

"May I have this dance?" Gabriel asks and holds out his hand for me. I look at him, confused by his offer.

"I thought you didn't dance," I say, recalling the one time he ran away from me when I asked.

"But I want to dance with you on your birthday. So, may I?" He simply takes my hand and leads me back to the dance floor when I don't respond. "Now, I'm not a good dancer, so you're going to have to do your best to make me look good." I laugh harder than necessary, feeling even more lightheaded now. Two shots on a somewhat empty stomach, and for someone who's never had alcohol, it's a lot.

"I could dance like this," I suggest and run my fingers through my hair seductively while my hips move slowly. "Or, like this," I continue, moving closer to Gabriel, putting my hand on his chest and squatting down in front of him. "Maybe like this?" I turn around and push my bottom against his crotch before I start moving my hips again. I don't know what's happening to me, but I have an incredible amount of confidence, especially because Gabriel isn't pushing me off. His hands move to my hips, and he goes along with my movements. By then, the alcohol has got me feeling amazing, and Gabriel's body pressing against mine is only adding to it. His hand drops lower, and it feels like I'm on fire.

"Fuck, Valentina. You turn me on so quickly, baby," he whispers into my ear, and I lean my head against his shoulder. I can't believe he's saying this to me; I can't believe this is happening, but my body is throbbing, and I need some kind of release. "No, I'm sorry," Gabriel blurts out and disappears. Disappointment washes over me, and I walk back to the table where the other guys are standing. James is leaning against it, smiling stupidly, Adrian is on his phone, Cameron is looking around the bar for something, and Gabriel is nowhere to be seen.

"What happened to James?" I ask Adrian, and he shrugs. His water bottle is empty now, and he is rolling it around the table, playing with it absentmindedly.

"You left, and he had two more shots," Adrian says. James stands up straight and grins.

"Okay, I want two more, too," I tell James, and his face lights up. He gets them for us, and I don't bother with the salt or lemon. I'm frustrated because of Gabriel, and I am sick and tired of always getting left... left unsatisfied. My mind is completely clouded by the time the fourth shot settles into my empty stomach. All I realize is I start to laugh at something James is doing, but I can't quite comprehend what it is. The alcohol is making me giggle, laugh, and choke on my spit. I'm definitely tipsy when I bring the glass to my mouth for the... *fifth? sixth?* time.

Somehow, James and I make it back to my hotel room in the middle of the night. He stumbles over my backpack, and I start laughing at him.

"Hey, hey," he complains but also starts to laugh. My eyes drift to the chocolate on my nightstand, and it makes me excited. I stumble over to it, giggle a little, and then eat it. "Can I have some?" James slurs, and I put a piece in his mouth.

"Do you know how damn hard it is to get someone that'll get you off?" I tell him, unaware of what I'm actually saying. "Luke only cared about himself, and... and Gabriel is just so stupid," I slur the words, too, but then for some reason, start to giggle. It's probably the way the words sound coming out of my mouth. "I just wish someone could make me feel really good." I'm in his face then, trying to communicate my point to him. He needs to understand what I'm saying right now.

"I could make you feel good," he whispers, and my eyes drop to his lips. I don't know what's happening, but all I can think about are his lips. My mind is completely clouded, and I don't have any control over my body.

"Yeah?" I ask, and he nods eagerly.

"I can make you feel realst good," he assures me, and I laugh at his words, but James takes my face in his hands and looks into my eyes. "Do you want me to?" he asks, and my heart skips a beat. My body is drawn to him.

"Yes, I do," I reply firmly and lean toward him until our lips meet. I can't pull away; I can't move. All I do is enjoy the way his tongue slips into my mouth when my lips part slightly. I don't know what I'm doing, but I keep doing it anyway. James moves between my legs, and he pins me down on the bed. "You want this?" he asks me.

"I want you," I answer before focusing on his erection and how it is pressing against my heat. I wrap my legs around his hips, and James continues to rub against me while his tongue massages mine. It doesn't make any sense to me, nothing at this moment does, but my mind is also not in the moment with him. It imagines Gabriel between my legs. James' tongue runs over my hot skin, and I shiver.

"Can I touch you?" he slurs.

"Please, touch me," I beg, and his eyes focus on mine. We're both way too drunk, and it's probably a bad idea, but I need this right now. His fingers drop to my jeans, which he unbuttons when I tell him 'Yes'. His fingers slip into my panties, and all I can feel is the rubbing and the pressure he's applying to my throbbing area. I have to bite down on my lip to keep from screaming out a name, which I know isn't his. James' lips find mine again, and he cuts me off before I can moan by putting his tongue back into my mouth. His finger continues to rub in a steady movement, and I fall apart under his touch a minute later. He drops down on the bed next to me, and the last thing I see is him smiling as he tugs a loose strand of my hair behind my ear. A deep sleep consumes me as his eyes close too.

Chapter 28

I wake up with the worst headache of my life. I sit up in bed and rub my temples but have to run to the bathroom before my consciousness can catch up. I throw up until there's nothing left in my stomach. A big hand wraps around my arm, and I look up to find Adrian helping me. He sits me down on the rim of the bathtub, and I try to stop the floor from spinning.

"What happened last night?" I ask him. "All I remember is walking into the club, but that's it. I can't remember anything past that," I admit and drop my head into my hands. With all the strength in my mind, I'm trying to figure out what the hell happened, but I got nothing.

"You had a million shots, and then you disappeared with James. I found him passed out on the chair in my room this morning. I don't know how he got there, but he seems to be in a lot of pain as well." I nod and try to figure out what James and I did when we returned to the hotel room last night. Adrian puts a cold, wet towel against my forehead, and I already feel better. "Now that you have experienced how terrible it is to be hungover, can you promise me not to put yourself into this state again? I don't like seeing you this way," he says, and I nod.

"Never again. I can't remember anything from last night, and it's killing me," I tell him and laugh a little, only to flinch when pain shoots through my head. It's throbbing, aching, and I feel like I'm going to pass out.

Adrian helps me back into bed, and I fall asleep again. An hour later, I wake up and see Adrian is gone, but I also find James sitting on my bed, watching me sleep. I shoot up and realize the headache has gotten less painful. James lifts his hand to touch my cheek softly. I cock an eyebrow, surprised by the affectionate gesture, but focus quickly enough.

"Thank God you're here. What the hell happened last night?" I ask, and he drops his hand from my face. His expression briefly changes to disappointment but then goes back to a neutral one.

"You don't remember anything?" I shake my head and wait for him to tell me what we did. James rubs his face with his right hand before he looks at me again. "We came back here, watched a movie, and ate chocolate, then you fell asleep," he informs me, but I'm still confused.

"Why did you leave? You could have slept in my bed. It's not like we didn't sleep together before," I say, confused, and he nods. *He's acting so strangely! Maybe something awkward happened? I wish he would just tell me!*

"Yeah, I know." He shrugs and drops down onto my bed. "I'm sorry about last night, luv. I should have never let you drink so much," he admits, and I can see he feels guilty. I take his hand to comfort him, and he briefly pulls it away before letting me take it. *So strange...*

Of course he would feel bad for getting me drunk and blame himself for the pain I'm feeling today. However, if I point out that it was my choice, he'll tell me he's older and should have been more mature. I didn't see my brother jumping between me and the glass at any point during the night either. Then again, Adrian always wants me to make my own mistakes so I can learn from them. I remove the blanket from my body and lie down next to him on the bed. I retake his hand and intertwine our fingers.

"I'm sorry about getting so drunk last night, but I'm very thankful you got me into my bed and that I was safe and sound. You're an amazing friend,"

I say and lie on my side. My hand is still in his, and he turns his head to look at me.

"You don't remember anything?" he asks me again, and I shake my head.

"No, should I remember something?" Panic washes over me, and I'm scared I did or said something I shouldn't have. *Maybe I said something about Gabriel? Did I say something to Gabriel? Fuck, fuck, fuck.* I probably did, and it was most likely beyond embarrassing.

"No, babe, there's nothing you need to remember. I was just curious," he assures me and squeezes my hand. He puts it on his chest, and I feel his heart pump quickly against his ribcage. There is a sad expression on his face, which makes me frown.

"Are you sure there is nothing at all? I feel like you're not telling me something," I mumble, and James stares intensely at the ceiling. He's quiet for a couple of seconds before he answers my question.

"I don't remember too much either." His voice is quiet, and his hand is holding mine tightly. It is as if he is scared to let go for some reason. It worries me, but he isn't going to tell me what is bothering him.

James and I talk a bit about the symptoms of our hangovers, and I start to laugh when he tells me he dreamt the room was spinning, but once he woke up, he realized it was still turning.

A couple of hours later, someone knocks on the door, and I get up to reveal Gabriel on the other side of it. As soon as I look into his eyes, I remember the dream I had last night, that vivid dream of Gabriel and me. I still remember the way he touched me, the way his tongue massaged mine, and the way he unbuttoned my pants before he pleasured me. As I recall it, I could swear it happened, but I know better than that. Gabriel would never actually touch me like that.

"Valentina, can we talk?" Gabriel asks me in French, and my heart flutters. He never speaks to me in French. I step out into the hall and feel his hand on the small of my back, pushing me gently further. "We need to talk about what happened last night on the dance floor," he says, smoothly switching back into English. I welcome back his beautiful accent, but I'm also concerned about what happened between us last night.

"Why, what the hell happened?" I ask and start to pull on his sleeve. His eyes drop to where I am grabbing him before they lift to my face again. "Sorry," I mumble and remove my hand from his shirt.

"You don't remember?" There is a surprised expression on his face, and I sit down against the wall out of frustration. My head drops into my hands, and I sigh.

"No. I've been trying for hours, but nothing." Gabriel drops down next to me. "I feel terrible, and now I'm sure I said something stupid to you. I'm so sorry for whatever it was," I tell him, still incredibly frustrated with myself. I look away and hide the embarrassed flush on my cheeks. Gabriel's hand finds its way onto my thigh, and he squeezes gently, sending a shiver down my spine.

"No, you didn't say anything. It was me. I said something inappropriate, and I am glad you can't remember it, I have to admit." He lets out a sweet, soft laugh, and I wonder yet again what he said to me. "If you do remember it later, just know I'm sorry." I shake my head and stare at the wall on the opposite side of us. We're all embarrassed about things that happened or didn't last night, and I don't want to push it. Although, questions like: *What could it possibly be? Why are they so secretive? Should I just be letting this go? and Why am I just okay with this?* are roaming around in my head.

Gabriel takes my face in his hand and presses a sweet kiss onto my cheek before getting up and holding his hand out for me. I take it, and he pulls me up aggressively, slamming me against his chest. His laugh is deep, sexy, and it vibrates through my whole body as he holds me close for a few seconds longer. His breath is hot against my skin, and I have to pull away to find the ground under my feet again. My feelings are stronger than ever, especially after that dream, and I don't know what to do about them. Then again, I never have.

Chapter 29

Present...

Eduardo is landing in an hour, and I am not ready. I've never been in a position like this, where I had to ask someone if they wanted to be friends with benefits instead of being in an actual relationship. My feet tap the floor, and I hold onto the sheets on either side of me a little harder than necessary. After a little while, I lean back on my bed and stare at the ceiling.

"Hola, hermosa," Eduardo says as he appears out of nowhere in my room.

"Eduardo!" The handsome man sits down next to me on my bed, his hands resting between his legs and a perfect smirk playing on his full lips. "What are you doing here?" I ask, trying to calm my heart down. Instead of answering, he stands up before he leans down again and presses his lips to mine ever so gently.

"I may have lied about my arrival time to surprise you," he informs me, and I grin. Now that he is here, I'm excited to see him. Eduardo sits down next to me again and takes my hand in his, placing a soft kiss on the back of it. I feel an urge to reach forward and run my fingers over his cheek. So, I do, and his light brown eyes close from my touch.

"We need to talk," I whisper, and he opens his eyes once more. He nods and laces his fingers through mine.

It takes me a while to explain to Eduardo what I want. I share how miserable my old relationship was and even open up to him about having feelings for someone else. He's sitting in front of me, patiently listening to everything I have to say. There is no anger on his face, only a faint smile when I finally get to the point and ask him if he wants to fool around without actually dating. He sits in silence for a long time.

"This is truly what you want?" he asks me, and I nod. "You don't want commitment? You don't want to text every day and talk about our feelings? You don't want to have people see us together and say, 'Look at that cute couple!'? You just want sex?" He's not condescending. Eduardo seems completely genuine when he asks me those questions. Again, I nod. An embarrassed blush settles on my cheek, and I have to look away.

"I do want to have meaningful conversations and be good friends with you if we do this. Yet, I don't want to be emotionally available, nor be anyone's girlfriend. All I can give you is this, no strings attached." My eyes drift back to his face, and he cocks an eyebrow. "I got tested a month ago, and I'm clean," I tell him, and he nods.

"I got tested, too, only a couple of weeks ago. I'm clean, too," he assures me right before he puts his hands on my thigh and squeezes. "If this is what you want, we can try," he tells me with his delicious accent.

Eduardo leans forward to press his lips to my neck and then to the soft spot just underneath my jawline, making me forget about everything else. He takes my face between his thumb and index finger and tilts my head to get better access to my throat. My eyes flutter shut, and I enjoy the way this feels. It's nice, not as amazing as when Gabriel did the same thing, but it's not about that. This is about me enjoying myself. I put my lips to his and straddle his lap. My tongue enters his mouth, and Eduardo lets out a low moan which vibrates through my body. I can feel him grow underneath me as I rub my heat against his lap, which is only covered by my underwear since I'm wearing a skirt.

Involuntarily, I let my mind wander to the only person I know will get me over the edge. As bad as it is that I'm not thinking about Eduardo, I need to imagine Gabriel. I need to remember how his lips felt against my skin. Eduardo moans when my lips drop to his neck and my hands slip under his shirt. His muscles are rock-hard, and I can feel his abs move underneath my fingers.

He switches our positions in one swift movement so that I lie under him, and he has easy access. His fingers slowly slip into my panties, but not without making eye contact with me to make sure he is not going too far. I simply lie back and close my eyes as a response. He reaches into my panties, and I imagine Gabriel's touch from the dream I had once.

Seconds later, my fingers are grabbing Eduardo's hair, and I fall apart. It's not a big orgasm, but it's enough to make a small moan escape my throat. My hands drop from his chest to his bulge, and I start to rub him. I reach down into his pants to allow for skin contact.

"A little firmer," he begs, and I do as I'm told. "God," he moans when I grab a little tighter. Eduardo gasps and groans before I feel his pants getting wet. A smile spreads over my face when I look at him to find him completely out of breath and biting his lip. He opens his eyes and stares at me. Eduardo puts his hand against my cheek, and I give him a quick kiss on the lips.

"Valentina?" a familiar voice says from behind us, and I push Eduardo off me so I can sit up and look at the intruder. Gabriel takes a look at the scene in front of him, my flushed cheeks and Eduardo's stained pants, and a sad expression appears on his face. "I'm sorry, I didn't know you were in the middle of– Adrian let me in, and your door was a little open–" he cuts off before he finishes that sentence. He rushes out of my room, and as much as I want to run after him, I know better.

"I would have had to compete with that guy? It's a good thing we're only friends." Eduardo laughs a little, and I look at him with a confused expression. "Come on, Valentina. I can see the way you look at him. I could have never won you over." Eduardo gets up and walks over to his luggage, which I haven't noticed until now. "May I use your bathroom?" he asks, and I tell him 'Yes'. Minutes later, he comes back out wearing a pair of jeans and a new shirt. "So, what do you want to do today?" He drops down on the bed and smiles.

Eduardo and I end up going for lunch and then to a movie. It's a comedy movie, and I enjoy it, especially the witty comments Eduardo makes throughout. It's about six o'clock when the movie ends, and Eduardo and I make our way back to my house. We talk about racing and each other's childhood like we always do, and I smile. This feels comfortable and uncomplicated. Simply two friends hanging out, talking, and spending time together.

"Are you excited for the race weekend?" I ask when we're minutes from my home.

Bahrain is the second race of the season, and it is a great track, in my opinion. Eduardo tells me how disappointed he was by the result of the first race and how much he has been working ever since.

The Spaniard asks if he can sleep in one of the guest rooms, and for the fifth time, I assure him it is not a problem. He takes his luggage out of my room, gives me a brief kiss on the lips, which confuses me but doesn't make me uncomfortable, and lets me know he needs to get some rest. Sadly, as soon as he's gone, I start to overthink everything...

Chapter 30

My fingers trail over the packages Gabriel has sent me, and I contemplate opening one. The events of today replay in my head while an uneasy feeling spreads through my chest. Being with Eduardo was carefree, but my mind won't stop focusing on how I left things with Gabriel. We were finally together, and I pushed him away over the tiniest mistake. He was right, I am being a hypocrite, and I have no idea why. Part of me is convinced it's because I'm terrified of how much he means to me and pushing him away is easier than losing him in the future.

I rip the package open and pull out a framed drawing of me in Gabriel's Formula One car. My heart sinks a little as I take out the small note next to it. It reads: Chérie, I wanted you to have this even though we're not on speaking terms. I know I make your life difficult, and I'm deeply sorry for it. Please, never lose sight of what is most important: your dream. Yours only, Gabriel.

In all of the chaos, he's reminding me to think of myself and nothing else. My thoughts drift to the day he let me sit in his car, something very intimate and personal not many other drivers would allow, and I sink down on my bed. Gabriel is good for me. Despite all the fights and arguments, he's someone who cares more about my dreams than his feelings. Eduardo is kind and funny, but he's not goofy, charming, caring... he's just not Gabriel.

I take my phone out of my pocket and send him a message, telling him to meet me on the sidewalk outside my house. It's time I woman up and face the man I love. My grandpa didn't teach me how to walk, so I'd run away from my feelings like a coward. He raised me better than that.

Without waiting for a reply, I make my way outside and sit down. The full moon is the only source of light, but I recognize Gabriel from a distance. His hands are in his pockets, and his hair is messily neat. When he comes closer, I notice he's wearing Christmas pajamas and burst into laughter. I can see him smiling.

"Those were the only ones I could find, okay? The rest are in the wash," he informs me, and I cover my lips with my index finger to keep from laughing. Gabriel settles down next to me, his shoulder leaning against mine to nudge me ever so slightly. "What's going on, chérie? Why did you text me at midnight to meet you here?" he asks, and I tilt my head to look at him.

"I'm sorry," I start, and he lifts both eyebrows in response. "You were trying to protect me from getting hurt, and I thank you by being a bitch about it," I add, and he shakes his head.

"Don't apologi–" he starts, but I cut him off.

"Yes, I have to. You've been apologizing even though I was the one overreacting," I say, and he watches me with an intensity that makes my heart ache. I rest my head on my shoulder while my eyes focus on his. Gabriel reaches out to tug some of my hair behind my ear, and I close my eyes in response to his soft touch. My skin lights on fire where his fingers brush it, something only he can do. I take a deep breath. "I think when I went to your room that night, things suddenly got so real, and it scared me," I whisper and drop my head between my heads.

"May I speak now?" he asks, amusement faintly evident in his voice. I look back up again to show him I'm listening. "Does it feel like I'm forcing you to be ready?" he asks, and I shift my gaze from his eyes to his lips.

"No," I reply honestly. Gabriel gives me a small smile.

"Then don't force yourself either. If you need to be with Eduardo right now, let that be okay. If you don't want anyone right now, that's more than okay." This is my friend Gabriel, the one who only cares about my well-being. "I care about you a lot, chérie, and with that being said, I only want you to be happy," he promises, and I shift my body until I'm facing him entirely.

"I'm making a mess of everything," I mumble and take his right hand in my left. He studies our intertwined hands for a brief moment before focusing on my face again.

"So am I, which is why I understand you're not ready to be with me; maybe you'll never be. Having feelings for someone doesn't mean you want to be in a relationship with them. I won't pressure you, and you shouldn't do so to yourself either." This doesn't make it easier for me. If anything, I only fall more in love with him with every word. "You have to figure out what you want for yourself without any influence of what Eduardo, I, or Adrian want. I'll still be here when you've made your decision," he goes on, and I suck in a sharp breath while a tear rolls down my cheek.

"I won't ask you to wait until I've sorted everything out," I state, and Gabriel stands up, holding out his hand to help me up too.

"Don't think of it as me waiting for you. Think of it as me continuing my life with the hope of an answer one day," he replies, and I furrow my brows.

"The concept is still the same," I challenge, and Gabriel lets out a small laugh.

"Jesus, Val, just..." he cuts off, and we both chuckle. "Do what makes you happy. That's all I ask of you." I nod in response. Gabriel takes a step forward, his hand moving to my hips and his lips brushing over my cheek. "Good night, Lady Valentina," he whispers and bows as he leaves my house, but not before bringing a smile to my lips.

I lie awake for a very long time, trying to figure out what I should do. Eventually, Gabriel's words ring in my head. 'I won't pressure you, and you shouldn't do so to yourself either'. He's right. This isn't something I should decide at two in the morning. My head will tell me when the right time is, and for now, the second race of the season is my mind's primary focus. Bahrain will be a lot of fun.

Chapter 31

Gabriel and I haven't spoken much in days. He's giving me space, which I appreciate and despise at the same time. I don't like it when I don't speak to him. Eduardo and I haven't done anything more in the plus department of our friendship.

Today is Qualifying, and I am sitting and waiting impatiently for Q3 to finally be over. Gabriel takes pole, Adrian comes in third, James fourth, and Eduardo is in sixth. The day passes in a blur, and Adrian brings me back to the track after we were already at the hotel. He doesn't tell me why or what is happening, but I don't ask too many questions. He covers my eyes with his hands, finally making me impatient.

"Why are you so secretive?" Adrian leaves his hands on my face, and I follow him down a path. All I know is I am on the racetrack. When he uncovers my eyes again, I'm standing in front of a Ferrari 812. Adrian holds out a helmet for me, and a confused expression settles on my face.

"You're going to drive this baby around the track," he tells me, and my mouth drops. "I've arranged everything. All you have to do is try not to crash the car. After all, there is a race here tomorrow," he says and chuckles. *I can't believe he did this for me.* I take the helmet from him, put it on my head, and get into the car. Adrian gets into the passenger seat and puts his seatbelt and helmet on. He gives me some quick instructions and then lets me take over.

I feel the car under my control as I let my fingers run over the steering wheel, the buttons, and the rest of the gear. The helmet is tight on my head, but it feels secure. It is the same feeling I had for most of my life. My foot barely presses down on the gas pedal, and I try to get a feel of the car during the first lap. The track is lit up, and I have a clear vision of everything. When I arrive at the start and finish line, I come to a complete stop. Adrian counts down for me, and I get ready for a good start. When he says go, I rev the engine and make it speed down the track. Whenever I race, I feel free. Adrenalin shoots through me, and I feel more alive than ever. This is why I started racing in the first place. A scream of joy escapes me, and I hear Adrian laugh next to me. He trusts my driving enough not to be afraid.

Not much later, I'm driving back over the finish line and bring the car to a much slower pace. My heart is pounding, and the level of happiness I feel is overwhelming. Every corner of this track is so familiar because of the training I do in the simulator. However, being here is an entirely different feeling, and I prefer this over sitting in my room.

"Thank you," I say, and Adrian takes my hand in his.

"We'll find a way to get you into a Formula One car. I don't want to be the only one who gets to do what they love, especially when your time is better than mine," he informs me and holds up a stopwatch. "I was half a second slower than you in this car." Adrian shrugs and pulls back the stopwatch. "It's gorgeous, by the way, that smile on your face." Naturally, the smile only gets bigger, and I have to look away. He's going to make me cry if he continues.

I thank him repeatedly for letting me drive the car on the track, and Adrian assures me it is his pleasure. I pull the helmet off my head and hand it back to him. My brother disappears into his garage, and I wait outside, staring up into the sky. It is breathtaking.

"You're one of the best drivers I've ever had the pleasure of watching,"

Gabriel's familiar voice appears from beside me, and I grin at him.

"Likewise," I reply, and he smiles from ear to ear.

"One day, you'll sit in a Formula One car, and the only thing the other drivers and I will see is your dust on our visors," he says, and I let my mind wander to the image.

"Wouldn't that be something?" I mumble, and Gabriel winks at me before leaving me to stand by myself again, admiring the night sky.

There is no way. Anger courses through my whole body as I watch Adrian get stuck in the gravel because Kyle pushes him off the track. I'm furious by the amateur mistake Kyle makes, especially when Adrian has to bear the consequences. My brother's race is now over because of that mistake. On the monitors, I watch Adrian get out of his red car and kick the ground out of frustration. I understand him because I want to kick the ground, too. I also want to kick Kyle, but then again, Adrian probably imagines Kyle's face on the gravel.

Minutes later, Adrian is back with his team, and they are discussing something he will probably tell me about later. For now, however, I have to be patient and continue to watch the race, trying not to constantly wish something would go wrong during Kyle's pit stop that would cost him ten places. Unfortunately, the Mercedes AMG team is one of the fastest and most consistent in pit stops. The FIA eventually gives Kyle a ten-second penalty for pushing another driver off the track and causing a collision. That penalty will either be added at the end or, should Kyle do another pit stop, the pit crew will have to wait ten seconds before they are allowed to change the tires.

The race is a complete mess. Jonathan's car has to retire because of an engine failure, Gabriel crashes into Eduardo, but luckily, both of them stay in the race. I'm not sure what happened between those two, but I also don't seem to find more information. The best thing about this chaotic race is that James goes ahead and finishes in first place. Excitement shoots through my whole body, and I rush outside with the rest of the team just in time to see him get out of his car and hug the people on his side. I'm clapping enthusiastically while James is celebrating. It's only his second win in Formula One, which is why I am so incredibly proud of him. He deserves this, even if it was mostly luck that got him into first place. I then notice Gabriel only finishes fifth.

Adrian puts his ego aside and comes with me so we can celebrate our friend's victory. We go to a restaurant where James' team set up a congratulatory party for him.

"Well done," I tell James yet again, and he wraps his arm around my shoulder before he presses a kiss to my temple.

"Thank you, my love. Thank you for being here and celebrating with me," he says, and I smile. James takes a sip of his beer, and he continues to hold me close to him.

Sooner than I would like, the party is over, and Adrian and I go back to our hotel. We have separate rooms this time, which is why I can take my time showering. I lie down in bed, and my stomach starts to cramp. Without looking at a calendar, I already know what time it is. I groan and curl up into a ball on my bed.

Chapter 32

"Valentina, let me in," a voice says from outside of my door, and I groan once more before getting out of bed. Eduardo is standing there, a sweet smile on his face. "May I come in?" I step aside, and he walks into my room. The cramps continue to bring crippling pain to my body. Eduardo walks toward me before pressing his lips to my neck. I push him off gently and walk over to my bed again. "What's wrong?" he asks before he sits down next to me.

Tears roll down my cheek involuntarily, and I lean back in bed. "I'm on my period," I reply in all honesty, and he leans away from me. I frown as I watch an odd expression take over his face. He seems eager to go, so I tell him, "You can leave." And he does. How immature... I always thought Eduardo is the mature one out of the two of them, but then I recall the time Gabriel saw me cry and in pain and how amazing he was. *Gabriel is amazing... he's always been amazing. I want to see him.*

Before I can think about it more, I put on a pair of flip-flops, take my key card, and walk to the elevator. I press the eleventh-floor button and get out as soon as the doors open again, making my way to his room. He opens the door, and more tears leave my eyes. I don't know why, but I can't hold them back.

"What's wrong, chérie?" he asks me, but my attention is drifting from his face to his body. The only thing keeping me sane is the fact he's wearing boxers that reach to the middle of his thigh. His lean, muscular chest is exposed to me completely, and I forget why I came to his room. "Chérie?" he says again and brings me back to reality. His hands reach forward, and he wipes away my tears. "Are you in pain?" I nod, and so does he. "Okay, baby." My heart flutters, and he notices how much I like it when he uses that pet name.

"What are you doing?" I ask him, but he doesn't answer. Instead, he leads me to his bed, where he pulls back the covers and lets me crawl under the blanket.

"I'm going to go down to the lobby and see if the reception has a hot water bottle, okay?" I shake my head and hold onto his hand. "I'll be right back." He presses a kiss to my forehead and puts on clothes before he disappears out of the room.

Gabriel returns with a bottle of water, painkillers, and a hot water bottle. "Sorry it took so long, chérie, but I went to the store and got you the hot water bottle." He pulls back the sheets and places the bottle onto my stomach before handing me some water and painkillers. When Gabriel takes the bottle out of my hands, he frowns. "You're cold," he states and pulls his long-sleeved shirt over his head. "Here." Gabriel hands it to me, and I put it on. The tank top wasn't keeping me warm.

"Why are you doing all of this for me?" I ask him, and he runs his hand over my forehead. My eyes close from his touch, and a sigh escapes me.

"Is that a rhetorical question?" he replies, and another tear flows down. There's something seriously wrong with me. I'm not sad, but I also can't stop crying. His thumb caresses my cheek, and I pull his hand to my mouth to press a kiss against the back of it. I love how it feels to be with him right now, I love the affection, and I wish my cramps didn't ruin this moment.

"This shit hurts," I complain, and he chuckles softly.

"You know, I read something that helps with period cramps," he mumbles and smirks wickedly. "Having an orgasm helps," he whispers, and shivers run down my body. I can't talk or move. All I do is stare at his delicious lean body and imagine the things he could make me feel. There's another cramp, and I flinch involuntarily.

"You're very funny," I tell him, and he winks at me.

"I try." He runs his index finger over my lips so carefully, one might think he would break me if he pressed harder.

"Lie down," I command, and he gives me his perfect smile. He bites the inside of his cheek before he jumps over me and drops down on the other side of the bed. A sweet laugh, one I've never heard, leaves my throat, and I turn around to face him. Gabriel is lying on his back, his hand under his head, and a lovely grin on his lips. "I'm really sorry about today. I know you must be mad about the result," I blurt out, and Gabriel turns his head to the side.

"You're right, I was mad, but I'll never stop pushing. I will never give up because that's not the kind of person I am. I'll never give up..." As much as I want to keep staring at his handsome features, I know it is better to turn around and face the other way.

"Cuddle with me?" I ask and feel Gabriel's arms wrapping around me seconds later. His hands rest just underneath my breasts, and he puts his chin in the crook of my neck. A small sigh escapes him, and I run my fingers over his arms. "Don't think this changes anything," I warn him, and he chuckles. The vibration travels through my whole body, and I close my eyes to enjoy how it feels to be lying in his arms.

"Don't worry, baby, I won't think anything I'm not supposed to," he says before he presses a kiss to my shoulder. I don't need Eduardo in my life. He might like me, but Gabriel loves me.

Chapter 33

Gabriel's arms are still wrapped around my body when I wake up the following day. Somehow, I feel worse than yesterday, but also better. Worse because the cramps are more painful but better because his arms around me feel comforting. I turn around, holding back the groan threatening to leave my throat, and sigh when I'm finally facing him. It's difficult for me to comprehend how attractive he still looks, even when he's sleeping. His lips are slightly parted, but he's not snoring, nor is he drooling. *How's he doing that? If my mouth were open, I would do both in my sleep.* I shake my head and focus on his face again. His long lashes almost rest on his cheeks, and his curly hair is all over the place. He still smells like mahogany, just like he always does, and I can't help but place my hands on his muscular chest. His skin is smooth, and my curiosity is overpowering my self-control. I run my fingertips over his nipples, then his stomach, over the small line of hair leading from his belly button to his boxers. His eyes shoot open, and he looks down at me.

"You're getting me all worked up," he says with a raspy voice that makes my insides turn. His hand reaches out to touch my cheek, and goosebumps spread down my arms. "Can I kiss you?"

"Yes," I reply, and he grins sweetly.

His thumb pulls my bottom lip down, and he presses his mouth to mine, his tongue entering smoothly. He moans when he repositions himself, and my hand grazes his morning wood. Something inside me wants to reach for him and pleasure him to hear that sweet sound again, but I know better. Gabriel pulls back quickly and lies back down. He's right to move away. We shouldn't do something like this while we're unsure about where we are. "How are you feeling?" His hand runs over my stomach, and I smile.

"Good," I lie. "But I have to go," I tell him and attempt to make my way out of bed. He guides me back down and wraps his arms around me.

"No, you have to stay here so I can take care of you," he replies plainly and kisses my cheek. "Please, chérie, I will feel horrible if you leave." His arms tighten around me, and I try to wiggle free, unsuccessfully. I giggle and lean my head back against his shoulder.

"Gabriel, I have to go back to my room," I repeat, but he shakes his head.

"No, you can stay here. You don't have to leave," Gabriel mumbles, and I laugh.

"Gabriel, you don't understand. I *have to* leave," I try to tell him without having to say it out loud.

"Why? Why do you *have to* leave?" He says the 'have to' in the same way I did.

"I have to change my pad unless you want me to bleed on the bed." He slowly loosens his grip.

"Oh," is all he says before he lets go of me. "Sorry," he apologizes in a deep, sexy voice. I turn around to find him rubbing his neck with his hand and shake my head, laughing. "Will you come back?" he asks and finds my hand on the bed.

"No, but you can take me out for breakfast if you want. I'm starving," I complain, and Gabriel flashes me his perfect smile.

"What do you want to eat? Eggs? Pancakes? A whole cow?" He starts laughing at his joke, and I join him. I can't not when he starts laughing his pure, genuine laugh that makes my heart melt.

"You know, your laugh is funnier than your jokes," I inform him, and his mouth drops offendedly. "I'll wait for you in my room," I let him know, and he glares at me.

"Maybe I won't take you to breakfast anymore. You're too mean," he playfully whines, and I roll my eyes at him. He's covering his face with his hands and making crying sounds. Gabriel might be the most dramatic person I've ever met. I sit back down on the bed and put my hands on his, going along with his joke. When I remove them, he's smirking at me and pulling me down on the bed again before he buries his face in the crook of my neck. After a couple of minutes, he lets go of me but quickly presses his lips to mine. "Okay, go before you start bleeding on the bed," he uses my words, and I shake my head. He gives my ass a soft clasp when I get up, and I bite my lip in response before leaving.

Quickly, I take a shower and get ready. I put effort into my appearance, a little bit of makeup, and a beautiful black dress, and even let my curls fall down my back instead of tying them into a ponytail. There's a knock on my door. Gabriel is leaning against the door frame, a piece of paper in his hand and a grin on his lips. He hands me the drawing, and I stare at a perfect sunflower, then back at his face.

"What are you doing?" I ask, and he raises an eyebrow.

"It would have been a waste to get you an actual flower since we're flying back home today," he says and smiles. "This one is forever. I thought you'd like that," he mumbles, and I watch him for a moment. Gabriel is unbelievable.

"I love it," I reply before placing the drawing on my backpack to make sure I won't forget it. I kiss him passionately because I feel an indescribable need to be as close to him as possible. "Thank you." Gabriel winks at me before holding out his hand. My fingers lace through his, and he quickly holds up our hands to kiss the back of mine.

"So, where are you taking me?" I ask, and he grabs my hand more tightly.

"To the hotel buffet." We get out of the elevator once we reach the lobby, and he pulls me toward the breakfast area. Gabriel takes two plates in his hands. "I'll hold, you dish up," he commands, and I giggle when he stands in front of me, waiting to put whatever I want on my plate. Gabriel tells me what he wants, and I put everything in a large amount, making him smile. I know how much he eats better than anyone else. We sit down at an empty table and start eating our food. "Tell me, are you still taking me to *Les Misérables* in August? Or do I have to make other plans?" A smile spreads over my lips, and I wonder where we will be by August.

"You know, I've never been in your bedroom, I've never met your aunt or her wife, I've never watched you draw..." I remember his drawings and wonder when, or even how, he created them.

"As soon as we get back to Monaco, I'll do all of that with you," he promises me. His hand lifts to my face, and he runs his thumb over my bottom lip. "Whatever you want, I'll give to you." He retracts his hand from my face, and I almost whimper at the loss of his touch.

"I think we should head back to our rooms and pack our things. We have to be at the airport in a couple of hours." Gabriel nods absentmindedly.

"Okay." His eyes are searching my face for some kind of answer, and I feel a bit guilty for cutting our breakfast short. I get up from my chair, press a kiss to his cheek, and take his hand in mine again. He's done eating, too; I make sure of that before pulling him up from his seat.

"Let's go pack," I repeat. He has been increasingly pulling me in since yesterday, and I need to talk to Eduardo. He deserves an explanation before Gabriel and I move on with whatever it is we have.

Chapter 34

"Is it because of the way I reacted yesterday?" Eduardo asks, and I look into his light brown eyes, which are filled with guilt, and maybe even regret.

"A little, but mostly because I'm a mess. I'm so sorry for dragging you along, for doing this," I say, and Eduardo gets up from the bed. For a moment, he hesitates. Eventually, he walks out of my room and slams the door without saying another word to me. I let out the breath I've been holding.

"I just saw Eduardo in the hall, and he did not seem happy," Adrian tells me, and I flinch.

"How the hell did you get in?" I ask, my breathing uneven and my heart racing. Adrian only laughs and holds up a spare key card. He hugs me before he lies down next to me on the bed. "Eduardo and I were kind of fooling around, but I told him I couldn't do it anymore. Gabriel and I are trying to figure everything out, which is complicated when you've already fallen for one another." Adrian sits up and stares at me.

"He finally told you?" The brown in his eyes seems lighter than usual, but the green and blue are more dominant, as always.

"Wait, *you* knew?" I ask with disbelief on my face.

"Yes, since the day you slammed the door in his face. Gabriel came to me in tears and asked me what he could do so you would forgive him. He was frustrated and devastated, and he started yelling at me. I think his words were something like 'I don't know what to do anymore, man'," Adrian starts, horribly imitating Gabriel's wonderful accent. "'I've really messed up, and all I want to do is just tell her how much I–'"

"Don't," I cut him off and put my hand to his mouth, accidentally smacking him harder than I mean to. "He hasn't said those words to me yet, and I won't hear them for the first time from you, especially not with that terrible accent you are making." Adrian chuckles and removes my hand from his face.

"What are you going to do?" He leans back on my bed, and I start to fumble with my dress.

"For now, fly home," I reply, and he shoots me a 'you-know-that's-not-what-I-mean' expression. "I don't know, but Gabriel is not pressuring me to find out soon. I love him. I've loved him for a while. I want him, yet at the same time, I don't know if I'm ready." Adrian is watching me closely, and I know he's trying to figure out how to help me. "I think for now it's best if Gabriel and I don't commit to each other, which is fine because we're young, and we shouldn't commit anyway. Right? We can't all have relationships like the one Evangelin and Carlos have." I'm rambling, and Adrian and I both know it. My face drops into my hands.

"Only you can know what to do," he replies, and I let out a small laugh. "You have to know, Val." Adrian gets up and stretches his arms into the air. "By the way, if he breaks your heart, I'm going to have to break that pretty-boy face of his." I smile at my brother while I hold my breath from his words. "Come on, we have to catch our flight home." I nod and follow him, grabbing my suitcase and backpack.

Adrian and I check out of our rooms, and when I turn around, I find Gabriel sitting on a couch in the lobby, smiling at me. A blush settles on my cheek, and an involuntary grin spreads over my lips. Gabriel gets up from the couch, and my mouth waters. His dark grey sweatpants hang snugly on his hips, his white shirt is almost see-through, and his white sneakers fit the rest of his outfit. He turns around for a second to pick up his backpack, and as he leans down, my body starts to ache.

He makes his way over to where I am standing, but I smile and turn around, focusing on something inside my purse so he doesn't see me drooling. Adrian turns around and throws my purse on the ground.

"Shit, sorry, Val," he says, and we both bent over to get it.

"My, my, Romana, that's an impressive view," Gabriel says from behind us, and my eyes go wide.

"Thank you, I work out," Adrian replies, and I laugh. Gabriel winks at my brother, and Adrian fans air to his face with his hand. He then walks away to call for a taxi, leaving Gabriel and me alone.

"You know, I expected him not to react so playfully," I tell Gabriel, who is amused by what I'm saying.

"Oh, no, I'm sorry, beautiful, I meant your brother," he informs me, and I swat his arm teasingly. "Your ass doesn't create an impressive view; it creates a *heavenly view*," he jokes. I roll my eyes, and he grabs my elbows to pull me closer to him. My heart is racing when he drops his lips to my ear. "Let me kiss you," he whispers, and I shiver.

"No," I reply, using all of my willpower to reject him. Gabriel steps back but never lets go of my arms. "Although, I probably wouldn't be mad if you did," I admit in a low whisper. His eyes are on my face.

"Okay, chérie," he says before quickly grabbing my face and connecting our lips. I gasp, which only makes him take advantage of my open mouth to slide his tongue in ever so slightly. My stomach is turning upside down in the best way, and my skin lights on fire. Goosebumps spread over my arms involuntarily. His hands are at each side of my face, and he releases me before I'm allowed to get more. "I'll sit with you on the plane," he assures me, and I can only nod. I have no idea how he's going to make that happen, but I know somehow, he will. Gabriel touches my neck at the same place James punched me about two weeks ago, and I can tell he is glad about how well the bruise has healed. It is barely visible anymore.

The drive to the airport is quiet. Gabriel is sitting in the front passenger seat, I'm in the back on the left side, James is in the middle, and Adrian is on the right. It's hard for me to comprehend why we are all sharing a single taxi, but it's better for the environment. Except for James and I, who exchange a few sentences, no one talks. Gabriel turns his head every now and then to smile at me.

The metal detector shows up red as we go through security, and I'm pulled to the side to ensure I'm not carrying anything forbidden. At one point, the woman even has to frisk me down. After not finding anything and me getting annoyed at how they're treating me, they let me get back to making my way to my terminal. I look around for James, Adrian, and Gabriel, but I don't find any of them. I pick up my things, and strong arms wrap around me from behind.

"I almost punched that girl," Gabriel whispers before he nibbles on my earlobe, and I explode into a million pieces. What he's doing feels incredible. "The way she was touching you? No, chérie, that made me very unhappy," he goes on and touches his lips to the sweet spot just underneath my ear. We're in public, and I don't understand why he's not worried anyone sees, but no one seems to be watching.

"We should go," I croak out and, finally, put some distance between us. Gabriel grins and nods in agreement. He must know what he does to me because my cheeks are most likely a bright red, and my breathing is very uneven.

Halfway to our terminal, two guys and a girl come up to Gabriel, excitement written all over their young features. They ask him for an autograph and a selfie, and Gabriel begs me to wait for him before we continue making our way to the terminal.

It's unbelievable that Gabriel ends up sitting next to me, but he lets me take his window seat. Once I'm seated and organized, I turn to the handsome man, who is already watching me. The smile on his face brings one to my own.

"You know, you're starting to worry me. You've been smiling an awful lot recently," I state, and he lets out a sweet laugh.

"You can only blame yourself for that. Ever since you spent the night with me, I can't stop. Every time I look at you, I remember how it felt when you were in my arms, snoring peacefully." My eyes go wide, and I swat his arm.

"I do not snore," I reply firmly, and Gabriel chuckles. His long lashes frame his green-brown eyes, which makes them captivating. Yet the thing that makes his eyes the most beautiful is the sparkle in them, the one I know comes from happiness. When I realize I'm part of the reason why he's happy, I place my hand around his and pull it onto my lap. He gives me a confused look but doesn't remove it.

"Okay, you may not snore, but you did drool a lot," he tells me, and I get embarrassed immediately. My hand leaves his, and I cover my face with both of mine. "No, chérie, I'm kidding." He laughs a little and removes my hands from my face. "Valentina, I'm just joking, but even if I wasn't, what does it matter?" I look at him again.

"It's embarrassing," I point out, and he smiles at me.

"You know, if we were dating, I don't think it would be so embarrassing for you." He laughs, and I lace my fingers through his again.

"I'm not involved with Eduardo anymore, in any way." A slight smirk starts to settle on Gabriel's face, but he bites his bottom lip in an attempt to hide it. "I think it's best if we stay friends, no matter how badly we want each other," I tell him, trying to tease him, but since I am watching his lips more than his eyes, he notices my lie.

"Oh, really?" His hand moves from my cheek to my collarbone, stopping above my breast. "You don't want me?" he whispers and only moves his index finger to my breast. My eyes close involuntarily, and I force them to open again. "You don't want me to touch you like this?" He moves his finger from my boob to my cleavage and runs it down.

"I do, but I don't think now is the right time for us," I lie and grin, and he smiles more brightly. Gabriel removes his hand, and I try to calm my aching body. Everything inside of me wants him to continue to touch me, to never stop.

"And you don't want to touch me either?" He takes my hand in his and brings it underneath his shirt. My hand is flat on his abs, and I have to use all of my self-control not to pull his head down and kiss him. "Not like this?" He brings my hand down to his waistband, and my finger runs along there without him having to do anything. "You don't want me?" he asks again, lifting my hand back onto his stomach. I'm speechless, and all I want is to continue feeling his hard muscles underneath my fingertips. I started this game, but now I'm the one losing. "Because I really want to know what it feels like to be inside of you," he whispers in a raspy voice, so the other passengers don't hear. My insides turn upside down, and I have to cross my legs to make that persistent aching between them stop. Gabriel notices that too, and a victorious smile spreads over his full lips. "You want to know what it would feel like, too, don't you?" Before I can think, I nod. My fingers run over his hot skin underneath his shirt, and he leans back, making my hand lose contact with his body. "Too bad we're just friends." He puts his headphones on, and it takes me a minute to get back to reality. My hands reach out, and I remove his headphones and pull his head down so I can press my lips against his. Gabriel puts one hand on my cheek, but I lean away sooner than either of us wants.

"We are friends, friends who do this," I tell him, and he grins.

"Okay, friends who will have phenomenal sex," he says, and I shake my head, smiling. Gabriel plants his lips on mine one more time before taking out his sketchbook and pencil. I place one earpiece into his ear and the other into mine, playing some of the songs we both like. My eyes don't leave the page while he sketches a Formula One car on it. I'm confused until he draws the number nine on it, making tears shoot into my eyes. "One day," he promises as he hands the paper to me. My eyes meet his, and a small smile covers my lips.

"One day," I mumble, falling more in love with Gabriel Matteo Biancheri.

Chapter 35

"Come on, Val, push," Adrian yells, but I'm too exhausted. "The final corner, come on," he reminds me, and I force my body to cooperate. This is the longest I've ever been in the simulator, and every single muscle of mine feels it. Although I have no sense of how much time has passed, I know I've never lasted this long. It makes me smile. "Yes, come on!" Adrian cheers when I pass the start and finish line and can finally relax. I take deep breaths to calm my heart, and my brother gives me a soft smack on the helmet. "How do you feel?" he asks as he helps me out of the simulator.

"Like a champion," I reply, and he grabs my helmet, shaking my head out of excitement.

"As you should! Today you've truly worked out harder than I ever could." This morning, I went for a slow run that he didn't want to join me on, then we went on to do weights and our routine neck exercises, and lastly, the simulator.

My phone rings in Adrian's pocket, and I frown when he pulls it out. "Oh, sorry, I thought it was mine," he informs me innocently, but I reach out to feel his other pocket where his phone is. Adrian gives me an apologetic smile. "Oops?" I grab my phone out of his hand and laugh at my brother while answering the persistent caller.

"Hello?" I say as soon as I pick up.

"Hello, Ms. Romana? This is Colin Reiner. I am the head of the Ferrari driver academy," he states, and I feel my heart skipping a beat.

"Yes, Mr. Reiner, thank you for getting back to me," I reply, and Adrian whispers that I should put the call on speaker. We fight over it for a brief moment before he glares at me, and I cave in. Two days ago, when we returned from Bahrain, Adrian and I emailed Mr. Reiner because the Ferrari driver academy is the only one we had not contacted yet.

"I'm afraid I don't have the news you were hoping for." I want to punch a wall. Then again, I didn't expect anything else. "We see great potential in you, but unfortunately, we are unable to take in new drivers at the moment. As soon as a spot becomes available, we will call you," he assures me, but I only nod.

"Okay, thank you, I appreciate your call." We hang up, and Adrian squeezes my shoulder. "They're not going to call again, are they?" He simply shrugs.

"I don't know, but let's not give up hope yet." I can't help but be disappointed. They have put me on a waitlist, but who is to say they won't 'forget' about me? Plus, I'm almost nineteen, most likely making me the oldest candidate, and I'm a woman. "Hey, it's not over yet," Adrian reminds me, but when tears stream down my cheeks, he wraps his arms around me.

As much as I love my brother, I can't help the anger I feel toward him at this very moment. He never struggled as I have. It was easy for him. He did his two years in a junior league, scored enough points, and was recruited by Alfa Romeo to race in Formula One. Adrian was never turned away. Instead, he got sponsored and driven toward success. The complete opposite happened to me, and I've worked twice as hard as him, something even he admits. Before I push him away, I remind myself that it is not his fault and wrap my arms around him for comfort.

"What can I do to make you feel better?" he asks, rubbing my back and kissing the top of my head.

"Will you cook dinner for once?" I say, and he chuckles while pulling out of the hug to look at me.

"I think it'd be safer if we order takeout or go for dinner," he suggests, and I agree with a small laugh. He's absolutely right. If we want to eat tonight, Adrian cannot be the one cooking. Even James would be a safer choice, and he's set the kitchen on fire twice in my presence.

Adrian falls asleep ten minutes into our movie, but I can't sit still. My body is exhausted, but the news from earlier prevents me from relaxing. It's still early, and I write a quick note for Adrian to let him know I will be at James'. My friend is already waiting for me with open arms when I arrive at his house. I happily walk into them and sigh against his chest.

"Hard day?" he asks, and I let out a sarcastic laugh.

"Hard fucking decade," I reply, and we both burst into laughter. James leads me inside, where he hands me a cup of tea along with a piece of chocolate. I take both with a smile before sharing the news I received earlier. Obviously unsure whether or not it is good information, James leans forward on the counter to grab my hand.

"I have a good feeling about this. Be patient, and I'm sure something will open up," he assures me, and for the first time tonight, I feel a bit of hope too. James is not often optimistic, and I'm glad he is this time.

"What should we do?" I ask after a while of silence, and a small smile creeps onto his lips.

"Something that'll cheer you up," he replies, and I almost jump up and down in excitement. There is no way he'll do this with me to make me feel better. "Oh yeah," he promises, and I smile brightly.

"Yes! It's been forever," I cheer, and James leads me into the living room, where he gets everything ready before handing me a microphone and letting me pick a song.

Neither of us is great at singing, but it's not about our skill level. Karaoke is something I've always enjoyed very much, but Adrian and James have never cared for it. James, however, will occasionally, especially when I'm upset, pull out the karaoke machine he bought for me and cheer me up.

James' voice cracks and hits all the wrong notes, but we end up laughing so much, my stomach hurts, and we're on the floor. I choose one last song, but he, on purpose, sings even worse, and I can't even manage picking up my microphone to join him. It was a good decision to go to James' house. I already feel ten times better, and finally, my body feels tired enough to sleep.

"You better stay here, luv. I don't want you driving when you're tired," he says, but I'm already texting Adrian to let him know I'm sleeping here.

Chapter 36

"Valentina! Could you bring me the yellow dress with the floral print in a medium?" Evangelin asks, and I get it for her.

I cash out the people waiting in line and sit down on the chair behind me when everyone is gone. It's surprising how much I enjoy working in this small boutique. I would have never thought fashion would interest me this much, but it does, especially when Evangelin sits down with me before we choose the items she will order and stock.

As always, Evangelin connects naturally with her customers to find clothes she can suggest to them. I watch her run around the store for items to present to the tall lady that walked in a couple of minutes ago, and I hurry over to her to make sure she doesn't need any help. Evangelin tells me I can start closing the shop, and I do as I'm told. By the time I'm done, the customer ends up not buying anything and leaving. Evangelin rolls her eyes and saunters over to where I'm standing.

"Some people," she complains with annoyance in her voice. She runs her fingers over her forehead. "Who is that?" she asks me after a while and points outside. There is a shocked expression on her face, which makes me worry. I turn around, my eyes following her finger. The man holds a bouquet of sunflowers, and I can't keep the smile off my face. I haven't seen him in days, but I've missed him incredibly. After that day on the plane, I told him to give me a few days to get my life in order. But I never expected him to show up at Rush.

"Gabriel Biancheri," I reply and turn to look at Evangelin. She's smiling too, but there is also surprise on her face. "What is it?" I ask, bringing her attention back to me.

"Nothing, dear, he just reminds me of someone, that's all. Now, go, have a good evening," she tells me, and I grab my purse from the chair. I give her a kiss on the cheek and walk out of the store toward Gabriel. When he spots me, the corners of his mouth lift, and he lowers the bouquet so I can wrap my arms around his neck. His mahogany scent hits my nose, and before I can stop myself, I let out a small sigh.

"I've missed you," I admit, and he wraps his arms tighter around my body.

"I've missed you more, chérie, which is why I couldn't stay away anymore. I hope that five days were enough," he mumbles, and I step out of the hug. Gabriel puts the flowers into my hand before he leans down and presses a kiss on my lips. It's brief and leaves me wanting more, but it's also sweet and makes my body tingle.

"Well, I could have used a couple more days break from you, but seeing you're already here, we might as well hang out," I joke, and he chuckles. He takes my hand and leads me home.

Gabriel and I are walking home, talking about the simulators we're training with. I look at him, proud he's working hard to improve, but when I notice the redness in his eyes and the dark circles underneath them, I get worried. Ever since I met him, and probably for most of his life, Gabriel has had this tendency to get completely caught up in doing something to a point where he forgets to eat, sleep, or drink. Right now, he's hellbent on improving his results. His priority is to get faster times and win more races. My hand tightens its grip on his, and he gives me a confused grin before continuing to talk about all the different things he has to prepare for next week.

I tell Gabriel about work, and he listens attentively, asking me lots of questions about it. The way he's genuinely interested in my life makes my heart flutter. He leads me to my house but then pulls me past it and down the road to where I know his home is located.

"Aunt Domi and Aunt Nicolette aren't home this week. They are on vacation, but Jean is home, and I finally want to show you my room. If you would like that." Gabriel smiles at me.

"I would love that," I assure him, and we continue to make our way down the street to his house.

Gabriel's home is small, a two-story house with a simple beige façade and a few columns at the entrance. The front garden is fenced and well-kept. Flowers are growing on the left side, and I remember Nicolette likes gardening, which is why Gabriel gifted her lots of supplies last Christmas. He brings me inside his house, and a delicious scent hits my nose. It smells like tomato sauce. Of course, Gabriel made food for me.

"Are you cold? Hot? Thirsty?" I turn to look at Gabriel, a small smile spreading over my face.

"Just horny," I reply plainly, and his eyes go wide.

"What?" he asks, and I look at him casually.

"Just *hungry*," I say as if I had before, and Gabriel shakes his head, an embarrassed expression on his face.

"I thought you said something else," he tells me in a quiet voice, and I grin at him. He walks toward his kitchen before I can assure him he didn't misunderstand.

Strong arms wrap around my body, and when I smell Jean's familiar cologne, I jump up from my chair to turn around and hug him. We catch up for a couple of minutes before he tells Gabriel and me he's meeting up with Lia, some girl he met a couple of weeks ago. Jean walks out of the room, leaving Gabriel and me alone again. I sit down at the wooden table in the kitchen and put my chin on one of my hands, watching Gabriel closely.

"What's with the swooning expression?" he asks when he catches me staring. He puts down the kitchen towel he was holding and walks over to me slowly. "You look happy," he states and squats down in front of me. I place my hand on his cheek, feeling his usual stubble underneath my fingertips and tracing his features.

"I am happy," I admit, and Gabriel smiles. His eyes sparkle with joy, and the dimples imprinted in his cheek are breathtaking.

"Let's go. I want to show you my room." Gabriel leads me up the stairs, and before we enter his room, he covers my eyes with his hands. I'm about to complain, but he says, "Don't ruin it, just go along with it." I grin because he knows me so well. When he finally reveals his room to me, I gasp. There are ten bouquets of sunflowers spread all over his room, his bed is made, and the blinds are letting in the fading light of the setting sun.

"I can't believe you did this for me," I whisper, and Gabriel's arms wrap around me from behind.

"Can't you? You know how I feel about you. So, this can't be a surprise," he replies before he presses a kiss on my shoulder.

I turn around in his arms and kiss him, moving away from him soon after. My feet bring me to the bookcase on the very left side of his room, and I read the covers. He has classic novels, science fiction novels, romance novels, and more. I take one book out and open it, spotting notes written on the pages. The book is worn out, and I wonder how old it is. I also wonder who wrote inside of it because the handwriting is not Gabriel's.

"What are these?" I ask and turn to face him. Gabriel is sitting on the bed, watching me closely.

"All of them are second-hand. I like buying books that have notes written in them. In fact, I make sure the previous owner did take notes. Reading a book and then reading it from another perspective helps me see things I may have never considered," he explains, and somehow, my feelings for him run even deeper. I would have never expected Gabriel to collect something so pure. I put the book back on the shelf and walk over to where he is.

"Why haven't you ever told me about this?" I join him on the bed and look around his room some more. He has two large windows next to his bed, and two more that lead to what I assume is a balcony. His curtains are a light beige color, almost the same as his walls. Gabriel's room seems empty, with only a bed, a nightstand, and the bookshelf. There is nothing else, but I understand. Gabriel is hardly ever home, and when he is, he doesn't want too much to tie him to one place. I do the same thing.

"I've never shown anyone my books," he admits and lets out a nervous laugh. He's embarrassed about them, which doesn't make any sense.

"I think it's beautiful, Gabriel," I tell him, and he lifts his head so he can look into my eyes again. I don't know if he's trying to figure out if I mean it or not, but he can search my face as much as he wants. He shakes his head ever so slightly before he reaches up to take my face between his hands.

"This is why I showed you. I knew you would never make me feel bad about it, that you'd think this is something special. You understand me in a way no one else does, Valentina, and I never want to lose that sense of security I feel with you." Before I can respond, he presses his lips to mine sweetly, sending shivers down my spine. My hands rest on his thighs for a while until he pulls back. "Tell me when to stop," he says, and I nod with a smile.

He pushes me down on his bed and smoothly moves between my legs. His lips move from mine to my jaw, and he traces kisses along there. My legs are angled on the bed, allowing him to be closer to me. Gabriel's hands are on each side next to my head, and he is now tracing kisses down my neck. He starts sucking on my soft spot, and I moan into his ear, making him suck more aggressively. I'm about to tell him to be a little gentler when he stops and soothes the ache with his tongue. Feeling his wet tongue against my hot skin makes my most sensitive area throb rapidly. My hands move up to the loops on his jeans, and I press his body against mine. I want to feel more of him. Gabriel's hand moves from the side of my face to my neck, left breast, and stomach, and then he rests his index finger right above my underwear. His lips continue to make their way further down my body until he stops on the top of my breasts.

"Can I remove your shirt?" he asks, but I don't answer. I simply pull the thin fabric over my head and expose myself to him.

All I'm wearing underneath is a semi-see-through bralette, and Gabriel sits on his knees, looking at my body while pulling his bottom lip between his teeth. His eyes drop to my shorts, and I nod, telling him to take them off. Gabriel's index fingers move to the waistband of my pants before I lift my butt off the bed, and he pulls them down smoothly, leaving me in only my underwear.

"So sexy," he mumbles and pushes me back down on the bed. His lips find mine again, and I take his hand in mine, leading it back down near my aching area. Gabriel chuckles against my lips and moves his hand without my help. Finally, his fingers reach down, and he runs it along the outside of my panties, just above where my body needs his finger the most. "God, chérie, you're dripping," Gabriel says before placing his lips back on mine. My whole body seems to be on fire as he teases me with his finger that does not move. His tongue enters my mouth aggressively, but it leaves soon after, his teeth taking my bottom lip between them and biting gently. Everything he's doing is quick, but the combination makes my head spin. When he still doesn't move his finger after another minute, my hand covers his, and I remove it completely. "What are you doing?"

"Taking charge since you only want to tease me," I reply, and he chuckles before pushing me back down on the bed.

"You're so impatient." He lifts his shirt over his head quickly, and I smile victoriously.

I don't know if I'm smiling because he finally took his shirt off or because I know this man has feelings for me and no one else. My hands lift to touch his naked skin, and I smile. Slowly, my fingers drop to the buttons on his jeans, and I undo them carefully. Gabriel slides them down and then moves back between my legs. I spot black writing on his hip bone for the first time, which is mostly covered by his boxers. Confused, I reach forward and pull on the waistband, exposing seven different tattoos. They're small and near each other, and when I look closer, I see they are dates. Seven different dates. "My mom, my dad, my grandparents, and my godfather, who I lost a couple of years ago. Those are the dates on which they died," he tells me, and I can't help the tear that rolls down my cheek. "I've never told anyone this either. No one ever cared enough to ask." Gabriel wipes away the tear on my cheek and wraps his hand around mine, which is pulling down his underwear so I can look at his inked hip.

"Any other tattoos I don't know about?" I ask him, trying to lighten the mood. An embarrassed blush spreads over his face, and I look at him, waiting impatiently.

"I have a tattoo of the moon on my left ass cheek," he admits, and my mouth drops. "Yeah, I was drunk, and Cameron thought it would be funny to get a moon on... well, on my moon." The laughter that leaves my throat is uncontrollable. It's easy for me to imagine Cameron drunk and saying this to Gabriel, and I can also imagine Gabriel just going along with it. "Hey, now," he complains, and I try to compose myself. "In a way, the tattoo is your fault. If I hadn't gotten drunk, then I would have never done something so stupid."

"What? How is that my fault?" I ask but also laugh. I look at him with a confused and amused expression, and luckily, he elaborates.

"I got drunk because I heard that Luke and you were getting... serious, I guess." He means when he found out I had sex with Luke.

"Why did you get drunk? You were with Kira, which is why I got together with Luke in the first place." Gabriel grins, which only confuses me more.

"How ironic, don't you think? Us searching for other people because we thought that we didn't like each other," he states, and I frown at him. "At least now we know how we feel, and we can try and figure this thing out. Aaaand, I finally get to show you my moon," he whispers, and I know he doesn't mean his tattoo.

Chapter 37

Gabriel moves back between my legs, his hands wrapping around my breasts. The familiar ache returns, and I know this time there will be no interruptions.

"How far do you want me to go?" I'm barely listening to him because I'm too focused on how his hands feel around my breasts. He removes them, and I open my eyes to look at him. "You need to tell me, baby," he commands, and I take his hand in mine, pulling it close to my lips and pressing a kiss to his index finger.

"I want your hand right here," I say, leading it between my legs. Gabriel grins sweetly and finally slides his fingers inside of my panties. His cool thumb rubs over my most sensitive area, and my eyes roll into the back of my head. My head pushes against the mattress as he continues to move his thumb in circles.

"Is here where you want it?" I moan loudly, which answers his question and makes him continue his movements. His middle and ring fingers slide into me, curling at the perfect spot. I can't hold back the moan his touch is responsible.

I'm so close to coming, it's ridiculous. Gabriel leans forward to press his lips to mine, and I gasp in surprise, allowing his tongue to enter my mouth effortlessly. An unfamiliar feeling builds in my chest and my stomach, and Gabriel moves away from my lips. I open my eyes and find his green-brown ones staring into mine, an easy smile on his full lips. His thumb and index finger pinch my most sensitive area before he goes back to tracing circles and sliding his fingers in and out of me. I fall apart under his touch moments later. The sensation is heavenly, stronger than any I have ever felt. Gabriel's name leaves my lips, and he lets me calm down for a minute before he starts talking to me again.

"It's incredible how your body responds to me..." Gabriel trails off. He's lying next to me on his back, with his hands over his erection. I pull half my bottom lip between my teeth and move my fingers down to his waistband. "You don't have to," he whispers. He needs to find some kind of release, and I want to be the one to bring it to him.

"I know I don't have to, but I want to," I reply and slide my hand up to the waistband of his boxers. "What do you want?" I ask him, and a lovely grin spreads over his face.

"Too much," he responds and puts his hand on my cheek. "Whatever you're ready to do." I nod and move between his legs.

My hands roam over his naked torso, and Gabriel closes his eyes in response. My gaze lingers on his handsome face: the stubble of his beard, his long lashes, the dimples on his cheek, his full lips, and his perfectly shaped eyebrows. I slowly hook my fingers around the waistband of his boxers and wait for his permission. His eyes are open again, and he nods, watching me closely. I slide down his boxers until they drop to the floor. When I see him, I gasp quietly, and my body gets excited. He's much bigger than Luke and Eduardo, and even though I felt him through his boxers before, I had no idea. I must have been staring too long because Gabriel eventually sits up and puts his hand underneath my chin.

"You don't have to do this," he repeats, and I smile wickedly.

Without breaking eye contact, I lick my hand to make it wet. I lean forward, pressing my lips against his neck and wrapping my hand around his length. Gabriel places his right hand down on the bed, his left into my hair, and leans back ever so slightly. My lips move until I find the spot that makes him groan passionately, and my hand moves up and down his shaft. I go slow, making sure the pressure is just right. I want to make sure he's really enjoying my touch, just like I did his.

"A little faster, chérie," he says, and I do as I'm told.

My lips finally find his, and he moves his other hand into my hair, grabbing tightly each time he moans. I run my tongue over his hot lips, and he opens his mouth for me. Having his tongue in my mouth or putting mine in his is a different kind of pleasure. I could kiss him for hours and not get tired of it.

"God," he moans loudly, pulling away from the kiss.

"Cum for me, Gabriel," I say seductively, and he moans once more before spilling all over my hand and his bedspread.

Gabriel falls backward and breathes in deeply before exhaling loudly. I move off his bed and walk into his attached bathroom to get a towel and wash my hands. Afterward, I start cleaning up the mess Gabriel and I made. Luckily, a lot of his cum landed on the extra blanket at the foot of his bed, and I simply remove it.

"Valentina." Gabriel tears me out of my focused trance, and I look up at him. "I can do this."

"I know, but so can I." Once I'm done, I sit next to Gabriel, who is wearing boxers and a shirt now. I grab my shirt and pull it over my head. My eyes drift to his bookshelf again, and a hundred questions flood my mind, but I decide on one. "Which book is your favorite?" Gabriel takes a strand of my curly hair between his fingers, and a genuine smile spreads over his face.

"I don't have one." He pauses to think for a moment. "There is one series I've read many times. It's called 'Die For Me'," Gabriel informs me, and my mouth drops.

"Are you serious?" He puts his hand flatly on my collarbone, and his expression becomes more enthusiastic.

"Yes, it's an excellent book. The idea alone, I don't know how Amy Plum came up with it. Also, it plays in France, which I like." I shake my head in disbelief, and Gabriel smirks. "What?"

"I have read Amy Plum's revenant books at least ten times," I tell him. Gabriel walks over to his bookshelf, takes one of the books into his hand, and gives it to me. It is a worn-out copy of my favorite book.

"Read the comments the previous owner wrote inside. It will surprise you what they saw, I promise." I smile at him and place the book back on the shelf, planning on taking it home with me tomorrow. Gabriel drops down on the bed again, and his eyes meet mine. "Are you hungry?"

"No," I tell him, and his hand reaches out to touch my thigh.

"Do you want to watch a movie?" he asks me, and my heart skips a beat when his hand reaches further back and touches my butt. I nod, answering his question, and he gets up from the bed. My feet bring me to where he's standing, and I fling my arms around his neck, hugging him tightly. He hesitates for a moment, but soon enough, his arms wrap around my body too. "Are you okay, chérie?" he asks me, and I step out of the hug.

"Yes," I reply in all honesty. I'm more than okay. I'm really happy. "Although, I am getting a little hungry now. Maybe I can have some of your delicious-smelling food." Gabriel chuckles and places his hands on each side of my face.

"Sure," he replies, bends down to give me a quick kiss, and smiles.

After dinner, we move to his couch and start watching a movie. Gabriel is sitting on the right side, and I sit down on the left. Something inside me wants to see what he will do, whether he will come closer or stay on his side. After a few minutes, I find Gabriel fiddling with the hem of his sweatshirt. He's looking at me, and I cock an eyebrow, waiting for him to say what's on his mind. But he doesn't say anything. Gabriel simply pats the space next to him on the couch, telling me to come closer. I look away, not moving an inch. A small smile spreads over my lips, and Gabriel gets up from the couch. He pulls me into the air and sits down, so I'm between his legs. His jaw rests in the crook of my neck, and his stubble tickles my skin, yet I'm more than comfortable.

There is so much I want to ask him, so much I've never dared to. There is one dominant question lingering in my head. "Is the reason you chose number seven for your car because you lost seven people?" Every Formula One driver gets a number for their car; some get to decide, others don't, which is why I wonder if he chose it himself or if it is just a coincidence.

"Yes," he simply replies, and I nod. "But it is more than just that. Both my parents were born on the seventh of the month. So, seven just means the most to me," he explains, and I turn around to face him. "It's also a nice coincidence that I met you on the seventeenth of March," he says and laughs a little.

"You remember the day we met?" Gabriel's eyes move from mine to my lips and then back up to my eyes.

"How could I not? I started questioning everything the day I met you. It's kind of hard to forget." I lift my hand to touch his cheek. Gabriel closes his eyes at the contact of my skin against his. "You are everything I could have ever imagined, and the best part is, I didn't even have to look for you. You simply walked into my life without any warning, and I wouldn't have had it any other way." My eyes are studying his face, but I can't find anything that could prove he doesn't mean what he's saying. Panic settles in my chest, and I turn away from him. I'm feeling too many emotions, and I can't share any of them with him without admitting how much I truly care for him. Instead of overthinking things, I pull his hand to my mouth and press a kiss to the back of it.

Before the movie even finishes, I fall asleep.

Chapter 38

I shoot up in bed, trying to figure out where I am. My eyes scan the room, and I find the now-familiar bookshelf, the sun shining through the tall windows, and finally, Gabriel, sleeping peacefully next to me. My heart rate slows, and I lie back in bed. He must have carried me up here after I fell asleep on the couch.

Gabriel lets out a painful sigh. He's still fast asleep, but his eyelids are fluttering, and there is an odd expression on his face. I'm convinced he's having a nightmare, but I also don't wake him. Gabriel needs to rest to get rid of the dark circles under his eyes. I can't stand to see him as exhausted as he was yesterday. *Yesterday...* The memories come flooding back into my head, and I smile brightly. My mind replays how his lips felt on mine, how his hand felt on my skin. Nothing has ever felt that good.

I try to distract myself by getting out of bed and walking downstairs. When I reach the kitchen, I decide to make breakfast for the sleeping man upstairs and myself.

"Valentina?" I hear someone ask, and I turn to find Jean standing behind me. There is a handsome smile on his lips, and a blush settles on my cheek. Now there's one person I can't possibly hide Gabriel's and my... relationship? from. "Finally. Only took you guys three years," he blurts out and sits down at the kitchen table.

"Oh no, we're not..." I don't even know what to tell Jean. *Gabriel and I are just fooling around.* That wouldn't sound appropriate in any way.

"You're something, which gets you a step closer to becoming everything." Jean smiles at me, and I shake my head.

"You want breakfast?" He frowns and gets up from his seat.

"Yes, but you're not making it. You're the guest, and I will make breakfast for you." I recall the last time Jean tried to make a meal and flinch. Luckily, I can convince him to make it together. He starts to talk to me about Lia, and I listen closely, even though my mind is preoccupied with Gabriel upstairs.

"Chérie," a voice says, and I look up to see a half-naked Gabriel. "You weren't there when I woke up," he mutters, and I realize he must have woken up and run downstairs when he couldn't find me. His eyes are still half-closed, and he is rubbing them to wake up. "I thought you left." Gabriel rubs his left arm, and I close the distance between us. The left side of his face has marks all over it, probably from his pillow. I grin at the sleepy man.

"Nope. Jean and I were just making breakfast," I assure him, and he takes my face between his hands. There is a concerned expression on his face, and it worries me. "What's wrong?" Gabriel shakes his head, and his lips find mine before he even answers my question. He's aggressive, but I enjoy the gentle assault he's doing to my lips. The affection, his face and body, and his kindness all make me want to stay in his arms.

"I just had a horrible dream," he explains, and I nod. *I knew it.*

"Well, I'm here, and breakfast is ready," I inform him, and he places one more kiss on my lips before we walk over to the table and sit down.

Jean cut some fruits, and I made the pancakes. Both guys assure me they taste 'incroyable'. After we finish breakfast, Gabriel and Jean clean up the table, not allowing me to move an inch. When they're done, Gabriel walks over to me and reaches his hand out. I place mine in his, and he pulls me close to his body.

"Take a shower with me," he whispers, and shivers run down my spine. Gabriel grins at me when I nod slowly.

We walk into his large bathroom, and for the first time, I really look at it. The shower is oversized and has glass doors, and his bathtub is enormous. Everything is white and beige, and I'm too mesmerized by how lovely it is to realize Gabriel got naked, but once I do, I can't tear my eyes away. It is as if his body is calling out, and I'm the only one who can hear. His back is turned to me, which is why I finally get to see the infamous moon tattoo. It may have been a joke, but it looks... it looks terrific on his trained ass.

I undress before pulling my hair out of its messy bun. My curls fall loosely down my back, and when Gabriel turns around, my eyes drop down his body. He closes the distance between us, and I finally look into his eyes again, which are filled with lust. His hands move to my breasts, and I close my eyes as soon as his fingers find my skin. It's an automatic reaction, just like the familiar ache which has now returned to my needy body. There are goosebumps all over my body by the time he reaches the waistband of my underwear. Before he pulls them down, he leans down to press a kiss to my lips, my neck, my collarbone, and then my left nipple. He tugs on one of my hard nipples with his mouth, making a moan leave my lips. Gabriel leans down further, placing kisses along my stomach and then my hip bone. His fingers move down, pulling my panties with them. Although I ache for him, he's not touching me anymore. Opening my eyes, I search for the reason why, but Gabriel is simply standing back, admiring my body. My heart skips a beat when I see his erection, and the distance between us frustrates me. I take a step toward him, and he takes my hand, leading me into the shower.

"Hot or cold?" he asks me, and I lean against the shower wall, staring at his body. The heat between my legs makes me dizzy, but I can't describe how much I enjoy it.

"Hot," I reply, and he flashes me a smile, his dimples carved deeply into his cheeks.

"Yes, Milady," he tells me and turns the water hot. The shower soon fills with steam, and Gabriel turns back around to pin me against the shower wall.

His hands lift to my breasts, and he cups them softly, sending a thrill through my body. I wrap my arms around his neck and bring my lips to his in need of more contact. He makes me so impatient. His length pushes against my thigh, and I smile against his lips. I turn us around to push him against the wall, and my mouth moves to his jawline. His stubble tickles me, but I don't laugh. I'm too concentrated on what is going to happen next.

"You have to tell me what to do," I say, and Gabriel's eyes shoot open. He's watching me as I go down on my knees, in front of his erection. My hands wrap around him, and I start simply moving my hands back and forth.

"Val," he moans, and I glance up at him. His eyes find mine, and his legs start to shake long before I bring my lips to the head of his length. Seconds later, he orgasms in my hands.

"That was fast," I state, and he lets out a short laugh.

"I know, *trust me*, I know. The way you looked up at me through those thick lashes of yours and the way your naked body looks, I don't know, it just kind of happened." He is embarrassed by it, but there is no reason for him to be. He seems to panic a little bit. "Don't worry, it usually takes much longer, I can last much longer," he quickly adds, trying to convince me, or himself, I'm not quite sure. I smile at him knowingly.

"I know, handsome. I'm not worried." He nods, and before anything else can happen, there is a loud banging on the bathroom door, making both of us jump.

"Gabriel, Hector is here, and he is not happy," Jean screams from the other side of the locked door, and Gabriel's head hits the tile wall behind him.

"Tell him to wait a moment. I'm busy," Gabriel replies before dropping his hand to my second heartbeat. I press my lips together to keep from making a sound. "I would never leave you unsatisfied, chérie," he whispers before his fingers dip into my heat and his thumb caresses my swollen clit. My legs go weak, but Gabriel holds me up effortlessly. His touch has complete control over my body. I bite my bottom lip, but a low moan escapes me anyway. Everything inside of me tenses with every thrust of his fingers. His thumb applies just the right pleasure to make standing without his help impossible.

"Gabriel," I whine when he goes faster, and his mouth moves to my earlobe.

"Let me feel you cum on my fingers," he whispers with a raspy voice, and I instantly fall apart. The tension from before leaves my body and is replaced with pure joy and bliss. Gabriel slowly removes his fingers, pulls me close by grabbing my butt, and smashes his lips onto mine. I let out one last moan before he steps away.

"I'm sorry, chérie, I have to go deal with this." Gabriel opens the shower door and steps out. I want to answer him, but my mind is still in paradise, and all I can do is smile.

When I'm dressed, I roam around Gabriel's bedroom, and my feet carry me to the bookshelf. My mind still hasn't registered that Gabriel collects old books with writings in them. I grab 'Die For Me' from the shelf again. The copy is much more worn out than all of the other books on the shelf. There are three different kinds of handwriting on the pages, and I notice one of them is Gabriel's. I spot words like *confusion* and *desperation* on the pages. I have a deep feeling he's talking more about himself than the book.

I sit down on Gabriel's bed and continue to read his comments. *The struggle within her... fighting against her feelings... the revelation of his true self makes her leave... can she ever really love him if they're so different?*

I get so lost in the book I don't realize an hour has passed. There is no sign of Gabriel anywhere in the house, so I decide to head home. Also, I should probably text James back. He's been trying to contact me since yesterday morning, and I completely forgot to respond. It takes three rings until he finally picks up.

"'Ello, babe," he chimes into the phone, and I smile. His accent is unbelievably thick.

"Hey, I'm sorry I haven't texted you. Things have been a little crazy," I say while gathering my things, including 'Die For Me'.

"Don't worry, luv. I have some time today if you want to catch up," he offers, and I tell him to meet me at my house in fifteen minutes.

Chapter 39

James arrives at my house precisely fifteen minutes later. He's standing on my doorstep with one sunflower, smiling brightly.

"You know, you have to stop bringing me flowers. You might just give me the wrong idea," I joke, and a weird expression spreads over his face. Instead of addressing it, I simply invite him in so we can catch up.

The whole time I talk to him about what has been going on, James watches me closely. "I think taking it slow is the right choice for both of you. Gabriel is only starting his career, and you are still making your dream happen. There is no need to rush into something," he points out, and I smile at the tall Brit.

"You are an incredible friend. Ever since I can remember, you have always cared for me, and I can't tell you how much that means. I love you, James, and I hope I will never lose you." The words fall off my lips more easily than they would have a month ago. I realized a long time ago that once you let someone in, you have to make sure they always remember how much they mean to you. If you don't, and they get taken away from you, you will regret not reminding them for the rest of your life. "You're honest, protective, and I would trust you with my life." Tears flood his eyes, and I frown. I didn't mean to make him cry.

"You can't say that about me. You can't," he says and gets up. I'm so confused by his reaction, and panic floods my body.

"Why? What's wrong?" I ask and walk closer to him, but he puts his hands up, signaling me not to come closer. I almost start to cry when tears roll down his cheeks. "Okay, James, you have to talk to me because I'm freaking out." My voice is demanding but laced with concern.

"I'm a horrible man, and you should not say those things about me. I don't deserve it," he croaks out and sucks in a sharp breath. He's in pain. "I did a terrible thing." I am beyond angry at how vague he's being. Above everything else, however, I am terrified of what he's hiding from me.

"What have you done? Tell me," I demand, and James brings his hands to his hair, grabbing a handful.

"I lied to you," he cries in defeat and drops to the ground. A few sobs escape him, and I do my best not to join him. "On your birthday, we were both so drunk, and I couldn't think clearly, neither could you. I don't remember much, but I remember bits and pieces, and they aren't good. I'm so sorry, I'm so terribly sorry," he repeats over and over again, but I don't know what to do with myself. I try to search my brain for any memory, anything from that night, but I can't seem to find any...*oh. Oh my god, it wasn't a dream! And it wasn't Gabriel either, it was James, and it actually happened!* His fingers on my skin, the lust I felt, the sadness, it all comes back to me.

When I try to figure out why I was drunk and sad, I remember Gabriel and me on the dance floor. The things he whispered into my ear, things he should never have said to me in the first place. I don't know who my anger is directed at, but neither should be in my presence. I look back at James. He's on his knees, his face in his hands, and he's crying.

"Get up," I growl, and he does as I command without hesitation. Tears of anger roll down my cheek, but I am too mad to start sobbing and breaking down. "I remember being on the bed with you. I remember wanting you," I admit and swallow down the bile that is rising in my throat. "How could you not have told me?" I ask, my voice louder than intended.

"I didn't think we would be able to move past it, and if I am being honest, I was too in love with you to be able to lose you." *No, no, no, no. He's making this worse and worse by the second.* I can't breathe.

"Get out. I want you to get out of my house," I yell, and the pain that flashes across James' face makes me want to vomit.

"Out of your house or out of your life?" More tears flow, and I can't look at his face anymore.

"You should have told me a long time ago, and the fact that you didn't makes looking at your face unbearable right now. You're my oldest friend, one of the only people I have left, but I'm too mad. It's not what we did that angers me, it is the fact that you knew I didn't remember, and you chose not to tell me. I don't care about your reasoning, it was wrong, and I don't know how to forgive you right now. So please, get out of my house," I demand, and James nods in defeat, doing as he's told. My knees cave in, and I fall to the ground, sobs escaping my throat.

He lied to me, he deceived me, and all I can think about is how humiliated I am. There is one thing I never wanted James and I to do, and it turns out we've already done something along those lines. Still, that isn't even the only thing he was untruthful about. James lied about his feelings and what I mean to him, and I can't help the anger I'm feeling because of his betrayal. Nothing could have ever justified this deceit.

My body is overwhelmed by all the emotions flooding through me in a continuous, vicious cycle. It begs me to breathe, but I've forgotten how. James and Gabriel both lied. Two of the most important men in my life used my lack of memory to their advantage instead of being goddamn honest with me.

Finally, strength returns to my legs as anger consumes me. I grab my running shoes and sprint down the trail the guys and I followed not long ago. The memories of that night and the morning after replay over and over, taunting me for being so irresponsible. Grandpa always warned me about the effects of alcohol. *"You're an athlete. Your body is only as strong as your mind.*

If you let alcohol consume you, you betray your body." I should have taken his words more seriously instead of acting like an eighteen-year-old without a dream. I wonder what he would say to me now. I've been training but haven't gotten far. My feet bring me to a halt at the spot where Grandfather stopped me the first time we went for a run. *"Your determination and dedication will make you a champion,"* he'd told me. I bring my hands to my lips and cover my mouth as I scream as loudly as I can.

For the first time in over five years, I make my way to the one place I hate the most. I haven't been able to return because of the pain it brings me every single time I read my grandfather's name on the gravestone, but it's time. Grandfather deserves a visit from me, no matter how painful it will be.

My feet come to a complete halt once I'm in front of the stone Adrian and I had to choose. I wipe the dirt off the top and kneel in front of the grave while I let tears flow from my cheeks. My heart aches in my chest, and I have a difficult time breathing properly. This is much worse than I thought it would be. I wrap my arms around myself and rock back and forth while the same words fall from my lips.

"I'm so sorry." I repeat them over and over, ashamed of my actions and inability to make our dream come true. "I really tried, but I'm not good enough," I explain when I've calmed down enough to form a proper sentence. "I wish you were here. I love you and miss you so much," I go on, sending a wave of pain through my chest. "You must be so disappointed in me," I cry while I run my fingers over his name: *Josue Beau Romana.* "I just want to live my dream and make you proud, but I can't. I don't know what I'm supposed to do anymore." James and Gabriel have hurt me, my dream is slipping further away, and I miss the people I've lost.

All of the pain and anger fades for a moment when my phone rings, and I read Colin Reiner's name on my lock screen. My eyes drift to Grandfather's gravestone before I compose myself and answer the call.

"Hello, Mr. Reiner?" I ask, and my heart thumbs rapidly against my ribcage.

"Good afternoon, Ms. Romana. I'm sorry to bother you, but I have some news. A spot has opened up at our academy, and we would be delighted to have you join us. Are you still interested?" My eyes fixate on the gravestone again while goosebumps spread over my entire body.

Thank you, Grandfather.

Rush: Part Two

Chapter 1

Valentina

"You've been training for two years to get to this moment, little champion. How do you feel?" Grandfather asks as I settle down in my kart.

If I win today, I will become the champion of this year's karting league.

"I'm very nervous," I admit while he helps me get comfortable in my seat and readjusts my helmet to make sure the clasp is closed.

Adrian takes my hand and gives it a reassuring squeeze. Meanwhile, James is walking around my kart to check if everything is in order.

"I know, but you've got this, Valentina. There is no one like you, and you'll show them that today," Grandfather says before stepping back and nodding at my brother to let him know it's time to go.

"Go kick those boys' asses," Adrian adds in English, earning himself a frown from our grandfather.

"Adrian, watch your foul mouth," he warns, making my brother lift his hands in surrender. Grandpa leans down then so I'm the only one to hear his next words. "Go kick their asses," he whispers, going against his strict rule of solely speaking French to us, and I let out a little laugh. It relieves some of the tension and pressure on my shoulders.

"Breathe, race, and win, as long as it doesn't cost you a limb," Adrian, James, and Grandpa say in unison.

They stand in front of me for a moment before offering me one last nod and, involuntarily, the sadness of my father not being here creeps into my chest. Then they walk away, leaving me to enter my high-concentration mode. I shut everything out, focusing entirely on the task at hand: proving everyone who is doubting me wrong and winning the championship.

The race starts soon, and I manage to stay ahead for most of it. By the time the last few laps come around, my rival Christian Crovetto is right beside me, almost pushing me off track to get past.

I hold my ground, only giving in and letting him pass by so he doesn't force me to crash into the barriers. Then, at the next corner, I overtake him again, my kart touching his briefly before I'm ahead.

We race for one more lap, but I'm the one who makes it over the finish line first. Despite him playing dirty tricks, I win.

I drive my kart toward the little podium area where my family is waiting for me with big smiles. They clap and cheer the entire time while happiness fills my soul.

This is where I belong.

This feeling is what I long for every single day of my life.

It has taken a lot of disappointment to get here, but it was worth it.

I'm a karting league champion, and, one day, I will be one of Formula One.

The wind around me becomes more chilly with every minute I remain in front of Grandfather's grave. My fingertips feel like ice, but I can't bring myself to move yet. The thoughts in my head spiral, sometimes in a good way when I think about getting accepted into the Ferrari Driver Academy an hour ago. Other times, they fixate on the disaster between James and me. He said he was in love with me, and I begged him to touch me on my eighteenth birthday. We will never be able to take any of it back.

Embarrassment repeatedly settles on my cheeks when I recall what happened. I have no idea how we're going to find our way back to each other, but the ball is in my court now. James left because I asked him to, and he won't come to me unless I'm ready. He'd never put that kind of pressure on me.

Gabriel sneaks into my mind every so often too. I think about the way we danced that night, what he whispered into my ear... Yes, he should have told me the day after, *but what would have been the point?* All it would have done is allow me to overthink words I've always wanted to hear before he went back to Kira. My anger for him has long passed, even though I fear it will resurface the moment he steps in front of me. There is no way around it.

I have to speak to both of them.

For now, I revel in my success of getting what I've wanted since I was a little kid. My fingers brush over my grandfather's name on the marble stone once more. Josue Beau Romana. I hope he would be proud of me, despite the chaos in my life. After all those years of teaching me about balance, I've never been further away from it than I am right now.

I wipe the dirt off the top of the stone and place the flowers in the holder next to it, whispering 'I love you' before standing up. My hands straighten out my clothes while I turn around to see my brother a few meters behind me.

A smile dances onto my lips at the sight of him, and he opens his arms for me. I run toward him, excitement acting like adrenalin in my veins.

"I made it, Adrian. The Ferrari Academy offered me a spot," I say as soon as he envelops me in a hug.

He steps away, joy and surprise all over his face.

"Are you serious?" I nod with enthusiasm, and he jumps up and down. A few people around us glare at him for it, and he stops immediately. "Sorry," he apologizes, guiding me out of the cemetery to continue his cheerful behavior. "When? How?" Adrian asks and takes my hand to squeeze it. I've never seen him this giddy before.

"Mr. Reiner called me a few hours ago and told me a spot has opened up.

I took it. The first training camp starts the week after the third Grand Prix," I explain, my cheeks burning from the smile I can't keep off my lips.

"Fuck yeah! My sister has finally got her chance to become a world champion!" Adrian yells for everyone around us to hear. I try to shush him, but he's too excited. "Oh man, I'm going to be the brother of the first female world champion. Now that's a fucking honor, holy crap," he says and wraps his arm around my shoulder to pull me close while we walk toward his car.

Tears sting my eyes at the thought, but I swallow them down. There has been enough crying for today.

"Thank you for never leaving my side during this difficult and frustrating process." Adrian presses a kiss to the side of my head and opens the door of his Ferrari for me.

"I will never leave you, Val, no matter how hard times get." My eyes shift to the ground as the thought of my fight with James resurfaces.

I sit down in the passenger seat, and Adrian settles down in the driver's, letting the engine roar to life with a simple press of a button.

"What's up? Why do you look upset?" he asks on our way to a restaurant where he wants to celebrate my news.

"There is something we should talk about," I admit, and he cocks a curious eyebrow. "On my eighteenth birthday, when James and I went back to my hotel room, we kind of..." I trail off as my body cringes from embarrassment.

"You had sex?" His voice is loud, most likely from getting blindsided by my words, and he mumbles a quick apology. "Please, tell me I don't have to kill him." This makes me let out an awkward laugh.

"No, it was as much my decision as it was his. It wasn't anything big either... just his fingers." Adrian nods, but I can tell he's trying to figure out how mad he has to be at his best friend. "I remember wanting him at that moment, desperate to forget about Gabriel and what he'd said to me," I explain, covering my face as if I could hide from the memories.

I've never been so uncomfortable retelling a story. Then again, I've never done anything so stupid before.

"Gabriel?" His confusion grows, scrunching his eyebrows together.

"I was grinding my ass against him, and he said I turn him on," I say, and Adrian's mouth falls open as his eyes widen.

"As your big brother, I strongly advise you to never go near alcohol again," he says, and I give him an agreeing nod.

"Trust me, I don't have any intention to touch another drop," I promise, and he rubs his temple. "I'm sorry for this emotional bomb, but I have no idea how to fix any of it. How do I start forgiving James after he lied to me?" I ask, my eyes shifting to the *Casino de Monte-Carlo* as we drive by it.

"James is our best friend. He's been there since we were kids, and, no matter what, we will never be able to let go of him. Deep down, you know you'd do anything to save your friendship because he's family. A little bit more complicated family now, but still. He's been there for us for every important event in our lives. Yes, he screwed up, and I will most likely kill him for it, but he's James. There is no one more loyal than him. He's one of a kind," Adrian says, once again reminding me of the admiration I hold for my brother.

His willingness to speak about emotional things with me is why he's my favorite person in the whole world. Well, it's one of the reasons.

"I'll talk to him," I reply, but the words are so quiet, it makes me realize they are meant for myself and no one else. "For tonight, I just want to celebrate." Adrian briefly looks at me to reveal his smile.

"Anything for a future Formula One world champion," he tells me with a wink before focusing on the road in front of us again.

Chapter 2

Gabriel

I'm losing my fucking mind. Valentina has disappeared, no note, text, or anything letting me know where she has gone. I've tried calling her, but she's not answering her phone. My copy of 'Die For Me' is gone, and I wonder if there is anything I wrote inside that upset her, but nothing comes to mind.

"Jean!" I call out because worry has consumed every part of me. Thoughts of what could have happened to her take over, and I panic. "Jean!" I scream louder this time, and my brother appears in front of me downstairs, a confused look on his face.

"Why the hell are you screaming?" he complains, his French sloppier than usual. It irritates me, but I can't focus on scolding him right now. He might know where Valentina is and whether or not I've done something to upset her.

"Did Val tell you where she was going?" I ask because now I'm convinced she's angry with me for leaving her.

If Hector hadn't acted like it was the end of the world that I didn't go to one training session, I would have never left for so long.

"No, but try calling Adrian or James. They might know."

I dial James' number first because I remember her saying something about texting him back yesterday. The phone rings a few times before he answers.

"I'm not in the bloody mood, Gabriel. Leave me alone," he slurs into the phone, and I cock an eyebrow.

"Is Val with you?" I ask and hear him sniffle.

"No, mate, and she probably never will be again."

He hangs up before I can ask him what the hell that means.

My thumbs fly over my screen, searching for Adrian's number. I hate being like this, but Val told me she'd be here after I'm done. The fact that she didn't tell me she left bothers me. Something's wrong, and I need to make sure she's somewhere safe.

My heart is racing while I wait for Adrian to respond, but he doesn't. I'm about to have a panic attack when my screen lights up from an incoming text message.

Chapter 3

Valentina

My focus has been on the countless yachts in the harbor for most of the meal. The water barely moves, except for the occasional seagull, which disturbs the peace to collect some food. Gabriel has been trying to reach me, but I'm ignoring his texts. We need to speak in person, not over the phone.

"Can I bring you both something else? Maybe a little dessert?" our waitress asks, tearing me from my thoughts.

Her attention is on Adrian, a challenging look on her face. They've been flirting since we've sat down, which is why I can't keep the smile off my face. My gaze shifts to my brother, who gives her an easy smirk that turns her cheeks a deep red color.

"Depends. What are you offering?" he asks, and I roll my eyes when she slips him a note.

"Would that be of interest to you?" she replies, making me feel the urge to cover my ears. I don't want to know what she wrote on that paper.

"How could I say no to someone as beautiful as you?"

I smack my forehead, earning me a kick to the shin from him. It's not hard, just enough to serve as a 'stop that'. A laugh slips from my lips before I can contain it.

"Do you want to walk home?" he asks, and I cover my mouth with my hand.

He turns back to the patiently waiting waitress, Julia.

"I get off in ten minutes," she informs him, and Adrian smiles at her.

"If we follow the instructions on your note, yes, you will," he assures her, making another blush settle on her cheeks.

I suppress the urge to make a hurling sound but let it out when Julia leaves our table to get the check Adrian asked for.

"Give me the keys, please. I can't stay and watch more of that," I say and point at him. Adrian grins as he hands me the keys to his car.

"I'll be home later," he assures me, and I roll my eyes for the second time before standing up.

"You know, relationships aren't as bad as you think. They might be worth a shot." Adrian frowns in an instant.

"No, thank you. I've gotten hurt enough times in my life," he replies, and I bend down to press a kiss to the top of his head.

"Someday, a wonderful person is going to step into your life, and you won't be able to turn away from them, no matter our past. Trust me, *I know.*" Adrian squeezes my side, acknowledging my words without responding.

If I were smarter, I'd adapt his mindset to shield myself from further pain, but Gabriel is under my skin now. He's the reason why my walls have turned to dust.

I text him to meet me at my house. I don't want to torture him any longer nor do I want my anger to remain unresolved.

By the time I finally get home, he's sitting on my porch, his head between his arms, and his phone in his hand. When he looks up and sees me, relief washes over his face.

"Thank God, you're okay! Why have you been ignoring me? I was worried sick about you!" he says as he tries to close the distance between us. I hold up my hands to stop him, which he does at once.

"You've been keeping something important from me," I reply, and his eyebrows twitch from uncertainty.

"Chérie, please be a little more specific. As much as I'd love to, I can't read your thoughts." I would have expected him to be angry with me for avoiding him, but he's genuinely trying to make sense of how I feel instead.

"My eighteenth birthday party." His eyes go wide, and the confusion vanishes from his face. "The night you whispered naughty things into my ear, then brushed it off, and didn't tell me about it the next day."

Gabriel nods, a shameful frown now on his face. It makes the dimples on his cheeks stand out, but for once, it's not in the way I love.

"You should have been honest with me."

The more I look at him, the more I realize I want an explanation. I'm not angry, but he needs to tell me why he kept this a secret.

"You're right. I was a coward for not telling you because I was scared you would never look at me the same way. At the time, I had no idea how you felt about me, and I didn't want to risk our friendship because of one tipsy confession," he explains, and I wipe my face with my hands.

His words help me understand him, so I take a step toward him.

"I am so sorry for not telling you. I should have when we started this thing between us. God, I'm so sorry, baby." I move even closer until my hands rest on each side of his neck, pulling his face down to mine.

"No matter how scared you are to tell me something, you can always confide in me, especially when it's something like this," I remind him, and he leans his forehead against mine.

Our breaths intertwine, and his fingers slip onto my hips to guide me against his body. Electricity courses through me, making the blood in my veins hum to Gabriel's melody.

"I know. You're the most understanding person I've ever met. This won't happen again, chérie. I'll do better," he promises, the sincerity in his voice clear as day.

"Good because I'm understanding, but I don't tolerate lies."

Gabriel nods before leaning down and pressing a soft kiss to my neck. A wave of goosebumps spreads over my arms as my skin lights on fire.

"How can I make things up to you?" he asks, his lips moving to my jaw and then cheek. The affection clouds my mind for a moment, but I refocus quickly.

"Be happy for me when I tell you I got a spot in the Ferrari Driver Academy," I blurt out because, more than anything right now, I want to share this success with him.

Gabriel lets go of me to step back and stare into my eyes. A bright smile lights up my face, showing him I'm not joking. This is real.

"You did it! Oh my God, you fucking did it, mon tournesol," he cheers and kisses me all over the face.

My mind is stuck on this new nickname, 'my sunflower', but I'm also giggling as he attacks my face with love.

"I'm so proud of you! And happy for you. This is the best news I've ever heard in my life."

Gabriel's lips envelop mine then, and I almost sigh against them. It feels like it's been days since we last kissed, even if it's only been hours. His tongue slips into my mouth, making a little moan escape me. My knees go weak as he bites down on my bottom lip, but he holds me up, not ready for the kiss to end yet, and neither am I. Unfortunately, we're interrupted by the ringing of his phone.

"I swear, if it's Hector again, I'll fire him," Gabriel complains in French, causing a chuckle to escape me.

He rips his phone out of his pocket and cocks an eyebrow at the name before answering.

"Adrian? What can I do for you?" he asks, confusing me. I watch Gabriel, trying to figure out what my brother could possibly want right now. "I'll let her know. Yeah, okay. Bye," Gabriel says and laughs as he hangs up. "You forgot your phone at the restaurant, and he wanted to let you know he won't be back until tomorrow."

A yawn leaves me as I attempt to reply, and Gabriel brings his thumb to my bottom lip after, smiling.

"Let's go to bed, chérie, you must be exhausted." That's an understatement. It's been a long day.

He brings his lips to mine one more time before we go upstairs, and I take a shower. I give Gabriel an extra toothbrush so he can get ready too. We're in bed soon, and as tired as I am, I can't help but ogle Gabriel as he lies next to me without a shirt and pants on. The ink on his left hip bone stands out just above the waistband of his boxers, and I reach for it, like the first time I saw it. My fingers trace it for a brief moment, smiling because only I know about his tattoos.

Gabriel and I are facing each other on the bed, but we're too far apart for my liking. I inch a bit closer, desperate to feel his body pressed against mine.

"Are you hot?" I ask him after a while of silence, but he shakes his head and leans it back to study my face.

I'm only wearing a shirt, but it is so warm in my room, I'm jealous of him being half-naked. Frustrated because I want to cuddle, I sit up in bed, let out a heavy breath, and pull my shirt over my head. I feel like my skin can breathe again. Gabriel is watching my body with a toe-curling intensity, but there is also an amused smirk on his face.

"It's too hot," I complain, and he chuckles, his index finger reaching out to touch my cheek. It runs down from there to my neck and then to my breasts, leaving goosebumps in its wake.

"This is going to be a real problem," he says and pulls his bottom lip between his teeth. A blush settles on my cheeks, making me wish my body wasn't exhausted.

"What happened with Hector?" I ask, trying to distract myself and get him to stop touching my erogenous zones.

His green-brown eyes lock onto mine, and his full, round lips pull into a thin line. He's upset about whatever dragged him away from me this morning but doing his best to hide it from me. His gaze is on mine, a smile warming up his features when I give him a wiggle of my eyebrows.

"Don't worry about it, chérie, all that matters is I'm here with you now and we're okay." Gabriel's grin makes my heart weak.

It's ridiculous to me how much I love him and that, after three years, I finally got what I wanted. Gabriel is lying in my bed and he has feelings for me. I've been offered a position at the Ferrari Driver Academy so I can work toward my dream of becoming an F1 driver. Everything is slowly falling into place.

Now, I only have to figure out what the hell I'm going to do about James.

Chapter 4

Valentina

My eyes flutter open, and, like yesterday morning, I'm awake before Gabriel. A smile stretches across my face as I inch closer, and he wraps his arms around me in his sleep. My fingers trail across his naked torso, studying every birthmark and little scar they can find.

His heartbeat is steady, I can hear it perfectly with my ear flat against his chest. Gabriel's hand drops from my back to my butt, and I look up to see if he's still asleep. His eyes are closed, but there is a hint of a smile on his lips now. *Two can play this game.*

I reach for his morning wood but don't touch him. All I do is swiftly graze it, as if by accident, and then shove my hands between my legs. Gabriel squeezes my ass, making the smile on my face uncontrollable. My fingers move back to his chest, and I lean forward to press a kiss on his hard nipple.

Almost instantly, he pushes my behind toward him, and my aching clit presses against his groin. A low moan leaves me, my needy body happy because of the pressure against my most sensitive area.

I lift my head to see his eyes are open now, his lips are parted, and lust is all over his face.

"Good morning," I whisper, and the sweetest grin appears on his lips. His dimples seem to be everything I want to see at this point along with his stubble and green-brown eyes.

"Bonjour," he replies, his mouth brushing over mine. My body lights on fire when I feel him rub against me.

"Touch me," I beg and command at the same time, bringing a sexy smirk to his full lips.

His hand slips inside of my panties without hesitation, running over my swollen clit before his index and middle fingers slide inside of me. They curl at the perfect spot, making a loud gasp escape me.

"You're so wet for me, chérie, this early in the morning," he whispers into my ear, his voice husky and rough from just waking up.

He moves his fingers back out before he glides them in again, this time a little faster than before. Fire spreads through my stomach and chest, my eyes rolling into the back of my head at the same time.

"Look at me," he says, but I don't listen. "Keep your eyes on me or I'll stop," he demands, and I smile as I obey. He's so bossy... *I love it.*

His thumb rubs over my clit, tracing perfect circles. My moans are quiet, but they are also coming out fast and breathless. Gabriel brings his lips to mine and lets his tongue enter my mouth to massage mine with his. Pleasure grabs hold of every cell in my body, making them vibrate.

My eyes close in response, but he stops his movements.

"Eyes on me, baby," he reminds me, and I force them open again.

Gabriel keeps going before lifting his free hand to grab my chin between his fingers, tilting my head to face him completely.

"That's my girl," he praises, picking up speed and bringing back the familiar tension in my body.

I reach for his erection, the need to make him orgasm at the same time as me taking over.

"Shit, Val," he moans as soon as my hand glides down his hard cock. My eyes stay on him but his are closed now.

A wicked grin dances onto my face before I say, "Keep looking at *me*, Gabriel, or *I* will stop."

He half-chuckles, half-moans before obeying, his gaze revealing how good I make him feel. I rub faster, putting a little more pressure when he groans my name. It's so hot, I keep going to hear it over and over again. Every little sound from him pushes me further toward my release.

"God, baby."

His usually firm voice has lost its strength now. I feel his legs go stiff before his high takes over and his body starts to tremble. He pumps into my hand, riding out his pleasure for as long as he can.

Gabriel's lips crash onto mine a moment before my own orgasm pumps through my veins, releasing my entire body from the build-up he was responsible for. I cover my mouth to muffle my scream and grind myself against his hand to enjoy the orgasm and all of its after-effects.

"Fuck," I breathe and roll onto my back, trying to calm my accelerated heartbeat, which is useless until he removes his hand from my panties.

Gabriel disappears into my bathroom, but he returns soon, wearing his sweatpants from yesterday and smiling brightly at me. I'm still out of breath, and my mind is in a trance.

"Can we wake up like this every morning?" I joke, but Gabriel's expression is dead-serious.

"Say the word, I'll move in tomorrow." I shake my head, the smile on my face never fading. He cocks an eyebrow but grins too. That beautiful, handsome grin of his. "Fine, I guess we can just pretend we don't belong together for a bit longer if that's what you need."

He makes everything sound so easy, as if we could run away together into a fairytale land where problems don't exist and we could live happily ever after. Just trying to put myself in a mindset like that is absurd. Worlds like this don't exist, but mine is pretty good, even if I have to push through things, like my anger. James and I have to figure this out.

"What do you want to do today?" Gabriel asks me after a while of silence, and I take his hand in mine.

"I have to go make things right between James and me. We got into a fight yesterday, and I don't want this painful feeling in my stomach to be permanent," I explain, and Gabriel nods.

"I think that sounds like a great plan. You should talk to him," Gabriel agrees.

I place my hand on his foot and tickle him, making him jerk his feet toward his body.

"What are you trying to do?" he asks, a big grin on his face.

"I'm trying to be cute," I reply, and he chuckles.

Gabriel pulls me toward him by my wrists and starts to tickle my stomach. I don't know if he knows my feet aren't ticklish, or if he just wanted more surface to attack. I start screaming and laughing, and eventually, he just pins me to the bed.

"You don't have to try to be cute. It comes naturally to you." He gives me a swift kiss on the lips before he gets off me.

My hand has been in the same position, a few centimeters away from James' door, for about five minutes now. I cannot make my fist connect with the wood. I want to talk to him, I *need* to, but, somehow, my body is refusing to take the first step in the right direction.

It's been twenty-four hours since the fight started, and I don't know if it's the best idea to talk to him already. Maybe I'm too much of a chicken to find out what he meant when he said he was in love with me. If his feelings are still there, they will change everything.

But will they?

I don't know anymore, which is why I finally bring myself to knock on the door. Uncertainty is scarier than anything James could ever tell me.

When nobody answers, I walk around the side of the house and open the gate leading to his garden. James is sitting on one of the lounge chairs in front of his pool, his head between his arms and empty bottles of beer scattered around him. He must have slept out here.

"James?" His head snaps up, and I can see his red, puffy eyes and the dark circles underneath them. "Good God," I say and walk over to him. I wrap my arms around his head, ignoring the stench of alcohol coming off his clothes. "What the hell are you doing?" I step back, letting my eyes scan his sad face.

"I'm so sorry," is the first thing slipping out of his mouth. He's not drunk anymore, I'm sure of it, but he is exhausted.

His blue eyes seem lighter because the white part has turned blood-red, and his blonde hair is all over the place.

"I know, I'm sorry too. We should have talked yesterday, and I shouldn't have made you leave."

James probably spent the whole night hating himself, trying to forget about everything by consuming too much alcohol and putting himself in a dreadful head space.

"Let's talk," I tell him, and he nods.

"I should have told you the day after. I should have never kept such an important piece of information from you. But you have to understand why. You–you just have to," he tells me, his hand wrapping around mine and his eyes pleading with me. I don't know what he's begging me for, but it seems important. "I was in love with you for years, pretty much from when we were kids to only a couple of months ago."

My heart is racing in my chest, and I feel like throwing up.

"I've since realized we aren't supposed to be together. I am supposed to protect you, love you, care for you, and always be there for you in a brotherly kind of way. You need me as a friend, and I need you, which is why I never want to do anything to ruin that, even if I already did."

Tears are rolling down his cheeks, which bring some to my own eyes. We are two people who love each other too much for their own good.

"Once I realized what we both need, it was a lot easier to let go of my feelings. I even met someone a couple of weeks ago, and she and I have been getting along well, but I can't let myself connect with her fully. Until yesterday, I had no idea the reason for that was my deception. I've been lying to you for too long, and I just couldn't do it anymore, especially not after you were saying all of those things about me."

He rubs his face with his hands before he takes mine again.

"I should have always put protecting you first, and I'm sorry I let a ridiculous fantasy cloud my judgment. You deserve better, my love. You deserve a friend who would never do something like this to you, and it hurts me that I messed up our relationship. I know there is nothing I can do anymore, so I'm hoping you can find it in your heart to forgive the behavior of a stupid, immature boy, even if he doesn't deserve anything more from you."

His hand slips out of mine, but I take it back and lift it to my cheek. It lies flat against my skin, and I take a deep, calming breath. This is a lot to take in all at once, but at least I finally understand him. I can make sense of his feelings, which is all I've ever wanted.

"I'm sorry for all the pain I have caused you over the years. It must have taken everything out of you to give me advice and listen when I talked to you about Luke and Gabriel, or every time I friend-zoned you," I say and laugh a little.

"Yeah," he mumbles, and his thumb caresses my cheek.

"I'm so sorry something like this happened," I tell him, my voice cracking.

He's about to talk when I cover his mouth to stop him.

"You had your turn, now it's mine," I scold, and he grins at me. There it is, this is all I wanted to see. "There is nothing you could ever do that would make me hate you. You've made a mess out of a situation we could have dealt with a year ago, but we can also address it now. I wish you would have told me sooner, but I also know you won't ever lie to me again."

He shakes his head, shame in his features. I let out a strained breath.

"Let's just move on from this and get back to annoying each other." He nods, relief clear on his face. "I love you." James pulls me into a tight embrace.

"I love you so much, Valentina."

We hug for what feels like an eternity before I pull back to look at him. The smile on his face warms my insides because I'm glad to see happiness has taken over again.

"Now, tell me, what's been going on?"

A small, nervous laugh escapes me before I tell him about my spot at the Ferrari Driver Academy.

"Shut up, luv!" he says, shaking me out of excitement. "It finally happened! Soon, you'll be kicking all of our arses," he cheers, and I cover my face to hide the blush on my cheeks.

Soon...

Chapter 5

Gabriel

My fingers run over the soft skin of her cheek, tracing her features to memorize the feel of them. Valentina fell asleep as soon as she came home from James' house. I've been watching her like a creep for the past half an hour, but I can't help it. She's everything to me and admiring her face is the only thing I want to do while she's asleep beside me.

Val lets out a little, tired groan, her dream creasing the skin between her eyebrows. I smile at her, brushing her nose with mine as I inch closer. Just as my eyes are about to shut, a crashing noise shudders through the house.

"Hmmm?" Val says, raising her head, but she's still mostly asleep.

"I'll go see, chérie," I whisper, and she falls back onto her pillow, trusting me to check on Adrian.

He's on his knees downstairs, picking up the shards of the vase he broke.

"Are you okay?" I ask when he doesn't acknowledge my presence in the foyer.

His gaze shifts to my face, revealing to me that something is bothering him through the redness around his eyes.

"Is Val sleeping?" he says, and I nod to assure him it's just him and me.

I help him pick up the pieces, waiting for an explanation. "I'm having a bad night," he explains, but I already knew that. Adrian is more transparent than he thinks.

"You can talk to me about it, if you want," I offer, and he drops backward until he's on his ass, tears falling down his cheeks.

This is the first time since I've met him that he's felt comfortable enough around me to cry, and I'm not sure what to do.

"Do you ever have those nights when you get lost in your head, thinking about everyone you've lost and picturing the pain they felt when they left this world?" he asks, and I sit down too.

"All the time," I admit, doing my best to calm my racing heart.

He wipes his tears, wrapping his arms around his legs and leaning back to look more casual than he's feeling.

"I can't get my dad out of my head. The day he crashed into our living room, drunk out of his mind. A small part of me died with him as I watched the paramedics drag his lifeless body from the car. For some reason, I can't get the image out of my head tonight, and it's ripping open old wounds," he says, allowing me to envision what he had to go through as a child.

Chills cover my whole body.

"I'm sorry, I can't imagine how traumatic it must have been. I was only told what happened to my mom, but, every now and then, I will see an image in my head of her dropping to the ground in the grocery store. I didn't have to be there for it to haunt me, so I understand," I reply, and he gives me a compassionate smile.

"It feels surreal when I replay the memory, like a bad dream I had, or a nightmare that's consuming me." I nod, moving forward to pick up the shard I've been focusing on for a few moments. "Why can't my head let it go? Why does it have to show me what happened over and over?" he asks, pulling on his dirty blonde hair as more tears fall.

"You miss him, Adrian, and, unfortunately, that's the last memory you have of him. It's the most recent and traumatic, so your brain latched onto it.

It's difficult to forget, if not impossible."

His eyes shift to my face, studying me with an intensity that tells me he needs a distraction, to focus on something else to let go of what pains him.

"Come on," I say and stand up before holding out my hand to help him off the ground.

"Where are we going?" he asks, letting me pull him up. I place my hand on his shoulder, squeezing it to comfort him.

"You're going to show me where you keep the broom so I can clean up the shards. I don't want Val to kill us tomorrow for leaving pieces of porcelain on the ground," I start, and he chuckles at my words.

"She *is* really bossy," he complains with a smile, and I return it.

"Yes, she is, and rightfully so with us," I add and follow Adrian to the cupboard where the cleaning tools are.

"I'll take care of my mess," he says when he grabs the broom, but I rip it out of his grasp.

"No, you're going to set everything up for a card game of your choosing so I can kick your ass," I reply and make my way back to the broken vase.

By the time I've finished cleaning, Adrian is already at the table on the veranda, staring at the full moon in the sky.

"Are you praying to God to help you win? I think it's a hopeless case," I tease, and Adrian lets out a small laugh.

"No, I haven't prayed since I was a child. I don't even know if I believe in God anymore, or something like Him. I don't know." I was not expecting a serious response from him, but it's interesting how alike we think.

"I feel the same way, but what I'm sure of is that the people we've lost are watching over us, caring for us," I say as I settle down in the seat across from him. Adrian's eyes, the ones that remind me of the woman I love, stare into mine.

"I don't like how close we're growing, Gabriel. I think I need a break from you," he points out, and I burst into laughter.

There is the Adrian I know.

"You can try, but I'll still be here, at your house, bugging you with my presence because Val wants me here," I reply, picking up the cards to see what I'm working with this round.

"I really don't know what she sees in you. Your good looks? Your kind heart? *Pfft,*" Adrian says, and my jaw drops a little before amusement pulls my mouth into a smile.

"You're a dick," I say in Italian, and he winks at me.

"Just to you." I shake my head, leaning it back to let out a sigh.

"Remember who's teaching you Italian for free," I remind him while he plays down his first card, making it my turn.

"Remember who's not beating you up for doing unthinkable things to their little sister," he replies, shutting me up for good.

Touché, I think to myself before smirking at my cards.

Chapter 6

Valentina

It's been a few days since everything happened, and things have slowly been settling. Since all four of my favorite guys wanted to celebrate my news, we decided to go for a round of bowling.

Cameron holds my hand the entire walk to where we get our shoes and pay for the lane. He's been quiet, something obviously weighing heavy on his mind, but he continues to bring a smile to his face whenever I look at him.

Adrian, James, and Gabriel follow behind us, discussing something about the new tires I don't catch or even attempt to hear. Instead, I wrap my arms around one of Cameron's and lean my head against his shoulder.

"Would you like to tell me what's bothering you?" I ask, earning me an inquiring yet amused expression from him. His blue eyes pierce into mine before he lets out a small sigh.

"You know me too well," he complains with his thick Australian accent before nudging my head with his nose. I smile to myself as I wait for an explanation. "I dunno where to start," he says, but I don't rush him into telling me anything. "I'm in love with my friend. His name is Elijah, and we've known each other for a couple of years now. I don't know whether I should tell him or if I should just pretend I don't have any feelings. I've been fighting with myself for weeks, Valentina. What would you do in my place?"

I'm about to encourage him to go for it, to tell Elijah exactly how he feels because I think it is what I would do, but it's not. I'm not that forward nor that brave.

"I probably wouldn't tell him but only because I don't have the guts. If you're sure he's the one you want, that you're in love with him, then you should tell him. Don't put yourself in the same position as me because it only overcomplicates things. If I'd been honest with Gabriel from the start, and vice versa, we wouldn't have wasted our time searching for love in someone else," I explain, and Cameron stops dead in his tracks.

Adrian runs into him because, as always, he wasn't looking where he was going. He barely holds himself up on Cameron's shoulders before we all burst into laughter.

"Sorry, mate," Cameron says, but Adrian is crying-laughing now.

James and Gabriel go ahead already to get a lane, but my brother takes another moment to compose himself.

"It's all good. Sorry I ran into you, but, Jesus, you're built like a fucking wall. Nice," Adrian compliments our friend before squeezing his shoulders and arms with an approving nod. "You know, Elijah would be an idiot to shoot you down." A big smile spreads over his lips before he blushes. "I overheard your conversation a little. Your voice is very loud and firm," Adrian says, but Cameron doesn't seem to mind him knowing.

"Well, let's hope he doesn't shoot me down." He nudges my brother's side but then takes my hand again. "Thank you for the advice. I knew you would understand," Cameron says, addressing me, and I wink at him.

I understand the constant and threatening conflict inside of you, the one you can't figure out how to solve. The constant wondering: S*hould I do it? Should I risk our friendship over feelings that cloud my judgment? What if he doesn't feel the same way?* I hope Cameron is as lucky as I am.

"Go ahead, you can call me wise," I joke, and he bows before me.

"Oh yes, wise Ms. Romana, you are the greatest of them all." He shakes his head while laughing, and I drag him close again as we continue walking. "So, you and Gabriel? Since when? How did I miss that? I'm usually very good at spotting these things," Cameron complains, and I chuckle.

"I don't know what Gabriel and I are, so maybe that's why your radar is off," I suggest, but he shakes his head.

"No, my radar easily spots two people horny for each other," he explains, earning him an attack from my elbow to his ribs. It's soft enough to barely move him. "I mean, I knew he had feelings for you, but that you have the hots for him is a surprise. After all, he's been moping about you for years, even if he tried to hide it." *Moping...* I almost laugh. "Did he tell you about the time he let me convince him to get a tattoo on his ass because he got drunk when he found out you slept with someone else?" he asks, and I squeeze his arm while swallowing a chuckle.

"You're evil for that, you know," I remind him, but he brushes my comment off with a shrug of his shoulders.

"Hey, it's a cool tattoo." Even though he's right, I shake my head once again, disbelief in my chest. "So, are you two dating now or...?" He trails off, but I have no idea how to answer his question.

"We're not there yet. Plus, I'm going to start training at the academy soon while he has to work, and I don't know where that leaves us," I admit to myself and him.

This is a conversation I should have with Gabriel first, but I also didn't expect this realization to sink in right now.

"He's crazy about you, Val. Gabriel will take you any and every way he possibly can."

Cameron kisses the side of my head before we speak to the woman at the counter, telling her which shoe sizes we need. Gabriel hands me mine as soon as I try to talk, smiling before shifting his attention back to the person handing out the equipment.

"Alright, darling, ready to lose against me?" James asks, and I raise both eyebrows in response.

"The last time I lost against you was when—when I—" I cut off abruptly, touching my chin as if I was thinking. "Never mind, I've never lost against you," I tease, making him frown while he tries to think of a time he won.

"Fine, then today will be the first of many. You'll see, you will all see," he announces to the rest of our group, but they give him a confused look. James clears his throat, and I stretch my lips into a straight line to keep my amusement at bay.

"Sure we will," I reply and pat his shoulder, but he takes advantage of that vulnerable position and attacks my sides, tickling me until I squeal. I run away from him and to our lane.

Adrian and Gabriel are the first to join me, smiling at each other as they discuss who will win tonight. All of us are very competitive, especially Adrian and me. We don't handle losing too well.

"Come on, Gabriel, we all know I'm the best. This will be an easy win for me," Adrian says, and I look up at the ceiling, rolling my eyes while I beg karma to make him lose after that comment.

"Actually, I think we all know Val will beat us without even breaking a sweat," Gabriel replies, and a blush heats up my cheeks.

I can feel his eyes on me as I tie my shoes, making me shake my head with a smile. We agreed to keep whatever it is we have on the down-low, at least until we have had the inevitable conversation: *Are we dating?*

I love him, and he cares about me, but it doesn't uncomplicate things as much as I'd like. My career comes first, and now more than ever, it will require most of my time. It's not fair to ask him to have half a relationship. The thought makes my chest sting, but I push it away to focus on tonight.

"Luv, do you need a refresher course on how to hold a bowling ball?" James asks as he steps in front of me and brings me back to reality. My eyes shift to his face while a wicked grin dances onto my lips.

"You would be the best person to teach me about balls considering you were single most of your teenage years, wouldn't you be?" I tease, and Gabriel and Adrian break out into laughter. James' eyes widen and his mouth falls open.

"What did I miss?" Cameron asks when he finds my brother and Gabriel hunched over, and James still searching for a witty comeback.

"I taught James a lesson on how not to speak to a woman," I explain before winking at my best friend and walking over to the ball rack, grabbing one that looks like a universe.

Everyone watches me as I throw it down the lane, and it speeds toward the pins. Impatience combines with the hope to start off strong, which I do. All pins drop, earning me the first strike of the night. I jump up from excitement but straighten out my back and dress to pretend as if that was easy, no big deal.

All four of them have the same slightly annoyed, mostly impressed expression on their faces when I sit down to watch them have their turn.

Gabriel goes next and gets a spare. He smiles at me when he walks back, and I pat the space next to me, wanting him to be close. His arm wraps around me as he sits down, pulling me against his side. My eyes fixate on Adrian, whose first throw is so horrible, his ball lands in the gutter.

"I'm just warming up!" he defends when I laugh, and I raise my hands in mock surrender.

"You look stunning in that dress, mon tournesol," Gabriel compliments and runs his fingers over the soft cotton material. My heart does a few summersaults, unable to contain its excitement.

"'My sunflower', huh?" I ask because last time I didn't, and it's been gnawing at me.

"The beauty you find in sunflowers is the one I see in you every time I look at you. They're your favorite, and you're mine," he explains without hesitation. I forget how to breathe.

"I'm your favorite flower, Mother Gothel?" I joke, and he gives me a small chuckle before placing his fingers under my chin to lift my face to his.

"You're my favorite everything, chérie."

He kisses my forehead but then brings his attention to Cameron as he throws his bowling ball. I lean my head against his shoulder, the familiar mahogany scent filling my nose.

Damnit, he needs to stop saying all the right things at all the right times.

There is only one round left. Adrian somehow managed to catch up, and we're head to head now. Gabriel, James, and Cameron haven't done well compared to us Romanas, but that's no surprise. My brother and I are too competitive to lose in a game we've been playing since we could walk.

I grab the bowling ball for the last time this round, glaring at my brother before moving toward the lane.

"Come on, chérie, you got this," Gabriel cheers followed by James and Cameron.

"Is no one on my side?" my brother complains while a warmth spreads through my chest from their support. "So, when Val and I race against each other in the future, you'll be on her side too?" Adrian asks, and I turn to see him faking a pained expression.

"Most definitely," all three of our friends reply, and he lets out a laugh.

"Well, then that makes four of us. Go, Val!" he yells and claps, and I turn back around to throw my bowling ball.

I manage to get a spare with another throw, and my very last one is a strike. Adrian playfully rolls his eyes when I walk past him.

"Be careful. I wouldn't want you to trip over your big elephant feet and then use that as an excuse for losing," I tease, and he goes into attack mode. Adrian pulls me into the air just to drop me back on the ground and run like an idiot to the ball rack.

His first throw is a strike, which is why I grab Gabriel's arm and hold on tight. I'll never hear the end of it if Adrian wins tonight. My brother gives me a smug smile, but when he throws once more, he only knocks down a single pin. He doesn't manage to get a spare either, handing me the win.

"Oh yeah!"

My voice is louder than I intended for it to be, but my friends start celebrating with me, patting my back, or, in Gabriel's case, kissing my cheek. Adrian pretends to be deeply wounded by his loss before hugging me.

If happiness could be described as one single moment, this one would come very close for me.

Chapter 7

Gabriel

There is nothing I hate more in the world than this god-forsaken graveyard. I come here seven times a year, but it never gets easier. My heart doesn't get used to the squeezing from pain, and my lungs always burn from my uneven breaths. Still, I come here on every date tattooed on my hip because it's the closest I can get to people I've lost.

I wish there was another way for me to feel connected to them again.

"Hi, Max," I say as I settle down in front of my late best friend's and godfather's gravestone.

My hands start to shake while I get ready to talk to him like I always do when I'm here. The first time, it felt weird because I know he can't hear me, none of them can, but it's gotten easier over time. Valentina told me once 'You're not speaking for them to listen. You're speaking for yourself to process and heal.' That was the first day I realized I couldn't be without her again, the day I understood just how in love I am with her.

"The season is going alright so far. I managed to win the first race, but then only came in fifth in the second one. James is currently leading the championship, which you know how I feel about," I say and let out a laugh.

The Brit and I have never been close, and the only reason I tolerate him is Val. He makes her happy, so I try my best to get along with him.

"But I'm going to keep pushing, don't worry," I assure him and myself at the same time.

"Excuse me, I don't mean to bother, but my granddaughter fell and I don't have a tissue to clean the wound. Do you perhaps have one for me?" an elderly man asks, and I stand up to reach into my back pocket.

"Of course. Here," I say and offer him a whole pack. "I hope she's okay," I add, and he smiles at me.

"She will be," he replies, and I give him a slight nod.

The man walks away, and my eyes shift to the gravestone across from Maxime's. The name Josue Beau Romana is written on it, and I sink back down to where I was before. Next to his stone is another with the name Esmèe Rolande-Romana.

How have I never noticed that Valentina's grandparents are buried right across from Maxime?

I always knew our fates were entangled, but this takes it to another level.

"Aunt Domi and Aunt Nicolette are doing well, they're almost back from vacation. Jean is much better than the last time we talked. He's worked through his grief. You'd be very proud of him," I say, focusing on my godfather. "I wish you were here. I have so many questions to ask you," I admit and rub my face with my hands. "I've made mistakes with Valentina, but I'm trying to be better. I'd do anything for her, for her happiness. And yet, I can't shake my fear of losing her. I know she's the only person I want a future with, but I know I have to let it go. For Valentina's sake, my paranoia needs to turn into devotion. I won't turn away from her anymore. I can't feed into the fear when both of us know mere friendship isn't going to be enough."

My rant comes to an abrupt end when I remember to breathe. A laugh I don't mean escapes me before I can hold it back.

"I need you, Maxime, to tell me everything will work out in the end. I need you to assure me I've experienced enough loss. I need you to be here, not wherever you are!" I say, feeling the pain in my chest taking over.

Tears shoot into my eyes, and I can't stop them.

"Fuck, when will this get easier? When am I going to stop bawling my eyes out because you're gone? I can't change it, so why the hell am I crying?" I ask, fighting the urge to throw grass like a little child. "I love my job. I love racing, but I will hate it forever for taking you from me."

I lift my hands to his name as the pain finally rolls down my cheeks. No other place can bring tears to my eyes and no person besides Valentina. They turn into sobs until I break down completely, no longer fighting my feelings.

"I miss you," is the last thing I say before my heart falls into that all too familiar black hole in my chest, numbing my body to prevent it from feeling the same pain my soul and heart are experiencing.

This will never get easier, will it?

Chapter 8

Valentina

"I hope I will still get to see you occasionally," Evangelin says after I tell her my big news. I give her a small hug, the comfort of it running through me in waves.

"Spending time with you and in your shop always makes me very happy. I hope you know I will come and help out as much as I can," I promise with a smile that reaches my heart.

I don't think I will ever get used to the thought of joining the Ferrari Driver Academy in a week's time. The third race of the year will be the last one I'm attending for the foreseeable future, which makes me sadder than I'd like to admit. Then again, I've never been so excited for the next chapter of my life.

"You need to focus on your career now, belle, don't worry about *Rush* or me. We'll be fine," she assures me, her flawless French smooth in my ears.

She wipes away a tear I hadn't noticed leaving me.

"Don't be sad, Valentina. Adrian and Carlos are best friends now so we'll spend lots of time together," Evangelin says and points at her husband and my brother on the couch, talking about Adrian's performance in Bahrain.

Every time the former world champion speaks, my brother's face lights up. He's happy to have someone to look up to in his life again, a role model that acts as a father figure.

"You're right. You're always right," I reply, making her cheeks turn a wonderful pinkish color.

"Yes, I am. Now, tell me, do you know who will be training with you at the academy?" she asks, and I pull my phone out of my pocket to check.

"They sent me an e-mail this morning with the list of names. I haven't checked it yet," I explain before reading the names to her. "Oh, yes! There is another woman," I blurt out when I read 'Luciana Sanchez, she/her'. "The rest of the drivers are all men. Haru Satō, Pedro Angeles... No, oh God, no, no, no," I say when I read the last name on the list. "This is a fucking joke. Please, tell me this is a joke," I croak out before apologizing to Evangelin.

My vulgar language caught her off-guard, I could tell by the way her eyes went wide, but she seems more confused than anything.

"What's wrong?" I cover my face with my hands and groan into them.

"You know the prince of Monaco? The younger one, not the one next in line for the throne?" I ask, and she gives me a small nod.

"Yes, Christian Crovetto. I've heard of him." My heart beats rapidly from the image of his face as it pops into my head. "Why? Is he on the list?"

It's my turn to nod then.

"He was my rival when we were children, and he always, and I mean always, tried to cheat. Christian didn't like losing to 'a weak girl'," I explain, raising my fingers to show I'm quoting his disgusting words. "I can't believe I'm going to have to train with him. I hate him. Besides his inability to lose, he's a spoiled brat, and a royal one at that," I complain and drop onto the chair in her kitchen.

Evangelin clicks her tongue before handing me a glass of water.

"Then you need to show him who the fuck you are and that you're not to be messed with," she replies, causing me to almost spit out the sip I took. This woman will never cease to amaze me.

Evangelin pats my back to help me get the water into the right pipe, and

I thank her once I can breathe again.

"He's never had a chance against me anyway," I eventually tell her, earning me a proud smile from my friend.

I stare down at my phone once more, wondering why the hell I've been punished like this. Out of all the race car drivers in the world, it had to be the most arrogant one, my nemesis, the guy I despise the most in the world.

This is bullshit.

My eyes scan the list one more time just to make sure I'm not mistaken, which, unfortunately, I am not. I shake my head before my attention drifts to the date in the corner of the e-mail. It stands out to me for some reason, and when I check Gabriel's and my chat, I realize he hasn't texted me back all day.

A light bulb goes off in my head before I jump out of the chair.

"Evangelin, I'm so sorry. I know we're supposed to have lunch, but I have to go," I tell her with a rushed tone, but she assures me it's fine.

I let Adrian know where I'm going, but Carlos isn't ready for him to leave yet, so he decides to stay. My brother throws me the keys to the car, and I run toward it.

I can't believe I forgot!

James holds my hand as Grandfather talks about the kind of man his son was. Tears stream down my face, and Adrian sits beside me, his own falling down his cheeks. I want to take his hand, but I know he needs to hold onto Dad's cap with both of his.

James' thumb rubs circles on my skin, and I try my best to listen to Grandpa. Still, my eyes drift to the coffin he had to choose to bury his only son in, and I cry even harder. My friend's arm slides across my shoulders until he can pull me close and press a kiss to the top of my head. He is only three years older than I am, but he is much taller, which is why he can easily reach it.

Adrian stands up to move to the front so he can talk about our father.

"I know all of you are expecting a beautiful speech, but I can't give

you one. It's too difficult for me to do." He takes a break to wipe his eyes. "I loved my father very much. He introduced me to a life full of excitement, and I won't ever have the chance to thank him for it. But I will race for you, Dad. Val and I will both continue to race for you. We know how much it meant to you that we continue this legacy, and we will. Even in death, we will make you proud."

Adrian turns to our father's coffin, places the cap on top of it, and walks back toward where I'm sitting. He takes my hand in his, and James lets go of me so Adrian can pull me close. With both of them holding onto me, I know I'm going to be okay.

My dad's oldest teammate comes to the front, and I watch him force a small smile.

"Jo and I talked a lot about the day he or I would die, and I had to promise him I would lighten the mood, but I'm going to have to break that promise. No one here wants me to make some stupid joke about how I was the better driver and that he ate my dust for years."

Laughter fills the room for a brief moment, and Grant McGullen brings a real smile to his lips.

"I guess I don't have to break it after all," he says proudly. "Being teammates in Formula One, and rivals for that matter, created a strong bond for us. From the beginning until the end, there was respect between us. We fought, we argued, and we even hated each other at one point, but he was my best friend. When we sat in the car, we risked our lives, but we did it together. You will forever have my respect, brother." Grant walks away, and I let more tears stream down my face.

"Goodbye, Daddy," I whisper as they lift his coffin into the ground.

I'm never going to see him again. He's gone, and I barely spent any time with him. I wish he hadn't prioritized his work. I wish he would have realized what was more important: his children.

Now, he will never have the chance.

Chapter 9

Valentina

The flowers in my shaking hand are heavy. I don't know what to do or what to say. With slow steps, I make my way down the path that leads to Maxime Thomas' gravestone.

When I met Gabriel, Maxime was still alive and healthy. Four years ago, he died in an accident in his Formula One car. It flipped ten times before landing upside down, no halo on top to protect him. I was at that race, and it was horrible. None of the drivers left the hospital and neither did I until the doctor came out and gave everyone the news no one wanted to hear. I'd never seen Gabriel break down like he did that day. Losing Maxime was like losing a sibling, a mentor, his moral compass.

When I finally reach Gabriel, he doesn't hear me, and I do my best not to scare him. I hear sobs leaving his mouth, and the tears welling up in my eyes are out of my control. I love him too much not to feel his pain.

My hand moves to his neck, but he doesn't even flinch. All he does is look up at me with his tear-stained face. I squat down on the ground next to him and place the flowers in front of the gravestone that reads:

Maxime Arthur Thomas

Friend, Son, Godfather, Formula One Driver

"I miss him so much," Gabriel says, and I wipe away his tears with the back of my hand.

"I know, baby," I reply softly, and before I can move another muscle, Gabriel pulls me into his lap and wraps his arms around my body.

Another sob escapes him, and he hugs me tighter. We sit on the ground for a while, giving Gabriel time to calm down.

"You can't ever die, chérie. I could never live in a world without you in it." I lean back, place my lips on his briefly, and then slide my hands on each side of his face.

"I'm not going anywhere. I'm sorry I didn't remember earlier." Gabriel's gaze shifts from my lips to my eyes.

"Don't apologize, and don't ever stop taking care of yourself. You're–you're–" He cuts off, and more tears fall from his eyes.

"I know," I say.

I'm not supposed to disappear, not like everyone else he's ever cared for. Seeing him like this, heartbroken and vulnerable, makes me want to take all of his pain and put it on myself.

The redness in his green-brown eyes makes my heart thump rapidly against my ribcage. It's hard for me to understand how so much pain could be focused on one person. I put my thumb on his bottom lip and the rest of my fingers on his cheek.

"I know it hurts, but you have to remember one thing: you are strong, you can do this," I tell him, and his full lips form a straight line. "You are talented and wonderful, and I am so proud of you. I am proud of the man you are, the driver you have become, the friend you've always been, the whatever-you-are-to-me you are."

We both laugh a little, and I go back to building him up.

"Having you in my life has brought me so much joy, happiness, and love. Yes, it may have brought me heartache too, but from that pain, you have taught me how to be stronger, more independent, and most importantly, you've taught me how to love someone in a messy and exciting way." His eyes fixate on my lips, and I smile at him. I didn't say the words, but we both know what I meant. My love for him is consuming and thrilling.

"Let's go," he says and stands back up on his feet.

Gabriel holds his hands out for me, and I slide both of mine in his. He helps me up, and his lips find mine before he leads me away from the one place that is strong enough to drag him down.

Gabriel and I go back to his home and spend most of the day cuddling on his bed, watching movies on his laptop. We decided to watch all the Marvel movies in chronological order, and he got snacks for us. He rubs my back and plays with my hair for most of the first film, and by the time we reach the second one, I get up and take off my jacket. Gabriel is watching me closely with warmth in his eyes but doesn't say anything. During moments like these, I wish I could crawl into his mind to know everything he's thinking and feeling.

After another hour, I feel his fingers on my chin, and he lifts my head so my gaze meets his. His lips press onto mine, but the kiss feels different. It feels more honest, more meaningful than all of our other ones. It isn't rushed, and it's not suppressing any feelings between us.

"Gabriel! Aunt Nicolette and Aunt Domi are back, and they brought a surprise," Jean screams, and Gabriel groans.

I lean back from the kiss, but Gabriel guides me closer so he can capture my lips again. A giggle escapes my throat, and I push away from him. It sounded like Jean was excited, which means whatever the surprise is, it has to be good.

"Go, I'll be waiting here," I say, and he frowns at me.

"No, you're coming with me, and you're going to meet my aunts," he replies, and my heart skips a beat.

I'm meeting his aunts, now, at this very moment.

I swallow hard, and Gabriel flashes me a grin, revealing his perfect dimples. It calms me in an instant.

We walk down the stairs, and Gabriel laces his fingers through mine, trying to comfort me to the best of his ability. I take a deep breath, and by the time we reach the bottom of the staircase, a genuine smile is on my face.

He leads me into the kitchen, and surely enough, Domi, Nicolette, and Jean are all standing there, smiling at each other. Nicolette, a tall, beautiful woman with long, red hair and light brown eyes walks up to us and wraps her arms around Gabriel.

"We're having a baby," the woman says in perfect French, and the smile slipping onto my lips is entirely out of my control. She turns to me with a warm expression then. "Valentina, it's nice to finally meet you," she says before hugging me. "I'm Nicolette." She didn't have to introduce herself since I've seen videos and pictures of her. It does, however, surprise me that she knows exactly who I am.

"It's nice to meet you too. Congratulations," I tell her.

"Thank you, beauté."

Nicolette steps away, and I look at Domi, yet another gorgeous woman. She is a bit shorter compared to her wife and her curves are to die for. Her brown, coily hair complements her brown eyes, and her pinched nose highlights her full lips. Domi introduces herself as well, and afterward, I move over to give Jean a hug.

I find out Domi is the one who is carrying their baby and that the couple has been trying to have one for a year now. Finally, the artificial insemination worked and Domi got pregnant.

For the rest of the evening, I get to know Gabriel's aunts. Nicolette is Gabriel's father's sister, and she met Domi when they were sixteen years old. Eight years later, they got married, and four years after that, they started to try and have a baby. Nicolette is very open with me, she shares her stories and asks questions in return.

As much as I'm enjoying this, getting to know the women who raised two of my favorite people, this is an intimate moment. I feel like I'm intruding, which is why I decide it's time for me to leave.

"I have to go," I whisper into Gabriel's ear, and he takes my hand to lead me from the living room, up the stairs to his bedroom. He shuts the door, and I put my hands on his chest when he comes close to me again. "What's going on?"

"Don't leave," he says, and a small smile spreads over my lips.

"I think Domi and Nicolette want to spend some time alone with you and Jean," I tell him, and he frowns at me.

"Stay," he begs when I step back, and I don't have the strength to say no again.

"What would we do if I stayed?"

A wicked grin spreads over his face, and I know whatever he is going to say next is going to make my body ache.

"We could do a lot," he whispers as he bends down and his lips brush the lobe of my ear.

A shiver runs down my spine, and I'm close to letting him do whatever he wants to me.

"I could let my fingers roam into your panties or you could fall apart all over my tongue." I grab his arms because my legs no longer have the strength to hold me up. "Or, I could pin you down on the bed, spread your legs wide open, and make you mine." His lips find my earlobe once again, and a low moan leaves my lips. "I love that sound," he continues, and I make the same one again.

His hands drop to my ass, and he picks me up off the ground. A gasp escapes me, and I giggle when he slams me down on the bed. I like the aggressive side he's showing. I like that he can take things slow but also knows when to go fast.

"So, tell me, what do you want to do?" He pulls his shirt over his head, showing off his incredible abs.

"I think the last option sounds really good," I reply, and he takes half of his bottom lip between his teeth.

"Are you sure?" he asks, but I'm already removing my shirt and pants so I'm lying on the bed only wearing my underwear.

Gabriel hasn't moved a centimeter, waiting for me to reassure him.

"I want you inside me," I admit, and a smirk spreads over his face. His dimples alone excite my body.

"Fuck," he replies and pins my wrists down on the bed.

Chapter 10

Valentina

Gabriel is between my legs, his eyes never leaving mine. I'm watching his muscles as they flex with every movement, driving me crazy. I've been waiting for this moment for years. I've been fantasizing about what it would feel like for too long, and it's finally happening.

His hands cup my boobs, and my eyes flutter shut to fixate on the feeling.

"I love your breasts," he says, and I push my back off the bed to remove my bra and throw it to the side.

I look at him, waiting for him to put his hands back on me. I've never felt a need this strong to have someone's skin on mine. It feels like there's only one goal left in my mind and it is to have him inside of me. The odd feeling surprises me, but I'm too busy putting my tongue into his mouth to linger on it. Gabriel leans back from the kiss to slide down his pants.

"Your body drives me crazy," I say without hesitation, his V-line catching my attention and making my clit ache.

"I hate it when you say things like that. You make me feel like the sexiest man on the planet, and that is not an attitude I should have," he says, and I chuckle.

"But to me, you are," I reply before I can stop myself. Gabriel's mouth opens slightly before he closes it again.

"There you go again. I'm going to get cocky," he says, and I try my best to stay serious so my next words come across the intended way.

"Well, you're about to have sex with me, that must make you feel pretty awesome." He touches his tongue to the roof of his mouth, but I continue to hide my smile.

"Thank God, *you're* the cocky one." He leans down and starts kissing my neck, sucking on my sensitive spot.

Soft moans escape me as he leaves marks on my skin, drawing on me like he would on paper. My body goes back to its familiar begging for a release.

I let his mouth pleasure my neck for a little while until I get impatient and guide his lips to mine, his hands roaming my body.

Someone knocks on his door, and Gabriel immediately drops on top of me to hide me from the intruder. "Gabriel, do you have a–oh, fuck, I'm so sorry," Jean says as he steps inside without waiting for permission to enter.

Embarrassment settles in my stomach, and I cover my mouth with my hand.

"Get the fuck out," Gabriel yells, and Jean disappears. "God, I'm so, so sorry, chérie." I only nod because I can't move.

Why do things like this always happen to Gabriel and me? Maybe the universe just doesn't want us to have sex.

"Val, please say something."

For the first time in minutes, my eyes find his, and I can see the embarrassment on his face as well. I reach for the closest piece of clothing to cover my chest.

"Well, Jean almost saw me naked just now, so give me a second to process," I tell him, and Gabriel nods, a sad expression taking over his features. This is exactly what I don't want. I put my hand on his cheek, and my thumb moves to his lips. "It's okay, it's not your fault anyway. That brother of yours should really learn how to wait." Gabriel nods in agreement, and I laugh, trying to make us feel better.

"Trust me, I'm going to talk to him about that." He attempts to get up, but I stop him.

"Not tonight, not while you're this upset with him," I say, and he frowns.

"He'd deserve my anger for what he did," he replies, making an awkward laugh leave me.

"Well, we shouldn't have let our horny thoughts cloud our judgment either," I remind him, and he gives me a small sigh.

"You're right. I'll take you somewhere special and private next time, I promise." I press a kiss to his lips before leaning back again and smiling. "Moving out is starting to sound quite appealing too," he adds, and I cock an eyebrow.

"Why haven't you yet?" I know he's barely ever home, but there must be another reason for it.

"Jean. He needed me to stay while he worked through his grief, but I'm ready to leave now," Gabriel explains, his anger seeping through in his voice.

"He made a mistake, but he didn't see anything. It's okay," I assure him, but he doesn't agree with me.

If it was up to him, he'd be yelling at his brother right now, which is why I try to distract him by lowering whatever is covering my body.

"Don't be angry," I say and pout, his gaze shifting between my lips and breasts.

"That's not fair," he says and lets out another sigh. "Arms up," he demands, and I do as I'm told.

He pulls, what I now realize is, his shirt over my head, and I inhale the mahogany scent coming off it, *Gabriel's scent.* An unfamiliar, heartwarming smile spreads over my lips. It feels like... it feels like every piece magically falls into place.

"God, I never understood it, not until now," he mutters to himself, but I hear him anyway. He doesn't need to explain because I get it. I didn't understand it either until this second. "I want you to wear my shirts from now on," he admits with a playful yet firm expression.

"Okay, but then you gotta wear mine too," I reply, and he frowns at me.

"Please, you would feel awful when you'd see how much better I'd pull your clothes off." I swat his arm, and he chuckles.

He takes my shirt from today and slides it over his head. It fits him perfectly, and I pout when I realize how good he looks. *At least he would look stupid in my crop tops, right? Ugh, who am I kidding? He'd look gorgeous.*

"Screw you," I say, and he laughs. I join him because his laughter is contagious. "What do you want to do now?"

"I want you to pick out a book and read it to you as you lie on my chest." Gabriel's dimples appear with his smile as I nod.

I make my way over to his bookshelf, studying the row of books. A few novels I've been meaning to read stand out to me, and I turn to him.

"You've read them all?" I ask, pointing at the second-hand books. Gabriel rubs the back of his neck, a shy smile playing on his face.

"I may have bought them for you," he admits before sitting up and staring at me. "I remembered you telling me about them, so I added them to my collection a few days ago," he adds, and I shake my head in disbelief, shifting my gaze back to the shelf.

"You, Gabriel Biancheri, are something else entirely," I say, and the sound of his chuckle fills the room.

"Only for you."

We spent the rest of the night stealing looks until my eyes close and I fall asleep in his arms, listening to his soft voice.

"How dare you compare her to Kira?" Gabriel's voice echoes through the whole house, and I shoot up in bed. Panic settles in my chest, and I pull on my shorts before I run down the stairs. "Are you fucking kidding me? Are you?" When I reach the living room, I see Gabriel and Jean meters apart, yelling at each other in French.

"Come on, Gabriel, you're way too immature to see her as anything other than something to conquer. You probably want to fuck her just to be able to say you did it. You're too messed up to ever take her more seriously than that. That's why you were dating Kira, wasn't it? To try and prove you were better than that, but you're not." Gabriel takes a step back. "Valentina is way too good for you, and she will realize it soon enough, hopefully before you screw her and leave her."

I don't know how they got here, to this point in their conversation, but I get more worried by the second. Gabriel's breathing is heavy, and his hands are balled into fists.

"You really shouldn't have said that," he says, and that's when I know I have to do something.

I step between them and put my hands on Gabriel's naked torso, which seems hotter than it should be.

"Gabriel, stop," I say, pleading with him.

His eyes shift from his brother to me, and all anger leaves him. His hands open up, and confusion settles on his face.

"Yeah, calm down, man. Listen to your conquest," Jean says from behind me, and anger returns to Gabriel's handsome features.

"Let me handle this," I beg, and Gabriel finds my eyes again.

He looks back at his brother, groans loudly, and leaves the room. I touch my lips with my fingers, thinking about what I'm going to say to Jean. When I finally figure it out, I turn around and look at the boy I thought was better than this.

"What happened here?" It's best I don't insult or yell at him. Simply talking to him is my plan for now.

"Your lover got mad at me because of yesterday, which, by the way, I am really sorry about. I'm always going to wait from now on." I press my lips into a thin line, needing a better explanation. "Anyway, things got out of hand, Gabriel started yelling, I screamed back, we got to a point we shouldn't have gotten to, but what can you expect? Gabriel has always had a problem controlling his emotions."

"You know what, Jean, that's enough. I know he's your brother, but my relationship with him is none of your goddamn business. What did you think would happen when you called me a conquest, huh?" I defend the man I love, and Jean rolls his eyes.

My hand darts out before it hits his shoulder, hard enough to serve as a warning but too soft to hurt him.

"You're my friend, but you're acting like a dick. Gabriel has done nothing but treat me like the queen of the world." Jean stays quiet, clearly ashamed now. "If you ever doubt his intentions again when you have no idea what's going on, remember this: it's none of your fucking concern." I leave him standing there without saying anything else, too bothered by his behavior.

The summer sun hits my eyes the second I leave the house in my search for Gabriel, and I lift my arm to be able to see.

"Chérie," he says from behind me, and I spin around to face him.

A sad expression decorates his face, and I take three strides so his body can envelop mine.

"I'm sorry, he was pushing all of my buttons, and I always get so angry with him." His body tenses again, and I run my fingers over his back to calm him down. He relaxes under my touch. "I don't know why," he admits.

I place my hands on each side of his face.

"Siblings. You love them, but sometimes, you just want to punch them. That's why I count down out loud with Adrian when he pisses me off," I explain, and Gabriel chuckles.

"Maybe I should start doing that as well." He brushes his nose against mine, an exhausted sigh slipping past his lips. "You're not a conquest to me, mon tournesol. You're the person I care about most in the world, nothing less. You know that, right?" he asks, and I put my palms on each side of his neck.

"I know." His hands move onto my hips, pulling me against his chest. "But I don't know what to do," I finally admit to him, and he lifts his eyebrows in surprise.

"About what, chérie?"

"About us. Things are about to get very complicated with me traveling to Italy for training and you around the world for races. We're not dating, so I know I shouldn't be this scared of what being apart will do to us, but–" Gabriel cuts me off with a firm kiss.

"I'm yours, Valentina Esmèe Cèlia Romana, all yours. No matter how you want me, I belong to you and you alone. I'll fly to Italy as much as you need me to, hell, I'll move there," he says, making a little laugh escape me, but he grabs my face to make me refocus. "You know how I feel about you, and I know how you feel about me. We will make it work," he says, and a blush settles on my cheeks, heating them up.

"I'm yours," I whisper in response, and he picks me up off the ground to lift me into the air.

"No more running away?" he asks, and I shake my head.

"No more. I want this, I want us."

Gabriel kisses me all over the face, making me giggle uncontrollably. It's taken us long enough to get here, and I hope more than anything that this pessimistic feeling in my stomach will be proven wrong. I don't doubt his feelings for me or mine for him, but life has a way of finding ways to hurt us when we expect it least.

Please, don't hurt us.

Chapter 11

Gabriel

My team and I are doing our routine track walk with Adrian's right behind us. Someone, and I wish I knew who, thought it would be a good idea to give him and his performance coach scooters. They've been battling each other for the last two kilometers, always interrupting my team and me when we try to talk about basics and strategies.

"Focus, would you?" I call out in French when he zooms past me for the fifth time.

"Fuck off, would you?" he yells back, and I flip him off when he turns around to roll back to his team.

He blows me a kiss, and I think about stealing the scooter from him both because he's distracting and because he makes it look like a lot of fun.

"Gabriel, watch this curb at the end of turn twelve, okay?" Tomasso, my strategist, says, pulling me out of my thoughts. I assure him I will, making a plan in my head to try out different ways to avoid it during free practice tomorrow.

"Watch out!" Adrian warns as he speeds down the straight again, this time with Leonard by his side instead of his performance coach.

Surprise settles in my chest as I watch the Brit race against my teammate on the little scooter. Leonard takes his job more seriously than any of us, never getting distracted in any way, shape, or form. This side of him, the laughing, playful one, is someone only Adrian brings out. They have a special bond I wish I knew more about. Out of all the drivers, Leonard chooses to be himself around my teammate. It tugs on my curiosity, but it's none of my business, so I don't ask.

When we get back to the pit box, Valentina is talking to one of the engineers, smiling while telling him a story. He laughs at whatever it is, bending over to let it out. No one, and I mean absolutely no one, should be as good-hearted as her. The way she speaks to everyone, managing to brighten up their days is something I've never seen before.

Then, her eyes drift to mine, her smile no longer directed at anyone other than me. *Fuck, she adores me. She's all mine.*

"How was the walk?" she asks when I'm in front of her, but I capture her lips with mine.

A little giggle escapes her, warming everything inside of me. My day might be long and tiring, but a single kiss from Valentina works like a shot of espresso.

"Good, except Adrian forgot how to be a grown-up for the entire duration of it," I explain loud enough for my teammate to hear.

"I'm sorry I know how to have fun. You should try it once in a while," he says and places his hands on his car to check something his engineer is pointing at.

"Riding scooters is not the kind of riding I prefer either," Val chimes in, knocking the air out of my lungs. I fucking love it when she's dirty.

"Now that sounds like fun," I reply, guiding her against my chest by placing my hands on the small of her back and applying the slightest amount of pressure.

She gives me a naughty smirk, licking her lips before speaking again. A little move like that, and my cock pushes against my tight jeans, my body begging me to find a private room with her.

"Yeah, horseback riding is my favorite," she whispers before kissing my jaw and attempting to walk away.

I manage to take her hand, spinning her around once and then bringing her against my torso again. Val is smiling from ear to ear, fully aware of the effect her words and actions have on me.

"You drive me crazy," I whisper in French and let go in case she wants to leave again, but she doesn't. She presses her hands against my stomach, biting her bottom lip.

"I know," she replies and steps back. "What are you going to do about it?" she challenges, and I'm about to throw her over my shoulder when Tomasso drags my attention away from Val. A knowing smile spreads over her face while I'm forced to focus on my job again.

By the time I'm done discussing technical things with my strategist, Valentina has fallen into a conversation with Adrian and Daniel, his performance coach. I sit down on the chair in my box, taking out my sketchbook to try and capture how beautiful she looks. It's impossible, but I always have a lot of fun taking a shot at it anyway.

"I can't believe you two are dating. I should buy her a pair of glasses," Cameron says, and I shake my head with a chuckle.

"Did you just come here to insult me?" I ask, and he crosses his arms in front of his chest, staring down at my drawing. I tilt my sketchbook toward him so he can see better.

"Why else would I be here?" he teases with a smile so contagious, I can't help but return it.

"Asshole," I mumble, and he lets out a laugh. Cameron squats down in front of me, his phone in his hand as he spins it around, a nervous habit of his. "What's going on?" I ask, putting my notebook and pencil away to focus on him.

"My team found a problem with the engine. I dunno if it's fixable until Saturday," he explains, and I give him a comforting look.

"They will, don't worry. You know how hard our teams work. They're incredible and deserve a little more faith from you," I almost scold, and he looks up at me with furrowed brows.

"Valentina really did a number on you. You didn't use to be so positive. It's frightening," he says, and I give his knee a nudge. It throws him off balance, making him grab my legs to keep from falling.

"Don't be an ass," I say, helping him stay upright and laughing with him.

"An arse? Me? Never," he replies, and I give him a playful frown.

"You made me get a tattoo on my butt cheek when I was drunk! I think that counts," I defend with amusement in my voice.

"First of all, we were both drunk, and, secondly, can you imagine how stupidly in love you were with Val to do that to yourself? And, now, you're dating her," he points out, and the corners of my mouth lift before I can stop them.

"It hasn't changed how much I care for her, only that I get to prove it to her now," I say and grab my sketchbook again, my attention shifting to Valentina. She grins at Adrian, who is obviously joking around, like always.

"Don't fuck it up, mate. There will never be anyone that can compare to Val, and, if you break her heart, I will destroy you," he says and stands up, making me tilt my head backward to look at him.

"I'm pretty sure Adrian should have that talk with me," I tease, but Cameron doesn't even crack a smile.

"There is nothing I wouldn't do to protect her, Gabriel. You're my best friend, but so is Val." I give him a reassuring nod.

"You have full permission to destroy me if I mess things up," I say, and he gives my head a pat, shaking it from side to side.

"I hope it'll never come to that." *Neither do I.*

Chapter 12

Valentina

I'm sitting in Adrian's box, praying the start will be just as good as the Qualifying. My brother got pole yesterday with Gabriel in second, Kyle Hughes in third, James in fourth, and Jonathan Kent in fifth. Eduardo, who I haven't spoken to since I ended our agreement, is in sixth, right in front of Cameron and Leonard.

All of the drivers are lined up on the grid, waiting for the green light to take the formation lap. They need to warm up their tires to have more grip and charge their cars' batteries before the start. Meanwhile, the nervous feeling in my chest is spreading until it's everywhere, and I can't sit still anymore when they line up again.

The lights go out, and Adrian gets a great start, but not as good as Gabriel, who pushes past him and moves into the first position. Kyle and Jonathan crash into each other and fall out in the first corner. Thankfully, it is not a bad crash and both drivers make it out without an injury. Their cars, however, are wrecked. I know the Mercedes team is probably cursing and screaming right now, but my full attention is on the small screens.

"Oh my God, everyone! Look who it is! Valentina Romana," a familiar voice says, sounding more condescending and sarcastic than anyone I've ever met.

I turn my head and almost lose my composure. I don't reply nor do I let him know how surprised I am to see him here. I keep it all inside as my mind screams at the universe for bringing this man back into my life.

"How've you been, beautiful?" he asks next, making terrible shivers run down my spine.

"I was great," I start and then look him up and down, placing a disgusted expression on my face. "Now I wish I was anywhere else in the world," I go on, focusing on the screens again.

"Don't be like that. I'm very happy we get to see each other," the prince says, but I roll my eyes.

"Well, then that makes one of us." The hatred I have for this royal brat is beyond any I've ever felt. He has this way of annoying me until I explode.

"Come on, Tina, don't give me the cold shoulder. I've missed you," he says and takes a step toward me, still keeping enough distance so I can't 'accidentally' kick him in the shin. Not that I would, considering he's a royal and I'd get arrested for touching any of his white-blonde bleached hairs.

"It's Valentina to you, Christian," I remind him because I don't like his nickname for me, I never have.

"Then it is 'Your Royal Highness' to you," he replies, and I shake my head. He's already pissing me off, and we've barely spoken three words. *How am I going to make it an entire season in one academy with him?*

"Isn't there someone else you can blind with your box-dyed hair, *Your Royal Highness?*" I ask, annoyed, and his brown eyes go wide. Amusement sparkles in them as he crosses his trained arms in front of his chest.

"There is no one better than you," he says, and I'm barely able to keep my palm from connecting with my forehead.

The rest of the fifty-six laps in the Spanish Grand Prix, the third race of the season, goes by but slowly so. Luckily, Christian leaves me alone for the most part.

Adrian and Gabriel are a couple of seconds apart now, and I watch James, who is battling with his teammate. Eduardo attempts to fight James' overtake, but my best friend's tires are younger, allowing him to move back into third place. Cameron somehow is up in fifth, and I'm hoping he will remain there.

After the longest one and a half hours of my life, Gabriel wins the race, Adrian comes in second, James third, Eduardo fifth, and Cameron sixth. I walk outside with the crowd of people and wait for the three most important men in my life to drive their cars to the first, second, and third place signs.

The first one to come is James, then Adrian, and lastly Gabriel. They all get out of their cars, and my brother walks over to where I'm standing with the rest of his crew to give all of us a hug. James moves to his team, but also comes to high-five me.

Meanwhile, Gabriel is getting out of his car and pulling his helmet off. He walks over to his engineers and mechanics, giving them hugs to celebrate. When he spots me on Adrian's side, he jogs over and grabs my face to plant his lips on mine.

It's a short kiss, a sweet one, that makes my body tingle. A blush settles on my cheeks, and I put my fingers to my lips as soon as he steps back. Gabriel brings a heartwarming, happy smile to his face, and I can't help but return it. I hardly ever get to see him this joyful.

He walks away to talk to the man, who is patiently waiting for him to do the post-race interview.

"Congratulations, Gabriel Biancheri," Günther Willhelm, a famous Formula One driver who has been retired for thirty years, says and pats my boyfriend's shoulder. Gabriel nods, his smile never fading. "You had good pace, a well-planned strategy, and this is your second win of the season."

"Yes, we had great pace overall this weekend, and although the tires lost grip toward the end, we made it over the finish line in one piece, and a one-two for the team, which is always a success."

They continue talking until Günther moves on to interview a disappointed Adrian. He's hiding his feelings better than I would have expected, but I see right through him, just like he would me.

My eyes drift over to Gabriel, who is now talking to James. When he catches me, he winks, and I melt. I feel like a fan in a crowd, catching the attention of a celebrity. No, I feel like I just grabbed the attention of the most handsome man I've ever met, and he winked at me, making my body react in all kinds of ways.

When the interviewer is done, all three boys whisper something to each other before they turn around to, not very subtly, blow a kiss at me. My face turns a bright red before I let out a small laugh. *My silly boys...*

They move onto the podium, and, soon, my home country's anthem plays through the speakers. Then follows the Italian one with everyone from the Ferrari team singing along. I'm smiling at the three idiots on the podium.

A wave of jealousy temporarily takes over my body when I think about how much I want to win a Grand Prix and stand on that podium. I push all those thoughts and every jealous feeling to the back of my mind to focus on how proud I am of Gabriel, Adrian, and James.

Each one of them receives their own trophy, and then they take out the champagne and start spraying it around, which is routinely done after every race.

The celebration is over soon, and I get pulled back inside by the crowd. I'm trying to find a way out of the cheering Ferrari team, but I'm struggling. Luckily, I feel a hand wrap around my wrist, and seconds later, I'm standing in front of Gabriel inside an empty room.

His mouth finds mine before I can even say a word. He tastes like champagne, and, for the first time in almost a year, I don't mind the taste of alcohol on my tongue. All I can think about is how addicting his full lips feel as they claim mine.

When he releases them, I have to hold onto his arms for support.

"That one just keeps going," I say when I can't stop my head from spinning. I hear Gabriel chuckle and bring my eyes to his. There is only pure happiness in them. "Congratulations on your win," I add, and he grins at me, flashing me his stunning dimples..

"Thank you, chérie," he whispers before he presses another kiss to my lips.

"So, where are we going to celebrate?" He purses his lips, and my mind drifts.

I don't know what he has planned, but I'd much rather take the celebrations back to our hotel. We finally have time to be alone, and I want to take advantage of it, to feel his hands all over my body. To have him study me while I memorize all of him. I want to touch him, make him moan my name over and over...

"Just a bar downtown," he replies, and I look at him with a confused expression.

"What?" I ask, not remembering my question from before.

"You asked where we are going to celebrate, and I told you a bar downtown, but if you prefer, we could also celebrate alone," he offers and presses his body against mine.

"Aren't you exhausted?" His hands drop to my ass before he grabs it, making an involuntary gasp escape me.

"Yes, but never too exhausted to pleasure you..." He trails off and lowers his head to my neck, nuzzling it to make me giggle.

"Okay, stop, you have to shower," I remind him, and he steps back, his bottom lip between his teeth.

"You don't want me all hot and sweaty?" he asks, and I bite the inside of my cheek before I respond.

"Not if that sweat doesn't come from us fucking all night long." A proud smile spreads over his lips, and I can't help the one on my face.

"You're so hot," he simply replies and smacks my ass. With one more kiss, he disappears from the room, probably taking a shower.

My mind roams, my heart throbs in my chest, and I smile from ear to ear. I run my fingers through my hair, trying to get it somewhat under control.

After a few minutes of consideration, I decide to go to the bathroom and figure out a way to make my outfit more 'bar' appropriate. I take out the small makeup bag in my purse and apply a thin line of black eyeliner to my lid. Then, I guide my red lipstick over my lips.

I pull my blouse out of my jeans and undo the first two buttons, then the last three. I take both ends and tie them together so the knot hangs just beside my belly button. My jeans and long-sleeved blouse don't reveal too much, even after I make some changes.

Without overthinking it any further, I step out of the bathroom and make my way to where I think Gabriel might be. He's wearing his team shirt and long black jeans, looking at the monitors in the conference room. His hair is messy, as always, but he's too gorgeous for his own good.

Gabriel walks out of the room, appearing to be in a rush. There is a team briefing after each race he has to go to, and it looks like he's late. His eyes scan my body, stopping him dead in his tracks.

"Wow," he says and steps toward me. "You're unbelievably beautiful, do you know that?" he asks, and I click my tongue.

"Tell me something I don't know, mon amour," I reply, and he lifts my chin to grab my entire attention. His eyes sparkle at the way I just addressed him.

"It doesn't matter how many times I look at you, you'll always have my heart racing," he says and gives me a peck on the lips.

He leaves the room too quickly for me to reply.

"I finally understand how you got into the academy. Your brother couldn't help you so you snatched yourself the other Ferrari driver. Glad he could get you a spot," Christian says from behind me.

I have no explanation for why my entire world comes crashing down on me from the thought or why tears sting my eyes. *What if the only reason they recruited me was because of Gabriel? Or Adrian? Or even worse, what if they bribed the team?* Anger consumes me as I turn to Christian Crovetto, but I don't stop it either. It laces hatred into my next words.

"Says the prince of Monaco, who merely had to snap his fingers to get a spot," I start and keep walking until I'm in his face. "I have worked harder than you've ever had to because society was built for you, for privileged white boys that treat women like incompetent, baby-making objects. Let me tell you something and listen closely now: you're nothing special. You may have a title, more money than you could possibly need, and an attitude problem, but you're nothing compared to me. I come from a family of racers, it runs in my blood. It fuels me, and I will have you choking on my fucking dust this season, Your Highness," I spit the last two words, but this man is smiling at me the entire time I speak.

"I'd rather have you choking on my dick, Tina," he replies, and it's my turn to smile then.

"I can't choke on something that doesn't exist." Amusement leaves his face, and I take a step back. "Sexually harass me again, and I won't be the one you'll have to deal with, the FIA will be." I walk away and back into the private room Gabriel and I were in earlier.

My knees cave in until I'm on the floor, my hands shaking as they cover my mouth to keep my sobs at bay.

I'm terrified he's right, that I wasn't enough and needed both Adrian and Gabriel to get into the academy. I hope Christian is wrong because my confidence has begun to fade, and it won't return if there's truth behind his speculations.

Chapter 13

Valentina

Time passes. I'm not sure how much, but my phone rings after a while, pulling me from my panic-filled trance. My brother's name flashes on my screen, and I hit the decline button. I don't want to speak to him. Doubts have taken over my mind, and he will drag them out of me if I talk to him.

No part of me is ready to deal with the answers to my questions, but someone steps into the room moments later.

"What happened, ma chérie?" Gabriel asks as he kneels down in front of me.

"Nothing," I lie, but my eyes shift from his face, and the tears I've been suppressing threaten to roll down my cheeks. "Did you have something to do with me getting accepted into the FDA?" I say, although it is the last question I want to be asking right now. Gabriel furrows his brows, confused about where this is coming from all of a sudden.

"What do you mean?" That's not a 'no'.

"Did you do anything that could have tipped the scales in my favor?" I clarify, and he shakes his head.

"I didn't do anything, it was all you, mon tournesol." Relief washes over me, and I take his hand to squeeze it. "The only thing I did was tell Colin Reiner you'd make a great addition to the team, but it was during a casual conversation we were having."

My heart stops for a brief moment before I drop his hand again and lean away from him.

"You did what?" I stand up to put more distance between us.

Panic washes over his face, settling in his eyes.

"I did nothing! He was already considering you, and I merely advocated. I promise all I did was tell him how talented you are," Gabriel assures me, but pain stings my chest now.

"Oh my God, Christian was right. You helped me get a spot."

Nausea bubbles up in my throat. I raise my hands when he tries to approach me, signaling for him not to get closer.

"Christian? Christian Crovetto? You're letting the royal with a walnut-sized brain get to you?" he asks, and the laugh that escapes me is out of my control. "Come on, chérie. Telling Colin you deserve a spot doesn't change the fact that you've earned this all by yourself. Unfortunately, this sport is all about connections, and I know everyone you'll be working with because I have worked with them before."

Grandfather used to tell me the same thing.

"I tell everybody you deserve a chance, even the lady at the coffee shop yesterday. She looked at me like I was crazy," he explains, making me laugh even more.

The tears finally drop while I close the distance between us.

"Please, don't let *His Royal Disgustingness* influence you. Adrian and I had nothing to do with your success. Christian wants to believe we did because he has a tiny, misogynistic brain. It can't process the fact that a woman is better than him," Gabriel explains, and I fling my arms around his neck.

"I'm sorry for getting so upset," I mumble, leaning my head against his chest, but he steps away quickly.

"You're apologizing now?" he asks before swearing in French and grabbing my face. "You're not the one who has to apologize. *His Nothingness* has to," my boyfriend tells me, and I chuckle at his name-calling.

"You're going to come up with all sorts of names for him, aren't you?" Gabriel gives me an easy smile, revealing his dimples.

"It comes naturally with a guy like him," he replies, and I nod.

"Agreed. After I told him to choke on my dust this season he told me he'd rather have me choke on his penis." A wave of disgust makes me shudder while Gabriel's eyes fill with fury.

"He said what?!" My brother's familiar voice fills my ears, and I turn around to find him in the doorframe, anger all over his face. "Okay, I've had it. I've hated that weasel from the day he became your rival, but this just took it too far. Give me a second while I go crush him like the bug he is," Adrian says, but my words stop him dead in his tracks.

"And deny me the pleasure of doing it myself through racing? Come on now, Adrian." He hesitates but then pushes his protective big brother side away to let his best friend one take charge.

"Fine, but if he says something along those lines again, I will kick him in his royal jewels," he replies, and I grab his arm to squeeze it reassuringly.

He's never doubted my ability to handle situations like these, but, when it comes to protecting me, there is hardly a line he won't cross. I know because it's exactly how I feel about him.

Cameron, James, Adrian, Gabriel and I decide to go to a restaurant. Leonard is the last to show, but, for some reason, he takes the empty seat beside mine. I give him a smile as he sits down, and, for the first time since I've met him, he somewhat returns it.

I can't linger on the moment too long when Cameron and my brother get into a heated discussion about who would be able to convince James to pierce his ears. I'm not sure how they even got here, but by the time dessert comes around, they finally settle on Cameron being the only one in our friendship group that can get us to do anything. Gabriel settles the debate when he tells them about his tattoo.

James almost chokes on his beer and Adrian's eyes are close to popping out of his head. I chuckle as they start bombarding him with more questions, but a soft touch on my arm shifts my attention to the owner of it.

"I know we haven't gotten along well, and that's mostly my fault, but I wanted to tell you how happy I am for you. I've been watching your career and your struggle for a while, and it's about damn time you got your shot," Leonard says, his brown eyes staring into mine.

"Thank you," I reply because I'm not quite sure what else to say. He's never been this open toward me, but I have a feeling this is the case for most people.

"But I also want to warn you. A lot of people will hate you for pursuing this dream, no matter what you do. They don't care how hard you work or about your talent. They will hate you because of who you are, and then add the fact that you are faster and stronger than most, it will make them furious. You're going to need an even thicker skin if you want to succeed," he says, and I nod, finally understanding him for the first time.

Leonard was the first black man to join a Formula One team. He's experienced discrimination and racism for the entirety of his career, and he's worried about me, a woman, joining a competitive driver academy.

"If you need anything, just know, I'm always here," he promises and takes my hand. "I make a pretty good mentor if I do say so myself." I bring a real smile to my face, my uneven heartbeat calming now.

"I couldn't ask for a better one, Leonard." He gives my hand one last squeeze before turning to my brother and starting a conversation.

My eyes drift to each of my friends, a sad feeling creeping into my chest as I think about how much I will miss traveling with them. Gabriel lifts his thumb to my face, running it over my bottom lip and leaning toward me.

"Soon, you'll travel around the world for your own races, ma chérie," he says, accurately reading why my mood has changed. "Until then, each and every one of us will do whatever we can to make you proud, especially me and that elephant-footed brother of yours." A small chuckle leaves me while he traces the shape of my mouth. "Mon tournesol," he mumbles more to himself than to me, and I lift my finger to push one of his curls backward.

"Mon soleil," I reply, and his face lights up.

He is my sun, the one that brightens up my life and helps me grow, and I can't believe he's mine.

Chapter 14

Gabriel

Jean has been avoiding me since our fight a week ago, hiding in his room whenever I get home from work.

As the big brother and the one that can't stand it when something's wrong between us, it's my job to make things right. I go upstairs, knocking on his door and waiting for permission to come in.

"Anyone but Gabriel may enter," he calls out, and I laugh as I step into the room anyway. If he wants to be a dick, fine, but I'm going to figure out what his problem is. "I thought I was clear, jerk, get out. I don't want to talk to you," he says while I lean against the doorframe, crossing my arms in front of my chest.

"What is your problem?" I ask because I don't understand how we went from brothers to enemies.

"You're my problem. Now, leave, I have schoolwork to do," he says, and I walk over to him, grab his folders, and storm out of the door.

If there's one thing that will make him spend the day with me, it's a threat to his homework. He takes it very seriously.

"Gabriel, give it back! I'm not playing around," he yells at me from his room, and I smile to myself.

"Come with me, and you'll get it back," I say, and he groans so loudly, it vibrates through the whole house. "Don't be like that. I want to show you something. You'll like it," I promise and move to where my Ferrari is.

I get in, throw his folder on the backseat, and wait for him to stop pouting. Moments pass, but, eventually, he rips my door open and drops down into the passenger seat.

"If you slam the door shut, I will tie you to the back of the car and make you walk," I warn because it is the only materialistic thing besides my books that means anything to me.

"Yeah, yeah, Jesus, you don't have to threaten me," he says, but we both know he would have slammed the door if I hadn't. "Where are you taking me?" he asks when I stay silent the whole drive.

"You'll see," I reply, pulling onto the street that leads to a secret path where Jean and I used to hike to a look-out point. We haven't been here since Dad died, which is probably why he doesn't remember it until we get out of the car.

"You think taking a walk is going to fix anything between us?" he spits as I shut my door.

"Fix what? You starting a fight with me about my intentions with Val? You walking in on us because you don't know how to wait for permission to enter a room? You ignoring and avoiding me for reasons you don't care to share with me? What the fuck, Jean?" I ask, but he storms down the path and toward the most beautiful view, besides Valentina, that I've ever seen, the view of my home country.

"We're broken, Gabriel. We can't love women like Valentina in the way they deserve. That's why I got mad at you! You're living in denial, and someone had to wake you up!" he yells as soon as I approach him.

Suddenly, everything makes sense to me.

"Who is she?" I ask, sitting down on the bench near the railing at the edge. Jean turns to me, surprise on his face.

"How did you–" He cuts off, closing his eyes and shaking his head. "I met her at university. Her name is Raegan, and I like her. I really like her, but, every time I get close to her, I panic. I run the other way, terrified of my feelings. I don't want to fall in love, but I'm afraid that's out of my hands whenever I'm with her. So, I mess it up, unwilling to let her get too close, even after she admitted how deeply she cares for me," he rants, and I take a deep breath, nodding along to his words.

I pat the seat next to me, and Jean sits down, his head dropping between his arms.

"I'm scared," he says, his words muffled because his mouth is turned away from me.

"You know, I only started dating Kira because I knew she'd never have the ability to break my heart. She was safe. Don't get me wrong, I did care about her, but I didn't love her just like she didn't love me. We were using each other as distractions, and it didn't end well."

He raises his head, listening to every word and waiting to hear exactly what he needs to right now.

"I've been in love with Valentina for years, but I was scared of my feelings, just like you are now. Let me tell you something important, something I wish I'd known before: running away is useless. She'll consume you either way, but you'll hurt both of you if you try to fight it. Don't do that, don't be that stupid," I say, and he lets out a harsh laugh.

"It doesn't change the fact that we're fucked up, Gabriel! How could we ever be the kind of men they deserve? How can we put them first if we're terrified of getting hurt? I can't feel any more pain, man. Is love really going to stop me from putting myself first when it comes down to it?" I can't help but smile at his question.

"I think you underestimate how powerful it is."

I stare at the ocean, searching for the right words to describe my feelings.

"It can swallow you whole until all you do is breathe for her. Valentina has consumed me, and I'd do anything for her, shield her from all the bad things in the world with my life. Yes, we've been hurt a lot, and I didn't think I was good enough for her either, but I wanted to be, so I try my best every day. That's how you become the right man, that's what you need to do," I explain, and Jean covers his face with his hands, groaning against them.

"I'm scared," he repeats, and I slide my hand onto his shoulder.

"But that's what makes you feel alive. You can't hide from life, and I don't want you to. Allow yourself to be a little vulnerable, not as recklessly as me, but, still, at least a little," I say with a laugh that he returns.

"I'm sorry for being a dick to you. I guess I was struggling with all of this and let it out on you," he replies, and I get up again, stretching on the spot.

"I'm not upset with you, Jean. I'm glad we've worked everything out and get to move on from this."

He stands up too, wrapping his arms around me.

"Alright, let's go home. Domi and Nicolette wanted to have a family dinner tonight," I remind him, and we make our way back to the car, leaving our fight on the bench at our former favorite spot.

Chapter 15

Valentina

In two days, I will be on a plane to Maranello. Adrian has been preparing me mentally for what I can expect, but he's only scared me this far. It's a good kind but scared nonetheless.

Gabriel and I haven't spent any time together since we came back from Spain a few days ago. He's been busy with training and family responsibilities, but I, annoyingly enough, miss him a lot. I asked if he had time yesterday, but Domi had already requested for him to go to an ultrasound appointment with her.

I sit up in bed, stretching and putting on Gabriel's shirt, which I should probably return. My legs are sore as I make my way down the stairs, and I have to stop halfway to laugh through the pain.

Maybe I'm pushing myself too hard, but knowing I'll be training with Christian Crovetto is enough motivation to drive me past my limits.

I eventually make it to the bottom of the staircase, walking toward my kitchen, when my heart skips a beat. Gabriel is singing and dancing along to *From Angels to Devils*, his favorite band. The urge to grab my phone and film this moment so I can look at it over and over again is appealing, but I can't prevent the words from spilling out.

"What are you doing here?" I ask, a smile creeping onto my face when he spins around to look at me.

A grin that reveals his dimples dances onto his face, heating up his cheeks. I caught him off-guard, but he doesn't seem embarrassed, merely amused.

"I'm here to make you breakfast and spend the day with you," he replies. "I make the best waffles. Trust me, Jean asks me to make them at least ten times a month," he jokes, and I laugh as I make my way to the high chair at the kitchen island.

"Well, don't oversell them. You like to make something seem really good, but it often is very disappointing. You know, *like some things*," I tease, and he cocks an eyebrow.

"If we measure disappointment by the number of times you've fallen apart under my touch, I must be the most disappointing man on the planet." My mouth drops, and he gives me a naughty smirk. "You're not the only one who can play this game." Excitement heats up my face because I'm too turned on to hide how his words affect me.

"I'm happy you're here," I admit as he walks over to the fridge.

"There is no place I'd rather be, ma chérie."

His gaze drops from my eyes to my lips as his teeth capture his bottom one between them, making my body ache for him. His eyes drop to the shirt covering my body, a satisfied little smirk slipping onto his features before he goes back to cooking.

I watch Gabriel's muscles as they flex with every movement of his. There must be a little bit of drool dripping from my mouth because I am fantasizing about all the different things we could do, the way his body would feel between my legs.

"Valeeentttinnnaaaa," he sings, waving his hand in front of my face.

"What?" I ask, stunned he said my name like that.

"I've been asking if you want strawberries on your waffles for the past two minutes." He chuckles, and a blush settles on my cheeks.

"Oh," I say, a small smile creeping onto my lips. "Yes, I would love some," I tell him, and he grins.

"Okay then."

Gabriel gets back to his waffles, and I distract myself by setting the table. If I keep looking at his trained arms, I might go crazy.

I walk over to where he is, taking a freshly washed and cut strawberry before popping it into my mouth. Gabriel watches me closely, his gaze stuck on my face. I run my tongue over my bottom lip, making his eyes widen ever so slightly.

"Stop," he begs, and I give him an innocent look.

"I'm not doing anything," I defend, and he shakes his head.

"Trust me, you are doing something."

I bite my lip to keep from smiling. I love having the same effect on him as he has on me, especially when he points it out.

"Oh, how's Domi?" I say and reflexively smack his stomach when I realize I haven't asked about his pregnant aunt yet. It's a soft slap, but, of course, he makes a big deal out of it.

"Oh man, go get the emergency kit. I think you might have broken a rib." He bends over, breathing heavily. I frown at him, and he straightens out his back again, smiling like an idiot. My idiot.

"You're so weird," I tell him, and he shrugs.

"That's who I am, and we're dating, so that also makes you weird."

I give him a confused expression, waiting for an explanation, but he doesn't give me one. All he gives me is a stupid, sexy smirk.

I forget what we were talking about almost instantly.

"Was my point so strong it made you speechless?"

"Just finish breakfast, would you?" I tease, and he laughs.

"Yes, dear," he replies as if we're some married couple.

Gabriel's waffles are as delicious as he promised them to be. They're fluffy, full of flavor, and the strawberries go well with the vanilla taste. He's sitting directly next to me at the table, which is why it's hard for me to concentrate on anything other than his face. Luckily, I can play it off, pretending I'm just listening to him talk.

I pick up the last piece of my waffle with my fingers and place it in my mouth. Syrup drips from them, catching his attention. He takes my hand in his, lifts it to his lips, and then my index finger disappears into his mouth. I press my legs together when my most sensitive area starts to tingle from his hot mouth on my skin.

A whimper escapes my throat before I can help myself. He smiles before letting go of my index finger and doing the same to my middle one. His eyes are focused on mine, studying my reaction.

"You like that?" he asks when he lowers my hand again.

I nod, unable to speak or calm my body.

"How about this?" he continues, his lips brushing over the back of my hand, then my arm until he can't reach further, and gets up to put his lips on my neck.

His right hand settles on my left cheek, and his thumb tilts my head so he can have more access to my throat. My body is on fire, and I'm ready for him to take me upstairs and continue this on my bed.

"No, no, no, no, no," Adrian says from behind us, and Gabriel backs away as soon as he hears my brother. "I don't want to see that, especially not at the table where I have breakfast," he continues, and I get up from my seat, taking Gabriel's hand in mine.

"Fine, we'll go upstairs," I tell my brother before I lead Gabriel past him and up the stairs. "Let's go take a shower," I say, and he follows me without hesitation.

I lift Gabriel's shirt over my head and let it fall down to the ground. I'm about to slide down my pants when his hand covers mine and his other moves to my hip.

"Let me," he whispers into my ear, and I let my arms drop.

Gabriel guides my hair to the side before he trails kisses down my neck, shoulder, and back. He tugs down my pants and underwear in one swift movement. There are shivers all over my body, driving me crazy.

He turns on the water while I do my best to control my need to be close to him. When he gets underdressed, my eyes linger on his moon tattoo. He spins around before my eyes are satisfied, so I focus on the dates on his hip instead, admiring the simple, black ink.

A faint scar catches my attention then. It runs down the outside of his left thigh.

"How'd you get that?" I ask, and his eyes follow my finger as I trail it along the mark.

"I don't lie to you, so I won't give you the excuse story I give most people, but I'm not ready to share this with anyone. I accidentally told Adrian once, and I don't think I can do it again at the moment. Is that okay?" he asks, and I bring my attention to his face.

"Of course. I understand."

As curious as I am, I would never be upset about something like this. If he's not ready now, he might be someday, just like me. There are things he doesn't know that I'm not ready to share, like my life with Aunt Carolina...

Gabriel pulls me under the water, letting it run over our heads and pressing his lips onto mine. His fingers slide over my hard nipples, making my body beg for more.

"I could spend all day in the shower with you," he admits, and I let out a small laugh as my hands run through his wet hair.

"Eventually, you'd have to go home, train, race, and all that kind of stuff," I remind him, and he smiles.

"But I'd come right back, and I'd stay as long as you want me to."

I think about his offer for a second. I would love for him to be here twenty-four hours a day, but I also need some time to myself, and I know he needs it too. Not to mention, there are responsibilities I have to take care of... *like helping out Evangelin in her store!* Damn, I forgot she asked for my help today.

"What, what is it?" Either my facial expressions always give me away, or this man knows me too well.

"I told Evangelin I would help her out today, you know for the last time in a while. Saturday is always her busiest day of the week," I explain.

Gabriel bites the inside of his cheek, clearly thinking about what to do.

Without being able to help myself, I reach out and touch his cheek. His expression softens, and his thumb brushes over my left nipple. It's so soft and intimate, my body shudders in response.

"We'll go, and I'll finally meet the woman I've heard so much about," he assures me, and I smile brightly at him. "But first, let's clean you up. I wouldn't want Evangelin to have to endure the smell coming off you."

My mouth drops, and I swat his arm. Of course, he's laughing at his own joke, just like he always does.

"For that rude joke, no shower sex," I retaliate, and he frowns.

"Don't do that to me, chérie," he begs, but I simply shrug.

"Shouldn't have said I stink," I reply, and Gabriel lets out a short laugh. It's a punishment for both of us, but I want to make him sweat a little.

"Fine, have it your way," he mumbles and picks up my loofah. He's putting soap all over it before he turns to me and starts washing my body.

"I'm more than capable of doing that myself," I remind him, making him frown once more.

"You want to rob me of every pleasure, don't you? Should I close my eyes too?" he complains before pressing them shut and reaching out to touch me, pretending he can't see anything.

His hands move all over my face, and I burst into laughter.

"Fine. Wash me then."

A content grin covers his face, and I shake my head in disbelief. Gabriel picks up my shampoo before looking at my hair. He puts some in, realizes it's not enough, adds more, and then groans.

"Jesus, chérie, I think I might need the whole bottle," he tells me, and I laugh. "My hair needs a fifth of what yours needs."

Gabriel keeps applying the shampoo to my curly, thick hair, and I enjoy the head massage he gives me. His fingers are gentle, careful. He's doing his best not to get stuck on any knots in my hair. Meanwhile, I haven't found a way to stop smiling.

"An hour later, and I have finally finished washing your hair," he teases, and I roll my eyes, not keeping the grin off my face.

When he turns me around, I see he also has shampoo in his hair. I love the way it sticks out all over the place.

"What?" he asks when he notices me staring.

"You're cute," I reply, and he laughs, his hand reaching for his head.

"My hair is always messy, I don't see how this is different," he jokes, and I nod.

"It's not. It's always sexy." He cocks an eyebrow, his fingers snaking around my wrists to guide me against his chest.

"Are you flirting with me?" he asks, but his lips are barely a centimeter from mine, making it impossible for my brain to focus on finding words. Gabriel brushes them over my cheek and jaw before letting out a muffled moan. "Hmmm, I see," he adds and releases my wrists, taking a step back. My body has been lit on fire and not even the water in the shower can extinguish it.

Without another sound, he starts washing out the shampoo in my hair, then his. My head is still spinning, trying to catch up with what just happened and figure out why it was so hot.

I turn off the water, and Gabriel gets towels for us. He places one around his lower body, quickly dries his hair, and then wraps one around me.

"Oh man, this is going to take another hour, isn't it?" He laughs, and I chuckle.

"Yes, now, dry my hair."

"As you wish, *Lady Valentina.*" I almost burst into laughter.

Gabriel does as he is told, but it only takes a few minutes until it doesn't drip as much anymore.

He takes my hand and leads me into my room. My heart is racing in my chest, and I don't have the power to calm my body. I sit down on the edge of my bed, and Gabriel kneels down in front of me, his hands sliding onto my naked thighs.

"You're the only one I'll ever kneel for," he says, his lips brushing over my thigh. I roll my head, a satisfied moan leaving me. "I want to taste you."

The words send shivers down my spine. Everything starts to tingle as excitement runs through my veins.

"We don't have a lot of time," I reply, but his burning gaze excites me more.

"I only need a minute," he assures me, and my breathing hitches. "I want you to come all over my tongue." *Fuck.*

His finger rubs over my clit, and I realize he's right. It won't take him long.

"Please," is the only thing I manage to say.

Gabriel smirks, his eyes on mine as he spreads my legs. He pulls my towel off and moves between my thighs, his lips firmly claiming mine. His tongue slips into my mouth, and I let out a small moan when his index finger runs over my swollen clit again.

"I'm yours," he mumbles between kisses.

I want to say it back, but my mind is preoccupied with how good his finger feels. All my voice does is form a moaning sound.

"You're mine," he says while making his way down, placing kisses all over.

"With everything I am."

He guides my legs over his shoulders before pulling me closer to the edge of the bed in one swift movement. A gasp leaves me as anticipation continues to grow with each second. His lips brush over the inside of my thighs, tracing my stretch marks.

"So soft, so perfect," he mumbles, and I smile to myself.

Gabriel looks up at me right before he presses his lips to my most sensitive area. My eyes flutter shut and my head falls back on the bed. He starts off with a simple kiss on my clit, but then his tongue takes over, and I can't hold back the noises of pleasure that continue to leave my lips.

With every sound, his movements pick up speed. His wet, hot tongue feels euphoric, but when he adds a finger and creates a perfect combination of friction and pressure, I have to grab the sheets for support.

"Oh fuck, Gabriel," I moan, my hips pushing off the bed, but he presses them back down.

His lips wrap around my clit, tugging on it and making my eyes roll into the back of my head. I slide my hands into his hair, holding on tight as his mouth brings a new kind of pleasure to my entire body. I can feel it all the way in my toes, making them curl.

His tongue slips inside of me before it swipes over my aching clit again, bringing tension to my stomach. Gabriel keeps going, and I scream for him.

My orgasm blindsides me, originating in my stomach and moving to my chest where my heart pumps it through my veins. I buck my hips, trying to savor this feeling of pleasure for as long as I can while my mind drifts back to its familiar high.

Gabriel presses a kiss to my stomach before he lies down next to me. I don't even notice I'm covering my face until Gabriel removes my hand. He presses a kiss to the back of it and then places it on his naked chest.

"Didn't even need the full minute," he says, and a breathless laugh escapes me.

No, he most certainly did not.

Chapter 16

Valentina

My heart rate skyrockets before we step into Evangelin's store. I need both of them to get along, and I'm afraid of how she will react when she sees Gabriel. So far, there has always been something off when I talked about him, and, even though I don't know what it is, it makes me worry.

The handsome man next to me grabs my hand, clearly also nervous. As soon as I feel his fingers intertwine with mine, I relax.

"Are you okay?" The words leave my lips and catch his attention.

His gorgeous face is making all kinds of worried expressions, and I smile to comfort him.

"She's going to love you," I assure him and pull our hands to my mouth, pressing a kiss to the back of his. "Just behave yourself," I tell him, but he frowns at me in response.

Before we can both panic and overthink things any more, I open the door to Rush and lead Gabriel inside. No one is at the store because it is too early, and Evangelin is hanging clothes on the racks. When she sees us, a beautiful grin spreads over her tired face.

"It's a pleasure to meet you, Gabriel." She holds out her hand for him, and he takes it, a polite smile on his face.

"The pleasure is all mine," he says, and it warms my heart. It is riveting to hear the French words fall off his lips.

Evangelin nods at him before bringing her attention to me.

"You should be getting ready to leave for Italy," she scolds, and I give her half a frown.

"I'm not leaving you alone on the busiest day of the week." She takes my hand in hers and squeezes it. "And I've brought reinforcements. Gabriel is going to help us," I assure her.

"Thank you, for everything you do for me and my store. I've been trying to hire someone to help out, but I've been struggling." The small woman in front of me is about to cry when she catches herself and starts explaining to my boyfriend what he could do to be useful. Meanwhile, I set up everything by the cash register to be prepared for our customers.

As soon as the first one walks in, Evangelin moves to greet them. The person asks her for a couple articles of clothing, and I cash them out soon after. More and more people come and, within an hour, the store is full. It's difficult to keep up with all the customers and their demands, but all three of us do our best.

Every now and then, I look over at Gabriel, who is doing much better than I would have expected. He's helping mostly men, although a lot of women walk over to him, asking for his help. I'm a bit worried about what they're asking him because his face is a deep red, and he seems to get uncomfortable sometimes. Luckily, the queue decreases soon enough, and I walk over to release Gabriel from a middle-aged woman, who is clearly asking him questions he seems unsure how to answer.

"I bet your girlfriend appreciates your great fashion sense," the woman says in English, which surprises me, but also doesn't distract me from the task at hand: protecting Gabriel.

Her fingers lift to his arm, and she squeezes it. His eyes find my face, and I see relief wash over him.

"Yes, I do," I reply, making the woman turn around. "I would also appreciate it if you would not touch my boyfriend without his consent."

The woman drops her hand, embarrassment in her gaze. She mumbles a quick 'sorry' before she moves away and toward Evangelin. I bring my focus to Gabriel, whose smile is bigger than ever before.

"Are you okay?"

"More than," he replies. "You have no idea how long I've been waiting for you to call me that." His lips find mine before I can reply. It's a short kiss, but it still makes my knees weak. "I'm going to get some coffee." I don't even have to tell him my order, he knows that my favorite drink is an iced vanilla latte. He says it out loud before giving me another brief kiss and walking over to Evangelin.

The store is almost completely empty when Gabriel leaves, and I check the time. My legs are already tired from standing for the past four hours. I sit down on the chair next to the cash, and Evangelin comes up to me, her grin making me nervous. I attempt to get up so she can sit, but she pushes me down onto the chair again.

"Gabriel is very sweet," she says, and, suddenly, her grin is contagious. "I'm glad the two of you have figured everything out. He seems to make you happy." She pulls her hair into a bun, and I don't know what to say at first.

"He does, he makes me happy, frustrated, crazy," I admit, smiling to myself. "I don't understand it, but I love it." I hide my face behind my hands and let the embarrassed blush settle on my cheeks.

"I can see that. You don't know how delighted I am for you, Valentina. Your love story has just begun. There are going to be many more ups and downs, and you have to realize relationships take work. You can't give up after every single fight, but you also can't let things pile up. Communicate with him and make sure you always talk about things that bother you. If you don't, you might end up getting sick of each other. Trust me, Carlos and I have been at a point before where we weren't communicating, and we broke up. It took us one messy year to find our way back to each other. So, remember, communication is very important," she says, and I nod.

"Thank you. I don't know what I would do without you and your wisdom," I admit, and she blushes.

"Stop it," she says, and I laugh a little. "Are you ready to start training?" Evangelin asks next, making me feel nervous again.

"I've been ready since my grandfather took me on my first run."

Gabriel steps back through the door, a tray with three coffees in his hand. He presses a kiss to the top of my head, and we fall into a casual conversation. He asks Evangelin about Carlos and her shop. She happily tells her story, and I decide to look around to see if there is anything I want to buy.

I scan the racks, and something catches my eyes. It's an evening gown with the most unique pattern of flowers that stretches from the bottom of the dress all the way across the chestal area in one line. The rest of it is white, highlighting the different colors of the floral pattern. It has a boat neck, and the more I study it, the fancier I realize it is. I don't know where I would ever wear this to, but I'll regret it if I don't buy this dress.

The price tag makes my heart skip a beat. It's more expensive than any other piece of clothing I have ever bought. It goes against my nature to carry it toward Evangelin, but I push past the feeling.

"Excuse me, ma'am, I would like to purchase this dress," I say, and she frowns at me.

"Since you called me 'ma'am', the price of it just doubled," she jokes, and I chuckle. "Just take it, dear, you've done so much for me, you deserve it." I shake my head as soon as she says it.

"No, I don't help you because I hope to get free clothes out of this. I help you because you're my friend. Now, I'd like to pay with my credit card," I inform her, and she sighs loudly.

"Okay, four hundred euros is your total," Evangelin says, and Gabriel's eyes widen.

"Let me pay," he offers, but I shake my head.

"No," I say, making him frown.

"Chérie, this is nothing for me, but you need to save your money."

I ignore his comment, digging around in my wallet to get my card. His hand slips around my wrist, stopping my movements.

"Let me pay, please. It's a selfish request, I promise. I like buying you things, especially dresses I will rip off your body," he goes on, whispering the last sentence.

I stretch my lips into a thin smile, but the blush on my cheeks reveals how much I like the image he has planted in my mind. Gabriel smirks, satisfied he's on the verge of convincing me.

"No," I repeat, firmer this time.

"Fine. I won't rip it off you then," he says, and, for a brief moment, I think about letting him pay just so he will do so.

I shake my head and insert the card, ignoring his upset expression. Grandpa has left me money, more than enough to live on until I earn my own. I hate spending any of it on something other than a necessity, but if I don't buy it now, Gabriel will.

"You can wear the dress to the Ferrari unveiling event of their new sports car. Adrian and I have to attend it next week," Gabriel lets me know as soon as we leave the store. "Would you like to go with me? As my date?" he says, and I bite the inside of my cheek.

"I would love to. Just to clarify, does that mean you are going to pick me up, drive me there, make me feel amazing the whole night?" He chuckles but also nods. "I never went to prom or any dance," I admit, and he squeezes my hand, which has been resting in his ever since we started walking.

"Neither did I." He steps in front of me to stop me from going any further. "I will give you the full experience," he says, his hands grabbing my hips and pulling me close to him. I focus on his bottom lip, which is tucked between his teeth.

"Oh, and what is the full experience?" I ask, desperate for more information.

His eyes drift from my face, and he touches his tongue to the roof of his mouth. I tug on his shirt, waiting for him to answer.

"It's in Rome, so I can pick you up in Maranello and we can drive there. We will probably stay in the same room so I'll be able to take you to the event and spend the whole night trying to find a way to touch you inappropriately without anyone noticing." I smile and my head drops, but he lifts it again, forcing me to make eye contact. "Then, I will take you back to the hotel room and make love to you all night long..." He trails off, his eyes fixating on my lips. My whole body tingles with excitement as I imagine it. "Not being able to touch you constantly today has been driving me crazy, but thank you for bringing me. I loved meeting Evangelin, she's great."

He got along with her, and they like each other. A weight lifts off my shoulders, and after today, I'm sure I was just imagining the weird expression on Evangelin's face the first time she saw him. Gabriel's grip tightens on my hips, bringing me back into the moment.

"You make me really happy," he says, and, for the first time in minutes, I find my voice again.

"And you me, mon soleil," I tell him, making a smile spread over his full lips, which exposes his gorgeous dimples. I lift my hand to his face, my index finger touching the one on his left cheek. "I love those damn dimples of yours," I admit, making a blush settle on his cheeks.

"I love the ones on your lower back," he replies, and it's my turn to blush.

I had no idea I had them, but the fact that he likes them makes me adore them too.

"Let's go home, ma chérie." The way he says the word 'home' sounds right. I don't know what it is, but I push the ridiculous feeling to the back of my mind.

It's not time for that... *yet.*

Chapter 17

Gabriel

"I fucking hate board game night. Who suggested we play Monopoly?" Adrian asks, and I cover my mouth to keep him from hearing my chuckle.

"You did, goldfish brain," Valentina responds, and everyone at the table starts laughing at her nickname for Adrian. He glares at her, but it fades the longer he listens to her laughter.

"Roll the bloody dice and stop complaining, would you?" James chimes in.

Cameron stares down at his phone, a serious look on his usually happy face. I lean toward him, worry settling in my chest.

"Is it your Mom again?" I ask, and he looks up at me, placing his index finger to his mouth to remind me he doesn't want anyone, especially Val, to know.

Cameron sees himself as the only person in her life who isn't a burden, that relieves some of the pressure and tension. He doesn't want her to know his mother keeps disappearing. Not because he thinks she wouldn't understand, I don't believe anyone would assume that about Valentina. He simply hates the thought of making her worry.

His mom shows up every once in a while, but only to tell Cameron everything is his fault because he left to focus on his career. Maybe part of him believes her and that's why he doesn't tell Val; he doesn't want her to think he's as bad as her father was.

In reality, he still takes care of his family as much as he can, providing them with anything and everything they could ever ask for. Since his father left to start a new life with his secretary, all the family responsibilities somehow fell onto his shoulders.

"She came home and screamed at my sister so, nothing new," he whispers while James and Leonard celebrate Adrian having to go to jail. "It's alright, don't worry, mate." I place my hand on his shoulder and give it a reassuring squeeze.

"Twice in a row? Fuck this game!" Adrian complains, and Cameron finally smiles again.

"You should just stay in there at this point," he tells my teammate, who flips him off without hesitation. The Australian grins before taking the dice to roll them and going straight into jail with Adrian.

"Shut up!" Adrian says before bursting into laughter. Cameron slaps his forehead with the palm of his hand and then shakes his head.

"I'll never hear the end of it now," he replies as Valentina brings his little plane figurine to the jail box.

She takes my hand in hers, guiding it onto her lap where I grab her thigh. Val clears her throat quietly, pressing her legs together as I squeeze harder. A smirk slips onto my face, and I run my thumb in circles near the inside of her thigh. She shifts in her seat, removing my fingers to grab my hand between both of hers.

"*Per favore, basta,*" she says to me when I try to slide them up her skirt. I cock an eyebrow and smile.

"Oh, you speak Italian now?" I challenge, but she doesn't understand it to that extent, at least not yet.

"*Solo un poco,*" she replies, using her Spanish to help her out and making me smile.

"I'll teach you," I promise in English, and she grins at me.

"I figured I should learn if I hope to drive for Ferrari one day," she explains, and I lean toward her to press a kiss to her lips. She tastes sweet, like the piece of watermelon she ate a moment ago.

"Yes, you should, chérie." Because one day, she will drive for them, and they adore the drivers that learn Italian for their team. It's why Adrian is taking lessons from me and the reason I studied it in school. I'll have Valentina fluent by the time she's part of the F1 team.

"Okay, this is getting ridiculous now. I'm spending all of my fucking money just to get out of jail," Adrian says, interrupting my thoughts.

Cameron is crying from laughter now, and Leonard is patting my teammate's back as comfort. James, on the other hand, is watching Val closely as she throws the dice and buys yet another property. When he notices me catching his dreamy look, he shifts his gaze to the board.

God, I fucking hate him.

My arms have been wrapped around Valentina's body for a long time now, unable to let go and watch her drive away in the taxi. I want to go with her to Maranello, support her because I know how nervous she is, but Hector put his foot down. He told me to go to Silverstone and stop getting distracted, to put my job first. When I told Val about it, she agreed with my performance coach in a heartbeat.

"I'll miss you," she says, her fingers running over my back and sending shivers down my spine.

"I'll miss you," I reply and lean back to kiss her. My tongue slips into her mouth, and I have to hold back the sigh bubbling up in my throat when Valentina lets out a little moan. "Fuck my job," I say breathlessly, my hands moving to her ass to guide her more against my chest.

"I don't want to see that!" Adrian calls out from the taxi, and I lift my fingers to the small of her back where I know *her* dimples are. She grins at me and steps on her tiptoes to plant her lips on my jaw.

"We'll see each other sooner than later, you'll see," I assure both of us because we still haven't found a way to let go. "And whatever you do, please, be careful, mon tournesol. If anything happens to you, I–" I cut off because she runs her thumb over my bottom lip to distract my mind.

"I'm not the one racing in an F1 car this weekend," she replies, and I cock an eyebrow.

"No, but you're going to be in the same room as Christian, which is even more dangerous," I remind her, and she lets out a small laugh.

"Yes, for him." Valentina steps on her tiptoes to press one last kiss to my lips and then moves back, being the stronger one out of the two of us. "Please, be safe," she says, and I dig my hands into my pockets.

"You too, chérie," I reply as she gets into the taxi and drives off into her new life.

Chapter 18

Valentina

"Would you stop that?" I hiss at Adrian when he eats his fifth cracker, making the loudest crunching noises I've ever heard.

This is not the first time today I've complained about something he's doing, which is, for some reason, bothering me all the way down to my bones.

"Okay, so, to summarize: I can't eat, drink, or breathe in your presence anymore. I'm going to sit over there now," Adrian says and attempts to get up, but I drag him back into his seat.

We're waiting for Colin Reiner to welcome the new and returning drivers. My brother insisted on coming along when he saw how nervous I was this morning. I asked him to travel to Maranello with me, and he assured me he could stay a day before flying to Silverstone for the fourth race of the season. James and Gabriel are already there, getting ready for the weekend despite their offer to join us here too. I didn't want to be the person with three emotional support people, one is enough.

"I'm sorry, it's not fair of me to act like this. Thank you for being here, but can you munch on those a little more quietly?" I ask, and he shakes his head with a chuckle.

Adrian fishes around in his pocket for a moment before taking out his phone and earphones. He places one bud in my ear and the other in his, playing a list of my favorite songs to calm me. It works like a charm, and I even take the cracker he hands me, ignoring the nauseous feeling in my throat.

"Hello, everyone, thank you for waiting. It's a pleasure to have you all here, ahead of this exciting new chapter of your life," Mr. Reiner says, his attention drifting to Adrian, who gives him a nod to tell him to go on without acknowledging his presence to the others.

I notice Christian didn't bother to show up today at the same moment he walks through the door.

"You're late, Mr. Crovetto," Mr. Reiner scolds, but the brat simply sits down at the back of the room.

"My bad. Had this annoying blonde in my room, who just wouldn't stop talking," he replies, and I shake my head. Mr. Reiner's eyes go wide, and Adrian sits up to face the prince.

"If you already find yourself annoying, how do you think we feel?" my brother asks, and everyone in the room bursts into laughter.

"That's enough, Mr. Romana, thank you. And Mr. Crovetto, if you could refrain from sharing your personal life with us, it would be greatly appreciated." The Royal Dickhead, a nickname I'm sure Gabriel will come up with too, leans back in his chair and balances it on two legs, smiling at the man in charge.

"What are you going to do about it?" Christian asks, challenging Colin Reiner.

"Me? Nothing. But they will," he replies before someone pushes the brat's chair back into place, on all four feet. "Drivers, meet Andrea Russo. They will be your instructor." Andrea is staring at Christian, their arms now crossed in front of their chest.

"You may be a royal in Monaco, but, here, you are a trainee. You listen to me and obey my commands, not the other way around. Piss me off, and I will have your royal ass kicked out of the academy before you can say the word 'sorry'. Understood?" Christian makes no sound or movement except for a single nod, and I grin from ear to ear. "Glad to see we're on the same page then," they add and give his shoulder a squeeze. "You may call me Andrea unless you get on my nerves, then it is Boss Russo to you. I will be your instructor, coach, and, if I do this right, friend for the duration of the season."

They make their way to the front where Mr. Reiner is standing, a content expression on their young face. Andrea can't be older than mid-thirties, their hair is cut into a bob, and the brown color compliments their tanned skin and brown eyes.

"You can leave now. I'm in good hands," I say to Adrian, who keeps checking the time on his phone.

"Are you sure?" he asks, and I lean over to kiss his cheek.

"I love you. Please, be safe this weekend." He assures me he will be before walking toward the exit.

I watch him shoot a deathly glare at Christian, who even leans away out of fear. Adrian looks over his shoulder to wink at me, and I mouth a 'thank you', although the biggest thank you should go to Andrea. I doubt Christian ever got put in his place as hard as he was just now.

"Training will include workouts, simulator time, mental preparation, and more I won't bore you with right now. You will be assessed every single day for the ultimate end goal: getting you a spot in your desired field." Andrea grabs a chair, settling down on it as they address us. "I will be brutally honest with those of you hoping it will happen like this," they say and snap their fingers. "Currently, there is one open position in Formula Three. We will have to make the hard decision in a few weeks' time to pick one of you. I know you don't all want to race in Formula Three. As I understand, currently, we only have two candidates interested," Andrea says, and I hold my breath.

Please, don't let it be him, please, not him. Anyone but Christian.

"Ms. Romana and Mr. Crovetto." *I'm going to fucking lose it.*

"Fuck," I say, louder than I intended, but only the person in front of me hears it. They turn around, and I realize it's Luciana Sanchez.

"Yeah, I get it. I wouldn't want to be up against him either," she says with a thick Spanish accent, and I let out a breathy laugh.

"I've been battling against that royal douchebag since I was a kid," I explain, and she gives me a sympathetic smile.

"Don't worry, his behavior has gotten him kicked out of three other academies. This one won't be different."

A strange feeling in my gut tells me it will be because I'm here. Christian Crovetto was put on this Earth to torture me, *why else would all of this be happening?*

"I'm Luciana, but I prefer Lucie," she says and holds out her hand for me to shake.

"Valentina but call me Val, everyone except *His Highness* does." Sensing that I was speaking about him, he waves his fingers at me. "I've never wanted to punch someone so much," I say through gritted teeth, making Lucie laugh.

"I will help you keep your distance from him." I thank her before our attention drifts back to Andrea.

"Okay, everyone, let's go. I'd like to show you around the Ferrari headquarters."

We follow behind them through hallways with photographs of famous former drivers. Andrea brings us to where the rows of old Ferrari F1 cars are. The last time I was here, my father had taken Adrian and me. I tried to touch one of them, earning me a furious lecture from my father. He even smacked my hand away in the moment, and I remember Adrian 'blowing the pain into the stars' before holding it the entire way back to our car. We were six and ten at the time.

I refocus on the cars, yet again fascinated by how much they have evolved. My feet bring me to the one my father drove during the year of his championship title, making a sad feeling spread through my chest.

"Your father's?" Andrea interrupts my thoughts, and I force a smile at them.

"Yes, it was," I reply and step back, away from the vehicle. My attention drifts further up the line toward Grandfather's car. "That one was my grandpa's," I say, and they give my arm a comforting squeeze.

"When I was younger, I always cheered for your father. He made me realize I wanted to become a race car driver," they explain, and I nod absent-mindedly.

"That makes two of us." And neither one of us had gotten any help from him when he was alive.

We stroll toward the cases of trophies next, past the row of helmets and portraits of Ferrari drivers. Gabriel's catches my attention, and I smile at his handsome face, the dimples causing a warmth to spread through my chest.

Someone beside me makes a vomiting sound, but I don't have to turn my head to know it's Christian.

"The love in your eyes is revolting to me," he says while my gaze stays on my boyfriend's photo.

"Revolting is exactly what I think when I look at you," I reply, and Andrea lets out a single laugh before catching themself and telling us to follow them again.

The tour continues past a room with desks, where Andrea tells us we will be learning how to analyze data and come up with strategies for races. It ends at the fitness and wellness floor. There are a dozen treadmills, bench presses, weight and neck training stations, and so on. I'm both terrified and excited when I think about this becoming my place of working out for the foreseeable future.

"Alright, everyone. That's it for today. I will see you tomorrow, bright and early for training," Andrea announces while handing out the schedule for the week, and all nine of us make our way back downstairs toward the exit.

My eyes study the paper to see we will be training for a little over a week straight, from Wednesday to Thursday, and then we have off until Tuesday the week after. It's a strange schedule, but I have a feeling Gabriel is responsible for it. I have time to go with him to the car unveiling event next week, which makes this a little too convenient. The chances of Andrea making this schedule to perfectly fit my plans are slim to none. I shake my head when I realize it was definitely Gabriel who requested it to be this way.

I turn around as I walk out the door to study the red color of the building. The horse, Champion, stares right down at me like a guardian angel whenever I move through the doors of the headquarters. I'd like to think it's a representation of my father and grandfather, a way for them to stay with me everywhere I go in this chapter of my life.

"Val, hold up!" Lucie calls out, and I turn around to look into her brown eyes.

"What's up?" I ask as she hooks her arm through mine.

"Do you want to have dinner tonight by any chance? Haru and I want to go out," she says, and I smile at the short man walking next to her. He has somewhat long, black hair and warm brown eyes.

"I'd love to. Meet you in the lobby at seven?"

They both nod as we walk toward the *Maranello Suite Hotel* where we're all staying.

I have a great time at dinner. Haru is one of the most caring guys I've ever met, and Lucie is hilarious. She has me laughing through most of the meal while he finds new ways to ask me about my life. I return them, trying to get to know them better.

Haru shares that he was born in Japan but has moved all over the world for his father's job. From Singapore to Australia and now Italy, he's seen almost everything there is to see. Lucie, on the other hand, was born and raised in Spain to her Venezuelan parents, who have always supported her dream of becoming a NASCAR driver. Haru is training to be an IndyCar driver. They both hope the Ferrari Academy will prepare them for what's to come.

By the time we're done and have paid, it's eleven o'clock. We're all exhausted and ready to get enough sleep to do well tomorrow, especially me.

I need to rest so I can beat the smug smile off Christian's face. If he thinks I won't do anything and everything to get that seat, he's gravely mistaken.

I fall into bed, checking my phone one last time to see if anyone's texted me. The biggest smile spreads across my face when I read Leonard's name on my screen, asking if I had a second to talk.

"Hi, Valentina, how was your first day?" he asks as soon as he picks up my call. I smile from ear to ear at his behavior.

"Good, how are you?"

Leonard briefly tells me about his busy day before asking me all sorts of questions about how they welcomed me at the academy. He even lets me rant about stupid Christian Crovetto, listening patiently and giving me tips afterward on ways to avoid him. It's sweet, but I also know my rival. He won't stop bothering me until I do something stupid like letting it affect my performance.

We hang up just in time for Gabriel's name to flash on my screen from an incoming text message.

Gabriel: Hi, chérie. I hope you had a great first day. Can't wait to hear all about it. I'll see you in my dreams. Bonne nuit, mon tournesol. I miss you.

It shouldn't be possible for me to fall more in love with him because of one text message, yet, here I am, grinning at my damn phone screen.

Val: Bonne nuit, mon soleil. I miss you more.

I don't expect him to respond, so when my phone lights up once more, my heart does a summersault.

Gabriel: Not possible.

Yeah, it is.

Chapter 19

Gabriel

"Get off your phone and focus, mate," Adrian says, and I turn it off, bringing my attention to Lincoln Nash, one of the Williams drivers this season.

It's his birthday tonight, and all of the twenty drivers were invited to dinner. The Alfa Romeo drivers, Robert Lin and Felix Stark, had to leave early, something I wish I could have done too. However, Adrian told me to stay put.

The McLaren, Mercedes, Alpha Tauri, Red Bull, Haas, Alpine, Aston Martin, and us Ferrari teammates all sing 'Happy Birthday' as the waiter brings out the dessert with candles for Lincoln to blow out. He's a nice guy, but I'd rather be anywhere other than at his party right now. I hardly know him nor do I want to talk to anyone. I'm tired and miss Val. Today was her first day, and I want nothing more than to listen to her tell me all about it.

Leonard and Cameron are next to me, discussing the weather forecast for this weekend. I turn to them, my interest piqued now.

"It's supposed to rain?" I ask, earning me a cock of an eyebrow from the Brit.

"Don't you do your homework?" he asks with a small smile, obviously amused. I give him a playful frown, but he's right, I should have prepared myself better.

"Yeah, Gabriel, don't you do your homework?" Cameron scolds, and I let out an annoyed laugh. He might be my best friend, but he's also the biggest pain in my ass.

"Excuse me, I was trying to have a conversation with Leonard," I reply, and the Australian bends forward to let out a low laugh.

"I think someone's a bit tipsy," Leonard says, patting Cameron's back.

"Gabriel Biancheri! What's with the serious expression?" Eduardo interrupts as he stumbles over to where Adrian, Cameron, Leonard, and I are standing. He's also tipsy, and I'm not in the fucking mood.

"If he touches me, I'll lose it," I whisper to my teammate a second before Eduardo wraps his arm around my shoulders.

Adrian presses his lips together, trying to keep from laughing. My hands ball into fists as my breathing hitches. We weren't close before he and Val became intimate, and we sure as hell aren't now.

"You should lighten up a little. You're kind of bringing the mood down," the Spaniard goes on, and I shoot Adrian a look that says 'get him off me before I break his nose'.

The only reason why I hate him is because he was, or is, interested in Val, but it's enough to make me want to punch him.

"Alright, Eduardo, let's get some water in you. You have to sober up for tomorrow," my teammate chimes in, and I mouth a 'thank you' when he pulls the Red Bull driver off me.

"Remind me to never piss you off," Cameron says from next to me, and a smile slips onto my face.

"Why?" I ask, humor now spreading over his face.

"Because when you dislike someone, they become your nemesis," he explains, making me let out a laugh that reaches my chest.

"Well, I don't hate many people, so that's fine, right?" Cameron grabs my shoulder, trying to hide his amusement.

"Let's just hope not too many other people do something to Val you don't approve of," he replies, and I nudge him in the side, our attention drifting to Adrian as he pushes Eduardo down in his chair.

"Stay," he commands, and the Spaniard gives him a sad look before my teammate walks away.

James, on the other hand, checks on the tipsy driver, making sure he's alright. As always, James, the super kind, always attentive, good fucking guy does the right thing. *Asshole.*

"That's the last time I help you. Eduardo was about to tell me his favorite sex position, and that's not an image I need in my head," Adrian says as soon as he's next to me again. Cameron and I chuckle in response, earning us a glare from the tall man. "Fuck off, you wouldn't have wanted that either! The only people who should tell me what they like in bed are the ones I have sex with," he goes on, and, as if on cue, a blonde woman turns to him, clearly having overheard his statement.

"Would it be of interest to you to know mine?" she asks, and Adrian licks his lips, offering her an easy smirk.

"Most definitely," he replies, and she takes his hand, pulling him to her table.

"Does that mean I get to leave now too?" I call after him, but he doesn't even turn to me while raising his thumb into the air. I shake my head, shifting my gaze to Cameron's and Leonard's faces. They're full of disbelief.

"How? Just, how?" Leonard asks, and I let out a small laugh.

"I don't know. Maybe it's his face. He looks a lot like Val, which means he's gorgeous and can enchant anyone," I say before almost laughing at myself. I swoon over my girl way too often.

"God, you're wrapped around her finger like no one I've ever met before," Cameron says, and I cock a challenging eyebrow.

"Is that so? How's Elijah, huh?" I ask, and his cheeks go red in an instant.

"I thought you were leaving," he says with a laugh, and I pat his back before assuring him I will.

As much as I care about him and like spending time with him, I'm done with the evening.

Chapter 20

Valentina

"You can do it, little champion, push!" Grandpa yells, and I hold my head in the same straining position, working all of the muscles in my neck. "And, relax," he says, and I let out the groan I've been holding back. "Well done!" He pats me on the shoulder while I try to catch my breath. "The new karting league champion is only improving. The other racers better watch out because you're going to triumph over all of them soon enough." I take the bottle of water he hands me and beam up at him.

"Adrian better watch out then," I tease, and my brother winks at me from the other side of the room where he is lifting weights.

He hardly speaks when we train. Grandfather mostly focuses on me, trusting Adrian to know what he's doing now that he drives in F3. It's my dream to get to where my big brother is.

Grandfather looks between us before settling down on the bench, a serious expression on his tired face.

"I need to speak to you both about something," he starts, and, by his tone, I can tell this won't be good. Adrian and I sit down on the floor in front of him. "It's been a few weeks now since your father passed away, and it's

time I told you what he put into his will," he goes on, and I swallow hard when tears fill his eyes. My grandfather has never cried in front of us, ever. "He wants you to move in with your mother's sister, Carolina." My heart splits into a million pieces.

"No. I want to stay with you. I don't want to leave you," I beg, tears rolling down my cheeks. Adrian takes my hand, but his attention is on Grandpa.

"Monaco is our home. Why are you making us leave? What about my career? What about Val's?" my brother asks, and I nod as if to say 'See, you can't send us away'.

"There is nothing I can do. I tried to fight it, get custody to keep you here, but Carolina accepted. I've tried everything, my loves. I'm so sorry, but you can come to visit. Adrian, you will travel back and forth as much as you need for races. It will work, don't worry." This doesn't make either of us feel better. "We'll see each other, I promise." I cry harder then, wrapping my arms around his neck to hold onto him, this life, for as long as I can.

"I don't want to be apart from you," I sob as he wraps his arms around me.

We're all he has left in the world and vice versa. Aunt Carolina means nothing to us. We don't know her, and I don't want to either, not if it means leaving Grandpa all alone in this big house. This isn't fair.

Haven't we lost enough?

No one is at the academy when I arrive the next morning. My fear of showing up late anywhere combined with my inability to sleep when I'm nervous woke me up very early. I tug on my yoga pants a few times and then fix the Ferrari shirt they gave us in the welcome bag yesterday. It's for working out, but I'm a bit scared I'll be the only one wearing it.

"Valentina, you're early," Andrea says, their Italian accent even thicker in the mornings.

"Yes, I'm sorry. I have a habit of showing up too early in order not to be late," I explain or ramble, I'm not sure which fits my fast words better. They smile at my tomato-red cheeks before signaling for me to go with them.

"Personally, I appreciate punctuality. Rather show up before than too late, like Mr. Crovetto," they reply and stop in front of me.

For some reason, and I can't explain it, I feel comfortable around Andrea. There is a warmth about them that reassures me everything will be fine.

"Don't tell him I said that. I have a feeling he'll tell his father about it, and I'd still like to visit Monaco in the summer." I let out a small laugh before assuring them I will keep my lips sealed. "Come with me. I would like to show you something."

I follow with hesitation because we're walking downstairs to the cars again. Andrea leads me to my father's, pointing at something written on a faded sticker inside. *For Adrian and my little champion.* My heart sinks into my stomach.

"I saw it after you left yesterday. I thought you'd like to see it too."

"I did, thank you," I manage to croak out, but I'm trying my best to hide how deeply this both hurt and healed me.

Dad wasn't the best father, but he loved us. If only he could have shown it before he passed away.

"May I?" I ask, gesturing toward the car.

"Sure, but it stays between us." I give them a small nod and smile, my hand gliding over the cool metal.

The feeling brings me right back to the first time Dad took me to his garage as a child. There is nothing I'd love more than to forgive him for what he's put Adrian and me through. Yet, knowing he took us from Grandpa to make us live with an abusive aunt will prevent me from ever reaching forgiveness.

"What, so because her daddy was the driver, she gets to touch the car?"

It's too early for me to deal with Christian's horrible personality, especially because I'm vulnerable right now. I raise all of my walls and drop my hand, straightening out my back as I get up.

"Careful, Andrea," I say and point at the floor where he's standing. Christian's eyes follow where I'm gesturing toward as I say, "Don't slip on the slime he's leaving behind."

Andrea sucks in a sharp breath as they try not to laugh. I'm definitely enjoying that they seem to be on my side. When I walk past Christian, I pretend to lose balance a little, as if I'm the one who 'slipped'.

"Might have to put up a sign." The words are meant for our instructor, but my eyes are on his.

"We both know, in reality, you're actually into me, and it scares you," he replies, smirking. My body cringes from disgust.

"Not even if you were the last living, breathing *thing* in the *universe.*"

"Okay, enough you two. Let's take this energy and put it into our morning run, yes?" Andrea asks, but I don't break eye contact yet.

I've never wished to be taller as much as I do at this moment. Christian is at least a head bigger than me, which is irritating when I'm trying to be intimidating. His smile makes me want to tackle him to the ground. It says 'I've gotten everything I've ever wanted, never experienced any real pain, and have no human decency'.

"After you, Tina." *Don't kick him in the balls. Don't do it. He's a royal. You'll get arrested.* I fake a smile instead.

"I hope you trip on your horrible personality and land on your face, asshole," I reply in Spanish because it's the only other language I'm fluent in that he doesn't understand.

As planned, his smile fades. There is nothing better than to wipe the arrogance off his face.

Training starts soon after everyone arrives. Haru and Lucie each give me a hug when they see me. We stay in a group of three for the run since it is untimed for today, simply to test our endurance. Andrea wants to make it a game. Whoever can go the longest gets to train in the simulator first. The rest will have to do analysis work.

Haru and Lucie keep talking as we do the same lap over and over, which is probably why they are the first two to give up and sit at the side. Christian goes at a much slower tempo, almost walking while the rest of us keep a good pace.

According to my watch, it's been almost an hour by the time only Christian and I are left. Naturally, he has to start matching my speed to stay next to me then.

"Give up, Tina. You won't win today and you won't get the seat either. You're just a little girl, nothing more," he says, but his voice is strained and reveals how exhausted he is.

"Ah, yes, the sexism, very original, Christopher," I reply, and he gives me a confused look when I use a wrong name to address him. If he can't say my real one, I won't use his either.

"Alright, you two! Sprint to me, whoever is first, wins!" Andrea says, but Christian's reaction time is slower than mine.

I get enough of a headstart to make it to our instructor long before he does. Andrea lifts their hand for me, and I high-five them.

"Nice job, Romana," they say, and I feel happiness take over.

Like the little baby he is, Christian goes to complain about it not being fair because those weren't the original instructions and rules.

"It's all about training your mind to react, Christian. You have a lot to learn from Valentina." This makes him ball his hands into fists.

"It wasn't fair!" I roll my eyes at him.

"Someone get him a bottle, for Christ's sake," Lucie chimes in, and Haru falls over from laughter.

"How sweet. You got yourself an admirer. Girls supporting girls, *woohoo.*" His voice is condescending, disgusted. Christian truly is the definition of 'sexist'.

"Do us a favor and crack a book, Christiano, preferably one on feminism," I spit, but he walks away without saying another word.

"Well then, the rest of you, follow me. Your day has just begun," Andrea announces, making everyone but me groan.

They might be tired, but I've never felt more awake.

Chapter 21

Gabriel

It feels strange to stand with all the drivers, listening to the English hymn without seeing Valentina's nervous face somewhere in the crowd around us. I miss the stupid smile that spreads over my face when she tries to give me a reassuring one, pretending like she isn't almost peeing her pants from nervosity.

Adrian gives me a nudge in the ribs, reminding me to pay attention and be respectful after my shoulders fell. I straighten out my back and place my hands behind me, listening to the young woman in front of us sing her heart out.

"What the hell is going on with you? Where is your head?" my teammate asks as we make our way back to our cars on the grid.

I got pole yesterday, but he's in third place behind Kyle Hughes. After what happened two races ago, the Mercedes driver being responsible for Adrian's DNF, I can tell this will be a tense battle for second place. I hope it will give me space to create a gap.

I need this win today.

"Hello? Jesus, it's like talking to a wall," Adrian says with a slight laugh, and I force my attention to him.

"Sorry, mate, I'm just in my head." I've been distracted today, but I can't drive like this. My mind needs to be with me in the car, not with Valentina at the academy.

"Get out of it then. I don't want you to drive into me," he says and winks at me, but I don't find that funny at all.

Maxime was distracted, he was in his head that day, and it cost him his life. It's the reason why I shut everything off when I get into the car. It's also the reason why I'm so glad Val works tirelessly to always be in balance when she races. If she ever got distracted for any reason, it would put her in great danger. The thought makes me shudder. I wish she was here right now. I need a hug after going to the dark place in my mind. *Fuck, I miss her so much...*

I'm about to walk away when Adrian grabs me by the shoulders and spins me back around to him.

"Hey, I miss her too. It's okay to," he assures me, and I sigh.

"It's annoying how you always see through me," I say because Adrian has this way of sensing whatever is wrong, even though I hardly ever share intimate details about my life with him.

"Well, it annoys me how in love you are with my sister, but here we are," he says, and I raise both my eyebrows.

"What, why?" Adrian drops his hands from my shoulders to cross his arms in front of his chest.

"You're my teammate, Gabriel, but you're also my biggest competition. The fact that my sister and you are dating isn't exactly ideal." It isn't ideal for either of us, but this wasn't a choice I made deliberately to mess with his head or mine for that matter. If anything, it's Val's fault for being so damn perfect for me.

"I know, but whether or not I'm dating her doesn't influence the inevitable. I'm going to win the championship this year," I say with a smile, which he returns.

"At least you'll have Val's shoulder to cry on when I wipe the floor with you," he replies, and we shake hands, both of us chuckling. "Fair race," he says, and I give him a slight nod.

"Always."

We're the last ones to get into our cars. Hector hands me my helmet before making sure I have everything I need. My team works to get the car ready for the race, running last-minute diagnostics and checking the tires. I try to get comfortable in the car and force myself into my zone, ready for battle when it comes to it.

Soon, we're given the green light to take our formation lap, and I do my best to calm my nerves. This is my job, I'm used to them, but that doesn't mean I don't get nervous. If I would be able to turn that part off, I'd start questioning my sanity.

"Okay, Gabriel, remember: strategy A. Strategy A," my strategist's voice fills my ears, and I take another deep breath.

Strategy A means staying ahead, creating a gap, and playing off what the others are doing when it comes to pitstops. The last thing we need is an undercut if Mercedes pits earlier than us.

"Are we expecting rain?" I ask when the clouds above me turn a dark shade of grey.

"Negative. No rain on our radar," Tommasso assures me as I drive back to my place on the grid.

Adrian is behind me while Kyle moves next to me, staying slightly back. I watch the lights, taking a long, deep breath and letting it out as they go on. Then, they turn off, and I slam my foot on the gas, pressing the right buttons at the same time.

I manage to stay ahead, but Adrian is in second place already, fighting me for first. I have no idea how he managed to start this well, but I can't linger on it. I have to focus on keeping my place, which is exactly what I do.

Chapter 22

Valentina

The past week has been the most exhausting one, physically and mentally, I have ever experienced. Christian and me bickering has drained me emotionally too, and I'm ready for Gabriel to come and pick me up today.

We've spoken every day, especially on Sunday after he won the fourth race of the season. He's been strong in these few Grand Prixes, proving he deserves the Ferrari seat more than anyone else but Adrian, who came in second place. James had an engine failure toward the end, and I spent a good ten minutes reminding him he did everything right and the next race will be better.

Being away from home and everyone I care about makes me homesick. As happy as I am to have been given this opportunity and found new friends, I miss how things were. I miss my brother's humor, James' warmth, and Gabriel's love. They try their best to give me as much of it as they can through the phone, but it'll never compare. That's why I'm more than giddy to pack my luggage and rush outside to wait for the man I love.

To my surprise, he's already here, leaning against a bright red Ferrari he must have been given by the team. I drop everything and run toward him, joy spreading through me. Gabriel catches me with ease, holding me as close to him as humanly possible.

"Ma chérie," he says softly, letting me hear how much he's missed me. I pull back, my palms moving to his cheeks. He smiles, bringing his dimples out, which I trace with my thumbs. "Hi," Gabriel adds, but I don't respond.

I press my lips to his, needing to feel his kiss after over a week of being apart. His tongue slips into my mouth, making me moan from happiness and pleasure. He moves on to my cheek, jaw, then neck, where he nuzzles his face and inhales.

"I've missed you," he says against my sensitive skin before placing a few more kisses on it. I'm finally home.

"Oh yeah? What did you miss?" I tease, and he steps back.

"You. Your face. Your scent. Your body..." Gabriel trails off and grabs my hips to guide me against his chest. His green-brown eyes stare into mine as his fingers slip onto my ass. "Next time, I'll find a way for us not to be apart for this long. I don't like it." A chuckle vibrates off my chest, my hands sliding under his shirt to feel his muscles.

"Neither do I." I lean my forehead against his, and my heart slowly calms down from the excitement of being in his arms.

"Let's go, we have a long way ahead of us," he reminds me before kissing me one last time and opening my car door.

Gabriel and I talk a lot for the first hour of the drive, trying to catch up on what we've missed in each other's lives. Even though we spoke every day, there are little things we want to share.

Eventually, silence fills the car, so he connects my phone through Bluetooth, telling me to play whatever I want. I shuffle random songs from my 'liked playlist' before turning my head to look at him. The bandana he put on is keeping his hair in place, his curls draping over the red fabric. I can't help myself as I lift my phone to take a picture of him and set it as my lock screen. He looks too beautiful, and I love how happy he is.

We arrive at a traffic light, and Grabriel hits the breaks a little too hard, the notebook he carries around with him everywhere falling into my foot space. It opened, and a sketch of me standing in the Ferrari box, looking at the screens, is drawn on the page. Before I look further, I close the book so I can place it back in the cupholder where it was before.

"You can look through it. It's mostly you anyway," he says, and my mouth drops.

"But isn't this like your diary?" I ask, and he smiles, his eyes never shifting from the road to keep us safe.

"I'm not ashamed to show you what is going on inside my head." He flashes me his dimples and perfect teeth.

My fingers run over the black, rough cover of the notebook, and I smile before I even reopen it. On the first page is a drawing of his Formula One car, and I scan it, admiring the detailed sketch. The next page has a wolf on it, which I know is his favorite animal.

The following ten pages are drawings of me either sleeping at the airport, doing yoga, lying on the beach, smiling, crying, laughing, or every other emotion I have ever shown him. Each drawing is so damn beautiful, and all of them have one interesting thing in common: I'm wearing a necklace with an F1 car and the number seven on it... *his number.*

I'm pretty sure I've forgotten how to breathe because, eventually, I silently gasp for air. I reach for Gabriel's hand and take it in mine, squeezing it. He lifts our intertwined hands to press a kiss to the back of mine while I skip through the empty pages and find another drawing on the last one. I don't recognize the woman in it.

"What's wrong, ma chérie?" he asks, but I'm too stuck on studying her features to respond.

She has straight, long, red hair and green eyes, the only two features in color, along with full lips and, unlike mine, a slim face.

"Valentina," he says, and I cover my mouth with my hand. "Talk to me," he begs, but I don't say anything to him. He pulls over on the side of the road, and I turn my head as soon as he parks. "What did I do?" His eyes are pleading with me now, and I swallow hard. I show him the page of his notebook that has my throat dry.

"Who is she?"

The answer terrifies me. There are no other girls in this book, only me, and all of a sudden I notice this woman, more beautiful than any other I've ever seen.

"Her name is Harlow. We slept together a few months ago, after you went on your date with Eduardo," he explains while I nod along to his words. "It was a one-time thing, chérie, a distraction. I have no intention of ever seeing her again," he explains, his hand reaching out to touch my cheek. I let him, even though there is something about this that still bothers me.

"Why did you draw her if she was just a one-time thing, a distraction?" My voice is filled with pain, and he flinches when he hears it.

"Chérie, I can explain," he starts, but hearing those words makes me realize I don't want to hear what he has to say right now.

"Don't, I just need a minute." Without a doubt, I'm being irrational. I should be listening to him, and I shouldn't be reacting like this.

"But I can–"

"Don't, just please, don't," I interrupt him and turn my head so I don't have to look at his defeated expression.

"I'm yours, baby, you have me, one hundred percent. I'll explain when you're ready, but I don't want you to question that, ever," he says, and I close my eyes in response. He starts the car again and drives to the hotel.

Gabriel wouldn't cheat on me, and this is far from it, but it doesn't sit right with me that he kept the drawing for some reason.

He checks us into our hotel room while I try to understand his desire to draw someone he slept with and then keep it after.

We take the elevator to an antique-decorated room. The colors on the walls are light pink and cream, and the couch in front of the television matches it. The bed is huge, and I wish my thoughts would move in the right direction.

Gabriel puts his bag on the chair on the far side of the bedroom, and as I watch him, I have to turn away. I sit on the couch and don't talk to him for quite some time. When he settles down opposite me, I can't control my feelings anymore. I've been quiet, thinking about what it could possibly mean for long enough.

"Why the hell did you draw her?" I ask, and his eyes drop to the floor. "Why? Why her? You slept with her, you drew her, and you kept the fucking drawing? What am I supposed to think?"

"I drew her because I hoped it'd take my mind off you. I tried everything and it was just another way for me to deal with the fact that I'm never going to be good enough for you. You went on a date with Eduardo, and I was hurt." This only irritates me more.

"Are you trying to make me feel bad?" I ask with a raised voice and stand up. He gets up too but keeps his distance.

"No, fuck no, that's not what I'm trying to do, I'm trying to explain!" he defends, his hands lifting to point at absolutely nothing in front of him.

"If she's still in there, maybe you do have some sort of feelings for her!" I don't know why I'm yelling, but it frustrates him.

"*Pour l'amour de Dieu, Valentina, je suis amoureux de toi!*" he says, his voice raised as he tells me he's in love with me for the first time. "I tried to get you out of my head by sketching her, but you can see I wasn't into it by looking at it. It's horrible, it's ugly, it's nothing compared to the ones of you. So, please, stop reading into this. I forgot it's even there, that is how meaningless it was." He is out of breath, and I tug on the hem of my shirt. "I know how much this must be bothering you, trust me. I am so sorry she is still in there, but you know what?"

He takes the notebook into his hands, goes to the page of *her*, and rips it out before he tears it apart and throws the shreds all over the room.

"I love you, I need you, I want you." Gabriel walks over to me, puts his hands on my hips, and shakes them while he is talking.

"I don't want you to draw other girls you slept with," I mumble, and he puts his forehead against mine.

"I never will again. I don't enjoy drawing anyone else," he admits and chuckles, relief settling over both of us. "I want to draw you, all of you."

I pull back so I can look at his handsome features and remember the time I thought about him drawing all of me.

My hands cup his face, the stubble of his beard rough against my soft skin, and teasingly press my lips to his. He groans in response, making me grin. I lean away, leaving us both wanting more, and then, remove my clothes, pull my hair out of my ponytail, and lie down on the bed.

"You want all of me?" I ask, and he nods. He seems to be in a trance as he looks me up and down. "Then draw all of me," I say, but he shakes his head.

"Not here. I want a big canvas for you." I smirk, and he looks at me with a confused expression.

"Well, I'm naked, so either draw me or fuck me," I offer, and he rips his shirt over his head before he moves between my legs, claiming my lips.

His tongue slides into my mouth, and I moan into his. He lets his hands roam my body and swiftly runs his fingers over my clit. My hips push off the bed so I can press my sensitive area even more against his finger.

"I love you so much," I blurt out, and his movements come to an abrupt stop as he leans back to look into my eyes.

"Say it again," he begs, both of us smiling like we just won the lottery.

"I love you, Gabriel Matteo Biancheri, with my entire heart and soul." He attacks my face with kisses, and I giggle underneath him.

"I love you," he repeats over and over again, his lips eventually settling onto mine. I'm sighing against them when he pulls back with wide eyes. "Shit, we have to go in twenty minutes," he says, lifting me up and off the bed.

He leads us to the shower, but I assure him I already took one this morning. He barely acknowledges my response before jumping in by himself.

"Fuck," he repeats every once in a while as he washes, and I can't help but laugh.

He's done within minutes, rushing past me and toward his suitcase. I finish my makeup in record time. It's simple, mostly brown tones that highlight my unique eyes. The dress I bought from Evangelin fits my body snuggly, showing off my curves. The white high heels match the dress with the flower-pattern well.

When Gabriel notices me, his eyes fixate on my face, then my body.

"You look..." He doesn't finish the sentence, he simply walks over to where I am and puts his hands on my hips, his favorite way to drag my body against his. "Let's ditch the event. I can think of a thousand better things to do." I laugh a little, and he presses his lips to mine, stopping my laughter.

"Let's go."

Gabriel does as he is told, and I have to take a few deep breaths to calm my body, which is making my life a lot more difficult than it needs to be at the moment.

Chapter 23

Valentina

My knees are shaking as I sit next to Gabriel in the rental car. He's driving us to the unveiling event, and I can't help the nervous feeling in my stomach. We're going to be seen and photographed together, and everyone is going to make a big deal of it. I'm the sister of his teammate. Drama is going to encircle us, and there will be no way of stopping it.

My thoughts are spiraling, and the only thing bringing me back to reality is Gabriel's hand as it wraps around mine. He's squeezing it, and I let out the breath I've been holding. Gabriel knows I'm terrified, but he doesn't point it out. All he does is comfort me.

I focus on how handsome he looks in his tuxedo and forget all about the rest of the world. He always looks mouth-watering. I've never seen him dressed in something that didn't highlight how sexy he is, but he looks especially attractive in this outfit. The suit makes me want to rip it off him and ride him in the car. I catch myself, smile, and turn my head in the other direction. If I keep staring at him, I might actually do it. However, a lot of people are expecting Gabriel to be at this event tonight, and I can't be the reason why he wouldn't go.

I remove my hand from his to scratch my other arm, and he glances over at me with an annoyed expression.

"Hey," he complains and takes it back.

I stare at him with a confused look but don't question his odd behavior. After another couple of minutes, I take my hand away again to see how he will react, and he gives me the same bothered face as before.

"Stop," he tells me right before he intertwines our fingers again. I can't help but smile.

I do it once more.

"Seriously, stop taking it away." He's even more annoyed with me when I start laughing.

"Why are you so clingy?" I ask him, and he focuses on the road again.

"I'm not. I'm nervous and holding your hand comforts me," he explains, making me melt on the inside. I put my hand in his, and he smiles at me. "Yes," he says, victory in his voice, and I grin at him. It surprises me sometimes that a confident man like him has such a soft center.

Gabriel and I arrive at the event minutes later. We take a deep breath at the same time before laughing. He leads me to a carpet surrounded by paparazzi, and, as soon as we step onto it, cameras start to make clicking noises, blinding us with their flashes.

My boyfriend brings me to the middle of the carpet and snakes his arm around my waist, clearly used to all of this attention. I try my best to give them the most beautiful smile I can muster. The one that follows after he presses his lips to my temple is the most genuine one I could ever bring to my face.

"You're doing amazing," he encourages, squeezing my side.

I look up at him and he stares down at me until we're grinning at each other. The rest of the world vanishes for a moment as I get lost in his eyes.

As we walk away, Gabriel whispers sweet things into my ear. I bite my bottom lip and turn my head to show him my smile, which he only takes advantage of by kissing me. People are screaming at us, but I can't understand a single thing. I'm too overwhelmed by the lights, the cameras, and the handsome man next to me to understand anything. We finish strolling down the carpet, and when we're finally out of sight, I relax my face.

"God, my cheeks are burning. I don't think I've ever had to smile that much," I tell Gabriel, and he laughs before leaning down to press a longer kiss to my lips.

He is very affectionate tonight, and I'm enjoying it a lot. He pulls back but presses another quick kiss to my cheek before we walk into the large hall. A server, probably Gabriel's age, leads us to our table, and I can't help but glare when she touches his arm.

"Hey," Gabriel says as he turns to me, and I look at him, my bothered expression fading from my face. "Don't be jealous. You know you're the only one for me," he assures me, and I nod. Still, I don't want her near him, just like he wouldn't want anyone else to touch me.

"If she places her hand on you again, I'm going to knock that innocent smile off her face," I whisper as we sit down, and Gabriel presses a kiss to my neck.

"She was smiling?" he asks, and I look at him with a 'seriously?' expression.

"Didn't you look at her?"

"No, I didn't. I was too busy looking at you," he replies, and I have to bite the inside of my cheek.

"Smooth," I say, and he smirks at me.

"Merci, ma chérie." He leans to the side and puts his hand in mine. I set my other one on top of our intertwined fingers and rest them in my lap.

Gabriel is greeted by an old friend, and they start to converse in Italian. His hand never leaves mine while I enjoy the way the words sound falling from his lips. I barely get to hear him speak in Italian, so I savor every moment.

"Ilyan, this is my girlfriend Valentina. Val, this is Ilyan. I used to race with him in Formula Three." I shake the short man's hand and smile politely at him.

Gabriel and Ilyan continue their conversation in English, and Ilyan even inquires about my life. He leaves after a short while, and Gabriel turns to me again so we can talk about the speech he has to give. Apparently, he is driving the car onto the stage, which is a high honor, and will be asked some questions. I had no idea he was this involved.

"Hello, hello, hello." I don't even have to turn around to know that voice belongs to Adrian. I get up to greet him, and he compliments my outfit. James walks up behind him, and I press my lips together to keep from laughing.

"Hi, luv," he says and kisses my cheek.

His dark blue suit brings out his eyes while Adrian is dressed in all black to make his green-blue-brown ones stand out.

"Couldn't find anyone besides James who wanted to be your date, huh?" I ask my brother, and he chuckles as he sits down.

"I needed a hot date, and he offered. How could I have turned him down?" Adrian replies, and I laugh. His expression turns serious then. "I mean it. I'm asking you how so I don't have to take him next time," he teases, earning him a slap to the arm from James.

"I dressed up for you in this uncomfortable suit, and this how you thank me?" Adrian gives him an evil smile, but our best friend returns it. "You know what? I'm going to cock-block you all night for that comment." Adrian leans toward him and glares.

"You. Wouldn't. Dare." My brother hisses every word, but James gives him a wicked grin.

Gabriel covers his mouth with his fist as he places his elbow on the table to lean forward. He's trying his best to stay quiet but squeezes my hand to let me know how difficult it is.

The waitress from before returns a while after my brother and best friend stopped arguing, and her attention instantly drifts to Adrian. Her hand moves onto his shoulder as she asks him what he'd like to drink. Naturally, James answers before my brother even has the chance to swallow the big gulp of water he just took.

"He will have a glass of warm milk and a bib, you know, in case he has another spit-up accident," James says, whispering the last half of the sentence. Adrian spits out some of his water from surprise, and our best friend goes to clean it from his face. "See, it's already happening. Please, hurry," he says, and the waitress leaves without hesitation.

"You know, the more women you turn off me, the more desirable you'll start looking," he warns, and James shakes his head.

"Fine, I'll stop," he replies and lifts his arms in surrender.

Mindy, our waitress, returns with a few napkins for Adrian before stepping next to him and offering a flirtatious smile.

"May I clean you up, Mr. Romana?" she asks, and he smirks at her.

"Only if I get to buy you a drink after tonight's event," he says, and she starts wiping away imaginary droplets of water from his shirt and thighs.

She drops her number into his lap before disappearing again. Meanwhile, Gabriel is shaking his head and drawing a sunflower onto the napkin before handing it to me with a kiss. He finds all of this amusing, but James has steam coming out of his ears.

"It's not fucking fair. You make a fool of yourself and get a date! How does that even work?" James complains, but my brother merely shrugs.

"With a face like mine, I could be sitting here in a tinfoil suit," he replies, and I smack my forehead with the palm of my hand.

Luckily, the event starts soon after. Giuseppe Camilleri, the current CEO of Ferrari, approaches the microphone and gives a long speech, welcoming everyone and making an introduction. Gabriel kisses me when he has to leave to drive the car, and I smile the whole time he is on stage.

He switches between English and Italian, and I don't ever want him to stop talking. It is either his accent or the fact he's speaking in Italian that makes my body crazy in all of the best ways. Adrian joins Gabriel on the stage. I'm sitting with James as I watch two of the most important people in my life stand up there, talking about their careers and achievements. I'm so proud of them.

When they finally finish, they walk back to our table. Gabriel kisses the top of my head before he sits down next to me and places his hand back where it belongs.

The rest of the evening goes by painfully slowly, but I enjoy spending time with my three favorite guys and getting to know the people Adrian and Gabriel work with. My boyfriend eventually starts playing with my curly hair, twisting it around his index finger.

My thoughts drift to the day I get to be on that stage, a celebrated Ferrari Formula One driver, like Grandpa, Dad, Adrian, and Gabriel.

"Let's go, ma chérie?" Gabriel says and brings me back to reality.

"I thought you'd never ask," I respond with a naughty smirk.

We say goodbye to the people I've been introduced to, Adrian, and James before Gabriel leads me back to our car.

"Tired?" he asks me when we're almost back at the hotel.

"Not even in the slightest," I admit.

My body has been waiting for us to get back since we left six hours ago. My mind has been running wild, and those thoughts are only strengthened when he briefly looks me up and down.

"Me neither," he tells me in a low, raspy voice.

His hand moves to my leg and his index finger starts tracing circles. Shivers run down my spine, but I stop his hand when it moves up and toward my ache. I need his fingers to be as far away from there as possible, otherwise, we won't make it back to the hotel room before I rip his suit off.

Chapter 24

Valentina

Gabriel's hand is wrapped around mine as I lead him through our hotel room door. We stop in front of the bed, and I turn around to face him. My heart is racing from anticipation, unable to calm itself as his fingers move to my sides and glide toward my breasts. I guide his head to me, pressing my lips to his and stepping out of my heels. He has to lean down more now, making me smile against his lips.

"You taste so sweet," he says before slamming his mouth back onto mine to get another taste. A moan vibrates off him and through me, exciting every cell in my body.

Gabriel drops onto the bed, dragging me with him until I straddle his lap. I massage his tongue with mine until I feel his erection pressing against my aching clit. My hips rock back and forth, desperate to create a friction to ease the unbearable tension.

"Oh God," I moan as pleasure rolls through me, and Gabriel smirks.

"You certainly make me feel like one, ma chérie," he replies before flipping us over so I'm on my back.

Gabriel stands up again, removing his blazer before unbuttoning his shirt. His muscular torso makes my mouth water as my fingertips reach out to run over it. He lowers himself down on me, his fingers wrapping around the fabric of my dress, pulling it over my head in one swift movement. Everywhere his touch grazes my skin, shivers appear.

Once the dress is completely off, Gabriel places a soft kiss on my neck and fire ignites all around the area. My underwear is the only thing covering me now, but it's still too much, especially when he cups my breasts.

"Take it off," I demand, rolling my head when he pinches my hard nipples through the fabric. Gabriel's touch is soft as he unclasps my bra, tossing it to the side.

"You are my definition of perfection," he says as he brings his lips to my neck, merely brushing the skin there on his way to my left nipple. His teeth capture it before his hot mouth tugs on it.

"Fuck," I breathe. The combination of his hand squeezing my tit and his lips sucking the sensitive skin makes my eyes roll into the back of my head. "Please," I beg, but I'm unsure what for. *For him to undress? Undress me? Release me from this intolerable build-up?*

"I know, baby, lie back," he says, sensing I need all of the above as he slides down his pants, keeping his boxers on for now. He removes my panties and moves between my legs.

A low moan leaves my throat when he sucks on my right nipple, and I let my head fall backward onto the mattress. Our bodies feel close but the stupid fabric of his underwear is in the way. My hands reach for the waistband of his boxers, and I tease him by running my index finger along the line of hair that leads to his cock. I need him to feel the same amount of aching, the same shivers that run down my spine.

Gabriel pulls away, and even though I know he is only doing it to remove his underwear, I want to complain. The loss of his touch drives me crazy, and I almost sigh when his mouth moves back onto my skin. He pins me down on the bed and slips his tongue into my mouth until I moan.

"Put on a condom," I say, breathless and impatient.

Gabriel leans away from me again, almost breaking skin contact entirely when his hands leave my body. The only parts of him touching me are his legs. I look at him to see what he's doing and find him staring at my body, his eyes shifting up and down. His erection makes me ache even more, but I'm worried about his serious expression.

"What's wrong?" I ask him, and his gaze drifts to mine.

"Are you sure you're ready? I don't want you to feel pressured," he admits in a low, quiet voice, and I sit up in bed.

"I've been ready for a while. Don't make me wait any longer," I reply, taking his hand in mine.

Gabriel means more to me than I'll ever understand, and having sex with him is going to be a whole new experience, one I've craved for a long time. I've never wanted this as much as I do with him.

He smirks at me before he moves off the bed to get a condom from his pants. He hands it to me, and I rip open the small package. Gabriel's cock is a lot bigger than anyone I've ever been with, which adds to both my nervousness and excitement.

I slide the condom down his length, making him suck in a sharp breath as my fingers roam over his erection. I lean back once I'm done and satisfied with my work, looking at Gabriel, who is watching me. The smile on my face seems to be contagious because he returns it.

His hands slide back onto my breasts, squeezing them before he pinches my nipples. My back arches off the bed to get closer to him, desperation seeping out of me in the form of a whimper. One of his fingers trails all the way down to my clit, running over the swollen area while a satisfied smirk settles on his lips.

"I'm yours, mon tournesol," he says, aligning his cock with my dripping entrance.

"And I'm yours, mon soleil," I reply, and he places his hands on my angled legs, one of them sliding onto my lower abdomen.

"Relax for me, baby," he says before he slips inside of me, causing an uncontrollable gasp to escape both of us.

Having him this close to me is the sweetest feeling, and I never want it to end. Gabriel seems to feel the same way because, for a brief moment, he is still. I pull his head down and place a kiss on his lips as we lock eyes. My hips lift slightly to animate him to do the same, and he complies.

Every movement feels better than the one before, and I want more, no, need more of him. His scent, the skin contact, and his kisses threaten to overwhelm me, but my moans allow me to relieve some of the build-up. My chest is on fire and every time he touches me, the feeling intensifies. I feel whole in a completely new way; it's addicting.

My brain can't form a coherent thought anymore, but I don't mind. His thrusts are deep then shallow, hard then soft, fast and slow. The switches have my head spinning and my body consumed with pleasure. I'm a moaning mess underneath him as our movements harmonize and my nails dig into his arms. Whenever he speeds up, my body naturally adjusts to his rhythm as if we're two pieces of the same machine. Gabriel is moaning my name over and over again, which only makes me enjoy everything more.

"You feel so good, chérie, so fucking good," he whispers into my ear before he nibbles on my lobe. He pushes my legs further apart, going deeper than before.

"Shit," I breathe because Gabriel has me feeling a type of way I've never experienced. I've had sex, but it never felt like this. Nothing has ever felt this fulfilling.

The friction between us loads me with energy as he manages to push against the perfect spot inside of me with almost every thrust. The tension in my stomach escalates, and I grab his arms even tighter for support. I wrap my legs around his hips, letting him go deeper and faster. His mouth moves back onto my nipples, his pumps never losing pace. The build-up gets closer and closer to my release, which I know Gabriel senses when he presses down on my stomach again, going as fast as possible.

"Gabriel," I scream and arch my back off the bed as the orgasm finally takes over my body, making it tremble.

My nails dig into his biceps as my breasts press against his torso. Gabriel continues his movements until he spills into the condom, his legs shaking and his arms barely holding him up. He stays on top of me for a bit longer, and I run my hands through his messy, curly hair.

"I love you," I tell him, and he pushes off the bed again to kiss me.

"I love you." I smile at him, and he pulls out of me. It feels weird, like part of me is missing now that he's gone, but I push the feeling away, too busy bringing his mouth back onto mine.

A couple hours and a few condoms later, we're both sweating and smiling. Gabriel leads me to the bathroom, kissing my shoulder and neck before walking over to the bathtub. He turns on the water, and I find a bottle called 'bubble bath' next to the sink. This hotel is a lot fancier than any I've ever stayed at. Gabriel pulls me toward the bathtub, and we get in before I can overthink how much money he spent on this weekend.

The water is warm, and the bubbles envelop our bodies with ease. I'm between his legs then, my back pressing against his front.

"Have you ever thought about marriage and children?" Gabriel asks after a while of silence, and my heart skips a beat. He kisses the side of my head and ear as his fingers run over my stomach.

"I've been so busy fighting for my dream and dealing with life's curveballs, I haven't had a moment to think about marriage," I admit and feel him nod behind me. My eyes meet his as I turn my head. "But every moment with you allows me to breathe, to take a break from all of the pressure I constantly put on myself." I stop, grinning at a realization floating into my head. "You are my pitstop," I say, and he smiles.

"A moment of pause in an otherwise exhausting battle we call life where we get to recharge?" he asks, and I nod because it perfectly describes what I meant. "You are my pitstop too, chérie."

His lips brush over mine, and I realize something that scares me all the way down to my bones. I can't imagine getting married to anyone but him. When I picture my future, it's us, and it terrifies me.

"Have you thought about marriage?" I ask, too curious if he feels the same way I do.

"Every day that I spent seeing or speaking to you," he replies, and I sink further into his arms. "I'd love to marry and start a family with you in the future, if that is what you wanted too," Gabriel says, and I close my eyes in response.

"How can you be so sure this is what you want?" His touch moves to my lower stomach, his hands running over my stretch marks there.

"Because in my short twenty-one, almost two, years, I've gone through hell seven different times. I barely have any family left, and you know what makes me hopeful? My career does, it makes me so damn happy I get to live my dream. The fact that one day I am going to be holding the championship trophy and I am going to make everyone proud does. But you know what else?" he asks, tilting my head to the side again to look into my eyes. "You, ma chérie, you make me beyond happy. So, yes, we are still young, but I have known what I've wanted for a long time." A tear drops down my cheek, and he smiles at me. "We've got time, there is no rush. Maybe you'll change your mind about me, maybe something will fall into our path and separate us. There is no knowing what the future holds, but I am dying to find out with you."

"So am I."

I lean my head back and against his shoulder, savoring every easy breath I get to take in his presence.

"Oh man, do you know what I just realized? I'd be marrying the weirdest guy on planet Earth. You know, considering how dramatic you are, and the fact that you laugh at your own jokes," I say, but he starts tickling me for being mean.

I giggle and scream, begging to be released. Water is splashing everywhere, forcing him to stop sooner than he clearly meant to.

"Yes, and I'd be Mr. I'm-a-little-too-competitive, so we're even," he teases, but I cock an eyebrow.

"You love how competitive I am!" I defend, and he chuckles against my back.

"And you love when I laugh at my own jokes because you always join me," he points out, and I can't contain my laughter.

"Yeah, you're right. We're perfectly flawed for one another," I reply, and he kisses my cheek.

"For one another only."

Chapter 25

Valentina

"Chérie, chérie, wake up," Gabriel whispers into my ear, the pad of his thumb running over my cheek.

I smile while enjoying the way the electricity courses through my body from where his skin grazes mine. The mahogany scent coming off him almost makes me sigh, but I control myself. It doesn't matter how many times he touches me or how many times we kiss, it always affects me in the same sweet way.

Even though I'm awake, I pretend to be asleep so I can hear him say my pet name again and feel his finger on my face for a little longer.

"I know you're awake," he says, and I bite the inside of my cheek to keep from laughing. "Are you going to make me kiss you?" he asks, and before I can help myself, I nod. "I knew you were awake."

I open my eyes and giggle, pulling his head down so I can press my lips against his. I taste the mint from his toothpaste when his tongue slides into my mouth, making me moan against his.

"Good morning." My voice is raspy and hardly audible. He chuckles, his hand moving from my face to my arm to my hip. "What time is it?" A yawn escapes me, but I cover my mouth, lifting my arms to stretch a moment later.

"Six-thirty," he replies, and I shove his arm away, an annoyed expression settling on my face.

"Why the hell are you waking me up at six-thirty in the morning?"

Gabriel rolls onto his stomach to laugh into his pillow. I want to stay mad, but he's being too cute and it causes a grin spreads over my features.

"Don't be an ass," I complain, but I'm also a bit distracted by the way his back muscles flex as he lifts off the bed.

He faces me, my eyes drifting to his messy hair, which, as per usual, makes him look a ridiculous kind of sexy.

"So, why did you wake me up so early? And how come you've already finished getting ready?" Gabriel pulls me upright, his hands cupping my face.

"We are driving back to Maranello because my team has asked me to test drive the new Ferrari sports car, and I convinced them to let you too." A bright smile covers my lips, and I crawl on top of him, straddling his lap.

"I'm going to drive it around the track?" I ask, and he gives me a nod. "Oh no, but that also means I'll be sitting next to you while you drive, right?"

"Yes, of course. That's how it works," he replies and chuckles, an unsure smile on his face. "Why?"

"Well, I'm going to be terrified when you're the one behind the wheel!" I tease. He touches the tip of his tongue to the roof of his mouth, and I hold back my laughter.

"Oh really?" he asks, his hands grabbing my ass and squeezing it, making me forget my own name. "Terrified, huh?" His hands move under my breasts, teasing me.

"Yes, maybe you should let me go first so I can teach you how to properly race. You could use a few pointers." My palms move to each side of his neck, my gaze holding his as he brings my aching clit closer to his groin.

"Maybe I'll cancel, and we'll stay here where I can fuck that attitude right out of you," he says, his dirty words surprising me as much as they excite my body. "Go, get ready. We have to leave in half an hour," he demands with a slap on my ass, and I sigh before I move off his lap.

"Tease," I groan and walk into the bathroom.

It doesn't take me long to brush my hair and teeth and apply some light makeup. I put on my black jeans and a tight, purple, long-sleeved shirt. My breasts look bigger than they normally do in it, and I smile when I think about how Gabriel is going to react. My hair falls loosely down my back, my natural curls more defined today than usual.

"You look absolutely breathtaking," he says when his eyes shift from his phone to me. "Thank you," Gabriel adds, and I give him a confused furrow of my brows.

"For what?"

"For making me the luckiest man in the world by being mine."

Gabriel has this way of saying all the right things at the perfect times, and I hate it. I hate it because it makes me fall more in love with him. I hate it because I adore how romantic he is all the time. To anyone else, Gabriel is this confident man, who isn't corny, but with me, he's wonderfully vulnerable. He blushes, he gets shy, and he lets me in. He's still that confident guy, but he also chooses to be himself with me.

"I love you," I say because nothing else would sound right.

"Every time you say it, my heart jumps in my chest." He smiles to himself for the swiftest second.

"Well, I do. I love you," I repeat and walk over to where he's sitting, placing both of my hands on each side of his face. I adore the way his soft skin contrasts his gruff stubble.

"You make me perfectly crazy, you know that?" I lean down to press my lips to his, but he stops me so my mouth is a centimeter from his. "I love you, ma chérie." I smile as I kiss him on the lips, cheek, nose, pretty much all over his face, like he always does with me.

His hands lift to my wrists, and eventually, he stops me, forcing me to look him in the eyes as he kisses me on the lips in the sweetest way.

"Okay, let's go before I make other plans," he says and chuckles, making me laugh a little too.

Chapter 26

Valentina

The sunlight illuminates the *Fiorano* track, making everything look vibrant. I enjoy how peaceful it is with almost no one here. It's nothing compared to race weekends where thousands of people are running around, but I enjoy both ways.

Gabriel takes my hand, leading me toward where his team is waiting for us along with a beautiful red and black Ferrari. For a few moments, he talks to his team, and when he comes back, he is holding up two helmets that both have his Formula One helmet design. The number seven is placed on either side, and black, white, and red stripes make up the rest of it. It's quite simple, but not everybody can come up with a unique design as I did.

He hands me one of the headgears. Gabriel puts on his, and I notice he is biting the inside of his cheek. There's something he wants to tell me, but I'm convinced he doesn't know how to.

"Spit it out," I say, and he stares at me, shock on his face.

"How did you know?" I look at him with an 'are-you-seriously-asking-me-that' expression.

"Because when something bothers you, you look away, most often at the ground, your eyebrows furrow, and you bite the inside of your cheek. You always do that, every single time," I say, and he shakes his head as if he can't believe how well I know him.

"My publicist says we have to film us driving so they can post it online. It has to do with the fact that we need to generate more popularity and get more followers. It will benefit the sport and the team," he explains, and I nod.

It makes sense, the sport isn't that popular amongst young people, and, even though the drivers are doing their best to create more buzz, there's still a lot of work to be done. A young Ferrari driver doing hot laps with a young female racer who is his girlfriend and the sister of his teammate would invite a more diverse group to watch.

"Are you alright with that? If not, we could–"

"I'm very okay with it. Now, let's do this. We'll entertain the world when I'm behind the wheel by showing them a Ferrari driver peeing his pants," I joke, and he smiles at me.

"Thank you." I don't know what he's thanking me for, but I don't press. "We have to ask each other a couple of questions while we drive. They are going to be about Formula One and racing, naturally, and it's supposed to help our followers get to know us." He's being very technical with me right now, which makes me grin.

We get into the car, and I buckle up. I'm getting a little nervous, but excitement has mostly taken over now. I've never driven in a car like this with Gabriel, but I trust him.

A tall, dark-haired man hands me a paper full of questions, and I read over them, preparing to ask Gabriel. He sits down in the driver's seat and puts his seatbelt on as well. I smile at him, and he returns it, showing me his dimples.

My eyes drift to the cameras and to the team working on the car while we wait for them to give us the green light. My heart starts beating faster in my chest, and I'm convinced Gabriel feels the same way.

"Are you nervous?" I ask him after his team leaves and tells us we can go.

"More than," he admits, and I watch him as he takes a deep breath in and then lets it out. It's strained and shaky.

"Are you okay to drive?" He tilts his head to look at me and lifts the corners of his mouth to form a smile.

"Yes, I'm fine. I've just never had so much to lose when I drive."

My head falls back against the headrest, the helmet hitting the patting. I run my thumb over his bottom lip, and Gabriel purses his lips against my finger. We stay like this for a moment, simply staring into each other's eyes.

"Okay, ready?" he asks, breaking the silence.

I nod, and he steps on the gas, making me scream out in joy. He's going fast, and my heart stops and goes with each corner, each straight. The adrenalin that shoots through my veins is heaven.

"Have you always known you wanted to be a Formula One driver?" I ask, reading the first question aloud. I have to cover my eyes with my hands when he drifts in the corner.

"Yes, ever since my dad took me karting for the first time, I knew this is what I wanted to do. Luckily, I had great opportunities, and my family fought with me every step of the way," he replies, and I smile. I'm proud of his courage to speak about his family.

"How many Grand Prixes have you started in?" The second question is pretty straightforward.

"Sixty-two."

He takes another corner in the same aggressive way as before, and I search for something to hold onto, careful not to swear on camera.

"Okay, you're doing that on purpose now," I say and he chuckles, which is the only response I get. He drives over one of the curbs, and my head bobs from side to side. "Gabriel!" I complain and laugh at the same time.

"I'm sorry, baby, I will be more careful, I promise." He is true to his word when he avoids the next curb by far.

"How do you feel about driving for Ferrari?" I continue asking him the questions.

"It's a once-in-a-lifetime opportunity, and I'm thankful I've been given it. I hope to race with them for many more seasons."

We get back to the start and finish line, but he drives past it to go for another round so I can ask him the remaining questions. We laugh and talk about his career until we arrive at the box again, and I take a deep breath to calm my heart rate.

"Your turn," he says before we switch seats.

Gabriel gives me time to familiarize myself with the car before I slam my foot on the gas.

"Alright, get used to the track first before speeding around it," he says and chuckles. I do as I'm told, although I know it well from the walks we took at the academy. "First question," he yells over the roaring of the engine as we speed down the straight of the start and finish line. "Are you trying to kill me?" he asks when I take the curb a little too hard in the first corner. I should really break earlier.

"Is that the question?" I reply with a laugh.

"It's my question!" he says and holds onto the door when I drift in the next corner.

"Fine, I'll go easy on you, you big baby," I say and go as slow as he did for me before. "Ask me the real question, would you?" Gabriel shoots me an amused grin.

"When did you first realize that Gabriel Biancheri is the hottest guy you'll ever meet?" I shake my head, taking the curb on purpose this time to make him bounce in his seat.

"When I saw your di–" He cuts me off.

"Hey, woah, chérie!" he warns, but I'm confused now. "Cameras are rolling," Gabriel says, and I burst into laughter.

"*Dimples*, Gabriel, when I first saw your *dimples*," I clarify, and his face turns a bright red shade.

"Oh, shit. Well, whoever looks through this footage later is going to have a laugh." I have to do my best to stay focused on the road ahead of us, but it's difficult to keep my amusement at bay. "First question," Gabriel repeats, and I smile. "How long have you been interested in racing?" I hit the breaks in the corner only to press down on the gas again as we rush down the straight.

"Almost fourteen years now," I reply, and Gabriel moves on to ask me about my journey and experiences.

By the time I've completed about three laps, we're done with the questions, and I drive the car back into the pitlane. Gabriel turns to me after we take off our helmets and brings his lips to mine, but, for the sake of not being inappropriate in front of the cameras, he leans back sooner than either of us wants.

"That was fun," he says, and I agree.

We get out of the car, and Gabriel starts talking to his team in Italian. My body reacts in all sorts of ways because he sounds too sexy to keep it in check. I can barely feel my legs anymore, which is why I walk over to Gabriel and grab his arm for support. He squeezes my hand, smiles at me, and goes back to talking to the members of his team.

I'm impatiently waiting for him to finish so I can kiss him or even pull him to an empty room. My thoughts drift to what we would do, and I forget all about him speaking Italian, or where I am for that matter.

"Chérie?" he asks to bring me back to reality.

"I love it when you speak Italian," I swoon, and he laughs a little. His dimples are enough to make my mind go back to that small room with the panting...

"Ti amo," he says. He kisses me again before he wraps his arms around me.

"I might actually vomit." Christian's voice fills my ears, and Gabriel tenses instantly. "Valentina Romana, always complaining about the unfair treatment she's received in this sport when she gets everything handed to her on a silver platter." Gabriel is about to step past me and, most likely, punch Christian in the face for his comment, but I hold him in place.

"You call being kicked out of Formula Three for no reason getting things handed to me? What about getting turned down by every other driver academy? And everyone else who had the power to help me succeed in this sport? I've been turned away, shut down, and pushed out of racing my entire life. What did you have to do, *Your Royal Highness*? Beg daddy to make it happen and then get kicked out of every academy because of your own actions?" Christian takes a step toward me then, but Gabriel moves me behind him.

"Oh, look, how sweet. Your boyfriend's protecting you," the brat says, and I see Gabriel smile.

"I'm protecting you from her, not the other way around." He moves closer to the prince. "When I'm not here, Val will deal with you, but as long as I'm in your presence, it'd be wise for you to fear me. She *might* hold back from punching you, but I won't." I've never seen him this angry, but I can tell he's as sick of Christian as I am.

"Are you threatening me?" the prince asks, but Gabriel continues to smile.

"No, I'm warning you, Your Royal Highness, simply giving some free advice." He moves away from my rival, taking my hand and leading me inside to get some breakfast. "I can't wait for the day when he hears that you got the seat instead of him," Gabriel says and kisses my temple.

Neither can I.

Chapter 27

Gabriel

"Guillaume, look at our son! He looks so professional," my mom says as I settle down in my F4 car, getting ready for the first race of the season.

This is an important day in my career, but I'm not as nervous as I thought I'd be. My parents have a way of calming me. They say it's magic, but I know better. I know it's love.

"Take a picture. No, take a dozen. I always want to remember this moment," she adds, and my father stands in front of me, pulling out his little camera to do as she wants.

"How many is enough?" he asks her with a grin, and she pinches him in the arm. He laughs at her, pulling her close to press a kiss on her lips.

"Ewww," Jean says from next to me, and I shake my head in amusement. He thinks they're disgusting, but I can't wait for the day I have that with someone.

"Yeah, yeah, come here," Mom says, holding her hands out for Jean and lifting him into the air to attack his face with kisses.

I smile at them before my team pulls my attention to them, reminding me of everything I have to do for the start.

"Don't forget to breathe," Maxime chimes in, and I look up at my godfather, whose brown eyes stare into mine. "Your power lies in your breath, Gabri. Focus on it, control it, use it," he says, and I give him a nod to let him know I'm paying attention to his words. "Don't get distracted. It can be deadly," he warns, and I let out a deep breath.

"Don't scare him," my father scolds, but Maxime is right to remind me. It's important. "We have to go now, Gabriel, but you got this, son. We're proud of you, no matter what," my father tells me, tapping the front of my car and grabbing Jean by the hand.

"We love you, Gabriel," Mom adds, blowing me a kiss for good luck like she always does. I 'catch' it, placing it on top of my helmet so it stays with me for the duration of the race.

"Don't crash," Jean reminds me, and I assure him I will do my best to stay away from the other drivers and the barriers. He gives me a thumbs up with his stubby, short finger, and I can't help but smile. Maxime gives me a wink and walks away with them.

Man, I have the best family in the world.

I stare at the photograph of my mom, the one I keep in my wallet along with the ones of my father, grandparents, and Maxime. Today is the last day Valentina and I get to be together before I have to fly back to Monaco. It's also one of the hardest days of the year, but I'm not planning on telling her. We should be enjoying our time with each other, and I have to stop looking at my mom's photo. It won't bring her back, nothing will, and studying the picture will only make me sadder. I was hoping it would make me feel connected to her, but it's only ripped open old wounds so far.

Val's hands slip over my shoulders before she starts massaging my sore neck. I don't remember a time in my life when it hasn't been, which she knows. It's also why she always tries to knead out the knots there.

"She's beautiful," Valentina says, rubbing them out one at a time.

"She was." I turn to hand her the photo, and she takes it from me, settling down on the bed to study it.

"You have her eyes," she points out and looks at me to reveal she's smiling.

I reach out to touch her cheek, running my thumb over her soft skin. Her light eyes watch me as she lifts her hand to cover mine. A tsunami of comfort collides with the pain in my chest, easing the hurt inside of me.

"I miss her more than anyone. We had a special bond, and I'd give anything to feel close to her again," I admit to someone else for the first time in my life.

I pull Val onto my lap when a sad look spreads over her features, and she places her palms on each side of my neck.

"Don't worry, chérie, I'm fine. I just miss her, that's all," I assure her to wipe the concern off her face, but she frowns even more.

"I don't like it when you lie to me about your feelings. It's okay not to be okay, Gabriel, don't hide from me," she says, leaning her forehead against mine.

"Okay, I won't hide. It hurts, especially today because it would have been her fiftieth birthday," I say, and Valentina's eyes go wide from surprise. She leans away, her hands remaining on my throat, sending a warmth through me.

"Why didn't you tell me? I would have prepared something to celebrate her life," she states, and a genuine smile creeps onto my face as I guide her against me by her hips.

"Do you do that for your late family?" I ask, and she wiggles from side to side, a shy look in her eyes.

"No," she lies, her voice cracking from deceit. "Okay, yes, I do, but I've never told anyone, not even Adrian, so you need to keep this to yourself, which I know you will because I trust you, but–" Val cuts off when she realizes she hasn't stopped to end that sentence. "Sorry," she mumbles, embarrassment turning her cheeks a wonderful shade of red.

"What do you do to celebrate their lives?" I ask to shift her attention away from her rant and back to the sweet thing she was trying to tell me about before.

"I buy their favorite flowers, food, drink, and then watch the sun set while eating and listening to music that reminds me of them," she explains while her thumb trails over my bottom lip, watching my reaction to see what I think of her tradition.

"Just when I thought you couldn't get more beautiful, here you are, showing me another piece of you to fall in love with," I say, and she places her lips on mine, smiling against me.

"Alright, let's go get her favorite things," Val announces, trying to move off my lap, but I hold her in place for a moment, not ready to let go when I'm mesmerized by her big heart for the millionth time since I've met her.

"Kiss me," I beg, but she tilts her head with a curious smile.

"I thought we were past asking each other that," she says, and I lick my lips, biting down on the bottom one to keep from smiling.

"I plan on those two words to be the last I'll ever say, right after 'I love you'," I reply, and she gives me the small eye-roll that always comes with my cheesy words. I squeeze her perfectly round ass, forcing her to focus on me. "Kiss me," I repeat, and Valentina lowers her mouth to mine, our breaths intertwining.

"Always," she whispers before kissing me, the watermelon taste from her lip balm making me groan against her. She always tastes too good. "Let's go," she says against my mouth and slides off my lap to grab her purse.

We go to a local supermarket to buy two bottles of lemon iced tea, some bread with mortadella, and a bouquet of tulips, all of Mom's favorites. Valentina holds my hand as we make our way through the store, finding new ways to bring a smile to my face.

I miss Mom and everyone else I've lost, but this woman, this perfect human I get to call mine, eases all the pain I've ever felt and still endure. Val makes life worth living, and I don't ever want to lose her, I can't.

I drive us back to the headquarters where we walk toward the track, sitting down on one of the grandstands just in time to watch the sunset. Valentina hands me a sandwich and bottle, grabbing the others for herself. She takes a big bite, and, for a moment, I'm too lost in her to start eating myself.

"Here, you can play her favorite songs, if you'd like," she says with a full mouth, which she's covering with one hand as the other gives me her phone.

I notice a playlist named 'Gabriel's favorites', bringing a smile to my face. My fingers tap on the screen, searching for a few songs to play that remind me of my mom.

"I'm going to miss you a lot when I go back tomorrow," I say after a while of silence between us. The music in the background is quiet so I can still have a conversation with her.

Val turns to me, a forced smile on her lips.

"I know, and I'll miss you, but we'll see each other soon, mon soleil. We always do," she promises, and I move toward her, pulling her between my legs and kissing her cheek. "I love you," Val says, leaning into me so I can completely wrap my arms around her.

"I love you, mon tournesol," I reply, nuzzling my face in the crook of her neck to inhale her sweet scent. "More than I'll ever understand."

Chapter 28

Valentina

My simulator times have been strong, a lot more so than Christian's. I have him beat in endurance too, and analysis, which has always been easy for me. However, he's physically stronger than I am, at least for the moment. Over the past few years, I haven't focused as much on lifting weights as I have on every other category. Seeing Christian do better in it is infuriating, especially because he keeps bothering me about it.

"Finally, Tina, you have all the proof you need to see you're weaker than me," he said yesterday after Andrea told us our results. I rolled my eyes. "Now, what does that show you?" he challenged me.

"It shows me you suck at analysis, considering you came to this conclusion by looking at one data point, Sebastian," I replied, pissing him off.

There is something that crosses his face every time I use a wrong name for him, and I'm convinced it's a combination of anger and disappointment. Meanwhile, victory floods my features whenever I manage to knock the arrogance off his lips.

Today, Andrea is taking us to *Extrema Kart*, a Go-Kart race track near the academy. Christian has been uncharacteristically quiet all morning, and

I enjoy the peace. Lucie and Haru try to tell me a story about what they did last weekend, but I only understand half of it because they keep laughing. He shoots her a longing look after a while, which she doesn't seem to notice. No one does, except me. I see the way he smiles at Lucie as she beams at the chaotic time they had at the track during our time off. Eventually, she gives up and simply takes Haru's hand. I grin to myself and can't help but wish Gabriel was here.

It's been two days since he left to go back to Monaco for work and family responsibilities. The last time I saw Adrian and James was at the event four days ago, and I miss them a lot. We text and call, but it's never going to be the same: James and Gabriel just barging into my house, and Adrian always being home after training. I'm alone here, and, as excited as I am, it also brings back the lonely feeling I always experienced in LA.

"Alright, everyone, here are the rules for today. Ready?" Andrea asks, and we all answer with a 'Yes, Boss!'. "Have fun, okay? You've been working hard enough this week. Take a break," they add, and everyone cheers, except Christian. He's been frowning the entire time.

The others and I move over to where the karts and helmets are, but Andrea calls me over to them. Christian is already standing beside them, a brooding frown on his thin lips.

"I have some news. This morning, I got a call from Lorenzo Mattia, the Ferrari F1 team principal," they start, and I hold my breath. "He said one of you can go to Baku for the fifth race and gather some experience working with the team." I take an involuntary step back, a nervous feeling spreading through my chest now. "I want you to take today's race to prove to me you're worthy of this opportunity, okay?" they ask, and both of us nod.

Andrea gives me a serious look, reminding me Christian is willing to do anything to win, that I should be careful.

"I'm going to grind you to dust," Christian whispers in my ear as we make our way back over to the karts.

"You never have before," I reply when all of a sudden, he places his leg in front of mine, tripping me. I lose balance, but, luckily, Lucie and Haru were watching the whole thing and catch me before I fall to the ground.

"Don't fucking underestimate me," Christian warns in French to ensure I'm the only one who understands him. *Asshole.*

"Are you alright?" Lucie asks, but I assure her I'm fine, the anger I feel for Christian fueling me now. My body was tired from training, but adrenalin replaces exhaustion. He can't win, I won't let him.

Andrea reminds us one last time to have fun and be safe before we get to drive around the track to get a feel for it. Then, we do a mock Qualifying to find out who will start where. Everyone simply takes one lap, and Andrea stops our time. Haru is fastest overall with me in second, Christian in third, Lucie in fourth, and the rest of the guys taking up places five to nine.

Our instructor stands at the side with a green flag in their hand, waving it when we're allowed to finally start. My reaction time is slightly better than Haru's, allowing me to overtake him in the first corner. I speed down the straight, breaking late to give me more of an advantage, but Christian is right behind me.

This race is only supposed to be two laps so that we can have careless fun after, but they are the longest laps of my life.

At the start of the second one, Christian bumps into the back of my kart, and I barely manage to keep it from swerving off the track. This gives him an advantage, allowing him to pull up next to me. I push ahead again, but he slams against me even harder than before.

My kart gets shoved into the barriers and off-track until I'm on a grass area where I'm thrown from it before it flips over itself. A stinging pain shoots through my left hand as I roll away from the vehicle. I distantly hear someone screaming my name, but my ears are ringing from hitting my head and helmet on the ground.

"Valentina," the voice repeats, and I identify it to be Andrea's.

They appear in front of me, a first-aid kit in their grasp. My hand starts to throb, and I lift my right one to hold onto it.

"Can you take your helmet off?" they ask, and I attempt to, but pain shoots through my left thumb.

I shake my head, and they remove it for me, the ringing finally stopping now that the pressure on my head is gone.

"What happened?" is the next question Andrea asks, and I look into their brown eyes.

"Christian, he–uhm, he–" I cut off, the shock confusing my mind.

"Did he push you off track?" I manage to nod before Andrea says something in Italian I don't understand. It sounds like swear words. "It's okay, Valentina, you're okay. I have some medical training in cases of emergency like this. May I check you for injury?" they ask, and I thank them.

Andrea puts pressure on every part of my legs, watching my reaction to see if anything hurts. They move on to my ribs and neck, but everything else is fine. The only thing bothering me is my left wrist.

"Nothing's broken, just bruised. It should heal in a few days," they assure me, and I offer yet another nod.

"I'm sorry for this. I tried to keep control of the kart, but he hit it so hard, I had no control," I explain when my brain clears up and sentences are forming again.

Andrea grabs me by the shoulders then.

"This was not your fault. I'm so happy you're okay, Valentina, and I'm the one who is sorry. I didn't think he would go this far to win the Baku opportunity," they say, but I give them a comforting smile.

"Don't worry, he would have done this whether you had told us about it or not," I reply while they wrap my wrist and hand in a dressing to keep it in place.

"Can you stand?" I try to, but the shock hasn't worn off completely, and my legs give in from shaking. "Okay, it's alright. Take your time."

This isn't my first crash, but it was a lot scarier than any other I've been in. After a few more moments, I manage to walk back to the main area to sit down. Andrea gets an ice pack for me and a bottle of water so I can take some painkillers.

As soon as the other drivers return, Andrea storms toward them, grabbing Christian by the collar and dragging him out of his kart. They throw him on the grass area before the prince has any time to react.

"Are you proud of yourself? You could have cost Valentina her life!" A wave of fear spreads through my chest at the thought.

"I won, so, yes, I'm very proud," he replies, and my fear is replaced by disgust.

"You're an arrogant, spoiled, childish boy, and, let me assure you, it won't get you far in my academy," they spit, and Christian stands up to step in front of them.

"It's not your academy, it's Mr. Reiner's. He is in charge, not you," he replies, as smug as always.

"Trust me, child, it's *my* academy. What I say goes, and you're no longer going to be a part of it anymore." Christian grabs them by the arm, making Andrea's eyes go wide.

"It was an accident. How will you prove it wasn't?" he asks, but our instructor realizes he's right.

They can't prove it, and neither can I. It'd be my word against Christian's, and, speaking from experience, people tend to believe the royal man over anyone else.

"Pull that shit again, and I won't need proof." Andrea moves him out of the way before walking back over to me. They squat down, a sincere apologetic expression on their face. "I wish there was something I could do," they say, and I smile.

"I know, don't worry. It'll be fine. He won't do anything again if he hopes to stay in the academy," I reply, trying to convince myself and Andrea. In reality, I have no idea what Christian is willing to do.

"Congratulations, Valentina, you have just earned yourself the opportunity to fly to Baku and work with the Ferrari F1 team," Andrea announces to everyone, and my rival turns abruptly, anger all over his face.

"But she didn't even finish the race!" he complains, balling his hands into fists. Andrea raises themself and turns to scowl at him.

"I said in order to get this opportunity, you have to show you're worthy of it. That did not mean you had to finish first or at all. Valentina drove a clean race and suffered from your immaturity. She is more than worthy, you are more than not," Andrea replies, their voice firm.

Christian storms off without saying another word. Satisfaction spreads through my chest, and excitement settles in my heart. I will get to spend an entire weekend gathering experiences with an F1 team. On top of that, I will get to be with my favorite people in the world. At least something good came from Christian's immaturity.

"Go home to Monaco, Valentina, rest, and pack for Baku. I'll see you when you return," they say to me, and I let out a deep breath. Tears almost shoot into my eyes at the thought of finally going home.

It's been too long.

"It's okay, little champion, you're okay," Grandpa assures me as I hold my pinky and cry from pain.

He took us karting for the last time before we have to move, and one of the other people here accidentally bumped into me.

"Let me see," he says, inspecting the damage, even though both of us know I'm not crying because of my stupid finger.

"It hurts," I lie to cover up the fact that I'm weeping because this will be the last time in a while we get to be together.

"Val? Are you okay?" Adrian's voice appears from behind, and he squats down in front of me too, wiping my tears and checking my face for injury. "What happened?" he asks Grandpa.

"Someone accidentally hit her kart, and she hurt her finger on the wheel," he explains, and I nod.

"Who? I'll make them apologize," Adrian replies and stands up, but

Grandfather places his hand on his arm to keep him here.

"Don't worry, Valentina is going to be just fine." My grandpa catches my tears with the back of his fingers and smiles. "When we Romanas crash, we keep pushing with our heads held high. The pain will fade, but the experience will stay forever. You'll learn from it, grow from it, and, ultimately, benefit from it. Okay?"

"Okay," I reply and smile back. "It doesn't hurt anymore," I assure both of them because Adrian is still looking at me with concern.

I move my finger to prove I'm not lying, and they each give me a proud look when I raise my head high.

"No one can ever take that strength away from you, little champion."

He's right because I won't let them.

Chapter 29

Valentina

I didn't let anyone know I was coming home, not even Adrian. All I told Gabriel was to please go to my room and find a ring I've lost. He didn't understand but agreed to go anyway, no questions asked. This man is wrapped around my finger, just like I am around his.

Adrian told me he'd only be back home in the evening, which gives Gabriel and me enough time to catch up on the three days we've been apart. Then, after, I plan on calling James, and the four of us will have dinner and play a few card games. My schedule for the day sounds too good to be true, but I'm going to do my best to make it happen.

The taxi driver gives me a strange look when I place the money on his middle console as soon as he parks and hurry out of the car. I run toward my front door, dropping my backpack in the foyer and sprinting up the stairs.

Gabriel is already in my bedroom, his attention on his phone before he lifts it to his ear. Mine starts ringing then, and his eyes shift to me as I hit the answer button.

"I'm finally home," I say into the speaker, and he throws his phone onto the bed, opening his arms for me. I jump into them, wrapping my limbs around his body.

"So am I," he whispers against my neck.

I slide my fingers into his hair and grin. This is pure happiness. Being in his arms and feeling his body pressed against mine is my personal heaven.

Gabriel drops me onto my feet before capturing my lips with his, letting me know how much he missed me by the way he sighs against my mouth.

"What are you doing here?" he asks before his gaze shifts to my bruised wrist. "Who did this to you?" Anger and concern slip across his face, but worry wins, settling in his green-brown eyes.

"I took the curb wrong when we were karting, and—" Gabriel cuts me off before I can finish the lie.

"It was the royal dickhead, wasn't it?" I have no intention of telling him how terrifying the crash truly was, but I answer his question with a nod. "How?" My face is between his hands, his thumb tracing my bottom lip.

Although his touch is soft, I know he's angry. He's probably never been this angry, and I understand perfectly. If he came home with even the slightest scratch on his body because of someone else, I would be furious with whoever hurt him.

"It was a karting accident, but it's okay, don't worry. It already feels a lot better," I assure him and step back to drop onto my bed.

"Chérie, it's not okay. At least tell me you gave back harder than he dished out," he replies, getting frustrated with me now.

"Not a scratch on him, you want to know why?" I ask, and he crosses his arms in front of his chest.

It momentarily distracts me, his muscles and veins sticking out from under his rolled-up long-sleeved shirt.

"Tell me," he replies in French, and I smile.

"Because I'm better than him. I don't resort to violence, and I never will. The seat will be mine because I'm the one who follows all the rules."

My answer doesn't satisfy him one bit so I slide my shirt over my head and crooked my finger, signaling for him to come closer.

"Get your sweet ass over here and fuck me until I can't walk anymore, Gabriel." He runs his tongue over his bottom lip before biting down on it.

"You want it harder today, chérie?" he asks, lifting his shirt over his head and moving toward me.

"Yes," I admit while he places his hands on each side of me on the mattress.

"You want me to flip you onto your chest, pull you in by the hips, and fuck you from behind?" I swallow hard when his face is merely a few centimeters from mine, my heart racing uncontrollably fast.

"Yes." I bring my lips against his, barely brushing them.

My hand moves to his bulge so I can palm him through his jeans. His confident composure fades ever so slightly, and I smirk at the control my touch has over him.

"Just watch the wrist," I say with a challenging smile, and he brings it to his mouth, pressing a kiss to the dressing.

"I'll be gentle with it," he assures me as he places it on my lap again. "Have you ever had rough sex?" he asks, pushing my curls out of my face to grab it and tilt it upward to him.

"No, have you?" Gabriel gives me a sad smile.

"You can't make love if you're not in love. Before you, that was the only type of sex I had," he replies, and I hold my breath as he guides my lips back to his. "Say 'tournesol' if it gets too much for you, and I will stop immediately," he says, and I can see in his eyes that he doesn't want to overstep any boundaries.

But I need this. I want him to be rough with me, to fuck me like never before. He's been careful so far, almost as if I'd break if he pushed harder. I'm not easily broken, and we both crave this, I can see it in his eyes.

"Bring me pleasure," I say before his lips crash onto mine.

Chapter 30

Gabriel

Valentina's tongue slips into my mouth, making a groan leave me. She smiles like she always does when I let her know just how much I'm under her control. I do my best not to chuckle at her proud grin and focus on her demand. Val wants it rough, and I'm going to give my woman everything she desires, starting by removing those tight yoga pants that hug her ass way too perfectly. She watches me as I bring them to her ankles, my eyes shifting to her drenched panties. Fuck.

"Did I not tell you to be rough?" she asks, and I cock an eyebrow.

"You don't like it when I tease you?" I challenge, smirking at her as I run the tips of my fingers up her thighs, watching goosebumps appear in their wake. She's just as horny for me as I am for her, and I love it.

"Why am I even still in my underwear?" Valentina challenges back.

I narrow my eyes slightly, tilting my head as my gaze drops back to her panties. I want them gone, need them so far away from her body, it makes me ache. But I love teasing her. I love watching her squirm a little as I run my hands over the sensitive skin near her pussy. My index finger slips down the curve between her thigh and mound, and if I go a bit lower... *there it is.* Her whole body trembles from my touch.

"Patience, chérie," I whisper, running my fingers over the smooth skin on her stomach now. "I need you wet for me, for my cock," I say, but she lets out a whimper of complaint.

"I already am," she says, and I lean my head down.

"Not enough."

My mouth trails kisses and bites along the inside of her leg, making her press her soft thighs against my ears. She's trying to ease her ache, but I won't let her. That's my job.

"A little longer," I say, leaving wet kisses along the same curve I traced a moment ago.

Val moans, making my already hard cock unbearably so. It's begging me to hurry up, to slip inside of her, but my brain is still in charge, and it's focusing on her hard nipples right now. They're still covered by her bra, irritating me.

"Arch your back for me, baby," I command, and she does as she's told. "That's my girl," I praise as I remove the ridiculous fabric, which does nothing to contain her breasts.

Once they're free from their containment, I don't waste a single second. I wrap my mouth around her left nipple, sucking so hard, she cries out from pleasure instantly.

"Fuck," she groans, her hand moving onto my arm.

Her nails dig into my bicep as I massage her tit, flicking my tongue over the ache I created a moment ago. Valentina rolls her hips against me, trying to bring my throbbing groin against her swollen clit.

"Not yet," I say and push her hips down, moving over to her right nipple and paying the same attention to it. God, she tastes so sweet, like candy. I need more of her, need my mouth to be everywhere on her body at once.

I curl my fingers around the thin waistband of her thong and rip it off her body. Valentina gasps, but I don't give her mind time to linger on the broken fabric before I press my mouth to her swollen clit, groaning against it.

"Gabriel," she moans, and it takes all of my willpower to pull away again.

I'm not nearly done tasting her, but that's not what Val wants right now. She wants me to be rough, and I've teased her for long enough. Not to mention, I'm going to go crazy if her walls aren't wrapped around me soon.

I stand up straight, taking in the sight of her completely naked in front of me, her curves perfectly on display. My already hard dick press against my jeans, and I suck in another sharp breath. My thumbs trail over her hard nipples, circling them until she rolls her head from pleasure. I place a soft slap on her left one, trying to see how she reacts first before I keep going.

"Shit," she gasps, biting her bottom lip. "That felt..." Val trails off, a satisfied, little moan leaving her. Fuck, that sound gets under my skin, lighting me on fire.

"I know, baby," I reply before kissing her.

Desire takes over completely, and I pull Val close to me by her ankles, flipping her around until she's on her stomach.

"Oh," she says and giggles.

My fingers move to her hips, guiding her ass upward and toward my throbbing groin. I run my palms over her skin before slapping her right ass cheek and leaning down to flick my tongue over the ache. She bucks against me, a soft moan leaving her.

"You like that, don't you, chérie?" I ask, repeating the same action again, this time on the left side.

"Fuck," she whimpers, grinding her ass against my cock again. "Please, Gabriel, no more teasing," she begs while I rub my hands over her round ass, squeezing and kneading it until I'm satisfied. "Please," Val repeats when I don't move, and I'm ready to hand her the fucking world, heaven, and hell.

I unzip my pants and slide them down just enough for my erection to be free of the uncomfortable containment. A sharp groan leaves me as I roll the condom down my aching cock, the need to fill her taking over.

I trail my hand down her spine, watching goosebumps spread over her skin everywhere my fingers touch. I keep going until I reach the back of her neck, guiding her into an upright position.

"I'm fucking you from behind, ma chérie, so I need you to do something for me," I start and bring my index finger to her clit, rubbing tight circles that make her moan.

"Anything," she replies and grabs onto my wrist to keep my hand right where it is on her pussy.

"Keep saying my name. Remember whose dick is pleasuring you, baby." Valentina nods, more moans leaving her as she grinds herself against me.

I spread her legs wider, replacing my finger with my cock and gliding it back and forth. She's so wet for me, it almost makes me explode right then and there.

"Gabriel!" she screams, and I smirk to myself. *Fuck, I need to hear it again.*

I align myself with her entrance, anticipation spreading through me like wildfire. The thrill of being with Val takes over, and I slam into her, holding her against my chest while she moans my name again.

My lips brush over the shell of her ear before I bite down on the lobe, making her tense. The feeling of her wrapped around my cock lights me on fire everywhere. Every inch of me is burning from the heat she's responsible for, and it's weighing heavy on me in the best way possible. *God, she feels too fucking good.*

"You were made for me," I whisper into her ear, moving on to suck on her soft spot.

A whimper escapes her lips as I cup her breasts and squeeze her hard, perfect nipples.

"And you for me," she replies, breathless and in pleasure.

"Yes, I was, only for you."

I guide her chest back onto the mattress, keeping her ass in place to stay inside her without moving for a moment longer. Then, once Val has spread out her arms and tilted her head to the side, I slide back out, thrusting inside harder than I ever have before. She grips the sheets, repeating my name over and over as I create a friction that makes us weak. This position allows me to go deeper, something both of us are enjoying. I slap her ass once again, her body trembling in response.

"Merde," she moans, and I can't help the smirk on my face.

I'm pleasuring her to the point where she switches to her mother tongue. The thought makes me go harder and faster, smacking her ass every once in a while to hear that same whimpering-surprised sound again. It surprises her that she likes it so much.

"You look so good wrapped around my cock like this, chérie," I say, slamming inside of her with another hard thrust.

The orgasm builds in my erection, slowly spreading through me, letting me know I'm close, *way too fucking close.* I push it down, for now, focusing on getting Val to her personal heaven before I let mine take over completely. My body is consumed by pleasure, thriving off it now like it would adrenalin.

"Gabriel, I'm gonna–fuck–oh fuck," she says in French, and I lift her up once more so my chest presses against her back.

"I know, ma chérie. I've got you," I say, my movements never stopping.

Val falls apart, her body shaking from the orgasm as she screams for me. I keep pushing inside of her, my own moans filling the room. She turns her head to me, claiming my lips with hers and sending me straight over the edge she brought me to in the first place. My whole body tenses as the build-up in my cock finally releases, my thrusts slowing as it pulsates, and I finally spill into the condom inside of her.

For the briefest moment, I feel invincible as my whole body is consumed by the feeling of relief. Relief both because the tension has dissolved within me and because Valentina is mine in the same way I am hers. We're addicted to each other now, and I plan on staying that way for the rest of my life.

"Shit," I say, my chest rising and falling abruptly against her back.

My fingers slip over her hips before I trace her stretch marks, trying to memorize their pattern on her soft skin. They're one of my favorite features on her.

She falls forward too soon, breaking our connection. I shove the desire to frown at the loss of contact aside and smile instead because Val's happy grin is everything to me. The way we fit together reminds me of a single gap on a bookshelf and the perfect-sized book to slide into the void.

Nothing compares to the rush of emotions I feel when Valentina and I are together like this, nothing but the rush of racing. Those are the two best feelings in the world for me, and I never want to give either of them up.

"I love you, mon tournesol," I blurt out, and she beams up at me.

"I love you more, mon soleil," she replies, but I shake my head.

"Would you really like to start an argument about that right now?" I challenge, and she chuckles, her full, plump lips pulling into a smirk.

"No, I'd rather make out a little more," Valentina says, her eyes bluer today than ever. Usually, the green color comes through more, in the sun the brown, but never the blue, not like this. "How about this? I love you *the same.*" I give her a satisfied nod.

"I like that," I admit and lean down to bring my lips to hers again.

There is no doubt in my mind that she was made for me and I for her in every way possible. I truly am the luckiest man alive.

Chapter 31

Valentina

Gabriel is fast asleep on my bed when I get up to get some water. He needs a nap after we've been having sex for the past couple of hours, and I need to see if Adrian is home. I haven't spoken to him since yesterday morning, and we haven't seen each other in almost a week.

I try to be as quiet as possible while I make my way downstairs and find Adrian sitting on the couch, watching television. He ignores my presence, pretending I'm not there even as I sit down next to him. I grab the remote from the table and press pause on his movie.

"I'm watching that," he complains in French, and I realize something is wrong. Adrian doesn't speak to me in French.

"What's going on?" I ask him in English.

"You want to know?" I nod, and he sits up on the couch. "Okay, well, my sister had a horrible karting crash yesterday, and she hasn't taken the time to speak to me once because she was busy with her boyfriend." My eyes go wide.

"How do you know about the accident?" I ask, and he takes a sip of his water, rolling his eyes.

"Andrea called me because they were worried about Christian's behavior, which doesn't fucking matter right now. I come home today, see your luggage, and think to myself 'Wow, I actually get to spend time with my sister today'. I hope you can understand how upset I was when I had to leave the house because you were fucking my teammate."

His words hurt me, and I wish he'd stop, but I also understand why he's upset.

"You have been distant, barely talking to me, and obsessed with a guy that's going to make you cry in a couple of days anyway. I feel like soon, you're going to be cheering for him instead of me. I'm still your family, Val, and as selfish as it sounds, I would appreciate it if every now and then you would think of me first!" Maybe if he'd approached it differently and told me in a calm tone instead of yelling, I wouldn't be angry.

"You know what, Adrian? That's bullshit. I came here to spend time with all of you, and I thought you were training today so I called Gabriel. I truly am sorry you came home early and had to hear that, but I'm not sorry I finally have a life."

He cocks both of his eyebrows, waiting for my explanation.

"In LA, all I did was stay at home every single day, train, and do homework, but I want more. I have Evangelin, James, Gabriel, you, and my shot at making it into F1. It's hard to juggle, and I am sorry about this morning, but I just want to experience things with Gabriel, things I have only dreamed of. I was hoping you would understand."

I can't believe he started a fight. It's as if no one wants me to stay happy for more than a day because someone always has to swoop in and ruin my good mood. It's ridiculous.

"Whatever, Val. You can fly out with Gabriel tomorrow. You can stay in his room, and you can cheer for him. Baku is one of his favorite races anyway. After all, maybe he'll be the world champion this year, and you can celebrate everything with him. Go for it, Valentina, live your life, forget about your brother, who has always taken care of you."

That's not fair. He's acting like I've forgotten about him when he's the one who barely has time for me too.

"How could you treat me like this when I'm the one who has always protected you?" he adds, and I lose it.

"Yeah, you protected me so well, Aunt Carolina abused me for years without you knowing!" The words leave my mouth before I can stop myself.

This is never how I wanted to tell him about that, but I couldn't help myself. The anger overwhelmed me. That's always what I do wrong, I throw things around without thinking about them. Adrian's eyes are wide open and so is his mouth.

"She what?" he asks, but I'm too surprised to talk.

I cannot believe I blurted this out to win a goddamn argument.

"I'm going to kill her!" he yells, but I am still sitting on the couch, unable to move or speak. "I can't believe this, I can't believe this," he repeats over and over again.

I cover my face with my right hand and let out a sigh.

"How did she hurt you? You know what? Never mind. I'm going to kill her," he says before he storms off, and I get up to run after him.

"Adrian, please don't leave!"

He's gone before I can catch up with him, and I sink to the floor by the entrance of my home.

"Chérie?" I lift my head to look in the direction of Gabriel's voice.

My brain is trying to process everything that just happened. He settles down next to me on the ground, and I take his hand in mine. We sit in complete silence for a couple of minutes until he opens his mouth.

"Do you want to talk about it?" I nod, and Gabriel gets up again, pulling me with him. "I'm going to get you some ice cream. My mom used to say ice cream never fixes any problems, but it tastes so good, it will make you temporarily forget about how bad everything else is," he says as we walk into the kitchen.

"I've never heard words I relate to more," I reply, and he chuckles.

Once the ice cream is placed in front of me, I take the spoon and bring some of it to my mouth. Gabriel watches me closely, unsure of what I need from him.

"I said something to Adrian I shouldn't have told him in such a sensitive moment." Even saying it out loud makes me mad. "I told him about what our aunt did to me," I explain, and pain flashes over Gabriel's face.

"I heard that part. I want you to know you don't have to open up to me, but you can. If you want to cry, ball your eyes out, if you want to scream, do it until you lose your voice. You have every right, and all I want to do is make you comfortable to finally talk to someone about it," he assures me, and I give him half a smile.

"I love you so much," I say, which sums up everything I want to tell him.

"I love you the same," he replies.

I take a deep breath and relax my facial muscles, which are twitching in response to my forced expression.

"I've never told anyone, except James, who found out on his own," I start, my hands shaking now. Gabriel takes them in his, pressing soft kisses to the back of them. "She didn't hit me often to make sure Adrian wouldn't find out, but it started soon after we moved in with her."

Tears shoot into my eyes, and I wish I could stop them. I don't want the mention of this story to bring me pain, but it's part of who I am now. I need to speak about this if I ever want to move on.

"It was easy for her to hurt me, to try and force me into being some-one she could accept. Naturally, she could never accept any version of me." I pause, unsure where to keep going.

"It's okay, take your time. You don't have to rush this," he assures me as I bring my legs to my chest on the chair.

"I don't know why Dad decided we should move in with my mother's sis-ter and not stay with Grandpa, but what could we do after his death? Grandpa tried to fight it, but Aunt Carolina had already accepted. To this day, I can't understand why she wanted us if she hated me," I say, but Gabriel gives me a look that tells me he has a suspicion.

"She wanted the money you came with, chérie," he replies, and I stare at something behind him. He's probably right. "Why didn't you tell Adrian?" His question is genuine as he tries to understand this dark time of my life.

"Telling anyone about Carolina was never an option. Adrian would have only tried to take me out of the house, meaning he would have had to give up his career, and he wouldn't have been able to keep me anyway. I thought about telling him everything and asking him to move back to Monaco so that we could live with Grandpa, but then he died, and I was stuck in the same situation again."

I pause for another brief second before I'm able to speak. Gabriel squeezes my hand reassuringly, his eyes focused on my face.

"Nothing I ever did pleased that awful woman, and every single time I wasn't who she wanted me to be, I paid for it. She only stopped because James threatened her, and she knew better than to lay a finger on me after." I take another deep breath and watch a tear roll down Gabriel's cheek.

"Sorry, I'm sorry," he quickly apologizes. "Just the thought of you going through that, I can't even begin to describe how it makes me feel. I wish I'd known, I could have done something to help you," he says, and I squeeze his hand.

"I know, but what happened, happened. It will never leave me, and I will never be able to forget how weak and helpless I felt. It's easier for me to talk about now than it was a while ago. The only reason why I haven't is because I know Adrian would blame himself for not knowing and protecting me. That's why I am so angry it came out now and in the way it did. It's not fair, and I'm sure he's punching a wall somewhere." Tears stream down my face, blurring my vision. Guilt settles deep in my chest, and I wish my brother hadn't left.

"You're allowed to let it come out in any way you want, chérie." He drops his head onto our intertwined hands and lets out a deep breath. "I can't believe I made your life even more difficult than it already was."

The shame in his voice makes my heart drop. He lifts his head again to show me that more tears have left his eyes. I admire the way he never hides his emotions, that he isn't ashamed to cry in front of me when he needs to.

"I am so sorry," he says, and I lift my hand to wipe his tears.

"When will you ever understand you've made me the happiest woman in the world? You love me in a way that can destroy you, I know because I love you in the same stupid, irrational way, and that's why you were scared. So was I."

Gabriel gives me an absent-minded nod as I look down at my ice cream. I push the bowl away when I see all of it has melted.

"Let's go to bed. We need to wake up early to catch our flight."

There is nothing I can do about Adrian right now. I know he needs time to process this. I also know he's probably at James', which is why I call my best friend. He picks up after one ring.

"Val, thank God, I was just about to call you. Adrian is crying on my sofa, saying he's the worst person on the planet. What the fuck happened?" More guilt washes over me in an instant.

"I told him about Aunt Carolina during a heated argument," I admit, shame in my voice.

"Bloody hell, okay, I'll handle it. Go lie down and rest, I'll talk to him." I let out the breath I've been holding, and, right before I can hang up, he says, "I love you, Val." A small smile creeps onto my lips.

"I love you," I reply, and he hangs up. I still feel guilty about Adrian, but at least I know he's safe and James will take care of him.

Gabriel and I walk upstairs, and he sits down next to me on my bed, tucking one of my curls behind my ear. He presses his lips to mine before he crawls back on the mattress and wraps the blanket around himself. His eyes close, and he starts snoring, which I know he's faking. Gabriel only snores very lightly sometimes, not this aggressively. It makes me chuckle.

I lie down next to him and remove my pants, pain shooting through my wrist.

"Oh, wait, here, take this," he says, pulls his shirt off his body, and hands it to me. "Put this on."

"What if I don't want to wear your old shirt," I ask, and he frowns at me.

"Well, until I can replace it with something more meaningful, you are going to have to wear this for me."

I switch shirts, making a content smile spread across his face. Gabriel's mahogany scent fills my nose, and I let out a sigh. I put my head on his muscular chest, making sure my wrist is resting in a good position on my side.

"When you asked me if I've ever thought about marriage and children, I only told you I haven't had the time to think about marriage," I start, and he kisses the top of my head.

"I remember," he says, pressing another kiss to the same spot.

"I have thought about having children," I admit, silence filling the room again.

"Do you want any?" Gabriel asks, making my breathing hitch.

"I didn't. With one mother abandoning me, and the other mother figure in my life being an abuser, I always thought I should never be one. I thought there was no way I could be a good mom, but ever since I met Evangelin and experienced the love of a mother figure, it feels different. I feel different." I look up at him, and he smiles down at me.

"She helped you realize you're neither of those horrible women," he says.

"Yes, she did. One day, I'll make a good parent, whether it is to a baby or a dog or a fish," I say, and he chuckles.

"You'll be the best mother in the world because of your experiences. You'll be everything you never had, and they will be the happiest children in the world," he replies, and I push myself up to kiss his jaw. "Of course until they reach their teenage and adult years, and all their friends will have a crush on you." I laugh at his comment, but he takes my face in his hand, forcing my eyes to his. "And then they'll hate me because I'll be living the dream of calling you my wife every day of my life." He kisses me, and I let that fantasy play out in my head.

"Twenty-one, almost twenty-two, and you're already done searching the world for someone else?" I challenge, but he doesn't find it one bit amusing.

"I've been done since I first laid my eyes on you, mon tournesol," he says and kisses me again, and again, and then one more time.

"So have I."

I wish this moment wasn't tainted by the fight between my brother and me.

I have to find a way to fix this.

Chapter 32

Valentina

After a five-hour flight, and a twenty-minute car ride, Gabriel, Hector, and I make it to the hotel in Baku. The fifth race of the year is one of James' and Gabriel's favorite places to drive, and I remember Dad saying how exciting it is. He always talked about his work and everything he experienced throughout his career. The same one that brought him more joy than his own children.

My heart aches in my chest when I recall the day he died, the car crash into our living room. I still remember how loud it was, Adrian panicking, and the fear that had settled in my chest. Adrian had told me to stay upstairs while the paramedics took a long time to get Dad out of the car.

I shake my head to force the horrific event out of my thoughts. I don't want to remember anymore, especially because thinking about Adrian and how protective he was that night makes me sad. I haven't spoken to him since he left our house, and he isn't returning any of my calls or texts. The last message I received from James said my brother is much calmer, which lifts a burden off my shoulders.

It also makes it easier to focus on Gabriel, the fact that we are going to share a room, and the way he flashes me his dimples when he smiles at me.

He hands me my key and brings me in close, his mouth hovering over mine as we wait for the woman at the reception to give him back his credit card. Gabriel takes it, not once kissing me, and I can't stand the teasing. The last time I remember him kissing me was after the take-off.

We get onto the elevator with Hector. When he leaves again, Gabriel wraps his arms around me and starts to nibble on my ear. A shiver runs down my spine, and I have to bite my bottom lip to keep from admitting how good it feels.

The elevator opens, and I walk out, leaving him without saying a single word. I unlock the door to our hotel room... *our hotel room.* A smile spreads over my face but I hide it from him. I throw my purse onto the bed, and Gabriel drops on it as well. His shirt lifts, and I temporarily forget about the rest of the world.

"Can you help me undress? I want to take a shower," I say, and he sits up more quickly than I've ever seen anyone do.

"Hell yes," he replies, and I laugh. "I'll help you take a shower too," he says, but I shake my head.

"No, thank you. I don't need you to, I'm only going to wash my body," I assure him, and he pouts.

"But I want to shower with you," he begs, and my knees go weak.

"Maybe later," I manage to say, and he nods, clearly thinking about something.

He undoes the zipper of my dress, his fingertips leaving goosebumps in their wake. Once he's done, Gabriel steps in front of me.

"Why are you teasing me?" he asks as he leans down to press a kiss to my lips, but I move my head so they connect with my jaw instead. "You know I want you, why do you want me to beg?"

He sucks on the sensitive skin below my jaw, and I let my head fall back. His accent has a way of making my body feel a million sensations.

"Don't make me beg," he says in French, and I am putty in his hands.

An involuntary moan leaves my lips when he tugs hard on the sensitive skin on my neck. He flicks his tongue over the ache, and I step back.

"No, nope, we're not spending the entire day in the hotel room having sex. I want to do some sightseeing, and you're coming with me," I say because we've spent enough days at home in bed.

I don't get to go to Azerbaijan often, and we're going to make the most of it while we're here.

"Under one condition," he says, and I roll my eyes with a grin, already knowing where this is going.

"Yes, you can shower with me," I reply, and he places a firm kiss on my lips.

"Some of the best words I've ever heard. Let's go, chérie."

Gabriel jumps in the shower with me, and we wash before getting dressed. He leaves the bathroom before I do, which gives me time to study the bruises on my wrist. They have gotten better, but they are still a deep purple. There is also a big red mark on the right side of my neck, which worries me until I realize it's from Gabriel.

"Gabriel!" I call out, and he storms into the bathroom, worry on his face. "You gave me a hickey." I point at the red mark on my neck, and he starts to smile. "It's not funny, I'm going to have to cover this with makeup all week," I complain, but I'm not actually mad. I find it more amusing than anything.

"We're not in high school, you don't have to cover it up. Better yet, wear your hair up and a low neckline." I can't help myself, which is why I start to laugh.

"For what?" I challenge, and he smirks at me.

"So I see it every time I look at you, reminding me how it got there. Reminding me I made you moan when I gave it to you, and so the sound replays in my head all weekend," he explains, and I swallow hard. He'll never cease to make me speechless.

"I have to wear a low neckline?" I ask in an attempt to break the sexual tension he brought back with his words, but Gabriel gives me an easy smile.

"The only thing you have to wear for me is my shirt to bed. Other than that, I'd never tell you what you can or cannot wear, not that you'd listen," he says with a smile, and I nod, placing my arms around his neck.

"You're right, I'd never let a man tell me what to wear." He brushes his nose over mine.

"Just my shirt to bed," he reminds me, and I laugh.

"Well, if I have to," I joke, and he grins.

The happy smile on his face reveals his sexy dimples. My eyes drop from his face to where my hands are on his neck, and I see I'm not the only one that has a hickey.

A victorious smirk spreads over my lips when I realize everyone is going to know he's mine. I finally understand how he feels.

Maybe I should make him wear my shirts, too.

Gabriel and I spend the rest of the day walking around in Baku. He takes me to the *Maiden Tower* in the Old City. The unique structure of the building mesmerizes me. Sadly, we don't have the opportunity to go inside, but I don't mind admiring it from the outside.

The whole time we're exploring the city, Gabriel holds me close to him, his hand in mine, and his lips always finding their way to my temple, cheek, and lips. Walking around the capital of Azerbaijan with the man I love while he finds ways to kiss me when I don't expect it makes me feel whole in a way I've never experienced.

I start to wonder if Dad ever felt this way, or even if Grandpa did, but I know if they were here, they would be telling me stories about it now. *Would they approve of my relationship?* They would definitely approve of Gabriel; he's everything they could have possibly wanted for me. He makes a lot of money, has his future planned out, is living his dream, and he loves me for who I am. Plus, he is a Formula One driver. He checks every box.

We walk a little further until we sit down on a bench near a park. I can't help but stare at his face as he lifts it to the sun, letting it shine on him. His stubble has been growing out more, but he told me he doesn't want it too long, probably because I let it slip once I'm usually not attracted to men with full beards. What Gabriel doesn't realize is I'll always be attracted to him because of his heart, not just because he's the most superficially beautiful man I've ever seen.

"Do you remember what happened the day we met?" I ask, and his attention drifts to me.

"Like it was yesterday, *Lady Valentina*," he replies, and embarrassment heats up my cheeks.

"You had me breathless from day one, Gabriel," I admit, and he takes my face between his hands.

"And you'll have me breathless until the last." His lips connect with mine, and I smile against them.

He tastes like home, and I'll never get enough.

Chapter 33

Valentina

Leonard and I have been sitting at the table in one of the empty conference rooms, looking over my simulator times and other results. Ever since I started at the driver academy, we've become better friends than I would have ever imagined. He texts me at least twice a week to make sure I'm doing alright, and, whenever we both have time, he calls me to discuss my performance. It's usually longer conversations, moving from racing topics to anything else I need to get off my chest, like stupid Christian Crovetto's behavior. I also attempt to get to know him better, but he keeps his personal life private from me. He'll occasionally share how his workout routine is going, but never how his girlfriend or family members are doing.

Gabriel is still working, and Adrian and James have avoided me all day. I pretend like it doesn't bother me so they don't worry if they see me, but it hurts. Fighting with my brother hurts. Having my best friend hardly communicate with me hurts. I wish I knew what's going on in all of their heads, but I can't, not until they talk to me.

"What do you struggle with the most in the simulator? Staying focused or endurance?" Leonard asks, staring at the paper with my results.

His question pulls me back out of my thoughts, and I look into his comforting brown eyes. There is something about having Leonard as a mentor that completes my life. After Grandfather died, I never thought there would be anyone who'd fill that position again. Adrian is my big brother, and someone I could have imagined taking the spot, but I think he didn't want to 'replace' Grandpa.

Leonard doesn't look at it this way. He merely wants to be for me what Carlos has become for Adrian over the past few months. I can't help but smile at him as the realization settles in my chest. *Who would have thought Leonard and I would become this close?*

"I struggle the most with controlling my nervosity before I sit down. Then, once I start, everything's fine, but I'm scared it will influence my results when it matters most," I explain, and Leonard leans toward me, a smile on his usually serious face.

"I know you'd like to control everything, Val, but nerves are one thing we can't. You may get used to them, but they will be there either way. They remind you that you care," he says, and I tug on a loose thread from my pants.

"I don't like that I can't control them." *Or anything else really.*

Leonard chuckles, his full lips pulling back to reveal his set of white, straight teeth. I've never focused on this man long enough to appreciate how handsome he is, but since we've been spending more time together, I can't help but notice it. I've never seen anyone wear a nose piercing as well as he does.

"Listen, if your biggest struggle is how nervous you get, you'll be fine. You may not be able to overcome it, but you can use your breath to ease the effects. Deep breaths will slow your heart rate, allow your mind to focus on something else, and bring much-needed oxygen to your brain. Okay?" he asks, poking my leg when I shake my head. "Come on, you know I'm right."

"I don't think there's been a time when you haven't been, which is the annoying part," I say, and a genuine laugh falls from his lips. *I made Leonard Tick laugh... Man, I fucking love that.*

"You flatter me, maybe a little too much. I should go call my brother. He has a way of humbling me," Leonard jokes, and it's my turn to laugh then. "Anyway, to get back to the serious topic, how is your neck strengthening going? You told me you struggle with it," he says, switching the subject to get back to business.

"It's been going great. Your tips have really helped me," I reply before going into detail about my improvements.

Leonard and I talk for a while longer, discussing everything about my time at the academy, excluding Christian because I don't feel like giving that asshole any attention today.

Eventually, he gives my shoulder a squeeze and leaves to get some rest before tomorrow. I text Gabriel to see if he's ready to go back to the hotel yet, but he lets me know he'll need a little longer to take care of something. It's a vague response, but I don't pry. He'll tell me about it if he wants to later.

Cameron, on the other hand, is sleeping in his pit box while his engineers work on the car. Seeing an evil opportunity, I creep toward him, trying to be as quiet as possible. His mouth is slightly opened, letting out the snoring sound instead of muffling it.

I take out my phone, capturing this innocent and hilarious moment. A tap on the shoulder pulls me from my concentration trance, and I look over my shoulder to see Leni, Cameron's performance coach, holding something up for me.

"Here, put this on. It'll scare him," she says with a mischievous grin, and I take the mask from her. It's a photo of my brother mid-sneeze, and I almost fall over from laughter. *Where the hell did they get this from?*

I place the elastic band around my head, forcing myself to keep it together while leaning toward Cameron until my face is merely a few centimeters from his. It takes everything out of me not to ruin this because Leni is filming now.

"Cameron, it's Adrian, wakey wakey," I say with a soft voice.

He moves his head a bit, crossing his arms in front of his chest as his mouth parts wider. So I try again.

"Cameron, wake up, mate. I need to tell you something," I whisper, running the back of my index finger over his cheek.

His eyes flutter open before they go wide and he screams. It is *the* most high-pitch sound I've ever heard in my life, and I cover my ears to spare them.

"Oh, you're so dead," Cameron calls out when I lift the mask off my face, and I run away screaming, but he catches me, holding me against him.

He places his mouth on my shoulder, blowing air against it to make a farting noise and send awful shivers down my spine. I burst into laughter, but he doesn't release me yet.

"You're pranking me now? Mean," he complains but joins my amusement with a chuckle.

"I'm sorry, I'm sorry," I squeal, trying to calm down at the same time. "I won't do it again," I promise, and he lets go of me, spinning me around so I can see his amused grin. *Damn, I love this man.*

"Do you have any idea how terrifying it is to wake up to your brother's face?" he asks, his Australian accent thick.

The mention of my brother temporarily sends a sting through me, but I disregard it to laugh at his words.

"I do know," I reply, placing my hand on his shoulder. "I'm sorry," I repeat, and he wipes away the tear of laughter that escaped my eye.

"Don't worry, I will get my revenge someday," he says, and my eyes widen, but he doesn't say anything more as his arm wraps around my shoulders. "Have you eaten yet?" Cameron asks, pulling me closer to press a kiss to the top of my head. A warmth spreads through me, the familiarity of his touch comforting.

"Not yet. I was waiting for Gabriel, but he seems to be busy," I say as I check my phone for a message but find nothing.

"Then I'm taking you to dinner. You can text him to join us when he's done, but it's late enough already, and you need to eat." I don't even try to argue with him as he leads me out of his pit box and toward his rental car.

On our way to the restaurant, I text Gabriel to let him know where we're going. He responds a lot quicker than I was expecting him to.

Gabriel: I don't think I'll make it to dinner, but enjoy. I will see you at the hotel, ma chérie. Je t'aime.

I smile at my phone before answering.

Valentina: I love you the same.

Chapter 34

Gabriel

"Listen, Adrian, you either start talking to me or I'm leaving because I want to get back to Val. I haven't seen her all day," I say, and he finally lifts his head from between his arms to look at me.

Half an hour ago, he walked into my private room, sat down against the wall, and has stayed quiet ever since.

"I want to talk to you, isn't that weird? I feel this need to share how I'm feeling with you because you love my sister more than anyone, except James and me," he says, and I do my best not to roll my eyes at the mention of his best friend. *Fucking James.* "Why is that? I hate that," Adrian says, forcing my attention away from my dislike for the Brit.

"You hate that you want to talk to me?" I ask with a small smile, settling down on the floor in front of him.

Adrian watches me like a hawk, uncertain how to answer my question. Then, he almost screams.

"Yes!" he blurts out, and I can't help but chuckle. "We weren't close before you started dating Val, but now? We've spent so much time together, bonded for some inexplicable reason, that I want you to tell me I'm not the worst brother in the world. I don't rely on other people, but I want you to reassure me now, and I fucking despise it." I cross my arms, getting a little offended now.

"Would you like to know why, in this particular case, you feel most comfortable talking to me?" My words surprise him, grabbing his full attention. "James hid the truth from you, and you're too ashamed to face Valentina. I'm the only one who knows what happened that you don't mind looking at right now," I explain, and he nods absentmindedly as I speak. I can't imagine what he's going through, all the blame he's putting on himself.

"As much as I'd like that to be the sole reason, I think it's also because I trust you, and I don't trust many people." Neither do I, which is why we get along so well.

Silence fills the room for a moment before he breaks it again.

"Am I the worst brother in the world?" he asks, but I shake my head without a second of hesitation.

"No, you're not. Adrian, protecting Val has been your number one priority from the day she was born, and you thought she was in safe hands with Carolina. You couldn't have known unless she gave you a reason to doubt that safety," I say, and he shakes his head, tears welling up in his eyes.

"I never saw any mark or bruise. When I was home, Carolina was... almost kind. And, Val, she kept it from me so well, I never suspected anything. But that's the problem! I should have, Gabriel. I should have known, I should have protected her!" he says, throwing his hands around to argue with me or himself, I'm not quite sure.

"I know hearing Val was abused for years was one of the hardest things you've ever had to hear, but you need to stop putting all of this on yourself. The only person to blame is Carolina. You are still the best brother anyone could ask for, but, right now, you need to get it together for the one person that matters the most: Val."

He gives me a confused look, so I decide to elaborate.

"She's miserable. She hates herself for the way all of this came out, and you need to get over your shit and assure her everything's alright. Unless you'd prefer it if she continued to feel horrible about it," I challenge, and a smile slips onto his face.

"Tough love? That's not really your thing," he says, watching me stand up and hold out my hand for him.

"Well, you're breaking the heart of the woman I love. I'll become anything to make her stop hurting," I reply, and he allows me to help him off the ground.

"You're right. I'm being selfish. I just don't know how to face her," he admits, dropping his head backward to suck in a sharp breath.

I grab him by the shoulders, forcing him to listen closely to my next words.

"Val is not angry with you. She does *not* blame you, she never has. No part of her holds you responsible. All Valentina wants is for you to figure things out and get back to where you were before. It's as simple as that."

His head bobs up and down, showing me he's paying attention without responding.

"She's ready, but it's up to you to forgive yourself now. Don't hold onto something that isn't your fault, Adrian. It will break you," I remind him, waiting for a response this time.

"I hate you for saying all the right things," he replies, and I let out a short laugh.

"Well, someone has to, and if your best friend can't, I'll always be here," I say, but he laughs at the way I roll my eyes when I mention James.

"You really don't like him, do you?" Adrian asks, smiling at my disgusted look.

"Fucking hate him is more like it," I admit without shame, and my teammate starts laughing.

"Yeah, I would too if I were you, considering he's been in love with her far longer than you have."

It shouldn't piss me off, but it does.

"He's still in love with her?" I ask, resisting the urge to ball my hands into fists, which want to destroy that asshole.

Adrian's eyes go wide then, panicking when he sees how bothered I am by his insinuation.

"Well, I'm not sure, he never told me he was to begin with, but it's hard not to notice. I spent my whole childhood watching him look at her in the same, hopelessly in love way. He'd probably say he isn't, not anymore, but a love like that, does it ever truly fade?"

Yeah, I'm going to punch the fucking wall if we keep talking about James' feelings.

"We better stop discussing this. I'd rather not get kicked out of Formula One for knocking out one of the Red Bull drivers," I say and straighten out my back.

It's not jealousy that makes me angry. Val is mine as much as I am hers. I trust her and know she'd never cheat on me, let alone leave me for her best friend, but it makes me mad that James thinks he'll end up with her.

He needs to back off before I stop trying my best for Valentina.

"Good idea," Adrian chimes in and leads me out of the room, both of us ready to get some rest.

I can't wait for mon tournesol to fall asleep in my arms.

Chapter 35

Valentina

It's been a couple of days since my fight with Adrian. He's been avoiding me, but at least James gives me updates every few hours, letting me know he's alright, merely processing. I've been keeping busy with Gabriel's team, trying to learn as much as I possibly can. It's only Friday, but they have taught me more about F1 strategy in the two days I've been working with them than I have learned in my entire life.

For most of the afternoon, my guys are busy with interviews, and I find things to do around the track to keep me occupied. James hasn't replied to my message today, but I'm not mad. I'm sure he has a lot to do.

Instead of dwelling too much on the fact that my best friend and brother haven't reached out to me, I twist the infinity band on my left ring finger, the one Adrian gave me, and stroll past the booths.

There is one that catches my attention, and I walk over to it, examining the work displayed. A smile spreads over my face as I inquire about the drawings of the drivers. Each of them has its own colors, and there are two different ones. One of them is of the driver himself and the other is of their car. An explosion of colors surround the faces and cars: red for Adrian and Gabriel, blue for James, orange for Cameron, and pink for Leonard.

The artist who created these is incredibly talented, which is why I buy the ones of my family and friends without hesitation. The man at the booth thanks me, and I smile at him in response.

I keep walking until my phone vibrates, and I almost drop everything to rip it out of my purse. My heart leaps in my chest when I read James' name on my screen, and I quickly hit the... *decline button? What?*

I groan, annoyed with myself, and unlock my phone so I can call James back. He answers after seven rings, and I am so confused it takes him that long to answer when he was the one who called me in the first place.

"I was about to hang up on you as well, but then I miss you, and I really want to talk to you," he says, and I laugh a little.

"I'm sorry, I don't know why I hit the decline button. I was so excited you finally called me." I sit down on a bench.

"Meet me at my box in an hour." I agree, and we hang up. I have no idea what I'm going to do for another hour, so I simply make my way back toward the boxes.

I take my time walking, but I am still half an hour too early. My feet bring me to Gabriel's box to see if he is there. When I don't see him, I let out a sigh. *Why do I miss him this much?* I saw him a couple of hours ago, and now all I can think about is how much I miss talking to him, seeing his smile, and touching him. My heart feels like it's being squeezed when I think about his dimples and the sparkle in his eyes. I'm about to pout when I can't help but grin.

"Valentina," I hear Adrian say from behind me, and within seconds, tears fall down my cheek.

Before he said my name, before I heard his voice, I had no idea how deeply I was hurting. Not speaking to my brother and being in a fight with him for so long was taking a bigger toll on me than I realized.

I turn around and run into his arms. He wraps his around my back, and I fling mine around his neck. His familiar scent fills my nose, and I cry even more.

"I'm so sorry I put you through this. I should have never walked away, that wasn't fair, and I should have talked to you about it. I'm sorry I just left." I want to tell him it's okay, but I can't find my voice. I'm too happy he is speaking to me at all.

Adrian pulls back from the hug, and I can see even he shed a tear.

"I hate not talking to you," I say, and he laughs a little.

"Yeah, I missed your mean comments and warm heart too." It's my turn to laugh then. "Are you going to tell me everything?" he asks, but I'm not sure if it's really what he said. His voice was barely audible.

I nod, and he wipes away the tear that rolled down his cheek earlier. I wipe away my own.

I spent an hour explaining to Adrian what Carolina did, how I hid it from him, why I did it, and why it's taken me this long to tell him about it. The whole time I'm talking, Adrian tries his best to keep eye contact with me, but I can tell it's hard for him.

My eyes must show the pain I felt every day I was living with her, but there is nothing I can do to change it. It's burned into my body, just like it is into who I am. With every story, every slap, he flinches, and his knuckles turn more white. I can't imagine what he must be thinking right now, how he must be feeling.

When I'm done sharing, he looks off into the distance, thinking about how to respond after my long, horrifying story. I wouldn't know what to say either if he told me something like this. I would be so angry with the person who ever dared to harm him, which is exactly what his face is telling me. There is anger and sadness carved into his features.

I reach out to take his hand, and he lets me comfort him.

"It's not your fault. You are not responsible for what happened to me. I need you to understand that you didn't fail me," I say, causing the corners of his mouth to drop and more tears to escape his eyes. He covers his face with his hands, and I get up from the chair I've been sitting in to hug him.

"I am so sorry," he cries, and my heart breaks into a million pieces. I never wanted to make him feel this way.

We hug for what feels like an eternity, but at least when I step back, he isn't crying anymore, and neither am I.

"Are we okay?" he asks, and I shake my head.

"No, I think you have to buy me a bucket of ice cream first." I laugh, and so does he.

"You know, I always knew Gabriel and you were connected, but this is just another area in your lives you have in common. It's crazy," Adrian says, and I furrow both of my brows.

"What are you talking about?" I ask because I'm lost. My brother looks at me with confusion all over his face.

"A fucked up sibling of a parent that made your lives miserable," he goes on, but I'm about to slap him for being vague.

"Adrian, either tell me the whole story or let it go. I don't have the energy to play guessing games," I complain, and my brother sits up straight, clearing his throat before explaining his comment.

"Gabriel had an uncle, but he shut him out of his life a long time ago," Adrian says, but I shake my head and shrug. He's never told me anything about his uncle. "He's the reason why Gabriel almost didn't get to be a Formula One driver. He was drunk and driving Gabriel home from school. Gabriel was fourteen at the time, and they got into a terrible crash. Denis, his uncle, drove into another car, killing the other driver and severely injuring everyone involved. It took Gabriel almost an entire year to be able to walk normally again. That's why he has a scar on his leg." I recall the first time I saw it in the shower, a frown now settling on my face. "Anyway, after that, Denis went to jail and now he's in rehab, and Gabriel hasn't spoken to him since."

The thought of my boyfriend going through that breaks my heart all over again. Adrian looks at someone behind me, panic crossing his face.

"Damn, I've got to go do an interview, Val. I'll see you later," my brother says and jumps up, pressing a kiss to the top of my head and going back to work.

Chapter 36

Valentina

It's race day for Adrian and James, and I'm sitting next to my grandfather, watching the tiny screens in the loud pit box. My fingernails start to look appealing when I feel nervosity settle in my chest. I know it would help the feeling in the pit of my stomach, but I also know better than to bite my nails. Grandpa hates it when I do that.

"Come, little champion, we will watch from the sidelines."

Grandpa leads me outside, and I follow him to an area where we can watch the track. The only thing separating us from it is a big, steel fence. Every time one of the Formula Two cars races by, the loud noise makes my ears ring in the best way. I can't wait to sit in one of those myself.

"We're so close," I say, excitement coursing through me. It's always the same when we go outside. I feel exhilarated.

"That look on your face is exactly why I keep bringing you here," he replies, and I know what he means.

I'm in awe and completely mesmerized. The speed, the fans, the excitement, and the nerves are everything I need. Grandfather flew me out to Italy for this race, despite Aunt Carolina's objections.

The screeching of tires and a loud crashing sound grab my attention, and I watch as Juan Marquez and Oliver Jackson spin into the barricades, too close to where I'm standing. I am paralyzed with shock and fear. Every muscle in my body has turned to stone.

I continue to watch the cars for any signs of hope the drivers are okay. Except for the occasional bird chirping, everyone has forgotten how to make a sound, and I'm convinced no one else is breathing either.

"What is going on?" I finally ask after moments pass without anyone speaking.

Grandpa puts his hand on my shoulder and squeezes it. He is on the phone with someone, and I wait impatiently for more information.

"One of the drivers got out of the car safely, but the other one is unconscious."

More minutes pass until an hour is over, and then another one follows. Juan Marquez has been brought to the hospital, and Oliver Jackson is safe in his pit box. I'm sitting with Adrian, James, and Grandpa, waiting to hear about a change in Marquez's condition.

James holds my hand and squeezes it gently every once in a while. We are all praying Juan is going to be okay, although it didn't look good when they pulled him from the car.

Adrian's phone eventually rings, but he is too nervous to answer it. Grandpa takes it, and I try to listen for an update.

"He didn't make it out of surgery," he says once he hangs up. "Juan died from his injuries."

Today is the first day I truly realize how dangerous racing is.

Today, my respect for the sport has doubled, and I will never stop fearing the consequences that come with it.

I love it, but I will do my best to never lose sight of this danger again.

Gabriel is still out, analyzing data with his team, and I am beyond exhausted. I get ready and put on my pajamas before I fall into bed and close my eyes. For the first time in days, sleeping seems like something I have to do, not something that relieves me from my troubles. Even though I try to stay awake and wait for Gabriel, I'm too tired to open my eyes again.

A loud bang makes me jump up in bed, and I watch Gabriel struggle to pick up his phone and the water bottle he dropped. When he sees me awake, an apologetic expression covers his face.

"I'm so sorry, chérie. I was trying to be careful, but I had a dizzy spell," he says, and I rub my eyes to wake up. Gabriel sits at the foot of the bed and pulls down his pants. "Go back to sleep," he whispers, but I smile at him.

"It's okay. How was the rest of your day?" I ask him and remove the blanket from my upper body, a yawn escaping me.

"It was good. I got a lot of work done."

Gabriel smiles at me before he pulls his shirt over his head. He smells it before walking over to his suitcase and pulling out another one. However, he doesn't put it on; he simply hands it to me. My eyes drop to my chest, and I remove the tank top I'm wearing. Gabriel's gaze locks onto my bare breasts, but he looks away a second later. His shirt fits me perfectly, and I'm surprised it smells like him even though he hasn't worn it yet.

"How was your day?" he asks me when he comes back out of the bathroom and lies down next to me.

Before I answer, he brings his lips to mine, and I sigh when I taste the mint from his toothpaste. His hair is wet from the shower he just took, and he smells delicious.

"Hi," he says, making me grin at him.

"Hi," I reply. "My day was good. I bought some art prints I think are really cool, and I made up with Adrian." I go on, and he listens closely while playing with a strand of my hair.

My eyes drop to the side of his thigh, and I fixate on the faded scar that runs down from the middle to his knee. I can barely see it because Gabriel's hair covers most of it. I trail my fingers along the skin there, thinking about what my brother told me earlier.

"Adrian told you," he says, and I look up at his unreadable expression. "I can see it in your eyes." My gaze shifts away from him, but he places his fingers under my chin to bring my attention back to him.

"Are you mad?" I ask, and Gabriel leans down to press a swift kiss to my lips.

"No. I never asked him to keep it secret." He shifts around a little to get closer to me. "I hate my uncle, and I wish he never appeared in my life. His irresponsible behavior almost ruined my career."

I wait for him to tell me more, but I don't know if he will. My hand moves to his cheek, and he closes his eyes in response to my touch.

"I almost lost the ability to walk because he needed alcohol more than he needed me." His eyelids flutter shut as he takes a deep breath. "I can't talk about it more, chérie, not yet," he says, and I smile at him.

"I'm sorry," I reply, and he kisses me again.

"Don't apologize." He runs his hand over my thigh, sending shivers down my spine.

We talk a little more before I fall asleep on his chest.

Gabriel is ahead, leading since lap fifty. Adrian is less than a second behind him. They're racing, battling each other for first place. I can't take my eyes off the screen. I can't even decide which one of them I want to win. It's a problem, and it's exactly what Adrian accused me of, but I love them both, and I would be happy for either of them.

After another two laps, Adrian is right next to Gabriel, their wheels almost touching. I need to look away, but I can't. My heart is jumping in my chest, and I feel the urge to bite my nails.

Adrian cuts it closer and closer until there is no more space for Gabriel to drive on the track. My brother pushes him off, causing his car to flip and crash into the barrier. I don't know how to react, but I'm convinced a scream leaves my throat. I cover my mouth with my hands and watch the paramedics as they pull his lifeless body out of the car.

“He’s gone,” Hector says as he wraps his arms around me to hold me up. “He’s gone,” he repeats, and, this time, I’m sure screams leave me because I can’t stop.

I’m sobbing and crying, and I can’t comprehend what is happening.

No, God, no, no, no, not him, not him...

Chapter 37

Valentina

"Valentina, wake up, baby," Gabriel's voice fills my ears, and I shoot up in bed, my eyes opening and my heart beating too hard against my ribcage.

My gaze fixates on the half-naked man in front of me, and only when I see his full lips and green-brown eyes can I calm my body down.

"You're shaking, chérie. What did you dream about?"

I can't tell him. All I can do is wrap my arms around his neck and sob. I have a problem. I've had a dream like this twice before. One was about losing James, the other about losing Adrian.

After a couple of minutes, I pull back and explain my dream.

"You died, and there was nothing I could do about it." I put my fingers on his torso, and he takes my curly hair into his hands so he can drag it over my shoulder and let it hang down my shoulders.

"You know, my dad used to say if someone dreams about your death, you will live longer in real life. So, thank you."

He chuckles softly, and I drop my head against his naked chest. His skin is hot, and the steady beat of his heart calms my body.

"I'm sorry you had a bad dream. I just closed my eyes when you started moving around, and then you screamed," he says, and I lean away once again.

"I'm so sorry, Gabriel. I don't know what brought this on, or even why tonight, but I guess dreams are just as uncontrollable as..." I try to think of a good comparison, but my mind goes blank.

"My love for you," he finishes my sentence, and I roll my eyes. I run my fingers over his left nipple, and he tucks his bottom lip between his teeth.

"God, that was incredibly cheesy. I think we need to break up."

His jaw drops, but he smiles at me and wraps his arms around my stomach, flipping me onto my back. His mouth claims mine, and I can feel him grow against my leg. He pulls away sooner than I want him to, than either of us do.

"Cheesy, huh?" I nod.

"Are you done already? One kiss and you're done?" I challenge, and he shakes his head.

"Does this feel like I'm done to you?"

He rubs his erection against my leg, kisses me firmly again, and cups my breasts. A moan leaves both of us, but they are dulled by his lips on mine.

"And this," he goes on, guiding my shorts down, spreading my legs, and pressing his tongue against my aching sensitive spot.

My hands move into his hair, and I tighten my grip, making him groan. The vibrations make my back arch off the bed, and Gabriel's hands slip onto my hips to hold me down. His name leaves my lips, and his hands drag my body closer to his mouth.

It leaves my skin, and I am about to complain when he replaces his tongue with his thumb and uses it to trace circles. My head is spinning, my skin is on fire, and I don't know how to respond when he adds two fingers and pushes them inside of me.

"Oh God," I say, unable to keep the sounds of pleasures to myself.

The friction he is creating is heavenly, and the circles make me dizzy from pleasure. His lips move to my lower stomach, and I grab the sheets.

Too soon, I fall apart under his touch, and I cover my face with a pillow as I come down from my high. I press my legs together, enjoying all of the sweet after-effects of the orgasm. It's fascinating how alive he makes me feel. It's like every cell in my body gets its own heartbeat, and they dance with every touch from Gabriel.

He pulls the pillow from my face, and I smirk at him.

"Don't look at me like that. I'm already aching," he says, and the smug smile fades from my face.

"Let me help you with that, Monsieur Biancheri."

Addressing him like that excites me, and it obviously does the same to him. I can see it by the way he looks at me and how his body responds.

I remove his shirt from my chest, letting my breasts bounce free. His eyes close, his head falls backward against the pillow, and he lets out a loud groan.

"I don't understand," he states, and confusion washes over me. "It's not fair, you know." He sits up in bed and puts his hands on my face, then drops them to my breasts. "No one should have a body like yours," he says, and his eyes focus on my lips.

"Why?" I ask, a little distracted by the way his big hands are cupping my breasts.

"Because you have me addicted," he says.

I lean forward until our lips are a centimeter apart. My right hand moves down to his boxers, and I tease him by rubbing my thumb up and down on his cock. He moans, but I cut him off by bringing my lips to his.

"Tell me what you want," I whisper, and he opens his mouth.

No words come out, only groans of pleasure.

"Tell me," I say, but he doesn't answer.

I remove my thumb, and he opens his eyes to look at me. I love that I made him this speechless, but I need to know what he wants.

"That pretty mouth around me, if you're ready," he admits, and I smirk at him.

"I've been ready since that day in the shower."

He frowns for a brief second, but I distract him by placing a kiss to the soft spot on his neck. His head falls to the side, and I suck on the already purple mark there. For a brief moment, I wonder if anyone saw it today, but I concentrate on him quickly enough.

I kiss his neck for a minute longer until I get off his lap and kneel down in front of him. Gabriel gets up, pulls his boxers down, and sits on the edge of the bed, in front of me. The thought of taking all of him in my mouth makes me anxious. I won't be able to, will I?

"You're so big," I say, and he puts his index finger under my chin, lifting my head and forcing me to look at him.

"Go slow, and let your hands do what they do best on the part that doesn't fit in your mouth."

I nod, put my hands on his thighs, take a small breath, and sit up so I can press my lips against his again. I feel like I need some more time to prepare, even if I've been ready to do this for weeks already.

His hands are cupping my face, and his tongue massages mine. I lean away and trace kisses down his body until I reach the thin line of hair that leads to his cock. I lick up his torso one more time, making him moan, his hand slipping into my hair. He's under my complete control, which excites every cell in my body.

With another deep breath, I move down to his length and press a kiss to the head of his penis.

"Mhmm," he says, and hearing him motivates me to go further.

I run my tongue down his cock, ignoring the unfamiliar taste of what I assume is precum. I switch between licking him and sucking, and he moans loudly.

"Yeah, just like that," he says.

I look up at him and see his eyes are closed and lips slightly parted. My focus goes back to pleasuring him, and he grabs a handful of my hair, tugging. This is so unfamiliar to me, but at the same time, I like it. I like pleasuring him this way, to hear him moan my name.

"You're doing so well for me, chérie," he praises, and I go a bit faster.

His hands grip the edge of the bed while I take him all the way down my throat until my gag reflex sets in, and I lean back again. I repeat the same thing when he starts to let out little moans for me.

"Fuuuuuuck, I'm gonna–" He cuts off, and I keep going until I feel his warm liquid shoot down my throat. Gabriel's legs shake, and I give him a proud smile.

"Hmmm," I say as I stand up and straddle his lap. He pulls my mouth to his, kissing me fiercer than ever before.

"You didn't have to swallow, you never do." I lick my lips before I answer.

"But I wanted to," I whisper in a seductive voice, and he falls onto the mattress.

"You can't say those things to me, otherwise I'll be proposing sooner than either of us is ready for," he jokes, and I lean forward until my lips are a centimeter from his.

"You mean things like how fucking good it felt to have you in my mouth?" I ask, and he flips us over so I'm the one on my back.

"Yes, things like that," he says, indecisiveness on his face.

I can tell he wants to keep going, but he needs to rest. Tomorrow is Qualifying, and he has to be fit for it.

"I love you," I tell him, taking away the sexual tension and making a soft expression cover his face.

"I love you the same, mon tournesol."

Chapter 38

Valentina

"Come on, come on, Adrian," I whisper, my hands shaking and my legs bouncing up and down.

I hate watching him struggle in seventh place, but there is nothing he could have done. Eduardo pushed him off the track in the first corner and by the time he rejoined the others, he was in eighteenth place. He's been making his way back up while Gabriel is occupying the second position, fighting Kyle for first. I keep watching Adrian, and I can't help but smile when he shoots past James and holds up his pinkie into the air.

"Why is Adrian showing James his pinkie?" someone asks next to me.

I don't tell them. That story is too personal, and if anyone knew, it could be trouble for both of them. But I can't help that stupid grin on my face when I replay the memory of the pinkie incident in my head.

It happened about fourteen years ago, and it was one of the funniest things I've ever witnessed. I remember it as if it happened yesterday, despite the fact that I was so young.

It was on a Saturday, and Grandpa took Adrian, James, and me karting. I was racing against my brother and best friend for a little while, and I remember winning every race against them. Eventually, I had to go to the bathroom, which meant Grandpa went with me, leaving the two idiots alone on the track.

When we came back, Adrian had driven into James, and the Brit broke his pinkie. I don't know how or why it happened, but I also know a couple of children like them didn't have common sense. Grandpa took James to the hospital where he had to get his pinkie in a cast and couldn't move it for an entire month.

From that moment on, Adrian started teasing James about it. Soon, because they were young and not allowed to show each other the middle finger, they chose to use their pinkies instead.

My eyes focus on the screen again, and my heart stops when I see Gabriel trying to move past Kyle. Their cars touch and Gabriel's front left tire gets a puncture, causing him to spin off the track. I gasp and groan when I see it. I can't believe he is out of the race now when he was so close to winning. Gabriel gets out of his car, and I sigh with relief when I see he's okay.

He is frustrated. I can see it in the way he kicks the dirt and puts his hands on his helmet. When they replay the incident, I notice Kyle didn't leave enough space for Gabriel and practically forced him off the track. That's why I'm glad when the FIA is investigating the accident.

"You see this here, Valentina, this is what we deal with when a driver crashes," Tommasso, Gabriel's strategist says, interrupting my thoughts.

I've been working with my boyfriend's team the entire weekend, studying their strategies, methods, and procedures. I listen to his explanation of the course of action they take.

Moments later, my boyfriend walks through the pit box and toward me. I give him a confused look, but he merely grabs my hand and leads me into his private room, the one where he gets massaged after races.

He rips off his helmet and balaclava, throwing them to the side and closing the distance between us. His arms wrap around my chest, and I lift mine to hug him back, ignoring how sweaty he is.

"Are you sure I should be here?" I ask, and he pulls back to look at me.

Sweat drips down the side of his forehead, and I reach for the towel next to us to wipe it away. His eyes are glassy, making the green in them even more dominant.

"I want you right here and nowhere else," he replies, claiming my lips. "I need you," he whispers, sucking on my soft spot and making me forget about his responsibilities.

"Hmmm," is the only response I give him, although I know it's wrong.

He lifts me onto the table where his performance coach usually massages him, his tongue slipping into my mouth.

"Gabriel," I half-say, half-moan. "You have to go talk to your team," I manage to tell him, but he doesn't stop kissing me.

"No, I don't, I don't have to–" He cuts off, moaning when his groin rubs against my clit. It was a bad idea to wear a skirt today. Well, good because what he is doing feels amazing, but bad because this is not the time or place. "I need you," he repeats, and I lean back on the table.

I'm trying to focus on the right thing to do, but I'm unable to get into the proper mindset. Instead, I roll my hips, my clit rubbing against his erection. Gabriel's hand wraps around my neck in a tender, sensual way. I moan in response, and when I open my eyes again, I find him smiling.

"I knew you'd like that." I bite my lip involuntarily, close my eyes, and my head falls back on the table again. "God," he moans, and I know I have to stop this. We can't have sex with his team waiting for him. It's not right.

"Gabriel, stop." Without questioning my request, he lets go of my neck and steps back, concern on his face.

"What's wrong?" he asks, and I put both of my hands on his cheeks. My body is aching, and I wish I hadn't told him to stop.

"You need to go out there. They are waiting for you," I remind him, and he pulls on the strap of my bra, making my heart jump.

"Fuck that. I need to feel you, be inside of you..." He trails off but then looks away with a thoughtful expression. I force him to look at me again.

"But not here, not like this." He nods and lets out a deep breath.

"You're right. I'm sorry." Gabriel steps back and guides me off the table. I straighten out my clothes and wipe my lipgloss off his face.

"Don't be. I'm sorry about your race. I know you were fighting really hard, but you know what, mon amour?" He smiles at me when I call him that, like he always does. "I'm so proud of you, no matter if you win or lose. You are an incredible man, an amazing driver, and I know in the next race you are going to be on top again. I have absolutely no doubt."

"My pitstop," he mumbles, and I grin at him.

"Go and talk to your race engineer, look over the data and footage." His green eyes are focused on my face, and his hands are on my hips.

"This bossy side of you turns me on," he says, and I step on my tiptoes to press my lips to his.

"Go," I command, and he smirks at me.

His hands leave my skin, and, as he walks past me, I smack his ass. He turns around again, looks me up and down, and then disappears out of the room with the biggest grin on his face.

Before I leave, I adjust my skirt and tank top, reapply my lipgloss, and then retie my ponytail. I don't need anyone to know we were making out in here, if they don't already notice by the way Gabriel's erection is pressing against his race suit. It was quite tight in the front when he walked out of the room. My smile reveals my feelings, but luckily, there is no one around to see my wicked expression.

I stroll back out just in time to see Adrian overtake Eduardo and finish in third place. I clutch my hands together in excitement and jump up and down.

"Yes," I whisper when I see James is in second place. He must have overtaken Adrian sometime during the race again, and Cameron is in fifth.

My happiness soon fades when I see Kyle didn't even get a penalty.

"What the fuck?" I say more to myself, but Gabriel's arms wrap around me from behind, and he answers my unspoken question.

"I know, apparently it was a racing incident and nothing to investigate any further. Trust me, I'm just as angry as you. Well, probably not as angry.

I mean there is steam coming out of your ears." I turn around and nudge his arm. "Hey, ouchie," he playfully complains but then smiles at me. "I'm going to go and be interviewed, but I'll see you later, ma chérie." He kisses my cheek, and I make my way outside to give my big brother a hug and celebrate with him.

Adrian, James, and Kyle get out of their cars, and, unsurprisingly, while Kyle is being interviewed, James and Adrian hold up their pinkies to each other. They're laughing and talking until it is their turn.

Before they go up to the podium, James and Adrian come to hug their team and me. They are both sweaty, but, yet again, I don't mind. They are my family and I love them, even when they're sweaty, smelly, and all.

After the celebrations, Tommasso and Hector do their best to give me a few more lessons on what a driver is meant to do after a race. I take notes, unwilling to forget even the smallest detail I've learned this weekend.

"Valentina," a familiar voice fills my ears, but I can't identify who it belongs to until I turn around.

Lorenzo Mattia, the boss of the Ferrari team, approaches me, an approving smile on his face.

"How are you?" he asks and offers his hand for me to shake.

"Very well. Thank you so much for this opportunity, sir," I reply in Italian because I spent all weekend memorizing this sentence to impress him, which he seems to be.

"You're welcome," he states before switching back to English. "I must say, I am very impressed with you. There has hardly been a trainee as determined to learn as you. You've shown nothing but kindness to my team, and I will let Andrea know how well you've done," he says and squeezes my shoulder.

I'm about to respond when he starts a conversation with Tommasso instead.

"Come on," I hear Adrian say from beside me, taking my hand to lead me away from the team I don't ever want to leave.

I belong here, this has become more than clear to me over the past four days. There is nothing I won't do to get back here.

Chapter 39

Gabriel

Domi and Nicolette have been staring at my computer screen for the past few minutes, looking through the photos of the apartments I've chosen. They both have a sad look on their face, but we all know it's time I move out. The only reason I stayed was to make sure Jean was okay, and he is.

I need my own space where Valentina and I can have privacy, where I can finally have that art studio I've always dreamed of. With the baby on the way, they will need my room to convert into a nursery anyway.

"You sure this is what you want?" Domi asks, a tear slipping down her cheek. I wipe it away and take her hand in mine.

"I'm sorry it has to be now, but we all know it's for the best," I say, and Nicolette gives me a reassuring smile.

She's been on my ass to move out for a year now, telling me to live my life and stop worrying about everyone else. This will be easier for her than for Domi.

"But, what if we need you to help out with the baby? You won't be here," she points out, and I feel worse than I did before when more tears stream down her face.

"I'll always be here, Domi," I promise, and she stands up to hug me.

"He's moving ten minutes away from us, Dominique, it's not the end of the world," Nicolette says, earning herself a frown from her wife.

"He's my little racer," she says, and I smile at her.

She's called me that since I was ten years old, when she met me for the first time at a karting race. *Damn... that was a long time ago.* The realization almost makes me shudder.

"It's going to be hard not to have him here when he isn't away winning Grand Prixes." She settles down on her chair again, letting Nicolette hug her.

"I know, ma colombe, but he needs his space, and we can use his room for the baby," she says, kissing Domi's cheek and rubbing her stomach. "It'll be fine, don't worry," Nicolette adds with a smile that reveals how happy she is.

I shut my laptop and push it to the side, settling down in the seat across from them.

"Alright, baby names. What have you got so far?" I ask to change the subject.

Their faces light up, and we spend the next hour or so discussing what would fit best in our family. Eventually, Nicolette stands up to braid Domi's coily hair, something she's trying to get better at, and I make them a cup of tea.

"What about, if it's a boy, Maxime Guillaume," Domi suggests, and a pain shoots through my chest.

It's been a while since I've heard my father's name.

"If it's a girl, maybe we could name her Vivienne Juliette," she goes on, and I fight the urge to walk away from this conversation.

Vivienne was my grandmother's name, Juliette my mother's. What Domi is trying to do is wonderful and kind, but it rips my heart into several pieces. More pain crosses me, and I struggle to breathe.

"Those are perfect," I reply and get up, grabbing my phone to dial the number of the only person that can put my heart back together right now. "I have to get some work done, but I'll speak to you both later."

I kiss their cheeks before sprinting upstairs and shutting my bedroom door. The phone rings against my ear, and she picks up soon, her soft voice coming through the speaker.

"*Bonsoir, mon soleil. Est-ce que je te manques?*" she asks, and I enjoy the way the French falls from her lips.

"I do, I miss you more than anything," I reply, the grip on my phone tightening as I try to calm my heart.

It's getting more difficult to be apart from her, especially since the last time we were together was almost a week ago. I tried to visit her, but I had to do some photoshoots for the new sponsor my team got.

"I miss you the same, Gabriel, but I can hear there's something else bothering you. Do you want to tell me about it?" Valentina asks, and I realize for the millionth time I'm going to marry her.

One day, I will put a ring on her finger because she's the love of my life, and nothing will ever change my mind.

"Domi and Nicolette were choosing baby names, and they decided on some that honor the family we've lost. I don't know why it hurt me." The control she has over me is dangerous. I'd never share this with anyone who isn't Val because it's too personal.

"I can't hear any name of the people I've lost without feeling pain. If I had to hear it every day... the thought would hurt me too," she says, and I sink to the floor, holding onto my knees while I listen to her soothing voice. "But I think it would also help me move on, in a way. The name would be given a different meaning, a happier one. It could be beautiful," Val adds, and I can sense the hint of a smile on her lips.

"When are you coming home?" I ask because I'm starting to feel homesick.

With my schedule, I won't be able to fly out and see her, but I'm hoping Valentina will be back in a few days.

"I don't know, mon amour. Andrea is pushing us past our limits since they have to decide who to give the spot to in a couple of weeks. Tomorrow we'll be setting our final simulator times, which they will use when they make the decision." Nervosity slips through in her voice, making it crack with the last word.

"You've been kicking Christian's ass for the last four weeks, ma chérie. You got this." And I have no doubt she does.

The day he gets the seat over her is the day Adrian can walk past a mirror without fixing his hair and admiring himself.

"I hope so, but there are more categories I have to beat him in, one isn't enough," she reminds me, and I nod before realizing she can't see me.

"You were born to be an F1 driver, tournesol. One way or another, it will happen," I reply, and she sighs into the phone.

"Never stop dreaming with me, okay?" she asks, and I smile to myself, standing up and walking over to my bookshelf to look for something to distract my mind once she hangs up.

"It's not a dream, it'll be reality, and I need you to start believing it too," I say, almost scolding her.

Val laughs into the phone, the soft sound sending another wave of homesickness over me. My heart misses her, my head misses her, my entire existence misses her.

"I will believe it when it happens, not a moment before," she says, shutting down any further discussion on this subject. "Now, tell me, how is the apartment hunt going?" she asks, shifting our focus to a lighter topic.

"Pretty good. I've found a few places I like, but we need to see them together when you're back," I explain, grabbing one of the books I bought for Valentina.

"Why? You want to put me in different positions there and see if it looks good?" she teases, and I can't hold the chuckle back.

"Come on, baby, we both know you could make a dumpster an appealing place to live for me if you spread your legs on top of it," I reply, making her go silent for a brief moment.

"I'm going to ask Andrea when we next get the chance to go home. I hate this distance," she says, and I click my tongue in response.

"It won't be like that for much longer, you'll see."

My optimism is probably annoying her, but I can't turn it off anymore. Valentina is so close to getting everything she's worked for her entire life.

"I'm going to read one of your new books tonight," I say when she doesn't respond.

"Read it to me?" she asks, which is exactly what I was hoping she'd say. The only reason I picked it up was to hear this question.

"Always, chérie."

Chapter 40

Valentina

I've been nervous, but how I'm feeling right now takes it to another level. If my time is worse than Christian's, I'm going to struggle with my confidence in the rest of the categories too, which is what this test is about.

Am I capable of pushing everything aside to focus on the task ahead? Can I disregard my emotions?

It's what my grandfather taught me to do, but I've never had this kind of pressure on my shoulders. I've never had it all come down to me fighting only against my rival, the person I despise the most in the entire universe.

"Is the always collected Tina nervous?" Christian asks as he steps into the room, his white-blonde hair even lighter today and his brown eyes full of amusement.

"You know, there is a processing time on the box. Maybe don't leave the dye in for that long next time. I wouldn't want your hair to fall out," I say, and he laughs at my comment.

"This hair cost me two thousand euros, sweetheart, it's not box-dyed, and you know it," he replies, but I give him a confused look.

"My bad. I underestimated how spoiled you truly are for the last time,

Your Royal Highness," I spit, and he takes the seat next to mine.

I stand up immediately, trying to get as far away from him as possible. My body cringes from disgust every single time he comes close to it, and I need to stay in control right now. *Balance.* I have to find balance. I'm already struggling emotionally, I don't need him to throw me off physically because of his nausea-inflicting presence.

"How was Baku, by the way? Did you learn anything new? Like sucking off your boyfriend before the race?" He laughs at his 'joke', but there's nothing funny about it.

His family would understand if I punched him in the face, right? I know Andrea would be fine with it after everything they've witnessed him put me through, but I don't know if his family would allow me to stay in Monaco if I messed with their precious, little boy. *Probably not.*

"You truly think that's all a woman is good for, don't you? Just attending to her man, making sure he has everything he needs, giving him head, and disregarding her own desires?" Christian gives me a wicked smile then.

"Not all women, just you."

I won't let him succeed in his attempts to throw me off my game. He's trying to get under my skin, piss me off so anger will take over when I'm in the simulator.

"Although you're being very selfish with Gabriel at the moment. You're here all the time now when he probably needs you at his races. You're only focusing on your career, on what you need."

His words hit me hard, but not just because of Gabriel. They hit me because I know Adrian, James, Cameron, and Gabriel all miss me. It also doesn't help that I've been feeling selfish for the past week, but Christian will not be the one to guilt-trip me. No one will.

"I might be selfish, but there is no question about you being a sexist, misogynistic asshole."

His eyes go wide for a moment before he composes himself again.

"Please, how much longer will you fight your attraction for me?" he asks, and I make a vomiting noise.

"You disgust me, and I will never, ever be attracted to you, Christos."

He furrows his brows at the new name, just like he always does, and I almost smile. It feels like I should pat myself on the back because he always gets so annoyed.

"What's it with the fucking incorrect names? I'm not here calling you Valeria or some shit," he complains, and I turn away to hide how proud I am to have gotten in his head. "You will answer me when I speak to you," he demands, and my shoulders go stiff. "You're a citizen of Monaco, and I'm your prince. You will show me respect."

Don't beat him up. You'll get kicked out of the academy. Don't do it. It will ruin your career.

I turn around, curtsying before I raise my head.

"Burn in hell," I say in Spanish, frustrating him even more.

"You know what? I'm so done with you! You act like you're so special when I have been training to be a race car driver since I was two years old!" I cross my arms in front of my chest as he yells at me, yet again pretending to be better than me.

"And you've been a spoiled dick since birth. What's your fucking point?" I challenge, and he takes an angry step toward me.

"I'm your prince!" he repeats, and I roll my eyes.

He grabs my shoulders, but I slap his arms away with mine, shoving him backward. Luckily, my wrist hasn't hurt in a few days, so this action isn't painful. Christian barely holds himself up, too surprised at my willingness to fight back.

"Touch me again, and I will do far worse than push you," I warn, but the shock on his face hasn't worn off entirely. "You're not my prince. You're nothing more to me than a rival that needs to be taught a lesson," I reply, and Andrea walks into the room.

They look us up and down before clearing their throat.

"We're ready for you, Christos, uh, sorry, I mean Christian," they say, and the brat walks away without saying anything more to me, anger making his shoulders vibrate. I laugh at Andrea, who turns to wink at me before disappearing into the simulator room.

I sit back down, more nervosity now washing through me. My phone rings and I notice a long message from my brother.

> **Adrian: I know you're nevous. I know you're scared you'll mess up, but you've got this. Out of the two of us, you've alway been the more focused one. There is nothing you cannot do. It's time they all found out too. No matter what happens, know I'm the proudest brother in the world. You've come a long, difficult way, but it's all going to be worth it. I love you.**

I manage to text him back just in time for Christian to walk back out of the room, a smug smile on his face.

"There is no way you'll beat that time, Tina." He takes the seat next to mine again, and I get up to follow Andrea.

"Watch me, Christoph." His frown fuels my confidence.

Andrea tells me to settle down in the seat of the simulator, handing me the helmet and patting my shoulder to reassure me. I take a couple of seconds to calm my heart and prepare myself for what is to come.

Lorenzo Mattia, Colin Reiner, and Andrea are all watching me do this, and I cannot fuck this up. There has never been a more important moment in my life, and this is the ultimate test to see if I've got what it takes. It's time I prove to them I deserve the opportunities I've longed for my entire life.

"Whenever you're ready," Mr. Mattia says, and I give him a slight nod.

They chose the Australian track, and I almost smile. I've been racing virtually on this one for years, longer than any other.

I take one last deep breath before the simulation starts, pressing down on the gas pedal as soon as I'm given the green light. I speed down the track, avoiding the curbs as much as I can, breaking later than I probably should, and accelerating to the maximum as soon as I know a straight is coming. Everything is going well. Adrenalin courses through me, pushing me further than ever.

Too far.

I almost lose control of the car as I take the curb, but, somehow, it stays on track. It probably cost me a lot of time, which momentarily distracts me. *Breathe, race, win.* My grandfather's voice echoes in my ears, and I push myself to focus.

I finish the lap, but I'm not shown my time. They instruct me to wait outside once I'm out of the simulator, and I do as I'm told, ignoring Christian's presence. After the horrible lap I must have done, I'm not up for another battle. I have to concentrate solely on not bursting into tears of disappointment.

Grandfather would scold me for losing my focus at such an important moment. He'd also give me a big hug and tell me everything is alright, but I can only do one of those for myself right now.

A while later, Andrea and Lorenzo appear in the doorframe, serious expressions on their faces. The team principal takes a step toward us, a piece of paper in his hands. His body turns to Christian, his shoulder rising and falling in steady motions.

"I heard about Valentina's karting 'accident'," he starts, making air quotations around the word, and my rival tenses. "We do not tolerate that behavior in our academy, let alone our Formula One team. Do you understand me?" I've never seen Christian look at anyone with as much respect as he does Lorenzo.

"I didn't do any–" He is cut off before he can finish lying.

"Do you understand me?" Lorenzo repeats, his voice firm and demanding now.

"Yes, sir," Christian says, and I almost pity him. His usual cold demeanor has vanished, a child-like one taking its place.

"Good. As for your results–" Lorenzo pauses, turning to me with a smile growing on his face. "Valentina was two-tenths faster." Christian's eyes go wide before he storms in front of Andrea.

"Which track did she get? She got an easier one, didn't she? You're taking pity on her because she's a girl!" Andrea wipes something off their face, and I realize he must have spat on them in his rage.

"If I were you, I'd sit my ass down before I drag you from the headquarters myself," they warn, and Christian shakes his head. "I really don't think you understand what it means for someone who isn't a cis-gender man in this sport. I'm done listening to someone who wasn't oppressed talk to me, *to us*, about fucking pity opportunities."

The prince suddenly becomes quiet as our instructor puts him in his place.

"Valentina had the same track as you, the same settings, and she even made a slight mistake in the tenth corner, but she was still faster. Let that speak for itself, *Your Highness.*"

I can barely hold back the smile that wants to light up my face. *I did well. I did better than him.* My legs vibrate, begging me to jump up and down from excitement. Somehow, I manage to stay grounded, at least for the moment.

"You can all suck my dick!" Christian says in French so the other two don't understand before he rushes out of the room.

My eyes go wide, but my attention shifts to Lorenzo Mattia, who is holding out his hand for me to shake.

"Well done, Valentina. I'm looking forward to seeing your next results," he says and leaves the room as well.

Andrea turns to me, and I let the tears of relief drop.

"You look like you could use a hug," they point out, and I nod before they wrap their arms around me, rubbing my back to comfort me. "I hope you know I will do everything I can to help you get that seat. You deserve it more than anyone I've ever taught here," they say, and I step back to show them my smile.

"I'm thankful for everything you've already done."

"You think I'd let you fight this royal brat by yourself? Never," they promise and give my shoulder one last squeeze. "Now, it's about time you got to go home. I'll see you in about a week," they say, and excitement fills my chest.

I finally get to see my family again.

Chapter 41

Valentina

Luckily, Adrian and Gabriel are busy when I arrive in Monaco, which gives me time to find out what's been going on with my best friend.

I knock on James' door, who I haven't heard from in days, and wait impatiently for him to open it. I'm concerned; he's never ignored me like this. Adrian hasn't seen or spoken to him either, which is odd. Something's wrong, and I am going to find out what it is. James doesn't have a choice, just like I wouldn't if the roles were reversed.

When minutes pass, and there is no sign of life, I walk around his house down the path that leads to the pool area. The door which is usually unlocked is locked for the first time in years, and I groan as I climb over the gate. James is making this a lot more difficult than it needs to be.

I make my way toward the sliding doors that lead into his living room and can't believe my eyes when I see James on his couch in front of his television. *Why didn't he open the door? Why is he ignoring me?*

I knock on the glass, and his head lifts up. That's when I get really worried. He hasn't shaven in days, there are empty beer bottles all around him, dark circles under his eyes, and even from far away, I can see they are a flaming red. He's either been crying or not sleeping, maybe even both.

When he sees me, he rolls his eyes and focuses on his television again. I know he wants me to leave, but I can't, I'm too concerned. My fist keeps knocking on the glass, and I don't stop until he opens the door.

"What the fuck do you want? Can't you see I want to be left alone?" He's yelling at me, and I know he's angry, but I don't think he's mad at me. "Leave me alone, Valentina. Just leave me alone."

He slams the door shut again, and I go back to knocking.

"Just go away," he tells me when he rips it open. This time, however, tears fall down his cheeks, and he's no longer furious.

"Let me in," I beg, and he nods, his head falling in defeat.

I wrap my arms around his torso, ignoring how bad he smells: beer and sweat.

"What happened?" I ask in a gentle, low tone. When he doesn't answer, I pull back and look at him. "Let me in," I repeat, but this time I mean it in a different way.

"I'm going to be a dad," he says and chokes on his own spit.

James covers his mouth with his hand before sinking to the ground, and I follow him. He's silent for a long time, and I rub the back of his hand with my thumb in an attempt to comfort him. My heart is racing in my chest as I try to process this new information.

"How–" I can't even finish phrasing the sentence before my voice cracks.

"About seven months ago, I was casually seeing this girl Annabel, and she came to my place on Thursday. She could not have been more pregnant, Val."

He shakes his head, but I can't comprehend anything he's saying.

"I even took a paternity test. I really am the father, there is no denying that." More tears roll down his cheek. "I'm twenty-three years old, I can't be a father! This isn't how it was supposed to happen. I'm supposed to fall in love with a girl, marry her, then think about expanding our family. This is not how it's supposed to go." James is yelling at me again, and I can't hold back the tears leaving my eyes.

I'm quiet for a while until I find words.

"I know it's not, but, James, you're going to be a dad. You're going to have a child that needs you, that relies on you. Even if you didn't want this, it's happening. This baby is going to love you, and you don't have to do any of it alone. I'm right here by your side, Annabel is going to be there, and she is probably just as terrified as you are. And you have Adrian, your sister, and your parents. We are all here for you. But what you have to do is, well, first of all, you need to take a shower. You smell absolutely disgusting," I inform him, and he lets out a laugh he doesn't mean, I can tell. "Then you gotta stop drinking because it's not going to make this go away. Afterward, you have to go talk to Annabel."

He nods, and I take his other hand in mine.

"I got you, James. You know that, but now, you have to meet me halfway." I get up from the ground and hold out my hand for him. He takes it, and I help him up too.

James tells me more about Annabel after he has finished showering and shaving. I find out she is from Monaco, has a sister, and didn't tell him she was pregnant for six months because she didn't want to ruin his life.

I can't imagine what she must have gone through. Finding out she's having a baby at twenty-two, unsure whether or not to tell the father because he just started his career, and then doing it all by herself must be terrifying. Her parents live in England, and she only has her sister here.

I want to say I don't understand why she didn't tell James earlier, but I can't. Annabel must be scared, like James is. I am too, in a way, terrified for him. Other than being here, there is nothing I can do.

I wipe my face with my hands, thankful I didn't put on any makeup today. James is in the kitchen getting some water, and I check my phone for any messages. I have three new ones, all from Gabriel.

Gabriel: I miss you.

Gabriel: I'm home now. If you want, you can come to my place or I'll go to yours.

Gabriel: I love you.

I shake my head and smile at my phone. It soon fades when I realize I can't go to his house. My first priority is to make sure James meets with Annabel and sorts this mess out. She's due in two months, and they need to figure this out before then.

Valentina: I miss you the same, but I have to take care of something, mon amour. I love you, and I'll let you know when I'll be home.

Within seconds, Gabriel texts back.

Gabriel: If you need me, I'm here.

James walks back into the room with a glass of water for me.

"Will you come with me? I don't think I can do this by myself." I bite my bottom lip and think about his request for a brief moment. Annabel might not want me there, but I can tell he needs me.

"Sure," I say, and he gives me a small smile.

Before I can overthink things any further, I get up from the couch and walk over to where his keys are.

Annabel knows we're coming, and it takes us ten long minutes, which are filled with silence, to get there.

"Come on," I tell James, who has been staring at the small home for a while.

I'm surprised by how well I'm handling this situation when all I want to do is scream. I'm scared of what is going to happen, how our lives are going to change, and about what James will have to do.

"I'm terrified," he whispers, and I put my hand on his. I lift it to my mouth and kiss the back of it.

"I know. You don't have to do this alone, I'm right here," I reassure him, and he places his head against his headrest while he studies my expression.

"I love you so much. You know that, right?" He's squeezing my hand,

and I smile comfortingly at him.

"I know, and I love you. Now, let's face our fear, yeah?" Once again, he only nods.

We walk down the short path that leads to Annabel's house, and I knock on the door before James can change his mind.

I feel like throwing up. This is too much for one person to process as quickly as I'm trying to. I keep reminding myself of James' feelings, and I have to continue to prioritize them. If I focus on mine, I might actually throw up.

A beautiful, very pregnant woman opens the door for us. Annabel has long, brown hair, and round lips. She takes my breath away, but I don't know why. I might be scared of what she represents.

"James," she says when her brown eyes find him standing awkwardly next to me.

I wonder why my best friend was only casually seeing her, but that's a question for later when things have settled.

"Who are you?" she asks me, and I hold out my hand for her.

"I'm Valentina," I say because I'm not quite sure what else to tell her.

"It's nice to meet you. I'm sorry, I wasn't expecting someone else to join us, but please, come in. Make yourselves at home. I'll be right there, I just have to run to the bathroom. This baby seems to think my bladder is a trampoline," she jokes, and I smile at her.

She shoots James a quick grin before leaving the room.

"Maybe it's that pregnant glow, but she is gorgeous. And she seems very nice," I say to James, and he gives me a brief smile.

"Yeah, she is, I guess. I don't know. She isn't the one I thought I would end up having a baby with."

He gives me a weird look, and I feel my heart skip a beat.

Oh.

"I had this whole dream in my head of how life was going to be, but now, everything is so messy," he replies, and I frown. James looks beat, and I lean forward to rest my hand on his.

"I understand, I really do, James, but you gotta take a deep breath. This is reality, it's not a fantasy, and saying it's unfair won't change what's going on. Now, Annabel doesn't need any more stress. I'm sure she has enough as it is."

"Yeah, well, so have I. My life is fucking upside down, and I don't want it. I don't want any of it," he yells at me just as Annabel walks back into the room.

I drop my face into my hands, and when I look up again, James has left the house while Annabel is standing in the same spot, tears filling her eyes.

"I'm so sorry, Annabel, " I say and step toward her.

She waves away my apology and dabs her eyes with a tissue.

"Don't be silly. It's not your fault. I'm sorry for creating this mess. I never wanted to do this to him, which is why I didn't tell him to begin with. Deep down, I knew this would happen," she explains, and I help the pregnant woman sit down on the couch. "Thank you." I smile at her.

"It takes two people to have sex, Annabel. This isn't your fault. Accidents happen. I'm just sorry James is reacting like this." I take a deep breath and look into her warm eyes. "I do understand why he is feeling this way." She nods and takes a sip of her water.

"So do I, but how can I make this easier for him? I'm not forcing him to be involved in this baby's life," she says, and I take her hand. It's not her responsibility to make it easier for him.

"It's up to James now. There's nothing you can do."

After a while of Annabel and I talking about where she grew up and what she studied in university, James walks back into the room.

"Val, can you give us some time? You can take my car home," he tells me, but I pull his keys out of my pocket.

"I'll walk home. It's not far," I assure him, and he nods absentmindedly.

He's not listening to me anymore, he's focused on the woman carrying his baby.

"It was nice to meet you. If you need anything, feel free to call me, you have my number." Annabel squeezes my arm, and I hand James his keys.

He gives me a brief kiss on the top of my head before I leave.

Chapter 42

Valentina

For the first time in hours, I inhale, filling my lungs as much as possible and letting out the breath through gritted teeth. I take my time walking home to be able to process everything that happened today.

James is going to be a father. He's going to have a child... I still can't believe it.

It takes me a moment to decide whether or not I want to see Gabriel or be alone right now. My body makes that choice for me when I walk past my house and toward Gabriel's.

My feet start to move faster with every step until I find myself running down the street. I know I won't be able to tell him about today, it isn't my secret to share, but I really need to be with him.

My fist connects with the front door, and seconds later, Jean opens it for me.

"Val, what's wrong?" he asks, and I try to force a smile.

His green eyes study my face, and I notice he's been trying to grow a beard now too. I wonder what made him decide to look even more like his older brother, but my mind doesn't linger on it too long.

"Where's Gabriel?"

I don't want to make small talk with him. All I want to do is find my boyfriend and feel his arms wrapped around my tired body.

"He's upstairs."

I run past him and to Gabriel's room. I don't bother knocking on his door either. When I step in, he's lying on the bed, notebook and pencil in his hands. His headphones rest on top of his head, which is why he doesn't hear me. His eyes lift from the drawing and panic settles in them when he sees me.

"Chérie?" he says and gets up.

I rush over to him and let his arms give me the comfort I crave. A sigh slips past my lips, but I don't try to stop it either. My pitstop. I can finally breathe again.

"What happened?" His mahogany scent fills my nose, and I sigh.

"I can't tell you," I reply, and he pulls back to look at me.

"Are you sure? Maybe I can help you," he says, and I smile at him.

"It's not my story to tell, but you can help me. Just distract me, take my mind off of it, please."

Although I can see the curiosity burning in his eyes, he loves me enough to drop it. He simply nods, kisses me on my lips, and leads me to his bed.

"Okay, so I bought a canvas today, and I was thinking about drawing you on it." My eyes go wide, and I stop moving.

"Naked?" I ask him, and he smiles.

"Naked, clothed, whatever you want," he responds, and as much as I try to hide my smile, I can't.

"Where would we hang it? We can't just put it in your room. Jean and your aunts will see it! And we can't hang it in my room because of Adrian and Mrs. Beaumont." Gabriel nods and puts on his thinking face: biting the inside of his cheek and staring at the wall.

"The only solution I can think of is buying our own house," he says, and, just like expected, my heart skips several beats.

"We've only been dating a few weeks, that's it!" I laugh, but he doesn't.

"I've waited long enough," he tells me, and I walk over to him to put my hands on his cheeks.

"Listen closely, Gabriel. We've only been dating for a couple of months, we can't buy a house. Are you crazy?" My voice is gentle, which is why he smiles.

"Yeah, crazy about you, about us, about our future," he says, and I let out a short laugh.

"We're not ready for that, and you know it."

Gabriel frowns, but I run my thumbs over his thick eyebrows. He closes his eyes in response and pulls his bottom lip between his teeth. I let go of him and guide the dress I'm wearing over my head.

"However, I am ready to get naked for you," I tell him, and his eyes linger on my breasts as his hands lift to them.

"To get drawn or to fuck?" My body reacts to his words instantly, and the familiar ache returns between my legs.

"Both offers are extremely tempting," I respond and put my index finger under my chin as if I'm contemplating which of his suggestions to take. "I'd say first draw me, and if you do a good job, maybe we can move on to the next part." He closes the distance between us to nibble on my neck and make me giggle.

I get completely naked and lie down on the bed. Gabriel walks over to me and adjusts my position, my hair, and asks me to change my facial expression before he gets a thin fabric and covers my sex and breasts. This solves the problem of where we will hang it because it is no longer inappropriate, at least no more than me in a bikini.

"Comfortable?" he asks, and I smile at him.

"For now, but I'm going to be sitting here for a while, so ask me again later," I reply, and he chuckles.

Gabriel sets up the canvas on his artist easel and starts drawing. I watch him with a genuine smile on my lips, and he grins at me when he catches me staring. Every now and then, we talk about something random, but he's mostly focused on the canvas in front of him.

It fascinates me how he goes from looking all concentrated and handsome to smiling at me and looking adorable.

Eventually, the hand on which my head is resting gets tired, but I ignore the uncomfortable feeling and continue to focus on Gabriel. He asks me a couple of times how I'm doing, and I continue to assure him I'm fine. He seems too happy for me to admit that my hand is asleep and I'm getting cold.

The more I watch him, the more I can't help but realize how far I've fallen. It's weird that I can't imagine my life without him anymore, but then again, he's become one of the few people I rely on. He has become the only other person apart from James and my family I have felt comfortable saying 'I love you' to, and it means more than anyone could ever understand.

I need him because he gives me something I can't live without anymore. He gives me hopes of a family, a beautiful life, love, and everything I could possibly want in the future. I'm going to make my dream come true, and we'll travel the world together. We're going to be truly happy because we want the same things in life.

Our passions overlap. We fit so well together, it scares me a little. I fear no one will make me feel the same way he does. I fear he is the one for me, which may be my naïve almost nineteen-year-old brain talking.

Then again, I don't think it is. I've never met anyone who could make me feel so... complete. The holes in my chest have become more bearable, and although I miss the ones I've lost, thinking of them doesn't bring me this awful pain anymore.

"Okay, I think I'm finished with the sketch, and I will add the colors later," he informs me, and I grin.

"You think you'll remember everything about my body when I'm not here?" I ask while he studies his work.

"I have memorized everything about you over the years, ma chérie. I will be fine," he replies, and I feel a warmth spread through me. "You are breathtaking," he mumbles at the canvas, and I smile at him.

He turns it for me to look at, and I forget how to breathe. Gabriel made me look like an angel. I stare back at him in awe.

"You like it?" he asks, and I tilt my head.

"I love it," I reply, and Gabriel smirks proudly.

A few moments pass before I get a little impatient and remove the cloth from my private areas.

"Why are you so far away?" I ask him, and he cocks an eyebrow at me.

The dimples in his cheek cause my insides to turn, and the way his smile changes into a sexy smirk makes my body ache. Gabriel removes his shirt, and I bite my lip in response. His muscles flex as he struts over to me and pins me down on the bed.

"I crave you," he says before pressing a gentle kiss to my lips.

"I'm yours," I reply once he leans back to look at me again.

I free my hands from his grasp and put them on each side of his face, guiding it down to slide my tongue into his mouth. His hard cock presses against me through his thin sweatpants, and Gabriel rubs it in circles, making me moan.

"I want to try something," I say when he moves on to kiss my neck, sending a wave of shivers and fire over me.

"Anything," he whispers against my skin.

"Tie me up."

Gabriel freezes for a split second before lifting his head to study my face. He's trying to make sure he didn't misunderstand.

"I want to be under your complete control," I admit, and he bites down on his full bottom lip.

The only place I'm willing to give up control is in the bedroom, something I'm convinced he's realized by now too.

"Are you sure?" I nod, waiting for him to do what I want him to.

He takes the same cloth that was covering me earlier and uses it to tie my hands together over my head. I'm curious about how it's going to feel but mostly irritated he's still wearing his pants.

"Take off your clothes," I complain, and he grins at me.

"One second, baby," he replies and tightens the material around my wrists. A gasp leaves me, and I press my lips together to muffle the moan.

Once he is happy with his work, he smirks at it. His hands roam over my breasts, and I push off the bed to get closer. The ache between my legs becomes unbearable, but he runs his fingers all over me, teasing me more. He glides one of them over my clit, only for the briefest second. I moan, rolling my hips to get more contact.

"You are so sexy," he says, and I bite my bottom lip.

I could swear I look like an idiot, but the way he smiles at me makes me believe the opposite.

Gabriel goes on to take off his clothes, removing them too slowly for my liking. As soon as he is naked, I smile victoriously, and he shakes his head. My eyes fixate on his cock as he slides a condom on it, moving back between my legs when he's done.

As soon as he starts kissing me again, I feel a wave of adrenalin rush through my body. I would have never thought being tied up would make me feel this alive, this excited.

The build-up sends a thrill through me, and I want more. My skin is on fire, and my nipples are painfully hard. His fingers run from my neck all the way down to my hips, goosebumps awakening in response.

Gabriel goes from kissing my lips to my neck and then my nipples. My back arches off the bed again, and I ball my hands into fists because that's all I can do while they are tied up over my head. Not being able to touch him frustrates me, but my body is too distracted by the way he explores it to care.

He takes his time pleasuring every single sensitive area of mine, making it impossible to lie still. My legs try to find a way to press together, to ease the pressure even a little, but Gabriel's body is in the way.

I moan with every lick, nibble, and kiss he plants on me. The anticipation drives me crazy, especially when the head of his cock presses against my wet core, but he doesn't move. He stays there, taunting me.

My head screams for him to slide inside, to fill and complete me in every way, but he doesn't. His hands roam over my needy body, and I almost let out a complaining whine.

"Please," I beg, something I've been doing a lot with him recently, but I adore the way I don't have to be in control when we have sex.

In all the other parts of my life, I need to be on high alert and in charge, but not with Gabriel. He gives me what I need, no questions asked.

"A little bit longer, chérie," he says, his mouth dropping back onto my nipples.

A wave of pleasure courses through me, and I wish I could touch myself to ease the ache. I pull on the cloth as Gabriel runs his tongue all the way down my body. He presses kisses to my hip bone, getting closer to where I crave his mouth the most.

"Gabriel," I moan, rolling my hips again, but he pushes me down on the bed.

The tension makes me dizzy, and I close my eyes while I wait for him to release me.

"You're so wet for me, chérie, always so wet," Gabriel says with satisfaction dripping from his words.

His fingers slip inside of me, curling at the perfect spot.

"So ready for my cock," he adds, thrusting his fingers inside again.

I'm already so close to falling apart that I whimper when he removes them. I open my eyes to see him move on top of me, kissing me until I forget my own name.

"Ready?" he asks, and I manage to nod before he slams inside of me.

I let all sounds of pleasure leave my lips, including one of relief. My hands tug on the cloth, looking for anything to hold onto while he slides back out and thrusts in again.

"I need you to stay quiet for me, baby, just this once," he says, and I breathe an 'okay'.

Gabriel creates a delicious rhythm, and the low groans that leave him only send more waves of pleasure through me. His hands bring my legs up to his shoulders, and he rests them there, his head between them.

His strokes go deeper and faster, and I feel the familiar tension build in my stomach. Too soon, I fall apart under his control, but Gabriel keeps going, despite my legs shaking and my body getting overwhelmed by pleasure. I press my lips together to keep from screaming at the top of my lungs.

He is rubbing my clit between his thumb and index finger, sending another orgasm through my body. The second one feels different but just as consuming.

"Oh God, Gabriel," I moan, and he smiles before bringing his lips to my leg.

His movements become sloppy, his mouth leaves my skin, and he groans my name as his body shakes from the orgasm. Gabriel lowers himself on top of me, sweat on both of our foreheads, and we let out small laughs of pleasure, which still washes over us. He kisses me all over the face, untying me at the same time.

"I'll be right back," he says and gives me one last kiss before disappearing into his bathroom.

I take my now free hands, running them everywhere Gabriel touched me.

When he walks back out, he's wearing nothing but a smile that warms my insides. I open my arms for him, and he drops his body onto my chest, nuzzling his face into the crook of my neck. My legs wrap around his torso, trying to get him even closer to me.

My hands slip into his curly brown hair, tugging a little until I hear him chuckle on top of me. The sound vibrates through me until it reaches my toes and fingertips, leaving my body with ease.

"I like this," he says, and I cock an eyebrow. "I like this a lot," he adds, and a small laugh skips off my lips and into the silent room.

"Being naked?" I ask, and Gabriel raises his head, showing me his dimple-filled smile and green-brown eyes. Both are full of happiness.

"Being naked *with you*," he clarifies, pressing a kiss to my stomach after.

"I like it too," I admit, bringing my hands to his face and tracing his dimples. "I like everything with you."

"Oh God, that was incredibly cheesy, too much so even for me," he says and attempts to get up, but I keep him trapped between my legs.

Gabriel is laughing from the bottom of his heart, and I join him, feeling lighter than ever.

Chapter 43

Gabriel

The doctor applies the usual gel to Domi's lower abdomen, and my aunt smiles from ear to ear, waiting impatiently to see her fetus. Nicolette grabs my hand, nervosity taking over for her as well. Jean is on the other side of the room, trying not to faint at the thought of a human growing inside of Domi. It's a good thing too because he's a fainter, and I don't think I'd catch him before he'd drop to the floor. As long as there is no blood, he should be fine.

"How are we feeling, soon-to-be Mom?" Doctor Alvarez asks, and Domi lets out a sharp breath.

She's not had the easiest of pregnancies this far with back pains, feeling extra sensitive everywhere, and nausea throughout the whole day. I've bought her more crackers and given her more backrubs in the past few weeks than I have for anyone in my entire life.

"Well, except for the fact that my morning sickness happens at any hour, I'm doing well," she says as the doctor runs the machine over her stomach.

My eyes shift to the screen just to see... absolutely nothing. I don't see anything at first, not until Doctor Alvarez points at the small bean that's going to grow into my cousin. The thought is weird and beautiful at the same time.

"That's good. From what I can see here, everything looks great. The baby looks healthy." All four of us start smiling at the news.

For a split second, my mind drifts to the day Val and I will look at each other in the same loving, joyful way Domi and Nicolette are right now, after hearing their child is healthy.

I shake my head, forcing the thought away to focus on my aunts, who are asking Jean and me what we'd like to do now.

"I have a date I don't want to be late for, but I'll see you tomorrow," I say, giving Nicolette and Domi a kiss on the cheek. Jean tells me he's fine, he doesn't need one, and I can't help but chuckle as I walk out of the room.

Valentina called me yesterday, telling me to put on something nice for dinner at her house. I decide on a white dress shirt and black pants, hoping it's fancy enough for her liking. The last thing I want is for Val to be disappointed because I didn't put enough effort into my appearance.

With my hair still dripping from the shower, I walk toward her home, excitement now filling my chest. Rose petals lead from the open gate all the way toward the veranda, where she's waiting for me in a long, red dress, the same color as my F1 car, and a smile that has my knees weak. Every curve of her body is highlighted in that damn outfit, and it takes everything out of me not to kneel before her.

"You're the most beautiful woman to have ever walked the Earth," I say as I approach the only person I want to spend the rest of my life with, pulling her against me by those hips that make my mouth drool.

"Ever?" she asks, amusement on her face as mine stays serious.

"Ever."

I wrap my lips around hers, needing to taste the watermelon flavor of her lip balm, which I've loved since the first time I kissed her. Her hands lift to my stomach, one of her favorite parts of my body, while I slide my tongue through her parted lips. My hands hold her face, and a little moan leaves her, driving me crazy.

"The food's going to get cold," she says, breathless and quiet, when I move on to kiss her neck, feeling the soft skin against my mouth. "Gabriel," she half-warns, half-moans, and I step back with a smirk on my face.

Her cheeks have turned a warm shade of pink, and I bite my bottom lip in response to the thought that she is definitely wet for me right now.

"Where do you want me?" I ask, and Valentina flashes me one of those naughty grins, which never fail to make me race more in love.

"For now, in that chair," she says, pointing to the one on my left.

I walk to the right one, pulling it out and waiting for her to sit down to push it back against the table.

"Thank you." Her voice is soft, full of love, and I press a kiss to the top of her head.

I settle down on my own chair, for the first time inhaling the aroma of the paella she made. Candles are on each side of the pot with more petals on the table.

"You look gorgeous," Val says, and my eyes lift to hers. "Thank you for dressing up. I thought it would be fun," she explains with a shy look, and I place my hand on top of hers, guiding it to my face where she traces my bottom lip with her thumb.

"It is. I just wish you would have let me help you cook or set all of this up," I complain, and she lets out a small laugh.

"That's not how it works, Monsieur Biancheri. I invited you on this date, so I get to organize everything." I shake my head, disbelief washing over me. I've never had someone do anything like this for me...

"I'm the one that's supposed to spoil you," I counter, but that makes her frown.

"Says who?" she challenges, crossing her arms in front of her chest to push her breasts together and knock the air out of my chest. "Well, whoever it is, they can fuck off because I get to spoil you just as much as you do me," she says, placing some of the food onto my plate.

I watch her with fascination, unable to speak.

"Bon Appétit," Valentina adds before bringing a spoonful of her meal to her lips, a mischievous grin on her face again.

"Uh oh, what did you do?" I ask, trying her food too. Naturally, it's the best paella I've ever tasted.

"I got a tattoo today," she states, folding both of her lips between her teeth to keep from showing me any kind of emotion. I, on the other hand, must have a thousand of them wash over my face.

"You didn't," I say, too shocked to believe her. Val merely shrugs, putting another spoonful into her mouth. "Where?" I ask, needing more information. The thought of her having a tattoo excites me to my core.

"Hmmmm, I think you need to search and find it," she replies, leaning back in her chair and wiping her mouth with the serviette she put on her lap minutes ago.

A smile tugs on the corners of my mouth until it has set itself on my face.

"Will you give me a tip?" I ask, standing up to walk over to where she is.

Her chest starts rising and falling more abruptly as I drop to my knees in front of her, one of my favorite places in the world.

"It's in the same place as yours," she says, and I forget how to breathe. *Fuuuuck.*

One of her legs rests on top of the other as I run my fingers over her ankles, guiding them apart. The slit in her dress lets me trail my hand over her right thigh, and I lean forward to press a kiss to it. Goosebumps instantly cover the area around my lips, making me smile.

"You have to stand, baby, so I can see your tattoo," I say, but she takes my chin between her fingers to grab my full attention.

"It's not on my ass." *It's on her hip bone.* I don't think I'll survive that.

My heart races while I lift her dress by the slit until the tattoo is exposed to me, two little words written on her skin: *Bon Appétit.* I lick my lips, my mouth watering.

"Do you like it?" she asks, but all I manage to do is nod. "It's not meaningful at all, but I think it's hot," Val explains, and I reach out to trace the outside of the clear bandage.

"It's too sexy, ma chérie. I don't think I can resist what it's saying." She spreads her legs for me, and I bring one of them over my shoulder, her black panties exposed to me now. I lean forward, my fingers pushing the thin fabric–

"I've just had the weirdest day of my fucking life!" Adrian's voice comes from the gate area, and I jump up, putting distance between Val and me.

He appears on the veranda just as I fall back onto my chair, panic in his eyes.

"Shit, am I interrupting date night? I'm sorry." An awkward silence fills the room as he passes by us, stopping to inhale the smell of the food. "Can I take a plate?" he asks, and my girlfriend clears her throat, forcing her head back into reality.

"Yeah, sure," she says, her eyes shifting to me as Adrian walks inside to grab a plate. "I guess we should eat first," she whispers, and I smile at her.

"We should, but let's hurry up. I crave dessert."

Chapter 44

Valentina

James has been cryptic for the past two days, only sending minimal texts to let me know he's okay and figuring things out. For the first time in the duration of our friendship, he's putting himself before what he thinks I may want, and I couldn't be prouder of him. I will give him as much space as he needs, and, once he's ready, I will be there for him in any and every way he needs me.

Gabriel and Adrian were asked to test out some of the changes the team has made to their cars, and we're all flying to Maranello together. I'm getting sick of traveling every week, but, at least with them by my side, it's more tolerable.

Gabriel keeps drawing me as I read the book we started almost a week ago. He turns his sketchbook whenever he finishes a drawing, a proud look on his handsome face. I give him a smile every time, and he goes back to sketching me again when I shift my position, careful not to put pressure on my new tattoo. It's been healing well so far, but I've only had it for a few days.

"How many more do you want to create? There will be too much of me in your book," I say with amusement, but he frowns at me.

"There is no such thing as too much of you, Valentina, stop being silly," he scolds, and Adrian chuckles beside me.

"I hope I will never be that wrapped around someone's finger. I don't ever want to say garbage like that," my brother says, earning himself a smack on the arm from me. "Hey, what? Gabriel didn't use to be this way, this romantic. I'm scared it'll happen to me," he explains, and I cover my mouth to keep from laughing.

Gabriel leans forward in his chair because he's across from us and wants to make sure his teammate hears his next words clearly.

"It will, Adrian, and, when it does, I'll remind you of this moment," he promises, briefly wiggling his eyebrows at him.

Gabriel winks at me and leans back in his chair, going back to drawing. My brother scoffs, and my boyfriend smiles.

"You're going to fall in love so hard," my boyfriend adds, and I let out the laugh I was trying to suppress.

"You're both annoying. I'm going to find someone else to sit with," he complains, catching the glance of a beautiful, curvy brunette across from him. She stares down at the seat beside her, inviting him to join her. "Whoever is in charge of my life, thank you," he says before walking toward her, a smirk on his lips.

I shake my head, my focus shifting back to Gabriel, who turns his sketchbook to show me a Formula One car with the number nine on it. Next to it, he drew me in a race suit with a helmet tucked between my hip and arm. A lump appears in my throat as I try to tell him how stunning it is.

"I know, it's not that great, but it'll be better when I get to draw it from real life," he says and turns his sketchbook again to work on his art.

"You're the most talented artist I've ever met, Gabriel," I finally manage to croak out, and he notices the change in my emotions.

He sits down next to me, taking my hand and placing a kiss to the back of it.

"It'll happen, I'll make sure of it, even if I have to give up my own seat to get you one," he says, and I lean away from him, surprise probably all over my face. His thumb traces my bottom lip as he smiles. "I'd do anything to see your dream come true, mon tournesol."

My eyes move to my brother, who's close enough to have heard this whole conversation. He mouths the words 'me too', and I bring my gaze back to Gabriel's.

"It will happen. We will make sure of it."

"No, you won't, I won't let you. You can't be my savior in this, no matter how much you want to be. This is my fight, and I'll make it happen, just like I was taught."

Both of my Ferrari drivers have been in the car, testing the new upgrades, for the past hour. Meanwhile, I've been talking to the strategists, engineers, and Lorenzo Mattia, trying to learn as much as I'm allowed to about the procedures. I watch an impressed look slip onto the team principal's face every time I add something to the conversation, like a suggestion about the front wing that could help them slightly increase their speed down a straight.

Grandpa taught me a lot about the workings of an F1 car, and I've been doing my best to study them as they evolve, something that seems to be earning me plus points with Lorenzo at the moment.

"You know, I remember the first time I ever saw you," he says to me as we're watching Adrian's lap time improve.

I turn to him, his smile contagious.

"You were this tall." He holds his hand a meter above the ground. "And you had this look of awe on your face that I haven't seen on many people, let alone little children like you were," he goes on, staring off into the distance as he recalls the events of that day. "Your father told me afterward that you wanted to be a Formula One driver, and I remember telling him if you proved to me you had talent, I'd let you race for my team one day."

I have no idea what to respond, but I do my best to fight the tears of hope shooting into my eyes.

"Your Nonno and Papà were two of the best drivers in the history of racing. What they had in them, I see in you," he says, pointing at my heart.

All my life, I've been told the opposite from the men in charge. I've been told I lack the spirit of a racer, that I lacked what my family had. The tears stream down now because I can't stop them, I don't want to anymore. Lorenzo gives my shoulder a squeeze.

"*Avere fede.*" Have faith.

"*Sempre,*" I reply, and he gives me another proud smile before walking away.

"It's going to rain," someone else says in Italian, and I'm impressed by how much I already understand. Gabriel is a great teacher.

Adrian is the first to return, his car already dripping from the sudden shower pouring down. He gets out and walks toward me, soaking wet. I try to run from him, but he catches me, lifts me into the air, and transfers the rain onto my clothes. Annoyance is replaced by pure joy, and laughter leaves me as he drops me to the floor again.

"If I have to suffer, so do you," he says, his words muffled because of his helmet. I nudge him in the ribs, but he doesn't even move a centimeter. "You should probably change. Your clothes are soaked," he points out, and I nudge him again, this time hard enough to make him bend over. "Yeah, I deserve that one."

We both burst into laughter. Adrian walks away, probably to put on some dry clothes, but my eyes fixate on the rain.

"Is anyone driving right now?" I ask the man in charge of giving the green light for any driver to go on track.

"No. Why?" he replies, and I smile at him.

"Do you mind if I–" I cut off, simply pointing at the track.

He follows my finger before giving me a thumbs up and focusing on his screens again. I spot Gabriel getting out of his car, but I'm on a mission.

Warm drops of water hit my skin as soon as I step outside and make my way onto the track. I spin around once I'm at the start and finish line. My feet carry me around while I let the rain drench my dress. I can't explain the feeling of freedom spreading through me, the adrenalin coursing through my veins, but it comes close to the one racing brings me.

Music fills my ears then, and I shift my gaze to the speakers at the fence next to me. James Arthur's voice comes through them, and I spin once more. The moment I stop, Gabriel's arms are around me, guiding me to the music. I beam up at him, and he uses the opportunity to wrap his lips around mine.

"You hate dancing," I remind him as water soaks his hair. My hands lift to it, pushing it out of his beautiful face.

"With you, I'd dance anywhere, anytime, even in the pouring rain," he says, twisting me around once just to bring me against his chest.

An uncontrollable giggle leaves me, and he smiles in return. I can barely keep my eyes open as more water hits them, but it's worth it; everything up to this moment has been worth it.

"I'm the luckiest woman in the world because you fell in love with me," I say, blinking away the rain to watch his features soften.

"I didn't *fall*, ma chérie, I *raced*."

He plants his lips on mine, smiling against my mouth before spinning me around one last time.

"I always want to be the man you deserve."

"You are, mon soleil, always."

Gabriel kisses me again as the entire world around us blurs into nothing more than the noise of drops hitting asphalt.

Chapter 45

Gabriel

It's been three weeks since Adrian and I were in Maranello for testing. Being away from Valentina is still not easy, but I've been to see her a couple of times. Apart from that, I had to be away for an entire week for the race in Montreal and then another for the one in Texas.

I won the Canadian Grand Prix with Adrian in second, *fucking Eduardo* in third, and Kyle in fourth. It was a great race with important points for the whole team, and it also expanded my championship lead again. Adrian won his first race of the season in the U.S., with me in second place, Jonathan in third, and James in fourth.

I shouldn't get my hopes up because the season isn't even halfway done, but I can't stop myself from imagining how it'd feel to finally hold that trophy, carry the title any F1 driver dreams of having. I push the thought aside, not ready to let myself linger on that scenario yet.

Valentina has been kicking His Royal Grossness' ass in every category except strength. For some inexplicable reason, Christian is a lot stronger than her physically, but one category, especially that one, won't stand in Val's way of getting the Formula Three seat. It can't.

She's excelled at everything they have given her, the practical and the theoretical, analysis and racing itself. If they give him the seat instead of her, there will be no other explanation except that Christian is a royal and a man.

"Are you okay? You're in your head a lot today," Adrian says as he stares at me from across the room.

We've just finished filming a video for our team to upload for the fans. I look outside the window at the Texas track, counting down the minutes until I can get on a plane and back to my sunflower.

"Would you hate me if I won the championship this year instead of you?" I ask, the question surprising both of us.

Adrian shifts in his seat, the awkward silence creating a veil of tension that makes us both uncomfortable.

"No, I wouldn't hate you. We're teammates, and we've been friends for years. This sport is brutal, and if you are the one to win this year, then I'll be happy for you." He truly is the best guy I've ever met. "I'll snatch the title from you sooner or later if that happens," Adrian adds, and I let out a small laugh. "You're family, Gabriel, whether you want to be or not. I could never hate you unless you hurt my sister. That's where I draw the line," he warns, and I nod.

"I'd never hurt her, not if I can do something about it." Adrian leans back in his chair, caressing his temples. My answer bothers him.

"What if you don't have a choice? What if something happens, and you have the power to spare her more pain if you did something that hurts you more than it will her? Are you capable of putting Val first, always?"

I want to answer him, tell him I'd give my heart and soul to her, for her, but Adrian lifts his hands to stop me.

"You can't answer because you haven't had to make that decision. I hope you never will," he says, shutting me up for good.

I go back to staring outside when Eduardo and James step into the room. *I can't catch a fucking break.*

"What's up, lads? Why the serious expressions?" James asks, and I have the urge to punch him in his fucking face for being who he is.

Adrian would never doubt the Brit because James has been proving himself to my teammate for their entire lives. He probably thinks his best friend would be perfect for his sister. *Great, now I'm fucking nauseous.*

"Oh, so you're talking to me again? Why, thank you, Your Majesty, for blessing us with your presence," Adrian says, annoyance in his voice.

I sit upright, surprised at this shift in the atmosphere. My senses switch to high alert as I watch the situation in front of me unravel.

"I think you've lost your bloody mind, mate," James replies, shoving his hands into his pockets.

"*I* have lost *my* mind? You're the one who's been a dick to me for the past month, and now you come in here like everything's alright? What the hell?"

Eduardo steps away when Adrian gets in James' face, but both of us are ready to separate them if they need to be.

"Figuring shit out counts as being a dick now?" Adrian rolls his eyes.

"When your best friend ignores and avoids you for four weeks without an explanation, yes, it counts."

His words come from a place of hurt, even if he's letting anger work as the spokesperson at the moment. Yelling won't do anything but frustrate both of them.

I'm about to tell him to calm down when James throws something into the room that knocks the breath from my chest.

"Maybe your best friend is struggling with the fact that he's going to be a fucking father!" He sinks down on one of the chairs while my hand lifts to my mouth, subtly covering it to keep it shut.

"You what?" Adrian asks, his tone soft now.

James drops his head, and I signal for Eduardo and me to give them some privacy. He gives me a slight nod, and the last thing I see is my teammate's arms wrapping around his best friend.

"Could you imagine having a kid right now?" the Spaniard asks when we're out of the room, and I give him a look that I hope says 'why-the-fuck-are-you-talking-to-me?'.

We make our way downstairs toward the exit.

"What? I just mean I'm glad Valentina and I always used protection. I couldn't imagine having a child right now." I stop dead in my tracks, anger making my shoulders vibrate. "What? Does it bother you she and I fucked?" he says, a smug smile on his face.

It takes everything in me not to punch him in his crooked white teeth. He's taken it too far now, but he knows it. This was his intention when he started speaking to me. Eduardo wanted to piss me off, and he has succeeded.

"Maybe if you'd done a better job, it would, but Val doesn't even remember you exist. That's how much of an impression you left." I walk past him, my shoulder hitting his.

There was a time in my life when I would have beaten him up, make him pay for his comments, but that's not who I am anymore. I don't start fights.

"Sure, if that's what you need to tell yourself," Eduardo calls after me, but I'm done with this conversation.

He's a coward for saying all of this to my face without Val present. He knows she'd mess him up for everything that just came out of his mouth.

I'd hold her fucking purse and cheer as she did it too.

Chapter 46

Valentina

Today Andrea is going to announce who got the Formula Three seat. Haru and Lucie have officially told me they are dating a week ago, which is why they're sitting across from me now, cuddling on the couch-like seating area. He presses a soft kiss to her lips, and she smiles against his. Such a simple action, but it makes me miss Gabriel with my entire being.

It's been a week since I've seen him, since I've felt his arms around me. What makes all of this worse is James has barely spoken to me and the last time I saw him was the day I found out about the baby.

Evangelin has been avoiding me too, but I don't have an explanation for that. Last we spoke, everything was fine. Maybe she's upset because I haven't gone to see her and *Rush* in a while. I'll have to check on her when I fly back tomorrow.

"I'll burn this place down if they don't give you the seat," Adrian says, ripping me out of my thoughts and bringing a smile to my face.

He was the only one who could make it here today. Gabriel has sponsor meetings and James has an ultrasound to attend with Annabel.

"It's a possibility you might want to prepare yourself for," I suggest, but he frowns at me in response.

"It cannot be, Valentina. What else do they expect of you? To not need a car and just run like you're The Flash or something?" he asks, and I laugh at his analogy.

"I don't know. Just, don't get your hopes up, that's all I'm asking," I say, and he wraps his arm around my shoulder, pressing a kiss to my temple.

He doesn't reply, merely holds me while we wait for Andrea to bring us the news I'm expecting.

"It's so cute how you bring your brother everywhere. He's such a good boy, always following you around," Christian says, interrupting the peaceful moment Adrian and I were trying to have.

"Careful, he attacks on my command," I warn, and Adrian starts growling next to me. The brat takes a step back, a disgusted expression on his face.

"You're both so fucking weird," he says, but walks away, looking over his shoulder with an expression which tells me he's making sure Adrian isn't coming after him.

My brother and I burst into laughter as he raises his hand for a high-five that I give him without hesitation.

"Valentina, Christian, are you ready?" Andrea asks, and I shift my eyes to where they are standing.

An unreadable expression lingers on their features, and fear consumes me. My rival and I get up at the same time, moving over to where our instructor is. Adrian is right beside me, like he has been for every moment leading up to this point, holding my hand.

"I want to let you both know you've done an exceptional job, and no matter what I'm about to tell you, you should be proud of your performance." Their eyes are on me then shift to Christian throughout their speech.

"Whoever doesn't get accepted is allowed to stay in the academy and train for another opportunity, right?" The question leaves me before the words have a chance to be processed in my head.

"Who gives a shit? Just tell Valentina I'm the one who got the seat,"

Christian chimes in, and my stomach turns upside down.

Andrea stares at the ground before taking a deep breath. Their eyes carry back to me, sadness in them now.

Realization dawns on me.

"I'm sorry, Valentina, I tried everything I could, but Mr. Mattia and Mr. Reiner were firm on their decision to have Christian race in Formula Three. I'm so sorry," they say, and I feel my head nod as everything inside of me goes numb.

"Hell yeah! I got the seat!" Christian celebrates as I sink into Adrian's arms, the shock sending my body into temporary paralysis.

"No, fuck this! How is that possible? Valentina outperformed that prick in every category but one!" Adrian fights for me, and I regain my ability to speak.

"Do I get to stay in the academy?" I ask, but tears fill Andrea's eyes then.

"No," they reply, and I nod again, my mouth turning into a desert as swallowing my own spit becomes impossible. "They don't want you to be a part of this academy."

I can't listen to any more, even though Adrian is arguing with Andrea now, demanding to have an answer they can't give him. I turn around, ready to run away from all of this when I see Gabriel in the doorframe.

His face is full of pain, letting me know he heard everything.

"Chérie," he says, his voice so soft, it shoves the tears out of my eyes and down my cheeks.

My body is frozen again because I'm not sure if I want to sprint into his arms, run from everything, or sink to the ground to let darkness swallow me.

"It's okay, I've got you," he says in French, and I rush into his arms.

He wraps them around me, enveloping me as if to shield me from all the pain and hurt my heart is trying to process. I sob against his chest, breaking down as he caresses the back of my head.

"Adrian, Andrea is not the one who decided this. Focus on what's important, would you? We'll get answers later," Gabriel tells my brother before attempting to lead me out of the room. Christian's words stop us.

"I told you I'd get the seat, belle. Don't take it personally. It's just how the world works, nothing you can do to change that, no matter how determined you are."

"You know what, Christian? I may not have a dick to get me ahead in life, but at least I don't act like one either. I hope you have a successful, long career. May lots of disappointments come your way so you can produce a better fucking personality," I reply and step out of the room.

My feet don't stop until I'm outside of the building where I collapse onto the ground. Breathing, crying, being, it all hurts. I cover my mouth and let out a scream, unable to hold it back any longer.

I scream for my grandfather, who gave everything to make my dream come true.

I scream for my father, who raced for me, but I'll never be able to race for him.

I scream for Adrian, who yet again has to help me pick up the pieces.

And I scream for Gabriel, who feels my pain deep in his chest because our souls are intertwined.

They didn't even let me stay in the academy...

"Mon amour," Gabriel says from next to me.

I don't know how long I've been in this position, crying over what I've lost, but the sun is setting now. My sobs have slowed, only shaking my body every few minutes. Tears still stream down my face, but they come as naturally as breathing now.

"We will get to the bottom of this, Val, I promise. There must be a reason why—" I have to cut my brother off then.

"Please, stop. Please. I can't do this anymore, Adrian. This ripping pain in my chest, I can't take it. I can't fight anymore. Please, don't make me fight," I beg, treading closer to the dark hole in my mind I've been balancing around my whole life.

Adrian takes my face between his hands, forcing me to focus.

"You listen to me, little champion, you will race in a Formula One car. This academy? It means nothing! It was supposed to help you, and, now that it didn't, fuck that. We don't need them. Lorenzo Mattia might be my boss, but I will make his life a living hell for what he's taken from you today. We can't stop fighting now because you haven't made it to where you want to be yet. You're not alone in this, you'll never be. This is not the end of your story, Valentina, this is not where you give up on your dream," Adrian says, standing up and holding his hand out for me. "I won't let you, just like Grandpa and Dad wouldn't. Fight for them, fight for us, but, most importantly, keep fighting for yourself."

I slide my hand into his, unwilling to argue with him when he's so full of hope.

"Okay," is all I answer, but we know it's done now.

There is nothing more we can do. I'll let him figure this out on his own while I do my best to walk in the opposite direction of the darkness.

"Whatever it takes," Gabriel adds, his hand cupping my face and wiping away the physical representation of my emotions. "Adrian is right. This is not the end. How could it be? Your story has hardly begun."

I lean toward my boyfriend, kissing his lips in an attempt to relieve some of the tension in my chest. It works for a brief moment, until I pull back and reality sinks in again.

"I hate agreeing with anyone that isn't me, but Gabriel is right. Then again, he's recycling my words, so..." Adrian trails off with a shrug, and I let out a small, genuine laugh.

"Let's go home, as far away from this place as possible," I say, and they both give me a nod.

It's time I get back to Monaco and figure out what the hell I'm going to do with my life now that my last chance has been ripped from me.

Chapter 47

Gabriel

The rooms are too small, the windows barely let in any light, and the kitchen is a disaster. This is the third apartment my realtor has taken Valentina and me to, and all of them have looked better in the photos than in real life. I can't see myself living in any of the spaces we've seen, which is quite disappointing. We need our privacy, and I was hoping one of the apartments would be a place I can see myself and Val spending our time, but none of them felt right.

I drop my head in response.

"Mon amour," Valentina says, her arms wrapping around me from behind. "We'll find one, don't worry," she assures me in French, sending a thrill through me. I love the way it falls off her lips.

"I know," I reply, running my hands over her arms before I guide her in front of me to capture her lips with mine.

She smiles, kissing me a few times and then stepping back. The bags under her eyes break my heart, especially because they're not from crying.

They've appeared because she isn't sleeping. We've been spending our nights reading, but every time she closes her eyes, I feel her heart accelerate and then they open again. I can't imagine what's going through her head when that happens.

"Listen, bébé, I had a feeling we wouldn't find something you'd be happy with today, so I got you this," she says, and I smile at the pet name before focusing on the ring-sized box she lifts up for me to take.

"Are you proposing?" I ask and cock an eyebrow. Her cheeks turn a bright red.

"No, it's way too early for that," she says with a small laugh, making me smile.

"Promise when it isn't, you'll let me propose. I want to be the one." Val lets out another little laugh, straightening out her back.

"We'll see," she simply replies, urging me to open the box.

I do as I'm told, raising the lid to see a key sitting inside.

"To my house. I discussed it with Adrian, and we both agreed it's time for you to have one. I want you to be comfortable in my home," she explains, stepping back and touching the tips of her fingers to her mouth while she waits for a reaction from me.

"Are you sure we're ready for this?" I know I am, but I want her to be too.

This will be a big commitment for us, for our relationship, and it shouldn't be because she doesn't like that I wait for her outside.

"Gabriel, this is long overdue. My house, my grandfather's house, it's my safe place, but so are you. I want you to be able to feel at home there too."

I reach for her hips, her now healed tattoo no longer at risk of me applying too much pressure and hurting her.

"Wherever you are, I'll feel at home."

She pretends like she hates my cheesy, corny words, but the corners of her mouth always stretch into a smile. She secretly loves it, which is why I never hold back from saying them out loud.

"I'll still text and ask for permission before coming over. I won't just show up," I say, and Valentina chuckles, her hands lifting to my neck.

"I know, which is why I feel so comfortable giving you this." I'm about to kiss her again when my realtor interrupts us.

"Ready to go?" she asks, and I turn to the short woman.

"Yes, we're ready," I say, grabbing Val's hand and leading her toward the door. She needs to get some sleep, and I have to find a way to get her mind off what haunts her at night.

"I'm going to look for places with more windows and bigger rooms. Also one with a balcony that overlooks the ocean. How does that sound?" Kim, my realtor, says, and I thank her a few times. Valentina does so as well before we make our way to my car.

"What can I do to make you happy?" I ask my sunflower when she sits in the passenger seat, staring out of the window and getting lost in her thoughts.

She tilts her head to me, a tired smile on her face.

"You already have," she replies, closing her eyes as I place my hand on her thigh.

Val falls asleep before we even make it home, and I carry her to bed. I wrap the blanket around her, caressing her cheek for a moment. My heart beats a little more evenly now that she's getting the rest she needs.

"How is she?" Adrian's voice comes from behind me, but I signal for him to leave the room with me. I don't want to risk waking Val under any circumstance.

"She's sleeping now, which is an improvement." He nods, rubbing his face and revealing how tired and frustrated he is. "When's the last time you got any sleep?" I ask, but he shakes his head as if to dismiss my question.

"I got better things to do. I've been trying to contact Lorenzo Mattia, but he hasn't answered any of my calls, texts, or e-mails. I think he's scared to face me," he jokes, a yawn slipping past his lips.

The usual white in his eyes is a fire red, and there are dark circles underneath them.

"Well, it's too late now, he won't get back to you at this hour. You, mate, need to rest. We all do," I remind him, and he gives me an agreeing wink.

"Yeah, you're right. I have to get up early. Daniel wants us to go for a run."

He rolls his eyes, giving my shoulder one last squeeze before disappearing into his bedroom. I walk into Val's, undressing and sliding under the blanket to get close to her.

Chapter 48

Valentina

"Will it ever get easier?" I ask Grandfather, who raises his bushy, white eyebrow in confusion. "Getting turned away?" I add, and he takes my hand as we walk away from the karting track where none of the talent scouts were interested in sponsoring me.

"Listen, little champion, success wouldn't exist without failure. Often, we need to learn how to fall before we can get up, do you understand?" he says, but I shake my head.

He's not making any sense to me.

"If everything was simply handed to you, you'd never know how to deal with rejection. Today is not something to cry over, it's something to grow from. You need to learn in order to be worthy of an F1 seat. In races, you won't always get the results you desire. It'll be difficult, disappointing, and frustrating, but you'll know how to deal with it better than anyone. It won't cloud your judgment during races, not like it would for people that never handled rejection." He leads me back to his car, but I stop before we reach it.

"But why don't they want to recruit me? I won the Karting Championship," I defend, and my grandfather grabs me by the shoulders, making sure I

pay close attention to his next words.

"You are a girl, Valentina. They will always look at you like the weak one because of that. I tried to shield you for as long as I could, but you have to understand boys will get top priority. That's why Adrian is doing so well. He's just as talented as you, has gotten the same opportunities, and the scouts were interested as soon as he arrived at the same event we went to today. It's how the world works, which is why I'm trying my very best to help you change that, okay? We will make sure, together, that the mindsets of the people will no longer be closed off. You will be the change the world needs," he says, and I nod.

"That's a big responsibility," I reply, and he gives me a proud smile.

"You don't have to do anything other than be yourself and keep on fighting. That's all you have to do," Grandfather assures me, and I grin at him.

I will do exactly as he said.

I will be the change.

"Oh, Valentina, this is beautiful. Thank you so much, darling." Mrs. Beaumont is holding up the cream-colored scarf I bought her, her smile contagious. I haven't truly smiled in a couple of days, since everything happened at the academy.

"Happy Birthday," I say to the sweet woman, and she hugs me. "I'm so glad you decided to come back to our house. I don't know what we would do without you."

I can't help but realize how much I rely on her. For most of my life, I haven't depended on anyone to help with cleaning my home. Since Mom took off before I could walk, and Dad was always gone, I had to figure out how to do all of the tasks in a household. Only when I stayed at Grandpa's home, I relied on Mrs. Beaumont and him, but he insisted I learn how to do all of these things, just like Adrian had to. He made sure I knew how to take care of myself when Dad wasn't home. I wish I could tell him now how thankful I am for teaching me to be independent, what an amazing grandfather he was, but I can't. I can't speak to him, ask him for advice, nothing.

Now, when I need him the most, he can't be my guiding compass.

Mrs. Beaumont squeezes my arm before she goes back to work. I find myself wandering around the house, searching for something to occupy my time, but I do so in vain. Adrian and Gabriel are out with their coaches, and James is busy filming a commercial.

When I don't find anything, I decide to go for a run on the beach. I want to work out. It'll clear my head and keep me from overthinking what happened only a few days ago.

I jog for a long time, not stopping once to breathe or rest. The burning in my lungs is a nice distraction from the constant pain I've been feeling in my chest, so I keep going. My legs get tired long before my mind does, and, somehow, I end up in front of *Rush*. I don't know how I got here, but I know why.

Evangelin.

My feet are cemented to the ground, keeping me from walking into Evangelin's store. I watch her roam around in there, smiling at her customers. I've kept my distance from James and her because it doesn't feel real yet. I've spent my entire life working toward one specific goal, and I know as soon as she hears about what happened, reality will set in for me.

She spots me before I can walk away, waving me inside with a smile. After she's been avoiding me for the past few months, I'm relieved to see her face light up from my presence.

"Ma belle Valentina," she says and wraps her arms around me, hugging me tighter than ever before. "It's been too long. How are you?" Evangelin asks, and I feel her trying to pull away, but I hold her close while tears fill my eyes. "What's wrong?"

She strokes my hair, making a sob leave me.

"Alright, it's okay, dear. Sit down." I do as I'm told, my hands shaking.

I don't want to tell this story, share my failure with someone I never want to disappoint. Evangelin locks the door to ensure no one will bother us before sitting down on the stool across from mine.

"What happened? Tell me," she encourages with a warm smile, and I wipe my tears.

"I didn't get the seat, and they kicked me out of the academy. My instructor, Andrea, had no idea why either. They just told me I couldn't be a part of it anymore," I explain, trying my best to be comprehensible. "This academy was my last hope, but it's over now. There is nothing left for me to do but find a new passion," I say, and Evangelin sits in front of me for a moment as silence fills the small boutique.

"I think you should get another passion anyway, whether you decide to give up or not." The way the words sound coming out of her mouth, 'give up', bothers me.

"I didn't give up on my dream, it keeps giving up on me," I clarify, but she merely shrugs, moving over to a pile of clothes and folding them.

"I know it does. I know 'unfair' doesn't begin to cover what you've gone through in your life, but why would you let it win?" I run my hands over my face and sigh.

"Because I'm done. I'm done trying to achieve something that's never going to happen," I defend, and her blue eyes shift to me, skepticism dancing in them.

"Do you think your grandfather would want that?"

I don't have words for the stinging spreading through my entire body, forcing tears back into my tired eyes.

"I didn't have to know him to tell you this is the last thing he would have wanted for you," she says when I don't respond to her question.

"He thought I'd change the world, Evangelin, but how am I meant to do that when the world doesn't want to be changed?" I challenge, and she places her hands on her hips.

"You do it by setting an example! Demand answers. Don't allow them to take away what makes you unstoppable, and that is your ability to find positivity in the darkest times. If you can't do it for yourself, do it for all the little girls out there, who share the same dream as you."

I forget how to breathe as I imagine my own daughter giving up on whatever dream she may have one day. The thought breaks my heart.

"Demand answers," Evangelin repeats as she finishes folding the last dress. "I'm not ready for you to lose faith in yourself, my child, not yet, not ever," she adds, and I give her one more hug.

"I love you," I blurt out before I can stop myself. "I should go," I say and step back, but she holds me close for another moment.

"I love you too, Valentina." My emotions overwhelm me, which is why I make my way back home.

A box, identical to the ones Gabriel sent me a while ago, sits on my doorstep, and I walk over to it with a smile. I rip the tape off, sitting down on the steps to study the contents. Just like the first one I've ever received, there is a drawing of me and a letter.

I pick up the art first, admiring how talented he is. The details and the pencil strokes are beyond incredible. He makes me look like an angel, simply lying on the beach. The way he drew my face, lips, lashes, and curly hair reminds me yet again he sees me in a way no one else does. He notices things I've never even seen in myself.

No one is ever going to look at me the way he does, there is no doubt in my mind.

I put the drawing on my lap and take the letter into my hands. I tear it open, my hands shaking now. My emotions are all over the place, and I don't know if I'm nervous to read his words or overwhelmingly excited.

Ma Chérie,

You and I know better than most how difficult life gets. We've experienced its cruelty more often than not, especially you, but I need you to remember one thing: you are a sunflower. You follow the sun's light wherever it goes, even when it seems to have disappeared right now, you never let that stop you. You stand in the pouring rain, finding happiness and growth in the water. Let this rainy time fuel you, not stop you. I'll forever be your sun, but you don't need me to tell you that. We all know I'd do anything to get rid of the thundering clouds you're experiencing. I know you well enough to see this situation for what it truly is: your villain origin story.

I lower the letter for a moment to let out a laugh that reaches my heart, shaking my body from amusement.

I'm just teasing. We all know the world would have no chance if you became the villain, especially because you'd have three idiot sidekicks, who would carry backpacks with your weapons in them. Anyway, I think I got a little distracted in my attempt to remind you of the unforgiving strength lying beneath that warm smile of yours. No one can take it from you, mon tournesol.

Only yours,
Gabriel
Je t'aime, chérie.

How could I have made someone like this fall in love with me?

I never have an answer that satisfies this question. I also don't have a justification that pleases the part of me, which wants to keep fighting. It doesn't care about getting hurt. All it gives a damn about is doing what my supportive family keeps telling me to do: keep fucking going until I make it.

Chapter 49

Valentina

"What's this for?" James asks when he holds up the present I gave him.

"For being you."

He's been having a hard time accepting this new part of his life, and I wanted to brighten up his day.

"I am pretty awesome," he says, and I cock an amused eyebrow. "Most of the time," he adds, and I continue to smile at him.

His blue eyes stand out even more as the sun shines onto them, and his blonde hair seems thicker and curlier today.

"You are. I love you, James Oliver Landon. I don't remember much from before I met you, and I'm glad I don't. Life is better with you in it, and I hope this small gift is something that can show you how deeply I care about you."

A tear drops down my cheek, and I quickly wipe it away. I can tell James is about to cry too, which is why I point at the box, indicating for him to open it.

James opens the gift and pulls out the small canvas with a picture of him and me on the front. We are sitting at a table in a restaurant when he was visiting Los Angeles. It's a somewhat recent picture, but the reason I chose it is because it represents our relationship. James has whipped cream all over his face, I am laughing, and my hand is resting on top of his. The balance between fun and love is exactly what our friendship is like.

I ordered a bunch of canvases with pictures, a couple of Adrian in his Ferrari Formula One car, some of my friends and me, and one for James. For Gabriel, I ordered a photo canvas of him holding his first trophy in Formula One. He looks so happy in it, it always makes my insides warm.

"Thank you. This is absolutely gorgeous," James says, and finally, a tear rolls down his cheek. "I love you," he tells me with his thick English accent.

He flings his arms around my chest, and I wrap mine around his neck.

"Seriously, thank you for giving me this. I'm going to hang it in my bedroom," he informs me as soon as he sets me down. I grin at him and wipe under his eyes.

"I'm glad you like i–" He cuts me off.

"I don't like it, I bloody love it."

James takes the canvas into his hands and stares at it for a couple of moments. He then puts it back down and stares at me.

"How are you feeling?" he asks, a worried expression on his face.

"I'm not okay," I admit but being able to say it actually feels like a weight lifting off my shoulder. "But what am I supposed to do about it? It'll be easier to just find something new to do with my life." James nods before he picks up his blue mug and sips the tea in it.

"If it's what you want," he says, and I shrug.

"I think so." *I have no idea.*

James wraps his hand around mine, picks it up, presses a small kiss to the back of it, and then puts our intertwined fingers back on the table.

"Where has my Valentina gone?"

His question takes me aback, and for a second, I'm not sure I want to answer it.

"I don't know. I'm trying to get her back, but with every 'no', she drifts further away." I look past James, taking a deep breath. "I don't want to be the one to lose every single time," I say, the last few words coming out in a whisper.

James studies me for a few seconds before he nods.

"I know, darling, but you have to hold onto who you are, okay?" he asks, his gaze shifting to the canvas on the table in front of him.

"I'm not going anywhere, James, I promise." I wink at him, and he smiles in return. "Anyway, how's it going with you and Emma? Did you tell her about the baby?" I ask, desperately needing to change the subject.

My heart is aching in my chest, and I feel like throwing up when I talk about racing.

"Oh, yeah, well," he starts, and I frown.

Something obviously went wrong between the two of them, which is weird since they only started dating a few months ago.

"Turns out she doesn't like what I do for a living, and naturally, I can't be with someone who doesn't support what I do. You should've heard her, Val. 'That is way too dangerous.' 'You're just driving around in circles'," he imitates her, and I start laughing. "She honestly said all of that to me with a straight face. You should have seen me run out of her house. I was faster than an F1 car." As I imagine it, I can't contain my laughter. James is not a sexy runner.

"I'm sorry it didn't work out," I tell him, wiping away the tears of laughter.

Another short laugh leaves my throat, and I look at him, the amusement still on my face. He gives me a brilliant smile, and I look at him, confused.

"What?"

"Nothing, I just adore how I can make you smile like this." I squeeze his hand and bring the most childish grin to my face.

"Like this?" I ask, pointing at my weird expression.

"Yup, like that," he teases before he pokes my cheek. "Now, get out of here, I have to go train."

A playful frown spreads over my face, but I gather my stuff and kiss him on the cheek before leaving.

Being back home for good hurts a lot, but it also gives me the chance to find myself and be with the people I love. I spent the whole day yesterday with Adrian, the day before with Gabriel, and before that, I had time to myself. I have to be able to see the positive side of things, especially when the glass seems empty. *I'm just going to fill it with my tears,* I tell myself and laugh at how ridiculous I am.

The afternoon sun feels like heaven, and I stop walking for a minute to take it all in. I'm sunbathing more often now that I'm home, and I love it.

After another minute of enjoying the warmth of the sun, I keep making my way home. Gabriel and I agreed for him to stay at my place tonight, and he texted me an hour ago, letting me know he's already there. Giving him a key was a big step for us, but I adore the thought of him waiting for me at home.

I sprint up the stairs, all the way to my bedroom where he is lying at the foot of my bed, sketching something as he listens to music. His eyes light up when he sees the happiness on my face, and I jump onto the mattress next to him.

Gabriel drops his notebook to pull me against him, tickling me until I giggle. His hands move to each side of my head on the bed as I look up at him.

"How was your day with James?" he asks and pushes a strand of hair from my face.

"I'm about to lose my fucking mind!" Adrian screams from downstairs, and Gabriel and I listen to him storm toward my room before knocking on the door like a crazy man. "Are you two decent?" he asks, and I sit up with a groan.

"Yeah, come in," Gabriel says, and I cock an eyebrow.

"You're allowing people to come into my room now?" I tease, and Gabriel lets out a small laugh.

"Sorry, chérie, I didn't know we're considering Adrian as people."

My brother interrupts my laughter as he drops down onto my mattress, like I did only a few minutes ago, steam almost coming out of his ears.

"I swear to God, I will strangle that man when I see him on Thursday!" Adrian blurts out without any context, his hands falling onto his chest. "All day I've been trying to reach him, but does he fucking answer? No! Of course not! I'm seriously going to lose it." He mumbles the last sentence, his frustration almost making him growl.

With a smile, I shift around on my bed, placing his head in my lap and massaging his temples.

"Relax, Adrian, everything will be okay. Now, why don't you tell us what's weighing on your chest," I suggest, and he lets out a groan.

"Lorenzo Mattia is a pain in my ass. I've been trying to contact him all week to get some answers, but that coward is hiding from me," he explains, pouting like a little child, who didn't get what he wanted.

I don't know whether to laugh at his cute behavior or stop breathing from his words.

"Just let it go, Adrian, there is no point fighting his decision." My brother shoots into an upward position to grab me by the shoulders.

"I understand you don't have the strength to keep fighting right now, but you have to let me at least try for you, okay? Let me try," he says, and I give him a small nod.

"You mean fail? You know, considering you can't even get a hold of him," I joke, but he doesn't even smile.

"I will, and when I do, hellfire is going to rain on him, mark my words!" Adrian announces before strutting out of the room like Hulk when he has to use the stairs instead of the elevator in Endgame.

"That brother of yours–" Gabriel cuts off, letting out a deep breath and shaking his head. "He's a lot of work," he adds, and I chuckle in response.

"Hey, at least *he* waits for permission to enter a room," I defend, and Gabriel bursts into laughter.

I join him until we're both lying on our backs, staring at the ceiling of my room. Eventually, he turns my head toward him, bringing my lips closer to his mouth.

"Thank you for the canvas you sent me. It's beautiful," he says and presses a soft kiss to my lips.

Everything inside of me summersaults and warms at this small gesture.

"But I don't like that you spent money on me."

I kiss him again, ignoring his comment. I will do whatever I want with my money, especially to see his dimple-featured smile.

No price is too high to see it, none ever will be.

Chapter 50

Valentina

"Gabriel?" I whisper, but he doesn't wake up. "Amour?" I say a little louder, and his eyes flutter open. I put my hands on his face, and he gives me a sleepy smile.

"You look so beautiful," he tells me in French, and my heart skips a beat.

"Well, I did get ready so I could wake you, looking like the angel you think I am." I laugh, and he does too. It feels wonderfully strange to speak in French with him.

"What time is it?" He sits up and slides his hand into my hair.

"It's six-thirty! *Ha*! How does that feel?" I ask and give him a victorious smile.

He starts laughing and falls backward onto the bed, covering his face with both of his hands.

"Okay, I'm kidding. It's eight-thirty. See, I would never wake you that early." This only makes him laugh more.

"You're still holding a grudge? That was so long ago," he responds, and I crawl on top of him.

"I guess you could make me forget about it," I tease and put my hands on his naked chest. His rest on my thigh, and he bites his bottom lip with seduction in his eyes. "But that's not why I woke you," I admit in a whisper, and he smirks at me.

"Is that so?" he replies and chuckles ever so slightly. "Then tell me, why did you wake me? If it's not to have sex." I lean forward to press my lips to his but stop before they touch.

"I'm hungry, and I thought we could go out for breakfast." The smile he shows me with his dimples carved into his cheeks makes my heart ache.

"I'm hungry too, but I'd love breakfast in bed. I think a compromise would be to have both," he says, his fingers trailing up my skirt before they squeeze my legs. "One day, your beautifully thick thighs will be the death of me," he adds, and I lower myself to feel his morning wood against my aching clit.

"What would you like to have?" I ask, and Gabriel licks his lips.

I run my hands over his naked torso, rolling my hips to create a friction that makes both of us moan.

"I want you to ride me, chérie, to use my cock and come all over it," he says, making me groan as I remove my shirt. "Keep the skirt on. It's so sexy."

I do as I'm told, earning me an approving smile. He pulls on the waistband just enough to expose my tattoo, smirking at it.

"Use me, baby," he says when I think about what to do. "Fuck me however you want," Gabriel adds, his fingers gliding further upward.

Confidence races through me as I lean down to trail kisses along his chest.

"Give me a condom," I command as I tug on the waistband of his boxers. He reaches into the nightstand, handing me one of the small foils.

"You're hot when you're bossy," he says, his eyes on me as I drag down his underwear.

"Is that why you're so hard for me," I reply, bringing my face closer to his as my hand wraps around his dick.

"Fuck, Val," he groans and pushes his head into the pillows when I start rubbing him in the way he loves.

"Mhmmm," I moan into his ear, and he tenses for a brief moment as the vibrations travel from my chest and through his.

"Please, I need to have you wrapped around me, chérie. No more teasing," he begs, moaning again when I run his cock over my covered clit.

Gabriel reaches for my panties, pushing them to the side just enough to expose my pussy to him.

"Let me feel you." I roll the condom down his erection, too impatient to keep denying us both what we crave the most: each other.

Gabriel aligns himself with my entrance, the anticipation now spreading through me, settling in my chest and stomach in the form of butterflies. I sink down on his cock, both of us gasping in response to feeling whole again. My mind revels in the pleasure for a moment, unable to move until my needy body demands a release from the build-up that has us out of breath.

"You're always so goddamn wet for me, it makes me weak," he says as I reposition myself to start bouncing on him.

I take the opportunity to press a kiss to his lips before placing my hands on his pecs and pushing off him. I stop right before he'd slip out of me and slam back down.

"Fuck," we moan at the same time, and I keep going, keep repeating that simple movement to experience the same sweet pleasure over and over.

Gabriel swears in French, his fingers digging into my thighs and his eyes rolling into the back of his head.

"You're doing so well, baby," he praises, encouraging me and sending a thrill through me, which settles in my lower abdomen. "Fuck, yes, keep going." He's breathless, but so am I.

Every time I come down, it feels like the feeling goes straight to my head, making me high. I never understood when people called their significant others a drug until I met Gabriel. He's mine, and I need more of him, as much as my body can take.

I roll my hips and then bounce, grinding myself against his thumb when it lifts to my clit. My breasts jump with every move I make, and I notice Gabriel's eyes keep shifting between them and my face. I smile at him, slamming down harder now.

"Holy shit," he moans as I feel him tense under me, growing closer to his orgasm as I do mine.

"Gabriel, fuck, I'm so close," I say, and he lifts my hips to thrust inside of me. He's desperate, going faster and deep as I fall forward, my hands barely keeping me off his chest.

"Merde," he says while I become a moaning mess on top of him.

His lips crash onto mine the same moment he slams inside of me, sending an orgasm through my body.

I start to tremble, shaking with pleasure as he spills into the condom and holds me close to him. Everything and everyone else disappears until there is nothing left in the world but us. I sink onto his chest, listening to his accelerated heartbeat.

"Ma femme parfait," Gabriel whispers before kissing the top of my head.

He's still inside of me when I sit up again to show him the happy smile on my face. He reveals his, the green-brown eyes I fell in love with half-closed.

"I'll get ready, and we will get some breakfast. Okay?" he asks, and his hands rub up and down my legs.

"Okay," I reply and kiss him again before getting off him.

Gabriel stands up and stretches his arms into the air. My mouth starts to water when I see his muscle flex, always on display for me. He turns around, and, when he catches me staring, he smirks. A blush settles on my cheeks, but I don't look away. I'm not embarrassed, I don't need to be.

When Gabriel walks out of the bathroom again, he's wearing a plain white shirt, light blue jeans, a bandana holding back his messy hair, and sunglasses hanging from his neckline. I feel overdressed, but then I remind myself even in such plain clothes, he looks absurdly attractive.

I make my way toward my purse, gathering everything I need.

"Ma chérie?" he asks, and my head shoots up. "What do you want to do for your birthday?"

My eyes go wide when I realize I'm going to turn nineteen in less than a week. I haven't even thought about my birthday. I've been so caught up in my messy, heartbreaking, and beautiful life, I didn't notice how much time has passed.

"You're turning nineteen, and I want us to do something special. Maybe we can have a nice dinner with Adrian, Evangelin, and Carlos, James, Jean, my aunts, Cameron and Elijah, maybe even Lucie, Andrea, and Haru. What do you think?" I smile at him and walk over to where he is standing.

"I think that's a really great idea," I say, and he beams at me.

"Okay, let me take care of everything. The only thing you have to do is be there." I let out a small laugh.

He gives me a quick peck, but I stand on my tiptoes when he pulls away just to give him another, longer kiss. I feel him grin against me. We've been kissing so much, my lips feel sore, but in the best way possible.

"What are we going to do for *your* birthday?" I ask, and he shrugs.

"I'm racing this year." Gabriel's birthday is five weeks after mine, which is going to be the Sunday he's racing in France. "I'll probably be too tired to do anything," he says and lets out a short laugh.

"Well, hopefully not too tired," I reply and stand on my tiptoes once again to press my mouth to the soft spot just below his jaw.

"Never too tired for that," he assures me, and I chuckle.

Chapter 51

Valentina

Adrian and I have been sitting in front of his phone for the past half an hour, waiting for the callback Lorenzo Mattia promised my brother. He's bouncing his legs up and down, his head between his arms. I've never seen him this nervous.

Out of the two of us, Adrian is the calm and collected one most of the time, but, right now, the roles are reversed. I know this call won't do anything, but he's clinging onto hope as if it's a drop of water in a desert.

"When will you let this go?" I ask after another long silence. My brother raises his head, anger on his features.

"The day you get an F1 seat," he replies, flinching toward his phone when the screen lights up. A groan leaves him because it's a message, not a call. "This man better call soon before I lose it." I stand up and move over to the seat next to him.

"You're going to break yourself trying to get it for me," I say, my voice soft as I take his hand. "Trust me, *I know*," I add, but he drops his face into his arms, resting them on the table next to the phone that won't ring.

"If you're going to be negative, please leave. I don't want that energy here." His words are muffled, but I hear them loud and clear, and they bother me.

"Pardon me for having lost my optimism," I spit and walk away from him.

"I get it, Val, I really do, but you can't–" I cut him off.

"You don't have the right to tell me what I can and cannot do, Adrian. You've been handed everything in your life. You never experienced the same rejection I have, so I don't expect you to understand how tiring it gets to live this part of my life," I scream, and he shakes his head.

"You're absolutely right. I have no idea. I've been by your side through it all, felt your pain as if it was my own, but I know I'll never understand. That's why I keep trying. You were taught to do your best by Dad and Grandpa, I was taught to do the same for you, okay? Now let me fucking do this because that's what they would have wanted, and it's what you need!"

Tears shoot into his eyes, making some sting mine as well.

"Please, Val, don't fight me on this. You've had the pressure of Grandfather's expectations on your shoulders your whole life, and the reason why getting rejected hurts you so much is because you see it as your failure. It's not. It's never been. The only failure you can put on yourself is giving up when I have the power to do something about what happened at the driver academy."

Adrian sinks back onto his chair after he stood up to yell back at me. There are a lot of emotions surrounding us, but I'm hung up on his words.

"What if you can't do anything about it?" I ask, wiping away my tears.

"Then it's not you giving up anymore, Val. It's having done your best in a society that hates women who succeed, but it hasn't come to that yet, and I won't let it," he says, and I suck in an uneven, sharp breath.

"I don't want to stop fighting, I'm not ready to," I admit to him and myself. I'm not ready to stop fighting.

A smile tugs on the corners of my brother's mouth.

"Good," he replies at the same time as our doorbell rings.

"Yoohoo, anyone home?" Christian's annoying voice comes from the gate area, and Adrian and I exchange a disgusted-confused look. "I can see you both," he says, and I storm toward him with determination.

Two bodyguards stand beside him, making me hesitate for a moment.

"Coward," I spit in French, and he whispers something to one of them. They step away as he brings his attention to my face. "What the hell do you want? You might be a royal, but I'm not obligated to let you inside my house," I bark, amusement sparkling in his eyes as soon as the words leave me.

"I love it when you deny me something, Tina. It's so hot," he says, and my body revolts.

"You disgust me," I respond, and he smiles.

"Yeah, yeah, you've said so before, but I just came here to talk. Please, may I come inside?" he asks, a genuine, serious expression neutralizing his usually smug features.

"Rot in hell," I say and walk away, but his next words make me stop dead in my tracks.

"I'm sorry, Valentina, truly." That means nothing to me, but I'm surprised at his humanity. "The seat should have been yours," he goes on, and I turn around to see someone else get out of the limo.

It's the crown prince of Monaco, Thomas Crovetto, wearing a suit that's more expensive than anything I will ever own. He adjusts his tie as he steps out of the car, making his way toward the gate more gracefully than anyone else I've ever met. The light-blue color of his clothes complements his dark skin. He has piercing hazel eyes and full, round lips.

The princes are half-brothers, with Thomas being the son of the king's first wife and Christian being the son of his second. The two could not be more opposite from appearance all the way to behavior.

"Good afternoon, Ms. Romana. How are you?"

I don't know whether to curtesy or drop onto my knees, but no matter who society has deemed them to be, I don't kneel for any man. *Well, just one...*

"I'd be much better if you removed your brother from my property,

Your Highness, thank you," I reply, and Thomas gives me a smile I'm sure has made people fall in love with him in the past.

"Forgive us, we're simply here for my brother to take responsibility for what he's done to you in the past. For one, he should have never endangered your life during that karting incident a few weeks ago. I hope your wrist has healed well," he says, sincerity in his tone.

I look down at the faint bruise, which hasn't disappeared yet before crossing my arms in front of my chest.

"I appreciate the sentiment, but I don't want an apology. However, I'd love to never see His Royal Slimeness again," I say and almost slap my mouth when I realize in whose presence I am.

Thomas assures me it's fine with a laugh, making me grin.

"She was doing that the whole time we were at the academy together," Christian complains, but there is something different about him with his big brother next to him. He seems... *almost childish?* He feels inferior to his brother, this much is obvious.

"Good, you deserve it. You're not better than Valentina or anyone else because of your title, Christian, and I'm glad she reminded you of that," Thomas says, and I give him a genuine smile.

"Would you like to have a cup of coffee or tea, Your Highness?" I ask, addressing Thomas and him alone.

He gives his brother a pat on the back before letting out a laugh.

"Go wait in the car, I'll be right there. George, crack the window for him, please," he yells the last sentence at one of the bodyguards, and I unlock the gate for him.

Thomas holds out his hand for me, and I slide mine into his, prepared to shake it. Instead, he lifts it to his mouth, pressing a kiss to the back of it.

"Pleasure to meet you in person. I've heard and seen a lot about you," he says, and, for some reason, a blush settles on my cheeks.

"It's an honor to meet you, Your Highness," I reply because I think it's the right thing to say. He drops my hand and waves my comment away.

"Call me Thomas. I don't like those titles, I'm not my brother."

"I know, that's why I invited you to stay for coffee," I explain, and he chuckles, his eyes staring into mine.

"I like you. You're not afraid to speak your mind in my presence. It's refreshing."

He looks off into the distance with a thoughtful smile before turning his attention back to me a moment later.

"How would you like to become my advisor on social problems? I've been searching for one, and my gut is telling me you'd be perfect for it," he says with an amused tone as we make our way to the terrace where Adrian is standing with a dropped jaw.

Panic settles in my chest, worry rising in my throat until a lump forms, preventing me from asking what has happened. Adrian lowers his phone from his ear, dropping it onto the ground.

"I'm afraid Valentina will be too busy racing for the Alfa Romeo F1 team next year to work for you," my brother states, and I feel my heart drop into my stomach.

What?

Chapter 52

Valentina

"What the hell are you talking about?" I ask, taking a step toward him with shaking hands. "Don't joke with me about this, Adrian," I beg, and he shakes his head, tears falling down his cheeks.

"I'm not, Val. Lorenzo Mattia is going to offer you a contract to be the test and reserve driver for Ferrari for the rest of the season with a guaranteed spot in the Alfa Romeo team next year," my brother says, making everything around me spin.

"I should go. Congratulations, Valentina," Thomas interrupts, and I thank him, still trying to process what Adrian has told me not even a minute ago.

"He's coming to your birthday party to bring the contract and tell you in person."

I sink to my knees because they are no longer capable of allowing me to stand. My whole body trembles as I try to let that information register.

"I did it?" I ask as my brother kneels down in front of me, more tears flowing out of his eyes.

"Yes, little champion, you did it. You proved to him, Mr. Reiner, Andrea, and the whole Ferrari team that you deserve a seat, and they listened. They saw you, and they've given you the chance to live your dream."

I grab his hand, needing to feel him to know this isn't a dream. Sensing it, he pinches my palm, and I let out a gasp which turns into a sob.

"I did it." He nods, and, for the first time in my life, I fall apart out of happiness.

All of the pain has led up to this point of pure, raw joy, and no one will ever be able to take it away from me. I fling my arms around Adrian's neck, and his wrap around my back, hugging me tighter and with more emotion than ever before.

"Thank you for everything," I say when I've managed to calm down a little.

"I did nothing. This was all you, Val, all you," he replies, bringing me closer to his chest.

I bury my face in the crook of his neck, inhaling his comforting scent. All these years, all those people who told me I wasn't good enough, they all got me to where I am now, proving them fucking wrong.

"I have to call James and Gabriel, oh, and Evangelin. I want to tell them," I say, still crying because I've never felt a combination of relief, happiness, and victory before.

"You can call James and Evangelin tomorrow. For tonight, go to Gabriel, celebrate. I'll see you for your birthday party tomorrow," Adrian says, kissing my cheek and standing up to help me. "Go," he encourages when I hesitate.

I give his hand one last squeeze before grabbing my phone and sprinting all the way toward Gabriel's house. My heart is racing both from running and the excitement of my good news.

I knock on the door, waiting for anyone to open it for me. Domi does, a warm smile resting on her face.

"Valentina, it's so nice to see you. How are you, belle?" she asks, giving me a kiss on each cheek.

“I’m well, how are you? How is the baby?” I reply, her face lighting up at the mention of her unborn child.

“Everything is great, but I know you’re probably here to see Gabriel. He’s upstairs. Go ahead,” she says, stepping out of the way to let me go past. I smile at her before rushing to his room and knocking on his door.

“Come in.” Gabriel’s voice is soft, and I hesitate.

I know how he’ll react. This will be a moment I’ll never forget, another core memory to add to today, but I’m nervous anyway.

I open the door to reveal a painting Gabriel, who is dancing on the spot to his favorite song. His lips pull into a smile when he sees me, and I jump into his arms, my legs wrapping around him.

“What’s going on?” he asks, his hands moving to the underside of my thighs to hold me up.

“I’m going to race for Alfa Romeo next year,” I blurt out, and he drops me onto my feet, his hands moving to each side of my neck.

“Shut up! Shut the fuck up! Oh my God!” he cheers, jumping up and down from excitement. He attacks my face with kisses before stepping back and shaking his head. “I don’t even know what to do with myself, that’s how happy I am,” he admits, and I let out a small laugh as more tears fill my eyes. I don’t care about them anymore. Today I get to cry as much as I want.

“Neither do I. It seems very surreal. Maybe I need to have the contract in my hands first,” I say, and Gabriel shakes his head in disbelief and awe once more.

“It’s not going to feel real until you have your number on the car and sit down in it for the first time,” he replies, rubbing his face with his hands. “I can’t believe this! I’ve never heard better news in my entire life. Fuck, I have to sit down,” he says, and I chuckle at his behavior. “What do you want to do? We can pop a bottle of champagne and spray it all over ourselves to help you practice what happens on the podium,” he suggests, but it’s my turn to shake my head then, laughing as I do so.

“Honestly, mon soleil, I would love nothing more than cuddling up against you while you read me a good book," I say, and he stands up, walking toward me to kiss me.

"Get on the bed then," he whispers, and I run toward it, dropping on it with a dramatic motion and waiting for him to grab a book from his shelf. He lies down next to me, a book in his hand and a pen in the other. "Tell me what you think, and I'll write it down in here," he says, and I place my head on his chest before we start annotating the book together.

This moment is my personal brand of happiness.

"Since it's already past midnight, Happy Birthday, ma chérie," he tells me right before he presses his lips to mine and lowers the book again. We've been reading for longer than I thought.

"Thank you," I say when I lean back, and he grins at me.

"Wait here," he commands and gets up from the bed.

A small box lies in his grasp when he walks back over to me.

"This is the first gift I have for you, but it is the most important one."

Gabriel hands me the box, and I don't bother telling him he shouldn't have bought me anything because he seems too happy. Within it lies the same necklace I have seen countless times in his sketches. The number seven, his number, is carved into the charm. I have no idea what my face is doing. I try to smile, but I'm mesmerized by his gift. It's the most magnificent necklace I have ever seen.

"Val?" he asks after a moment of silence. My eyes lift from the jewelry to him.

"This is so beautiful," I say in a low voice and laugh at myself for being so emotional. I throw my arms around his neck.

"I haven't explained the meaning yet, hold on." I pull back and stare at him. "I guess in a way this is like a promise ring, but it's also not. It's more than just a stupid promise. The necklace is supposed to remind you that you're on my team. My Formula One career is my life, and you are my life. You wearing it is supposed to symbolize that all of it means nothing to me without you. I love you, Valentina Esmèe Cèlia Romana."

"I love you the same, Gabriel Matteo Biancheri." I take the necklace and put it on. Gabriel watches me, and I smile at him once it's securely fixed around my neck. "I will wear this with pride."

I wrap my fingers around the charm before I look at the man in front of me again. There is nothing but love in his eyes as he watches me bring it to my lips and press a kiss against it. Gabriel lifts his hand to touch my cheek, and his thumb traces my bottom lip.

"Tired?" he asks, and I nod.

It's been a long day, and tomorrow will be another. We both need some rest for the party he has planned and organized.

"Good night, mon tournesol," Gabriel whispers into my ear as he spoons me on his bed.

"Bonne nuit, mon soleil."

Chapter 53

Valentina

I wake up to the smell of coffee, Gabriel's famous waffles, and freshly cut fruits. My eyes open to find my boyfriend sitting in front of me with a tray of food and, thankfully, no shirt on his body. There are at least five gifts next to me on the bed, and I frown when I see them.

"Gabriel, you shouldn't have bought this many presents!" I bring my attention back to him, but instead of answering, he leans forward to press his lips to mine.

"Happy Birthday. It's ten in the morning, I hope I didn't wake you too early," he says, and I let out a short laugh. God, he makes me sound so lazy. "I made you some breakfast, but before you eat, open your presents," he commands, but I shake my head.

"Before I open them and eat, I want to do something else."

I cock an eyebrow, and Gabriel smirks at me. He puts the tray with the food on the nightstand, and I remove the blanket from my chest. His delicious body moves between my legs and his tongue enters my mouth.

We make out for a while before he pulls back to look at me.

"Open your presents," he says, and I laugh.

I groan a 'fine', and he hands me the first gift. It's an envelope, and I retrieve a single piece of paper that reads 'Andrea, Lucie, and Haru are coming to your party'. My jaw drops, and I look at Gabriel in disbelief. All of them told me they were busy and couldn't make it only a couple of days ago.

"Yes, they are all coming. I called them again, and they were easily convinced when I told them food and drinks will be served," he jokes, and I let out a small laugh. "I'm teasing. They were trying to figure out a way to come before I contacted them. Andrea is particularly excited to see you, and I can't imagine how happy they will be when you tell them you're racing for Alfa next season," he says, and a wave of excitement courses through me.

"Thank you, mon amour. This has already made my day." Gabriel nods, the smile on his face enchanting.

He leans over me to get the second present, and I take it from him with a grin. This one is much bigger, and I have to put it on my lap to open it. Inside the box is the most beautiful blue, silk dress. It has white flowers at the bottom and will reach just above my knees. It's quite poofy, but not too much that it'd look silly.

"It's for your party tonight," he explains, and I beam up at him.

"It's gorgeous. Thank you."

He hands me another box without wasting any time. This one is small, and inside of it lies a dried sunflower.

"It's from the first day I brought you into my room. Remember? When I had dozens of sunflowers?" he asks with a shy laugh while I pick up the dried flower.

"Baby," is all I can say.

Before I get too emotional, he hands me another present. In it are fitting shoes to the dress.

"Where did you get the dress and shoes? They are stunning," I tell him, and he offers me a mischievous smile.

"Evangelin and I picked them out for you. So, I can't take all the credit." He chuckles, and I put my hand on his cheek. The stubble on it is rough against my skin. "Okay, last one," he says and hands me the biggest package of all of them. "I stole this idea from James, kind of," he admits, and I furrow my brows.

The all too familiar helmet I designed when I was a child lies inside the box, sucking the breath from my lungs. It is the full-sized one, not the small version that stands on my desk in my room.

"At first, I got this because you are going to need your own helmet when you drive with me around the track, like we did in Maranello, but now—" Gabriel cuts off, joy glistening in his green-brown eyes. "Now you get to wear it when you test drive, reserve drive, or next year."

I swallow down the tears. It's starting to feel less surreal with this gift in my hands. I'm speechless as I look at the helmet covered in flowers. Everything is in its proper spot.

"I don't know what to say."

We both let out a short laugh, and he wipes away the tears I'm no longer able to hold back.

"This is freaking amazing." I put the helmet on, and it fits my head perfectly. "I can't believe you did this," I say, but I can barely hear myself, and I'm convinced he can't either.

I get up from the bed and walk into the bathroom to look at myself. A warm feeling spreads through my chest at the sight in the mirror. I never want to take it off, but I do. The smile on my face, however, doesn't fade.

I run back into Gabriel's room, put the helmet down on the bed, and kiss him to say thank you until I'm convinced it's enough.

"What do you want to do today?" he asks while we eat the breakfast he made.

"Uhmm," I say as I think about what to do, popping another piece of waffle into my mouth. Gabriel watches me with an amused expression, and I grin. "Maybe we can go mini-golfing," I tell him and clap my hands together in excitement. He chuckles and nods.

"All right. We'll go mini-golfing. We just have to be back by four because I've got some preparations to do."

Gabriel leans forward and touches his lips to my forehead before he gets up, and I remind him I have to go home and change. He assures me he will come with me and disappears into his bathroom to get ready.

I wait for him on his bed while putting on my clothes from yesterday. Gabriel comes out again, completely naked. There is water dripping from his hair and it's curlier than ever before. My eyes fall to the moon tattoo on his ass cheek, and they linger there until I find the faint scar on the side of his thigh.

I wonder if he will ever speak to Denis again, but I don't ask. The last thing I want is to bring up a painful time of his life on a day that is meant for celebration.

Gabriel and I walk to my house, and when Adrian sees me come through the door, he jumps up from the couch. He sings 'Happy Birthday' and hugs me, pulling me into the air. When he drops me back onto my feet and leans away, tears glisten in his eyes. He composes himself when he remembers that Gabriel is right behind me.

"I'll give you your present later," he says, but I scold him with my eyes for spending money.

He gives me a kiss on the cheek before telling me to take a shower because, according to him, I stink.

"It's my birthday, you have to be nice to me," I remind my brother, who rolls his eyes with a smile. I poke his stomach, which only makes him laugh. "We're going to play mini-golf, asshole. Are you going to be nice or should I not invite you?" I ask, and he straightens out his back until he stands before me like a soldier.

"Ma'am, yes, ma'am, I will behave," he promises, and I shake my head at his silly behavior.

Gabriel stays downstairs with Adrian while I rush through my routine. After my shower, I put on a short, green dress that brings out my eyes. I leave off the makeup, too lazy and comfortable to bother.

My eyes shift to the necklace Gabriel gave me, but I doubt my reflection does it justice. I've never owned a jewelry piece as special and meaningful as this one.

When I step outside onto the veranda, Gabriel and Adrian are in a heated argument. I have no idea what it's about, but I see my boyfriend's hands balled up into fists and my brother's face redder than a tomato. They are glaring at each other like they haven't been becoming close friends, as if they've been rivals this entire time.

"You are buying people now, is that what it is? You buy them so they prioritize you?" Adrian is beyond angry.

"I am not *buying* anyone. They may prioritize me because I have more fucking points than you, but other than that, I have no explanation. How dare you accuse me of bribing the team?" Gabriel asks.

With every heartbeat, they get closer to each other, and so do I.

"Hey, what's going on?" I say as I step between the two angry men.

There is one motivation able to calm down their fury, which is my safety. They might hit each other, but they'd die before anything happens to me.

"Your boyfriend is getting special treatment because he's been paying people," Adrian says, and Gabriel takes another step closer to the guy who is accusing him.

When his chest touches my arm, he takes a step back again.

"You got proof?" I challenge, and Adrian's expression changes.

"No," he admits, and I frown at him.

"Then what the hell are you doing? Why are you starting a fight with him, a fight you know neither of you will win? Control yourself," I warn him, and he looks at me with a guilty expression.

Gabriel's breathing is still heavy next to me, so I take his fist in my hand, and he opens it so I can put my palm against his.

"We are going mini-golfing. Will you be able to drop this and pick it back up tomorrow?" If it wasn't easy to tell how defeated Adrian was before, it definitely is now.

"I'm sorry, Val, but I don't want to be in his presence right now." A wave of sadness storms through me for a brief moment, but I shove it away.

"Fine, we'll see you later." Gabriel squeezes my hand, and we leave my brother standing by himself on the veranda.

I get the keys to the Mustang, and as soon as we leave my driveway, I turn to Gabriel.

"Why would he think you bribed the team?" I ask, needing more information.

"Because there have been a couple of meetings now where the strategists have favored me, but I don't have anything to do with it. I swear on us, and that is the highest swear I could ever make."

I look at him again, sensing there is more he wants to say.

"I know why they do it," he admits, and I cock an eyebrow, waiting for him to tell me. "They think I have the potential to win the championship this year, they think I'm faster than Adrian, stronger." I forget to breathe as soon as the words leave him. "I promise, I will talk to them–"

"Don't," I say, and, from the corner of my eye, I can see the confusion on his face. "If Adrian has a problem with the strategists, he has to talk to them. This isn't your problem, as noble as it would be. Adrian is a big boy."

I look over my shoulder while I make a left turn.

"It took a lot out of you not to punch him in the face, didn't it?" I ask, curiosity in my voice.

I'd like to think they're both mature enough to get upset without starting physical fights, even if I hadn't shown up.

"I don't cheat, and he was questioning my integrity. So, yes, I wanted to punch him for doing so. He has this way of pushing my buttons." I park the car at the mini-golf spot.

The *Princess Antoinette Park* is where Grandpa used to take Adrian and me, and I have those memories stored securely in my mind. They've been packed away for a while, but now, they all come crashing to the front of my mind, filling me with nostalgia.

"He would have deserved it," I joke, and we both laugh. "But please, don't hit my brother, ever. I'd have to kick your ass, and we both know I can," I say, and Gabriel licks his bottom lip in response, making a wave of shivers run down my spine.

"I'd take any punishment from you," he replies with a smirk, and I touch my tongue to the roof of my mouth.

"Do you think you could handle a punishment from me?" I lean closer to him, teasing him with my hand as it glides up his leg and toward his groin.

"Depends. How would you punish me? Spank me?" The smirk on his lips deepens, but I shake my head.

"No, that wouldn't be a punishment. You'd probably enjoy that." He gives me a shameless nod, bringing a smile to my lips. "Yeah, so I'd have to do something to drive you crazy." I think for a moment, getting closer to his lips and my fingers to his crotch. "Maybe tie you to a chair and make you watch while I fuck myself," I say, noticing his breathing hitch.

"I guess I better not do it then," he says and clears his throat.

I peck his lips before I open my door and get out of the car, leaving him with that image.

The hot summer air almost instantly makes me sweat. It must be at least thirty degrees outside.

I wrap my fingers around my new charm and enjoy how it feels in my hand.

"I knew the necklace would be much better than a ring," he mumbles when he stands next to me. I smile at the man who makes me the happiest woman in the world.

"It is," I say with pride.

Gabriel presses a kiss to my temple and wraps his arm around my shoulders, letting out a content 'hmm' into my ear.

"But, don't worry, it will come," he says, and I let out a nervous laugh.

"Eventually," I remind him, and he rubs his nose against mine.

"Eventually," he whispers, returning my smile.

Chapter 54

Valentina

Gabriel pays for the round of eighteen holes, and the guy at the counter hands us two putters with an expression of awe. He knows who he's helping, and my boyfriend even asks if he wants to take a photo. The man gives him a few excited nods, and I take their picture before we walk outside.

Gabriel hands me a golf ball and a putter, winking at me as he does it. I set it at the start line and move into position to hit it. The summer sun is hot on my skin, but I ignore it as I get ready to kick Gabriel's butt.

Naturally, while I position myself, I push my ass out a little more than necessary to mess with his head. I swing my putter and the ball lands close to the hole, making me stick out my tongue at him. He shakes his head, his smile bright and his dimples deeply imprinted into his cheeks.

Gabriel hits his ball, and it rolls almost directly next to mine. However, he's closer than I am, which is why I go first and sink the ball on my second try. Somehow, it takes Gabriel three more until he succeeds, which I can't help but make fun of. I'm only joking, and he knows it, making him roll his eyes with amusement.

The next four holes are uneventful, but he is ahead when we arrive at the sixth one, and I have to find a better way to distract him. If he wins, he's going to brag about it for the next few weeks, and I am not going to let that happen.

I clear my throat before I start my distraction plan.

"Mon amour, did I tell you how hot you look today? Your abs, your arms, and, especially, your ass look fantastic in that outfit."

It does exactly what I want it to. Gabriel turns around with a shocked expression, but there is also something else on there. Pride? I'm convinced he's proud, not of himself, but maybe of being with me, or because I'm confident enough with him to say things like that.

"Man, I really love your tight–"

"Okay, chérie, we're in public."

I hold up my hands in mock surrender and mumble a 'fine' before I let him get into position again. I get up and stand behind him, my hands covering his ass. He chuckles in response, but, for some reason, he doesn't make me stop and doesn't remove my hands.

"You're being very naughty," he tells me, and I grin.

"I know, but I also know you love it." He hits the ball, and, just as expected, it lands far away from the hole. "Too easy," I say more to myself than him, but he hears me anyway.

"Wait, does that mean you don't actually like my ass?" Gabriel pushes his bottom lip forward, and I laugh.

"Of course I do," I assure him, and he looks at me with a confused expression.

I don't think he believes my intentions to be pure, which they aren't. When I get a hole-in-one on my try, I jump up in disbelief and turn to Gabriel, who is shaking his head.

"Doesn't count," he says, and I let out half a laugh.

"Of course it does!" But Gabriel is shaking his head, his curls bouncing a bit from the movement.

"Nope, it can't. It's not fair," he explains, and I burst into laughter, jumping onto his back when he tries to walk away. He catches me, holding onto my legs. "Don't try to cheer me up when you're kicking my ass," he says, and I press my lips to his ear, whispering a 'sorry'.

A couple of holes later, I'm barely ahead on the scorecard. I lie the ball on the line before me, for the fifteenth time, and position myself to hit the golf ball. Sweat drips down the left side of my face, and I wipe it away.

It is getting hotter now that it's noon, and I look over at Gabriel to see if we have any water left. He hands me the bottle, and I give it back to him once I have taken a few sips.

"Do you mind if I empty it?" he asks, and I shake my head.

Gabriel takes the bottle, and, not very subtly, pours the content over his white shirt. It becomes see-through in an instant. The fabric clings to his abs in the most delicious way. My heart forgets how to beat, and my head forgets how to breathe. No matter how many times I've seen him shirtless, his body never ceases to make mine ache.

"Oops," he says, but we both know it was no accident. He's doing the same thing I was.

I clear my throat in an attempt to bring my head back to reality, and it works, somewhat. I force my full attention to the ball and hit it. It lands centimeters from the hole, and I turn back to look at my frantic boyfriend.

"What you gotta know is, mon soleil, I may love your body, but I also love winning." He bites his bottom lip and nods.

"You know what I love? That beautiful smile on your full lips. However, I'm going to win and wipe it off your face."

My mouth forms an O-shape, but then I giggle when he sticks out his tongue and puts on a concentrating face I have never seen before. It's cute and weird at the same time, his nose scrunched and his tongue pressing against his teeth.

"I got this. Watch me, baby." I'm a little disappointed when he misses the hole by at least two meters.

"Hittin' the hole isn't your strong suit, is it?" He touches his tongue to the roof of his mouth and stares at me with a 'seriously' expression.

"We both know no one fucks you as well as I do." I give him an agreeing nod before we both grin at each other.

By the time we arrive at the last hole, Gabriel and I are head to head, and he ends up winning the game. My hand lifts to the necklace he gave me, and I smile to myself. I'm on his team, whenever he succeeds at something, I'm going to be happy for him because that's how much I love him. If he fails, I will be upset. So, it's a good thing he won, otherwise I wouldn't have enjoyed my victory as much anyway.

At least that's what I keep telling myself to feel better.

Gabriel turns to me with his smile bright and sweet. I take two steps toward him, closing the unbearable distance, and put my hands on his hips. He places his on my neck and leans down to kiss me. I grin against his lips, and he kisses my cheek before pulling away.

I wrap my arms around him, and he hugs me back just as tight. I could stay like this forever, but Gabriel has to get back to my house soon to start his preparations. Somehow, I manage to peel myself off him, frowning as I do. He smiles at my expression, running his thumb over my bottom lip.

"And you say I'm the clingy one," he says, causing me to grin from ear to ear.

I hand him the keys to my Mustang and let him take me home. For the first time in my life, no part of me feels like driving. I'd rather look out of the window and appreciate how breathtaking my home is. There are no clouds in the sky, all of the plants are in full bloom, and birds are chirping happily.

Then, I turn my head to admire Gabriel. The way his veins stick out on his arm as he drives, the way he bites the inside of his cheek as he concentrates on the road ahead of him, and the way his stubble complements his green-brown eyes make me swoon.

I love his stubble. It's short, clean, and I think it fits his face very well. It was patchy when I first met him, but that was only because he was so young. Now that he's almost twenty-two, it is full and makes him look mature.

When we arrive back home, Gabriel tells me to stay in my room and get ready until he's done and my guests have arrived. All of the presents he gave me this morning are on my bed, and I take out the helmet before placing it on the nightstand on the other side of where I sleep. My eyes drift to the mini one James gave me exactly one year ago. James...

I'm worried about him. I've texted him a couple of times, but he won't answer any of the messages. Everything was fine, and now he's distant again. I hope he'll be at my party, but he hasn't even called to sing 'Happy Birthday' to me like he does every year.

James' life is upside down, and he doesn't have the time nor the energy to deal with anything other than getting it back under control. I would probably do the same if I was in his shoes. *Would I? Ugh.* It's frustrating that I have no idea how he's feeling, or even how Annabel is.

Before I can overthink things any further, I go into my bathroom and put on some makeup to match the silk dress Gabriel bought me. I slide it on, the material smooth against my skin. I'm not surprised my boyfriend chose a dress that highlights my breasts, I am, however, surprised it doesn't accentuate my ass.

I can't help but notice ninety percent of my clothes have flowers on them. It's the only connection I have to my grandmother. She loved flowers and buying clothes with floral patterns for me. I've been doing it without realizing it, but I don't mind it one bit. We didn't have the best relationship, but it doesn't change that I loved her.

I let my mind freak out about the fact that Lorenzo Mattia will be at my house in less than an hour, contract in hand.

It's really happening.

I'm going to be a fucking F1 driver.

We did it, Grandpa.

Chapter 55

Valentina

"Ma chérie?"

I step into my shoes when I see Gabriel leaning against my doorframe, admiring my appearance with his arms crossed in front of his chest and a smirk on his face.

"Haven't you ever heard of knocking? What if I was indecent?" He chuckles as he walks closer to me.

"Nothing I haven't seen before," he explains in such an arrogant and cocky way, I can't help the next words leaving my lips.

"What if I was touching myself?" I ask, and he bites his bottom lip.

"You would call me first because you know I'd take care of that for you." He's got an answer for everything, which pisses me off as much as it makes me smile. "Now, I would love to continue this, but your guests are waiting for you downstairs."

I nod, but nervosity is settling in my stomach now. A lot of people are going to be there, and it is beginning to unsettle me.

When I reach the bottom of the steps, I'm greeted by everyone. Each and every one of them comes up to say 'Happy Birthday'. Evangelin hugs me and tells me how happy she is for the opportunity she heard I've received. Cameron introduces me to Elijah, a gorgeous dark-skinned man with brown eyes. Elijah is a lot taller than me, which is why I have to look up at him when he speaks.

Lorenzo and his wife Maria come up to me next, and I have a captivating conversation with both of them. The Ferrari team principal informs me personally of his decision and offer before handing me a contract he demands I read as thoroughly as possible. I assure him I will, placing the papers on the stairs.

Domi and Nicolette grab my attention then.

The whole time I talk to them, or anyone, I can't help the bubble of sadness rising in my throat. I had a feeling James wasn't going to come, but I would have never expected him not to call.

"Valentina," Andrea says, walking up to me and wrapping their arms around me. "Lorenzo has informed me of his decision. I'm so proud of you!" I hug them back, happiness consuming me like it always does now at the mention of my success.

"Thank you for coming. I'm so glad to see you," I say, earning me a smile from them.

Lucie and Haru appear next to Andrea, grinning at each other like the two people in love they are. They shift their gazes to me eventually to make conversation.

"I hope you'll invite us to one of your races next year," Lucie says, her accent thick.

"Of course."

An arm wraps around my waist, pulling me against the owner's chest.

"I'm sorry, I can't help myself. You, in that dress, have me at your mercy," he whispers into my ear.

I smile while I attempt to listen to Haru tell me how things have been at the academy. I keep getting distracted by Gabriel's warmth and mahogany scent, but I manage to nod every so often to show my attention is on Haru.

"You're kidding! Holy shit, Val!" I hear Cameron scream from beside me where he's speaking to my brother and Leonard.

He skips over to where I'm standing, picking me up and raising me into the air.

"I'm so fucking excited!" he yells, and I let out a joy-filled laugh that vibrates through the whole room.

He drops me back onto my feet, making sure to be gentle, and presses a big, wet kiss on my cheek.

"Adrian told you?" I ask, giving my brother a teasing angry look. He shrugs, his smile bright and contagious.

"I'm sorry, I don't know what came over me, but I want to tell everyone," he says, rubbing the back of his neck in response.

I give him another scolding expression, and he chuckles.

"Hey, you're going to be the first woman racing in F1 for an entire season, Val. It's a big deal, and you should be very proud!" Adrian says, and everyone in the room starts applauding for me.

My cheeks heat up in an instant, and I feel the urge to bury my face in my boyfriend's neck to hide from the attention.

"Let's pop some champagne, yeah?" Gabriel interrupts, bringing everyone's focus to him.

"Thank you," I whisper, and he leans down to kiss the bridge of my nose.

"I know my woman," he says, and I blush.

"I love you."

Before he can reply, my eyes drift from his face and land on James as he walks through the front door. I step out of my boyfriend's arms and rush over to my best friend so I can have his wrapped around me.

When he sees me, he lets out a long breath, and I see relief wash over his face. He gives me a firm hug, his head resting on my shoulder.

"Happy Birthday," James mumbles against my skin.

"Thank you for coming." I pull back and put my hands on his shoulders.

"I'm sorry, things have been hectic, and I needed some time to figure everything out by myself. I shouldn't have gone MIA, forgive me," he says while I study his tired features.

"Don't apologize, I'm not upset." A sad smile spreads over his lips as he takes my hand to kiss the palm of it. "I have so many questions," I admit.

"Tomorrow, darling. Tonight, let's celebrate your birthday." I squeeze his shoulders before he hands me a present. "Read the card later, please," he says, and I nod.

I take his hand and lead him inside the house. Leonard gives me a brief squeeze on the shoulder as I walk by him, congratulating me on my seat, which I told him about through text yesterday. At least he's one person besides Gabriel I got to tell myself.

My boyfriend walks up to us, handing the Brit a glass of champagne. I let go of James' hand and take Gabriel's, but he wraps his arm around my shoulders instead. He taps my collarbone, and I lift my hand, allowing him to take it and intertwine our fingers.

We make casual conversation until Gabriel makes us sit down to eat the catered meal. The decorations are wonderful. He placed sunflowers all over the rooms, there are banners with my name hung on almost every wall, and he picked out some brown and yellow tones for the table decorations to match the sunflowers.

"This is stunning," I say to Gabriel, who pulls out the chair for me and then pushes it back in when I've sat down.

"Anything for you, chérie," he replies before Lorenzo Mattia grabs my attention.

I love that my friends and family are all here to celebrate me, but whenever I turn my head, someone else is trying to make conversation. I'm convinced my social battery is going to run out long before the evening is over.

"I need you to read over the contract as soon as possible so we can get you ready to start working with the team in Austria for the next race," Lorenzo says, and I nod with more enthusiasm than is necessary.

"I will look over the contract with her tomorrow," James chimes in, and

I realize Adrian must have told him too because I haven't had the chance yet.

I look at my brother, who immediately turns his head away from me to hide the guilty expression on his face.

"Big mouth," I call out in French, and Gabriel snickers next to me.

We both know my brother is the worst at keeping secrets out of everyone we know.

The food is delicious and for dessert, Gabriel carries a three-tier chocolate cake over to me, candles burning on top. Everyone sings to me first in English, then in French. Gabriel kisses me after I blow out the candles, and we all enjoy the cake.

After dinner, we scatter around the room, and I try to find Evangelin.

"Do you know where Evangelin is?" I ask Carlos, and the former F1 champion gives me an unreadable expression.

"She went outside to get some air," he says, and I go there to check on her.

I would have never expected to find her like this...

Chapter 56

Valentina

"Evangelin?" I ask, and she attempts to wipe away her tears. My heart is aching in my chest, and I'm afraid of what is happening.

"Oh, I'm sorry, Valentina. Just go back inside, belle." She doesn't know me if she thinks I am going to leave her by herself when she is crying.

"What's wrong?" I ask in French, and she lets out a sob.

"It's a long story, " I put my hand on her shoulder and rub it to comfort her.

"Would talking about it make you feel better?" She looks away from me and off into the distance.

"I've never spoken to anyone about this," she starts, and I take her hand to lead her to the chairs on the veranda. No one is outside, which gives us some privacy. "Gabriel is Carlos' grandson."

I swallow hard because I can't comprehend that sentence. At first, I think she is joking and I laugh, but then more tears flow out of her eyes, making me lose the ability to breathe.

"Fifty-one years ago, a year after Carlos and I got married, he had an affair with an Italian woman. Nine months later, she had his child, but she gave her baby girl up, and only told Carlos about her years later."

Evangelin stops to let out a sob, and I can't bring myself to move. Her words have paralyzed me. This is not happening. She cannot be telling me the truth right now. I swallow again to get rid of the lump in my throat.

"I don't understand," I croak out when she doesn't continue the story.

"There was no way to find her, or at least that was what he thought. He didn't tell me about the affair for ten years and let me tell you, it took everything out of me to stay with him, to forgive and offer him a second chance. Then, a couple of years after, we found out about the baby. Sierra, the Italian woman, wrote Carlos a letter, but we never received a call or any other form of contact. We searched for years, only to find out Carlos' daughter had a brain aneurysm the summer before."

Gabriel's mom had a brain aneurysm. No, this cannot be happening. Everything is getting too complicated, and I still can't breathe.

"We also found out Carlos has two grandchildren, and one of them is a successful Formula One driver, just like he was. Carlos didn't have the strength to find out their address. The only name he got was 'Gabriel'."

I get up from the chair I've been sitting in and try to find a way to start breathing again. I'm convinced I am hyperventilating.

"Then you came into my life, and you told me about this gorgeous man you were in love with, but I would have never expected it would be him. Seeing Gabriel at the store that first time, I couldn't help how sad I felt. Everything I had suppressed over the years came crashing back, but I knew I had to get a grip. I care a lot about you, Valentina, and I wanted to make this work, but I can't anymore. It's painful seeing him."

Evangelin lets out another sob.

"Gabriel only exists because my husband didn't love me enough. Don't misunderstand me, I am so grateful he does because Gabriel is a wonderful young man, and he makes you happy, but seeing him and Jean *hurts* me."

I look at her with anger and compassion. The paradox is making my head spin, but I can't control my feelings. This is too much all at once.

"I care about you as well, but you know I cannot keep this a secret. Gabriel and Jean have lost more people than you will ever understand, and I can't deny them the opportunity to know about their biological grandfather, to maybe have a chance to have some family." I run my fingers through my curly hair, get stuck on seven different knots, and groan in frustration.

"You can't tell them," she mumbles, and I look at her, only with anger now.

"No, Carlos and you have to do that. I can't be the one, it wouldn't be right," I say, my emotions threatening to overwhelm me.

"Now?" she asks, and I sink onto the chair next to her.

"Please don't ask me to hide this from Gabriel. It will ruin our relationship, break the trust I have earned by never doing anything like you're asking of me right now. Gabriel would never forgive me," I explain, but she shakes her head. "Please, get your husband, Jean, and Gabriel, and sit down with them. I am not keeping this from my family because that is what they are, *my family.*"

Evangelin looks down at the table, tears still running down her cheeks, and I want to apologize for being so harsh.

"I'm sorry, Evangelin, I didn't mean for it to come out that way. It's not your fault. I just wish you would have warned me before dropping this huge bomb. You are asking too much of me, and you knew that when you started this story. And it's okay, just please, I love him too much to keep such a big secret," I say, and she stops crying. "Imagine keeping something like this from Carlos." Evangelin looks at me with a soft expression. "You wouldn't be able to, would you?" I ask, and she shakes her head.

"No, I couldn't do the same thing he did. It's too big of a betrayal."

The tender woman gets up from her seat and walks inside without saying another word to me.

A minute later, Gabriel, Jean, Carlos, and her step outside. I can't look at any of them.

"Chérie?" Gabriel asks, his voice soft and worried.

"I'm inside if you need me," I say and press a kiss to his cheek before making my way over to Adrian.

"Val?" he asks, and I look at him. "I'm sorry about this morning. I shouldn't have accused Gabriel of bribing people. I know he doesn't, and I am going to talk to the team."

I honestly don't give a shit about that problem anymore. All I can think about is how Gabriel and Jean must be feeling right now.

"All good, Adrian. Don't worry about it." He nods, and I force a smile.

"You know I love you," he says to cheer me up.

"I love you, Adrian, no matter how stupid you act," I reply, giving him my full attention for the first time.

He nudges my arm, and I grin. It doesn't feel right, which is why the corners of my mouth drop.

"Luv?" James asks, and I spin around to look at him.

He seems tired. His blue eyes are faded, and I know he hasn't gotten much sleep.

"I have to go home, but open your present and read the letter." We also make a plan to meet tomorrow to look over the contract.

James disappears from my home, and then Elijah and Cameron do so as well. Everyone else follows shortly after, leaving Adrian and me alone inside the house. Gabriel and Jean are still on the veranda with Evangelin and... *their grandfather.*

It has been half an hour since they first went outside, and I get more impatient by the minute.

"What's on your mind?" Adrian asks me, but I shake my head and smile at him.

I feel like throwing up or screaming, or anything to let out the frustration in my chest.

Finally, after what feels like an eternity, Gabriel and Jean walk through the veranda door. The younger brother has a smile on his face, but my eyes focus on Gabriel. He looks confused and shocked, but he doesn't say anything.

For one short second, he simply looks at me with too many emotions to identify and then moves upstairs toward my bedroom. I thank Jean for coming, but he is in his own world, probably dreaming about what is to come in the future. I'm glad he's happy about it, someone should be.

My feet bring me to the steps of the staircase, and I take two at a time to get to my room faster. I open the door to find Gabriel staring at the large canvas I got him. We hung it over my bed a few days ago, intending for it to stay there until he finds an apartment.

"Gabriel?" I ask in a soft tone, and he turns to me with tears running down his cheeks.

They are bright red, and his eyes are bloodshot. A pain shoots through me when I see how devastated he is.

"Everything is upside down. I need time to think, to sort out my feelings." Another pain courses through me when I realize he doesn't want to stay with me.

"What can I do?" I ask him, and he looks at the canvas again.

"Nothing. You can't do anything." Gabriel walks over to me and puts his hands on each side of my face. "I love you, ma chérie, and I will call you. Just give me some time."

I want to throw a tantrum, tell him he can't leave, but he should never feel like he can't take some time for himself.

"I love you the same, mon amour. Please, please, text me or call me if you need me. I don't want you to leave, but I understand. Just don't think you are alone. I'm right here." Gabriel's eyes shed more tears, and he takes a deep breath before he envelops my lips with his and rushes out the door.

I can't imagine how he's feeling. His mom was adopted. He has a grandfather, who is still alive and well, and maybe a grandmother out there somewhere. She might have more family too. He could have twenty more blood relatives. This could be huge for him and Jean, even for Domi and Nicolette. Gabriel is still in so much pain from losing almost everyone he's ever loved, and this news, it's not purely positive. His thoughts are probably spiraling right now... just like mine are.

What are the fucking chances Carlos Klein turns out to be Jean's and Gabriel's grandfather? What are the chances of that?

I want to scream at the top of my lungs. Nothing makes sense to me anymore, which is why I don't bother trying to figure it out. I remove my dress and makeup before lying in bed only wearing underwear. There is no energy left in my body to put on some clothes.

He's going to come back to me, right?

I lie awake for a long time, unable to keep my mind off Gabriel and what he's going through right now. Every part of me longs to be with him, comfort him while he processes what he heard tonight. I can't imagine how he must be feeling, which is why I wish he hadn't left.

A groan leaves me as I sit up in bed, sliding out of it to grab James' present and card. I open the envelope first, feeling my heart settle into a calm speed for the first time in hours.

Happy Birthday, my love.

I'm sorry I've been distant and haven't been the friend you deserve. If I'm being honest with both of us, I struggle to be in your presence now. You support me through it all, but you represent something to me that makes it difficult to look into your eyes.

Do you know what's harder though? Not seeing you. Not speaking to you. Avoiding you because of things that should stay in the past. I want to move forward, and I need you, darling. I need you more than anyone else in my life (don't tell Adrian I said that), and I'm sorry it has taken me so long to realize it.

Please, forgive me. You deserve better, and I will

be just that.

I love you.

James

He was in love with me, imagined a life with me, and wanted to grow old with me. It was a fantasy, a hope even, he had since we were children. When we got older, I may have no longer been the woman in that dream, but in itself, it didn't change. The principles remained, and this baby turned everything upside down for him.

It ripped the fantasy away, and now, I've become the representation he spoke of in the letter. I hate that. I hate how much pain I bring him without being able to do something to change it. It does, however, allow me to understand him better.

Maybe distance wasn't the worst idea, but neither of us wants that. We're happier when we're together.

My fingers wrap around the little gift he gave me, undoing the ribbons to open it. In it lies a keychain with a photo of Adrian, James, Gabriel, Cameron, and me on my eighteenth birthday. I smile to myself and grab the letter and gift, hugging it close to my body.

Finally, sleep consumes me, even if it's the most restless one I've ever had.

Chapter 57

Gabriel

I've never turned to alcohol to solve anything because I know it won't. I also know the consequences it will have on my body, but I don't give a shit right now. It numbs the overwhelming feelings in my mind, not that I could accurately name any of them. *Shock? Pain? Happiness? Fear?*

Shock definitely describes what my body is experiencing, but I'm not sure about pain and happiness. I am afraid, of what this will mean, of whether or not I can get my shit together and finally call the woman I love.

Valentina has been patient, giving me the space I asked her for when in reality all I want is to be with her, but not like this. Not when I'm fucked up and all over the place.

I should be excited about this like my brother is. I should be happy about having a shot at getting more family, but I'm not. *Why the hell am I not excited? What the fuck is wrong with me? Why can't I have the same reaction as Jean?*

I take another gulp of whatever alcohol I found in Nicolette's liquor cabinet, barely feeling the burn as it slides down my throat. Tears fall from my face, staining my shirt and the carpet.

"Gabriel, would you like some food?" Domi asks through my bedroom door, and I swallow down the lump in my throat to speak.

"No, I'm fine," I reply, my voice cracking because I haven't heard it in days.

I've avoided everyone, loneliness camping in my chest now, unwilling to leave me alone.

"If you change your mind, I will leave a plate for you in the oven," my wonderful aunt says before walking away again.

The urge to throw the bottle against my bookshelf is strong because it feels like my world has turned into one of those goddamn fiction novels that sit on there.

My phone vibrates, a message from Valentina lighting up the screen. I think about ignoring it because whatever she said will make me break down more than I already have. It'll make me realize that, right now, I'm not the man she deserves.

I made a promise to Adrian and myself to always put her first, no matter what it means for my own feelings. I need her more than anything, but I'm a mess she doesn't deserve to deal with after getting the news of a lifetime only a few days ago.

Fuck, she's going to have everything she's ever wanted, and I'll drag her down. I'll distract her from the most important thing in our lives: her career. I can't do that. I won't do that.

Another message appears on my phone, this time it's one from Adrian. I know I can't hide from reality forever, even if I should, at least until I figure out what's going on in my head. My fingers tap my screen faster than my brain can react to stop them, and I read Valentina's message first.

Valentina: Hi, mon soleil. I don't mean to bother you, just checking in to see how you're doing. It's been a few days, and I wanted to remind you I'm a phone call away. You don't have to go through this alone if you don't want to. I know you don't want to bring any sort of negativity into my life, but I'm here to dance in the rain with

you. Let me be your sun for a little.

I love you.

My heart races by the time I finish the sweetest message I have ever received. I shift my attention to Adrian's text, unable to let her words sink in completely yet.

Adrian: Hey, man. Just making sure you're doing alright. Val told me what's going on, and I want to let you know I'm here if you need anything. You can come vent to me anytime if you need to speak to someone that isn't Val. Maybe you don't want her to see you in a bad place or whatever, I don't know. Just remember I'm here for you too, for anything.

I think about calling him, asking him what the hell I'm supposed to do with myself now. Then again, he won't understand how I'm feeling nor will he tell me what I want to hear. I'd need him to assure me I can go look for my family and stay with Valentina. I'd need him to make me feel okay about being the wrong man for his sister as I fall apart, and that would never happen.

If he were here, he'd tell me I have to let her go to protect her, at least until I figure everything out again.

Valentina deserves someone who isn't broken, who doesn't fall apart from hearing they have a chance to have more family. *But what is family? Is it blood?* I used to think so, but after meeting Adrian and Val, I've realized family is whoever makes you feel whole.

Then why the fuck do I want to find Sierra?

The answer pops into my head before I can stop it.

Because Sierra and Carlos are my mother's biological parents. I miss her more than anything, and if there is a chance I can feel connected to Mom again, I have to try.

Chapter 58

Valentina

I wrap my arms around James' back, and he hugs me. He looks much better today than he has in days. It looks like he's gotten some sleep and seems to have made peace with the fact that he's going to be a father.

"Annabel and I have worked out everything. I can be as involved as I want to be, I am going to help her financially, and take care of the baby whenever I'm here. She reassured me we are going to make this work as long as we both put in the effort."

James has a small smile on his face, and I'm glad he's no longer this drunken mess I have to take care of. Now, he's the sober mess I get to take care of.

"I know it's not supposed to happen like this, but, Val, I felt my son kick yesterday. It was the most thrilling feeling, apart from racing, I have ever felt." His eyes glow with euphoria as he explains it.

"You don't know how happy I am you feel this way, and I can't wait to hold him in my arms. He's going to be the most beautiful baby boy," I tell him, and he smiles.

"How do you know?" I take a sip from my water before I answer his question.

"Because he's yours," I say, and a shy blush settles on his cheeks.

"Stop it. You're making me blush." I laugh, and he joins me.

James and I talk for a little while, but the longer I stay, the more my thoughts drift to Gabriel. He hasn't texted me or contacted me in almost three days, and I'm worried. I wish he would speak to me, but he needs time, I guess I understand that.

With an interesting conversation topic, James pulls me back to reality and out of my thoughts. He lets me know he is going with Annabel to a doctor's appointment today and that she's coming over soon.

James asks me to stay so I can maybe feel his son kick.

"What's going on with you?" His question catches me off-guard, and I choke on my water.

It takes me a minute, coughing and him slapping my back until I finally get the water out of the wrong pipe in my throat.

"Nothing, why do you ask?" James studies my expression for a short moment, and I get nervous. He'll see through me, I know he will.

"Because you are unusually quiet and keep checking your phone. That's how you always act when something is wrong between you and someone. So, what's going on?" I shake my head and swallow the lump in my throat.

"I don't know. I don't really want to talk about it." James nods, and I take his hand in mine. "What did your family say when you told them you're having a son?" He sucks in a sharp breath and steps back, avoiding eye contact.

"Mia is excited, and my mom said she needed some time to process. The angry one is my dad, which he told me to my face. I never had his approval to begin with, so it's not that bad, but still. It's never easy to hear your father say he's disappointed in you."

He pushes his hands against the kitchen counter, which we have been leaning against for the past hour, and frowns.

Our conversation is interrupted by the doorbell. James goes to open it and walks back into the kitchen with a smiling Annabel.

"Valentina, it is so nice to see you again," she says. The pregnant woman gives me a kiss on each cheek to greet me.

"It's nice to see you. I hear you have a doctor's appointment today." Her face lights up, and it's hard for me to believe someone could look so happy at almost nine months pregnant.

"Yes, and James is coming with me. He's going to see little Claude for the first time," she says, and James snorts.

"Please, Annie, let's not call our child Claude." *Annie?* I can't help but crack a little smile. Annie... Maybe, after all, James will open his eyes and see how wonderful she is.

"All right, how about Beauregard?" she asks, and he rolls his eyes.

"Do you want him to get bullied? Because if you call him Beauregard it is highly likely he will get made fun of."

Annabel puts on her thinking face, and so does James, but both of them stay silent for a couple of minutes.

"You could call him Damian and then your last names," I offer because it has been a while since anyone has spoken.

Ever since I found out James was going to be a dad, I have been looking at baby names for fun. The name 'Damian' was my favorite, but I say it more as a joke. I don't want them to think I'm crazy for having looked at names. I only wanted to support them.

Annabel's mouth opens, and her eyes go wide.

"And then his middle name could be 'Parker', like my father." Annabel stares at James with joy in her eyes. "Damian Parker Rossi-Landon," she says, and James smiles at her.

"It's perfect," he mumbles before he looks at me. "Thank you."

"Don't thank me, I was just brainstorming."

All of a sudden, Annabel touches her stomach and lets out a little laugh.

"He's kicking a lot," she says, and I ask if I could feel it. She almost rips my hand off my arm to get it to her stomach.

The feeling is strange to me. I'm amazed someone is living inside of her, someone created by her and somewhat my best friend. The only two words that come to mind are: wonderful and weird.

Both of them thank me again, and I inform them I have to run some errands. It's a lie, but they seem eager to spend more time with each other, and I need to go see how my boyfriend is doing.

I drive the Mustang to Gabriel's house only to have Nicolette tell me they aren't home, neither Jean nor Gabriel.

"But you are welcome to come in. Domi and I were just having tea if you'd like some." She takes my arm, leading me inside.

The two lovely women entertain me for an hour or so, telling me about how and where they met, the way they got together, and stories about Jean and Gabriel. I could listen to them forever, but eventually, Adrian texts me he prepared dinner. I assume he means he ordered dinner because there is no way he cooked something without burning the kitchen down.

Just as I am about to walk out of the door, Gabriel steps into the house.

"Val," he says, shock on his face.

There are dark circles under his eyes, and I hate that so many people in my life seem to have them nowadays.

"Hi, amour."

I wrap my arms around him because I'm happy to see him, but he doesn't hug me the way he always does. It feels like he doesn't want me in his house, which is why I pull back and leave without saying another word.

Gabriel doesn't follow me, he doesn't text me for the rest of the night, and I know something bad is going to happen.

I just don't know when.

Chapter 59

Valentina

Leonard messaged me yesterday, asking if he could come over to discuss something important. I haven't been feeling very social since my last interaction with Gabriel a couple of days ago, but whatever he wants to discuss sounded urgent over the phone.

After everything he's done, I didn't want to deny him the one favor he's asked of me, no matter how badly I want to be by myself to overthink. Then again, I like Leonard, and spending time with him always brightens up my day.

I place the biscuits I baked on a plate to bring outside onto the veranda, making a plan to prepare the coffees when Leonard arrives. He should be here soon, and, in the meantime, I text Cameron to see how he's doing.

A minute after I sent the message, he calls to let me know he misses me. Since I feel the same, we take some time to catch up, but Leonard interrupts our conversation. He's perfectly on time, greeting me with a slight hug for the first time. His fresh scent fills my nose, and I smile at him.

"Thank you for seeing me on such short notice," he says as he settles down on the chair I point to, lifting a black folder onto my table.

A small smirk tugs at the corner of my mouth while I study his professional attitude.

"I feel like I'm in trouble," I tease, and he gives me a half-amused, half-challenging expression.

"Why? What have you done?" he replies, smiling.

I raise my hands in mock surrender, leaning away from him to show my innocence.

"Oh no, you've finally done it, haven't you? I know he can be annoying, but locking Adrian in the basement isn't the answer," Leonard says, and I burst into laughter.

"Please, I wouldn't put him in my basement. I'd lock him in James' so he'd take the fall for it," I reply, and the Brit gives me a chuckle while shaking his head. "Anyway, what's going on? How can I help you with whatever is in that folder?" I ask, and Leonard refocuses on business, his favorite subject to discuss with me.

He's been opening up more and more toward me, and I love that we've connected. I hope, one day, we can be good friends.

"Before I get into what is in this folder, I'd like to explain why I kept my distance from you in the past," he starts, and I swallow hard.

"You mean why you didn't like me?" I say to relieve some of the tension, but he frowns at my words.

"It's not that I didn't like you, Valentina. You were a constant reminder to me of what is wrong with the sport we love. You reminded me of what I went through, even if our experiences differ. We both had to fight harder than the rest of them, and I hated seeing you hide how much you struggled without being able to do something about it. It made the feelings resurface of when I was a child and tried everything to get accepted by any teams, but I couldn't do anything to help myself either. My father had to work three jobs to finance my dream, but we heard the word 'no' more often than I could keep count," he says.

I take a deep breath when I remember my body needs oxygen to function.

"Getting close with you wasn't an option, not until I knew how to help you. That's why I wanted to become your mentor. You needed someone, who experienced something similar, someone that understood you."

He opens the folder as he speaks, avoiding eye contact with me, which I'm grateful for. I'm convinced I'd cry if he looked at me.

"You were trying to find a way to help me get a seat?"

All this time I thought he didn't like me when he was fighting for me. Man… I'm the luckiest girl in the world to have a support system like no one else.

"Of course. I spoke to Mr. Reiner, sat down with him to analyze your times and compare them thoroughly with the rest of the drivers in line for the spot. I didn't stop until he listened because you, Valentina, have something inside of you that hardly anyone else has. You have the spirit of a true racer. You didn't give up," he says, and guilt spreads through my chest.

"I did give up. After they kicked me out of the FDA, I didn't want to fight anymore. I argued with everyone because they didn't understand how tiring it is to be rejected all the time. I was ready to find something else, a new career," I admit, and Leonard lifts his gaze to mine, a warmth settling in my cheeks from his comforting smile.

"But you weren't looking for anything else, were you?"

I think about the time between Christian getting the Formula Three seat and me getting the F1 one, but he's right. I said I'd have to find a new passion and couldn't bring myself to do anything else. I wasn't done fighting yet, even when I thought I was.

"I'll take that as a 'no'," he says and hands me the folder, but I'm stuck on something else he brought up before.

"You were responsible for getting me that spot in the FDA?" I ask, panic filling his eyes when he hears the disappointment in my voice.

"No, no, no, none of that! I sat down with your statistics, with your lap times, and proved to him you're worth taking a chance on. It's different for me, I'm already a Formula One driver with a good, reliable reputation. My word, my opinions, they matter to these people, but it doesn't change your talent. Don't you start doubting yourself," he scolds, pointing at me with a warning finger.

I let out a small laugh and assure him I won't.

"Okay, tell me, what's this?" I ask, looking down at the pages in front of me.

"It's an idea I had, and I want you to be my partner," he says, and my heart momentarily forgets how to beat.

The title of the first page reads 'Driver Academy for Kids Like Us'.

"I want to open a race school for children that have been denied a chance because of who they are, where they come from, and what opportunities they've been given. I came from a low-income family and only had enough money to get into racing because my dad found someone, who wanted to sponsor me. This school is going to be the place where talented children get the chance of proving themselves, and, based on their results, not the color of their skin or their gender, they will be judged. We'll need a lot of sponsors and partners in this endeavor, but I want your name to be right next to mine."

I listen to him, scanning the page of the folder to see what sponsors he intends on having invest.

"This is a wonderful idea, Leonard, but who the hell would be crazy enough to invest in something without foreseeable profit?" I ask, and he leans forward on the table, ready to prove me wrong.

"In the long run, they'll make money from the drivers. Plus, nowadays, Formula One, Two, Three, and Four pride themselves on being diverse and inclusive. This is their way of showing it to the world."

I nod, still reading over his papers.

"I know it won't be easy, but I'd like to try and make a difference, and, like I said, I want you to be my partner."

He reaches for the folder, flipping it back to the first page and tapping the name.

"'For Kids Like Us'," he says, and my heart sinks into my chest.

"I don't know how much time I can put into this academy with my career just taking off," I explain, but Leonard smiles at me.

"All I need from you is advice, strategy planning, and bagging investors. You're a force to be reckoned with, Val, and they will see that. You could be a key part of this school because you're the first woman to ever get a spot in Formula One. So, what do you say?"

I cock an eyebrow, staying silent to build suspense, but I already have an answer for him.

"Come on, luv, don't do that to me," he begs, and I can't help but smile at the side he's showing me.

"I would love nothing more than to be your partner on this," I say, standing up and holding out my hand for him to shake.

Instead, he walks around the table to wrap his arms around me.

"Thank you," Leonard says, and I hug him back, needing the comfort of it for more than one reason.

"Thank you for fighting for me."

Chapter 60

Valentina

It's been a while since I've seen my grandfather, and it's starting to hurt how much I miss him. Aunt Carolina has no sympathy for my homesickness, so I make sure not to show it in front of her. I don't want her to get angry with me.

"Val, I have a little surprise for you," Adrian says while I'm on my bed, trying to study. "Come with me," he adds, holding out his hand for me to take.

There is a serious look on his face, worrying me. It's a surprise, so it shouldn't be bad, but it looks like he just got the worst news of his life; his face is pale and his eyes are red.

"What's wrong?" I ask him as he wraps his fingers around mine.

Adrian stays quiet until we reach the bottom of the stairs. Grandfather sits on the couch in the living room, and I sprint over to where he is.

"Grandpa!" I call out, my arms wrapping around his neck.

"Hi, little champion," he says, hugging me back. "I'm sorry, this isn't going to be a happy visit, but I've been dragging it out for long enough. It's time we talked."

I hold my breath as he guides me down onto the couch next to him.

"I don't understand," I say, panic flooding my chest.

Grandfather's tired eyes fill with tears, and he lets out a heavy, shaky breath.

"I'm not going to be–" He cuts off, inhaling again to gather courage. "I'm not going to be around for much longer, Valentina. I'm going to see your Grandma soon."

Fear strikes through me.

"No, you're not. You're still healthy, you're not that old," I say, disbelief coming through as denial.

"I have lung cancer, sweetheart. I'm dying," he explains, but I shake my head.

"No, that can't be. You're not a smoker."

I don't know who I'm trying to reason with, his disease or him, but it's not fair. He can't leave me. There is so much we still have left to do. I haven't made it into Formula One yet! He needs to see me fulfill our dream. He cannot leave me!

"Listen to me. I know this is going to be very hard for you, but I need you to promise me you'll keep your heart. Don't shut it off, don't start pushing people away. Not everyone leaves, I promise."

I shake my head again, tears pouring down my cheeks.

"You need to let me go now, my children. You have to so you can keep focusing on your careers and stay in balance in all three categories. Do you remember?"

I nod, but I don't want to. I want to throw things, scream, break down.

"Good, remember them. Don't let your emotions throw everything off balance. You have to let go, even if it's the worst pain you've ever felt. You have to let go because this is out of our control. There is nothing we can do to change it, but you can't let it tear you down from what's important, okay? Don't allow anyone to put themselves before your dream."

He turns to me, grabbing my face to make sure I pay close attention to him.

"One day, I hope you'll meet someone who will prioritize you and your career no matter what. That person will be the one for you. When you find them, and they show you how much they value your dream, don't shut them out of your heart."

I don't know why he's telling me any of this. I don't care about the future if he won't be in mine.

"There is a lot I have left to teach you, but I'm afraid I'm out of time."

It's been days since I've last seen or spoken to Gabriel. I've texted him a couple of times, and I have tried calling him, but he doesn't answer. Evangelin has tried contacting me, but I'm not ready to talk to her yet. James is busy with Annabel, and Adrian is training with his performance coach.

Lorenzo Mattia has finalized everything for me, and I will officially drive for Alfa Romeo next season. He's also told me I have to work almost every day of the three-week Formula One summer break to test drive the car. It's going to be busy, but I'm excited to get started.

After not knowing what to do with my free time, I decide to spend the whole day taking care of myself. First, I work out, then I go for a swim in my pool before taking a shower and putting on a face mask.

I pick up Gabriel's copy of 'Die For Me' and continue reading from where I stopped months ago. My eyes go back to Gabriel's annotations, and they focus on a specific one.

If I ever got her, would I have the strength to leave her?

God, I hope he doesn't. I hope more than anything he will come back to me. Yet, with every day he doesn't talk to me, I grow more certain he is getting strong enough to leave me. I start to panic when I think about it.

He's going to leave me, isn't he?

Of course he is, otherwise, he wouldn't be avoiding me.

It's been a while since Gabriel and I have gone more than a day without talking to each other. Not texting or calling him every day feels unnatural, just like it does when I don't talk to Adrian or James.

My breathing hitches and I can't stop thinking about the fact that Gabriel is going to break up with me. After such a huge revelation, he must want some time for himself, some time away from the person who might hold him back from finding his long-lost family.

I distract myself by turning on a comedy show and removing my face mask. Adrian comes home from his workout, and I spend some time with him, desperate to get my mind off my own problems. He tells me he is prepared for Austria, and I let him know how proud I am. Adrian is working harder than he ever has before.

After dinner, I go upstairs to be by myself for a little. My head has been spinning, thinking about Gabriel the whole time I was with Adrian, and I can't stand it.

A knock on my bedroom door startles me, but I don't even flinch.

"Come in," I say, wondering who it could possibly be.

When he walks through my door, I stop breathing.

"NO," I say louder than necessary, and a tear rolls down his cheek. "Why did you knock? You explained to me you didn't have to knock anymore, and I was okay with it. So, don't start knocking again," I beg, and the tears that leave my eyes are full of pain.

"Valentina, please don't make this more difficult than it already is."

I get up from my bed, but I don't move closer.

"No, I am going to make this as hard as possible because you are about to destroy everything, and I want it to hurt you just as much as it is going to hurt me."

It's selfish, and I know it's wrong. I'm hoping he won't leave once he realizes it's so hard to say goodbye because he loves me more than anything else in the world.

"You don't think this is going to hurt? You think I haven't been battling with myself for the past four days? Baby, I love you so much, and doing this now is going to break me, but I have to. I haven't been treating you right since

I found out Carlos is my grandfather, and I am not going to be right for you again until I find Sierra and the rest of her family... *my family.*"

I sink down on the bed, trying to stay strong, but my bottom lip starts to tremble.

"Please, don't do that."

"Then don't leave. You said I am your life, you gave me this necklace to remind me of that, and now you throw me away like I never meant anything to you," I yell at him, and the tears falling from his eyes hurt me more than my own.

"I need to do this. I made a promise to put you first, and this is me doing that."

I nod and look at him with as much anger in my eyes as I can form. My heart is shattering in my chest in a way I have never felt before.

"I don't care that you think you're still keeping it. You're not, and you're making me break mine too." I'm yelling, which makes him take a step back. "Why can't you go out and search for your family with me by your side? Why do you have to leave me to do that?"

He walks over to me, but I get up to put more distance between us again.

"Because you need to focus on your career. You cannot be in your head, wondering about my feelings and picking up the pieces of my broken world! You need all of your attention on one task: preparing yourself to become an F1 driver. I cannot be the reason why you get hurt in the car or why your performance isn't at its best. Trust me, I know what happens when you lose balance in your mind. It fucks you over, and I will not do that to you. I won't lose you the same way I lost Maxime!" he yells and points at me, pieces falling into place in my mind. Maxime... "I love you too much, chérie, and that's why I have to do this. I won't be who you need me to be, and that's not fair. Your career has to come first, always," he whispers, and I look at him in disbelief.

I still cannot breathe, or think, and my heart is sending waves of fear through my bloodstream.

"You know what's messed up? That even though you're breaking up with me, I want you to find your family." I laugh at myself and watch pain shoot over his face. "I've lost many people too. So, I understand why you're doing this, but as the girl who is in love with you, I can't help but be angry at your reasoning. You are giving up on us as if we never meant anything to you to begin with."

I've never been more self-centered than I am at this moment, but I don't care. He is doing this to us, he is squeezing all of my organs, and he is making me want to throw up.

"I'm not giving up," he complains before he throws his hands into the air.

"Yes, you are." Gabriel sits down on my bed and drops his face into his hands.

"I'm doing this for you, for your career! Valentina, I love–"

"Stop," I interrupt him. "Stop saying that. If you really loved me, you wouldn't leave me." His head shoots up, and he shakes it at my response.

"Try to understand," he begs, and I let out a short laugh I don't mean.

"I do, I truly do, but let me put it this way. I love you, and I let you in. I never let anyone in, but I did with you, and you are ripping me apart from the inside out. So, as much as I understand it, I can't forgive you for this."

He nods but doesn't look at me. I want to scream louder than I have ever before. Gabriel is doing this, he is letting go.

"You walk out of that door and I will never be able to forgive you for this."

I put my hands on my hips because I'm trying to stand my ground. In reality, I want to lie down, curl up in a fetal position, and ball my goddamn eyes out.

"I hope you *will* be able to forgive me."

Gabriel stands in front of me, and I let him press a kiss to the top of my head. I can't help myself. Maybe I want to feel his lips on my skin one more time before I let my anger consume me.

"I'm broken, mon tournesol, and I won't tear you down with me, not while you're finally getting everything you've ever wanted." I shake my head as he steps away from me.

"Everything I've ever wanted includes you, Gabriel. You spoke about marrying me, but now you're pushing me out of your life during your darkest time. You don't trust my love for you, which is the saddest part of it all," I say, and he rubs his tired face.

"No, chérie, I know you'd help me work through everything, but it would be at the expense of your career. Don't you understand that? You can't have a split mind right now. No Formula One driver has made it far if their head wasn't focused entirely on their success in the beginning stages, in the one you're in. Please, please, Valentina, you have to let me go," he explains, desperation all over the beautiful face I've studied more than anyone else's.

Some of my anger drifts as I stare at him.

"My grandfather warned me about you, but I never expected it to hurt like this," I admit, unwilling to hide my emotions from him.

"My mother warned me about you too. She said I'd fall in love with the strongest, most beautiful woman in the world."

Without looking back once or saying another word, he leaves my room and my life.

I can't help but hope it's just for now...

To be continued...

Chase

I close the door behind me using all the strength my body has left, leaving my heart and soul with Valentina. She'll never forgive me for this. I'm choosing myself over her, but I have to. I have to do what's best for me to be everything she deserves. Since I found out Carlos Klein is my fucking grandfather, I've been the wrong man for her. Someone who drinks and wallows in pain and self-pity isn't the type of person Valentina deserves. My mess shouldn't become hers during the most important time of her life.

She's just been offered a seat in Formula One. Alfa Romeo saw her potential, and she'll be training throughout the whole summer break to prepare herself for the rest of the season. The woman I love will be the first female F1 driver, but for now, she'll be the reserve driver for my team. Ferrari. Which is already a big responsibility that's going to need her entire focus. I can't drag her into the dark space I've spiraled into. It's not fair. If I knew Val could be selfish, focus solely on herself, I wouldn't have left, but she's not that type of person. She loves me too much. And I love her more than anything or anyone else. Which is why I have to do this.

It's how I become the man she deserves again.

I straighten out my back, ignoring the tears streaming down my face as I walk down the stairs and the way my muscles try to fight against it. Every part of me is drawing me backward, back to Val, because I'm not whole without her. Half of me is her, just like half of her is me. We complete each other, and walking away? It goes against my survival instinct.

"What the fuck did you just do?" Shit. Adrian's voice is full of anger and frustration, and I spin around to show him how horrible I look. His eyes widen at the sight of me. "Jesus, Gabriel. What happened?" he asks, and I let the tears drop down my face.

"I ripped my heart out and left it with her. That's what happened," I reply and attempt to leave again when his hand wraps around my elbow to stop me.

"Don't. Don't leave her like this, mate. You'll do more harm than good," he says gently and firmly, understanding my pain as well as trying to protect his sister from harm. If he could look inside the dark hole in my head, he'd know letting me leave is the best thing for her.

"Let me go," I say when his grip tightens around my arm.

"If you do this, there's no going back," Adrian warns me, and I know what he means. There will be no undoing the pain I've caused. Val will hate me. He will hate me. My only hope is that they loved me enough at one point to forgive me once I've put myself back together.

"If I don't do this, I will be putting Val's life in danger," I whisper-scream, ripping my harm free. This has gone on long enough. I have to get out of this house that's somehow become more of a home to me than my childhood house before Valentina hears us.

"Don't pretend you're doing this for her," Adrian replies, pissed at me now. Good. Maybe he will let me walk out the door if he's angry.

"I am. And you have to promise me you will do everything in your power to ensure she's focused when she tests the car, you hear me? Her mind needs to be in her head, not stuck on wherever I am. Do you understand me?" I ask, grabbing his shoulders as I speak to be certain he's hearing me. Nothing can happen to mon tournesol, especially not because of me.

"Val is my little sister, Gabriel, the most important person in my life. I will do whatever it takes to keep her safe," he says like I should already know this, and I do. It's one of the reasons assuring me I'm doing the right thing.

"So will I," I reply, leaving him standing in the middle of the entrance before walking outside and letting the hot summer sun burn my skin.

My lungs are constricting, preventing me from breathing. My heart feels like it has stopped beating, slowing my steps. My head is screaming, telling me what a horrible man I am and, at the same time, reminding me this is for the best.

God, I'm so fucked.

Acknowledgments

To all of my readers, from the bottom of my heart, thank you.

Books by Bridget L. Rose

The Pitstop Series

Rush: Part One

Rush: Part Two

Chase (Coming in 2023)

Jump Start (Coming in 2023)

From Angels to Devils Series

From Devils to Angels

Standalone

The Inside of a Rainbow

Made in the USA
Middletown, DE
12 July 2023

34946387R00321